THE DAY
THE SUN DIED

Books by Dale Van Every

NOVELS

WESTWARD THE RIVER

THE SHINING MOUNTAINS

BRIDAL JOURNEY

THE CAPTIVE WITCH

THE TREMBLING EARTH

THE VOYAGERS

THE SCARLET FEATHER

THE DAY THE SUN DIED

HISTORIES

THE A.E.F. IN BATTLE

MEN OF THE WESTERN WATERS

OUR COUNTRY THEN

FORTH TO THE WILDERNESS

A COMPANY OF HEROES

ARK OF EMPIRE

THE FINAL CHALLENGE

THE AMERICAN FRONTIER PEOPLE

DISINHERITED

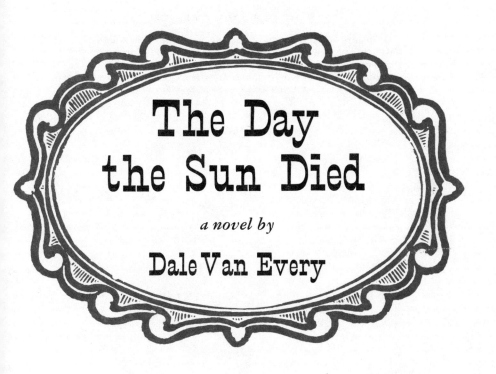

The Day the Sun Died

a novel by

Dale Van Every

Little, Brown and Company
Boston — Toronto

Published simultaneously in Canada
by Little, Brown & Company (Canada) Limited

PRINTED IN THE UNITED STATES OF AMERICA

THE DAY
THE SUN DIED

I

THE COURSE OF EVENTS which was so soon to grip the nation's attention was like a fuse which smoldered at first and only began toward the last to burn like lightning. The man who lit the match in the first place was a grizzled veteran of the Apache wars who was never to see Wovoka, or the dancing, or Standing Rock, or the dreadful field at Wounded Knee.

Major Wade had bolted his breakfast that morning. Eating too fast was one of the bad habits of which Rachel had not yet been able to break him. But his haste had had a purpose this time. It had given him an excuse to move a few feet away to a chair in front of his tent where he could ostensibly busy himself with oiling and cleaning his rifle. The piece was in good order, as always, but by seeming to give it his attention he could keep watching Rachel without her noticing. Watching her was for him a total delight. She was twenty years younger than his fifty-five, and sitting there laughing and talking with the others she looked to him like a girl of eighteen. She was holding her own, too, though even at the same table with the general himself and the general's lady and Hoyt's Boston wife.

It was pleasant to think how much happier she looked now than that rainy night he had first seen her behind the counter at the Santa Fe station restaurant in Kansas City. She had thought she was marrying well in taking a major in the United States Army. She had not foreseen that the first years of her married life would be spent in desert hellholes like Fort Bowie, with her husband away most of the time and nothing for her to do but look out at the blowing sand and the cactus and the blazing sun. Still, she had not complained. She had done her part, and her part had been enough to transform his whole life.

Those at the table were particularly gay this morning. They had reason. After the Apache surrender the general's headquarters had been transferred to San Francisco, but he had not forgotten men who had served him in the desert. He had invited a succession of his hardest-working officers to his vacation camp in the California Sierras. To them it was more than a holiday. They had spent the better part of ten years chasing Apaches across the scorched expanses of Arizona, New Mexico and Mexico and a leave in this cool land of stupendous trees and rushing streams was like a turn in paradise. Wade was especially grateful for Rachel's sake. She had deserved a reprieve. It was also a satisfaction that two of his captains, Pete Hoyt and Tod Ward, his closest and oldest friends, were in this contingent. Even young Lieutenant Stuart Kirk had been included. He was a cub compared to them, but on that last run after Geronimo he had outlasted everybody. He was sitting beside Rachel now. It was another pleasure to note that the mannerly West Pointer was making himself as politely attentive to her as though she were the general's daughter.

A certain forced note in the gaiety at the table stirred Wade's complacence. He felt a slight premonition like the smell of danger that came when working up a canyon and suddenly suspecting that there might be an Apache sniper lurking somewhere among the crags above. Wade's perceptiveness, once focused, became acute. Most of the people at the table were apprehensive. Only the general was at ease. They knew something that the general did not yet know. Their hilarity was part of their attempt to disguise their alarm that he would learn of it. Anybody could understand their anxiety. The violence of General Miles's temper was a byword in the army. His wrath, once aroused, took no account of the consequences to himself, to his career, or to the prospects of his officers. Even his wife Mary, whom he worshiped, could never hold him back. Since his notable successes in the pursuit of Sitting Bull and the captures of Chief Joseph and Geronimo, his resentment at Washington's failure to appreciate sufficiently these triumphs had made him even harder to handle.

Moreover, this was the worst of all moments to get him launched on one of his famous outbursts. Everybody knew he was again being considered for another star. His many enemies would be only too quick to seize upon any irregularity in his military household, which might have

4

escaped general notice if not magnified by the roars of his displeasure, to help them get him passed over again.

Wade began idly to speculate on what the people at the table could be concealing. He had been in such a doze of contentment these last days that he had given heed to nothing but his casual hunting and to Rachel's pleasure in their holiday. It was odd that Pete or Tod had not consulted with him so that he could be lending a hand in hushing up whatever it was. Anyway, the breakfast had now come to a safe end. An orderly was bringing the general's horse and the general was off on his daily three-hour gallop.

Young Kirk came back from his tent with the two fishing rods. A feature of his kindness to Rachel had been in teaching her to fly-fish. So far the two had whipped the stretch of the stream flowing through the mountain meadow in which the camp was pitched. Each day Rachel had become more interested.

"Let's get going before the sun gets too high," said Kirk, handing Rachel her rod and creel. "Today I want to see you hook that big one under the rock."

"No," said Rachel, to everybody's surprise. "Today I want to try it alone. I mean it, Stuart. I want to see how much I've learned and how can I do that when you're there telling me every second what to do next?"

"Good for you," said Kirk. He rattled on with the garrulous gusto of a man absorbed in a hobby. "Then you take the South Fork. Don't hang around here in the meadow. Wait to start casting until you get up into the canyon proper. That's farther than we've been, and as soon's you get into water that hasn't been fished for a while you ought to get some good strikes. I'll take the North Fork." He gestured toward the lesser of the two canyons debouching into the meadow. "There's a little lake up toward the headwaters of that which might have some big ones in it. I've been wanting to get a crack at them."

Wade got to his feet. "Want I should go with you?" he asked Rachel.

"No, sweet," she said quickly. "I really want to try this alone. Your watching would only make me nervous. And you know how much you'd rather hunt."

The big smile she gave him made him turn back to his chair to hide the flush spreading over his seamed, sunburned face. This was a weakness that invariably came over him whenever she signaled her affection for him in the presence of other people. This time the warmth of her smile had been as unmistakable as the flash of a heliograph. He picked up his rifle and binoculars and turned again to watch Rachel until she was out of sight. It was just then that the sudden chill hit him. For he had caught the glances of relief being exchanged by Pete and Tod and Mabel and Mary as they stared after Rachel and Kirk going their separate ways.

The fools. So this was the mystery. They had somehow gathered the impression that something was going on between Rachel and young Kirk. Nothing was so sure to stir the general into one of his rampages than any hint that one of his officers was fooling around with another man's wife. This was probably in part due to his extraordinary devotion to his own wife but also to his basic assumption that his officers were necessarily gentlemen. Wade chuckled as he considered the nonsensical anxiety they had nursed. It served them right, even though with the general's promotion hanging fire everyone did have so much excuse to feel edgy. His chuckle had drawn the attention of the others. They had been his friends for years. Now they seemed strangers. They had never quite accepted her. Not from the first.

"I'm having another go at the mountain," he announced, offhand, nodding toward the wooded array of soaring cliffs behind the camp. "Up near the timberline there's an old ram with the biggest horns anybody's ever seen."

Striding away into the big trees encircling that side of the meadow, he chuckled again. He could sense the relief behind as they watched him, the supposedly offended husband, making off in yet a third direction.

As soon as he was well up the wooded slope, he began circling swiftly toward the outflung shoulder of the mountain that became the ridge rearing above the south rim of the canyon of the South Fork. He had not for a moment intended to allow Rachel to wander off unattended. She was a city girl and there was no limit to the trouble a tenderfoot could get into alone in wild country.

When he came out on the more barren slopes of the ridge where he could see the camp in the meadow far below as well as down into the canyon of the South Fork, he began taking the most careful advantage of every patch of cover. He had no fear of Rachel's spotting him, but the trained eyesight of Pete or Tod, were they to glance up, would catch any sign of movement within miles. He hardly wished them to imagine he was out spying on Rachel.

When at length he had squirmed out on a brush-fringed ledge and focused his field glass, he could see Kirk far across the valley still on the lower reaches of the North Fork. Kirk had not pressed up his canyon toward the headwaters lake he had mentioned. Instead he was fishing the stream with a furious energy that suggested he was endeavoring to fill his basket quickly. Just as puzzling, Rachel must not have paused to fish at all, for she was nowhere in sight below the first sharp bend of her canyon.

Wade dropped into a belt of aspen, trotted half a mile farther in its cover, and crept out again to another outlook. With a grunt of satisfaction he adjusted his binoculars. He could see Rachel now a thousand feet below. But the oddities in her behavior caused his skin to crawl. She had left her fishing gear somewhere behind and was scrambling up the boulder-filled stream bed toward a waterfall beside which stood a great incense cedar and a high white rock. Despite her haste, from time to time she crouched at some vantage point to look back and make sure she was not being followed. Reaching the waterfall, she climbed the rock with the same feverish impatience that had driven her thus far and gazed up the slope of the three-thousand-foot ridge that divided her canyon from Kirk's. Wade knew what he would see before he lifted his glass. Kirk, having also forsaken his fishing, had scaled the intervening ridge and was leaping and sliding down the face of it toward the waterfall.

Rachel slipped down from the rock and was edging backward into the shadow of the cedar. Wade began to shiver. He steadied his hands and the image at the waterfall became again agonizingly clear. Kirk leaped from boulder to boulder across the stream. Rachel flew out of the shadow of the cedar to meet him. The ardor of their embrace betrayed the passion each had struggled to contain since they had begun planning this rendezvous.

The glass slipped from Wade's fingers. The sharp clatter as it broke against a ledge a dozen feet below echoed like a gunshot along the silent mountainside. But nothing could have distracted the pair sinking down in the shadow of the cedar. Immersed in the twin roars of the waterfall and of their emotion, for them all else was silent.

As Wade emerged from the trees into the camp meadow, he could tell by the faces of Pete and Tod when they looked up from their pinochle game that he must be walking with the same step by step automatic gait as that evening when he had struggled back to bivouac with three Apache slugs in him. He felt as near death now. But his mind was as clear as it had been then. He kept walking until he stood over them.

"How long have you known?" he demanded.

"Nobody's known," said Hoyt. "Not for sure."

"You had to keep it from me," charged Wade. "In order to keep it from the general."

His friends stood their ground.

"You wouldn't have believed us," said Ward.

"If we could keep it from the general," said Hoyt, "there was always the chance it'd blow over."

"Not now," said Wade. "Not any more."

"You really going to throw her out?" asked Hoyt, approvingly.

"No. I want her back."

Ward's fascinated gaze was on Wade's fingers, playing over the lock of his rifle.

"Rusty — you thinking of shooting him?"

"No. I don't want her shamed."

"Want us to bear down on him?" offered Hoyt. "We might throw a scare into him — though he's not a lad that scares easy."

"No. Like I said, I don't want her shamed."

"Then," said Ward, "you'd better take her away from here as fast as you can."

"No. I know her. She's proud. She'd leave me. You don't seem to get the hang of this. She's twenty years younger than me but she's ten years older than him. If she cut loose from me he'd drop her straight off. She'd have nobody. She'd be nowhere."

"Just where you are now," said Ward.

"I can stand it. If there's no big fuss she would get over this. Something might be worked out. And as I keep saying, I don't want her shamed."

"For God's sake," said Hoyt, "what do you want?"

"I'll tell you what I want. I want you to figure some way that I don't have to have anything to do with to get him sent away from here. Right now. Today. Because if he's still here tomorrow I will shoot him. And that'll be something you'll have a hell of a time keeping from the general."

Wade plodded slowly back into the refuge of the big trees. Hoyt and Ward looked at each other and then by common consent made their way to the general's tent to lay the case before the second highest court, the general's wife.

"That Rusty," said Mary. "He's such a good man." She continued to knit busily while considering the problem. "I'll have to take it up with the general when he gets back — much as I hate to do that. Rusty's right. It would be so much better for everybody concerned, for all of us, if we could hit upon some official excuse for sending Stuart off on some assignment — even though it meant the young scamp's getting off unpunished. But it will have to be an excuse the general won't see through and that's never easy. I tell you what. Leonard's riding up from the railhead this morning. He'll have dispatches and maybe news. So you ride down the trail to meet him and tell him the story. His news just might help with the excuse. But if not, Leonard's always so good at thinking of ways to get things done."

Dr. Wood waved cheerily when he saw Hoyt and Ward riding down the trail to meet him.

"So you couldn't wait, eh?" he said. "Well, the news is not all good but for sure not all bad. No promotion yet. But Miles is going to be transferred to command the Division of the Missouri. His headquarters will be at Chicago. Play your cards right and you might get taken along. Chicago has its drawbacks but not so many as Fort Bowie." He looked at them more closely, his grin still cheerful. "What's the trouble? Miles off the reservation again?"

They told him.

"That Rusty," marveled Wood. "They well say there's no fool like an old fool. Let me alone a minute while I think. Could be I've already got the bear by the tail." They walked their sweating horses up the rocky trail. Wood pulled up. "Now listen and tell me if you think this might work. Miles sets great store by how he understands Indians. Maybe he does, but if so he's the only white man that does. At any rate, he's always trying to puzzle out what it is they're really up to. What reminded me of this was running into MacMurray yesterday at the Presidio. He was telling about a time five years ago — back in '84 when Miles was commanding the Department of the Columbia — the Indians in the Northwest got all stirred up about a new religion. The Smohalla cult, I think it was called. It soon petered out and the Indians went back to scratching and fishing. But this is the point: MacMurray had rank — he was a major — and yet Miles put him on detached duty and kept him nosing around among Indian towns and fishing camps for a whole year trying to find out just what hold this religious excitement had on them. Now keep your shirts on. I'm working toward something. At a lunch yesterday I also met Senator Stanford. He's always more interested in his railroad than in anything about the government. He was telling that for the last two or three months his train crews have been reporting no end of trouble with Indians jumping rides on their trains. From as far away as Colorado, Utah, Idaho, northern California, they're heading for some place in Nevada where a Paiute — Wovoka, or something like that — has set himself up as a prophet. What's attracting his visitors is word of a new kind of dance that he's teaching. Stanford didn't know what was so special about this dance but we know that whenever Indians take to dancing there's always mischief upwind. We've had no reports on this from the War Department or the Indian Service. They're always the last to catch on to anything, of course. Now, wouldn't you say that when I tell Miles about this — dressed up, a little, of course — he'll first get mad because he hasn't been kept informed and then feel straight off like sending someone to Nevada to look into it?"

"Why?" objected Hoyt. "If he's moving to Chicago what's he care about Indians dancing in Nevada?"

"You've put your finger right on it, Pete. In the Division of the Missouri he'll be responsible for the Plains Indians and they can be a lot more nuisance than these Diggers or Bannocks or Snakes. You know how fast news travels among Indians. First thing Miles will think of is — suppose by next spring the Crow or Cheyenne or Arapaho begin to take an interest in this new dance? Or — worst of all — the Sioux? My guess is Miles won't want to waste a minute finding out what he can about this Wovoka."

Ward had a more cogent objection. "But why send this ignorant young sprout Kirk?"

"Miles seems to think Kirk is smart enough. And not being a West Pointer, he likes to prove he's got no prejudice against one. Anyway, you're forgetting the main thing. This is not yet this general's business. He won't want to make a show of his investigation. If he sends one of you old-timers you'd likely be spotted by the first Indian agent or chief you ran into. But the lieutenant can put on civilian clothes and pass anywhere for — say — a newspaper reporter."

"It just might work," agreed Hoyt.

It did. When Wade at twilight emerged again from the trees, Lieutenant Kirk was already halfway down the trail to the railhead. Taking a long breath, Wade drew aside the flap and faced Rachel in their tent. She turned toward him from her dressing with a welcoming smile. In the lamplight her gaze seemed as innocent and untroubled as it had that morning.

II

As it grew darker Kirk pulled his horse to a walk. He had no wish to chance a stumble on this steep trail that might interfere with his catching that train. Giving less attention to his horse allowed him to give more to thoughts of his immediate future. What he might expect of it had taken an incredible turn for the better in the last few hours. Here he was actually on his way to San Francisco. Next, after a decent interval for preparation, he would be off on that singular Nevada excursion. It would undoubtedly prove a good deal less interesting than the preamble in San Francisco. But at least it would postpone by some weeks his return to the regiment. Now that the Apache war was over, garrison duty in an isolated Arizona fort was dull beyond comprehension or endurance. And, best of all, for these same weeks he would be completely on his own. An independent assignment, an official secret mission, as it were, was not something that often came the way of a fledgling lieutenant in the first years of his service.

His pleasant reverie reverted from the immediate future to the immediate past. This had been a special day, uniquely distinguished by double good fortune. Of all his amatory ventures, his experience with Rachel had been in every aspect the most satisfactory. As an added delight to her inherent female endowments, all the arrangements had worked just right. This had been due only in part to his good management. Her contribution had been superb. She had balanced daring and discretion with a sure judgment of which he had never thought any woman capable. She had, moreover, eased everything by making it clear from the outset that her acquiescence was to be limited to the single episode. There had been no foolish pretense, no silly affectation of either sentiment or virtue. Her case had been as forthright as his. Each had recognized the grip of a tension that required release. The extraordinary risk to which he was subjecting his career had minimized any misgivings he might have felt with regard to Wade. The same had probably been true with her, for she had seemed genuinely attached to her husband. All the same, it was just as well that this assignment had snatched him away. The explosive sensuality of that consummation under the cedar had surprised them both.

The mountain camp and San Francisco seemed suddenly memories of events out of a far past and a remote distance when, a week later, he dropped off the narrow-gauge train at the Walker Lake Paiute Agency. The intense blue of the lake at the foot of the range of red and black mountains rising at the farther end to a snow-capped peak formed a backdrop of lonely grandeur. But the dismal foreground presented only a greasewood-dotted flat of sunbaked sand, a scattering of smoke-blackened wikiups, and a dozen filthy, naked Paiutes lounging about the ramshackle frame agency.

Kirk picked up his luggage and threaded his way among the blank-faced Indians to the porch of the agency. A door leading off it was boldly lettered:

C. C. WARNER

AGENT

He knocked. There was a squeak of springs from a couch within. A corner of a window blind was twitched as someone took a second's glance at the visitor.

"Be with you in a minute," called a deep, resonant voice. There was the faint rustle of some activity and then the voice echoed again. "Come in. Come in."

Kirk entered. The agent was a short, stout man, nearly bald, bushily bearded, foppishly dressed, with a heavy gilt watch chain looped across his flowered waistcoat. The collar of his worn alpaca coat was still askew and two buttons of his faded vest still unfastened, indicating the haste with which he had made himself presentable after rising from the couch against the back wall of the office. He had seated himself behind a large plank desk covered with carefully arranged stacks of official-looking papers and documents, on all of which, Kirk noted, lay a film of desert dust, betraying how long since they had been touched. Warner looked up with the tolerance of the important official whose time is being wasted.

"Well, sir, what can I do for you?"

"My name's Stuart Kirk. I'm here to do a series of articles for the *San Francisco Chronicle*. Thought I'd better check in with you first."

"Very proper. If you left your luggage on the porch — better have it in. Never safe to leave anything around here a Paiute can pick up."

Kirk brought in his things. Warner peered at the mountaineer's knapsack, rod case and big carpetbag.

"Expect to write about fishing? Mining? The fishing's good but the mining's gone to pot."

"Neither. I came to see Wovoka — the Indian prophet."

"Wovoka? Oh, you mean Jack Wilson. I suppose you could call him a sort of a prophet. He got sick last winter and came out of it with some crazy dream or other. Indians are always dreaming."

Warner had turned even more elaborately patient. His visitor was bringing up matters too trifling to be worth consideration by a busy man.

"What I want most," persisted Kirk, "is to see this dance he's been teaching."

"Then you've come to the wrong place. There's been no dancing on this reservation. None."

"You mean your Paiutes have taken no interest in it?"

"I mean that's the sort of foolishness my regulations forbid. I rule with an iron hand. No velvet in my glove. Not that my Indians don't regard me as their best friend."

There were some odd characters in the army, reflected Kirk, but you could trust the Indian Service to round up the real curiosities.

"Anyway," he said, "long's I've come this far I want to see Wovoka. How do I find him?"

"Well, he works as a woodcutter for Dave Wilson." Warner swung around in his chair and gestured toward the majestic panorama beyond the window. "The Wilson ranch is way off the reservation — in Mason Valley, the other side of those mountains." Now that he had sufficiently emphasized the importance of his office Warner was becoming less pompous. "It's a forty-mile trip and there are no horses around so you'll have to foot it. But if you're still bent on it, I tell you what I'd do. Charley Sheep, Jack Wilson's uncle, lives in the third wikiup past that split rock. He knows a little English. If you show him a quarter he'll jump at the chance to take you to see the elephant — I mean the prophet." Warner laughed heartily at his little joke.

Charley Sheep proved to be a one-eyed, excessively thin, old Indian who, so far as could be seen through the dirt encrusting his scrawny frame, was constructed of charred rawhide. He kept his eye fixed disinterestedly on the sky while Kirk addressed him. There was no hint in his expression that he was comprehending any part of Kirk's proposal. But when Kirk tossed a silver dollar in his palm Charley instantly reached for it. Kirk put it back in his pocket. Charley was galvanized into activity. Setting off at a trot toward the railroad, he beckoned Kirk to follow.

Veering toward the river, he crossed the railroad by going under the bridge and kept on up the river bottom which, unlike the open desert, was checked with thickets of tule and sage. Kirk began profanely to protest. Charley appeared not to hear. He continued to trot and beckon. Kirk had come to a disgusted halt when he saw that Charley had also paused and was pointing in triumph. Kirk joined him at the edge of a cleared area among the six-foot-high tule and sage where the surface had been stamped flat.

"Dance," said Charley dramatically, getting out at last a word of English. "Dance." He illustrated by taking a few shuffling steps.

So there was a secret dancing ground within a mile of the agency. Kirk wondered whether the agent was too stupid to know what was happening on his own reservation or merely striving to conceal his inability to control his Indians. Charley was extending his hand again for the dollar. Kirk shook his head and resumed with many patient reiterations his attempt to explain what he wanted. At last Charley caught on.

"Wovoka," he exclaimed. "Wovoka."

He grinned his reproach that Kirk had not stated what he wanted in the first place, nodded his forgiveness, and set off at a trot back toward the railroad. At the embankment he sank down and squirmed in the sand into a position to take his ease. Then, reacting to Kirk's scowl, he sprang up and by intricate pantomime disclosed that the first stage of their journey must be by rail. Therefore they must wait here for the next northbound freight, on which they would catch a ride. Kirk had a better idea. He remembered that the triweekly northbound passenger train was due.

Returning to the agency, he picked up his knapsack, left the rest of his luggage with Warner, and emerged in time to flag the one-coach train. Charley was ecstatic. He had obviously never before been a paying passenger or so much as seen the interior of a passenger coach. From the steps he stared down haughtily at the awed assembly of his fellow Paiutes who had gathered to see him off. Thereafter, as the little train rocked and rattled along, he kept patting the wooden seat on the edge of which he perched while repeatedly springing up to peer from the windows on one side and then the other. After some twenty miles it was with the utmost reluctance that he indicated they were approaching the point where they must get off. Kirk persuaded the conductor to slow the train and they jumped.

They had dismounted near the sharp bend of Walker River where it swung around the northern shoulder of the Wassuk Range and pointed southward toward its source in the Sierras. Kirk was gathering that the lowland along this stretch of the river was the area known as Mason Valley. The soil next to the river, more fertile than the general Nevada desert, had attracted ranchers to supply the market created by Nevada's mining boom and when the boom had collapsed the ranchers had hung on. The region was made scenic by escarpments of black volcanic rocks and the encircling ramparts of snow mountains.

Charley kept going at his tireless trot, evidently impatient for the moment when the dollar would be his. Kirk might have had trouble keeping pace had he not been hardened by his recent months of campaigning. Charley's route kept well away from the ranchland along the river, forcing them to scramble continually up and down the lower slopes of the rocky foothills.

Some ten miles up the valley they crossed a very old trail showing many signs of recent use. It curled down out of the mountains to their left. From Kirk's estimate of the topography it appeared to come out on the other side near the head of Walker Lake and therefore near the agency and the railroad. He questioned Charley about the trail but Charley failed to understand, or at least so pretended. The matter became more mysterious when, looking back from the crest of the next foothill, Kirk noted that the trail, upon nearing the valley bottom, entered a patch of greasewood from which it did not emerge. People using the trail to get across the mountains evidently scattered at this point to leave no further trace of their passing.

With the exception of the secret dancing ground, nothing had developed since Kirk had knocked on Warner's door that had not been disillusioning. There seemed no escape from the growing impression that everything about his mission was nonsense. The existence of the mysterious trail, however, stirred in him a second slight flicker of interest.

When they sighted the next ranch, Charley pointed and spoke again. "Wilson," he said. "Wilson ranch."

Kirk had assumed this was to be their destination but Charley shook his head and kept on. They passed near enough to a Wilson horse pasture to enable Kirk to note the horses. He saw a strongly built bay gelding that he liked. Were he to remain in this country for even a few days he would have to acquire a horse.

They began getting into higher country as the east branch of the river below them swung nearer the Wassuk Range. Presently there were occasional wind-twisted pines. They crossed a number of small streams tumbling down from the higher ridges. In one Kirk saw the shadows of trout. They had come what Kirk judged to be ten or twelve miles past the Wilson ranch when Charley paused and pointed with a solemnity that bordered on awe.

"Wovoka," he announced. "Wovoka."

Some hundred yards ahead across a flat there stood a solitary wikiup in a clump of stunted pines at the foot of a little cliff. Charley emitted a low-keyed howl. A naked Indian who had been asleep in the sun jumped up and ran into the hut. Kirk started forward but Charley restrained him. In a couple of minutes the Indian emerged while attaching something to his right elbow. He had donned a big white sombrero and a whitish garment that extended to his knees.

"Wovoka," repeated Charley. "Wovoka."

The prophet had evidently needed the brief delay to assume the regalia of his office before receiving visitors. Charley indicated that the time had come to make their approach, remembered the dollar, and held out his hand. Kirk gave it to him. Wovoka stepped forward to meet them, extending his hand in friendly greeting to Kirk.

The prophet was dark, nearly six feet, more thickly and strongly built than most Paiutes, and appeared to be possibly thirty years of age. His features were broad and heavy and altogether without expression in repose. His hair was cut off square on a line below the base of his ears in Paiute fashion. The knee-length garment was of pink-striped white ticking, evidently at some time stripped from a bunkhouse pad. The white hat and the eagle feather attached to his elbow appeared to have great ritualistic significance, for Charley extended a finger toward each without touching either and then bowed his head reverently. Kirk was unable to guess whether Charley's postures of piety were sincere or staged for his benefit.

Charley thereupon embarked on an animated account of the circumstances connected with his conducting Kirk here. It appeared by his gestures that he dwelt in detail on the novelties of his ride in the passenger coach while pointedly refraining from any reference to the dollar. Kirk took advantage of this lengthy discourse to survey his surroundings. The prophet's residence was a typical Paiute wikiup of tule rushes laid on a pole frame. There were no utensils, furnishings or living comforts in it. Whatever honor he was given, the prophet had certainly found no profit in his own country. A young woman, presumably Wovoka's mate, was squatted by the fire pit nursing a year-old infant.

Farther along the base of the cliff was a large, hard-trodden dancing ground. At its other edge was a grove of larger pines, among which were a dozen or more other wikiups. A fair-sized mountain stream wound through the encampment. Seated or stretched out on the ground among the wikiups were the blanketed forms of thirty or forty Indians. Most likely, they were visitors from other nations, Kirk decided, with another flicker of interest, since few Paiutes possessed blankets.

Charley came at last to the end of his recital. Kirk in his turn addressed Wovoka, alluding to his having heard of the prophet's renown and to having come from beyond the Sierras to pay his respects. Wovoka's command of English appeared sufficient for him to catch the general drift of Kirk's remarks but not sufficient to reply except in his own tongue. In the hope of extending their communication, Kirk resorted to the sign language universal among mountain and Plains Indians, to an acquaintance with which he had devoted many hours of practice. But evidently this was not an art that had penetrated this far desert. Wovoka's only response was a puzzled stare. He waited until Kirk had abandoned his effort, then sat down on the ground and benevolently invited his guests to do likewise.

Without preamble Wovoka embarked upon the performance which had apparently by now become his long-established routine when receiving strangers. He first tried several minor conjuring tricks which culminated in his producing three eagle feathers from his sleeve, removing the hat, turning it upside down in his lap and waving over it the three feathers in such a manner as to permit the onlookers only the narrowest glimpse inside the crown. Charley started back in apparent terror but Kirk had been able to see nothing. Then Wovoka got to his feet and undertook a reenactment of what seemed to have been the events of the day he had had his historic vision. Some of his pantomime was so graphic that Kirk could pick out bits and pieces of the drama. Wovoka had gone up that high mountain towering over the upper valley, which Kirk knew from his map was Mount Grant, and there to the accompaniment of shuddering rolls of thunder the heavens had opened to him. After that climactic moment the relation got into more esoteric detail, which Kirk was unable to follow.

Kirk was getting restless. The sun was near setting. He had no wish to spend the night in a wikiup. He had already determined to make his way back to beg shelter at the Wilson ranch. Wovoka came suddenly and unexpectedly to his peroration. Kirk got up at once, proclaimed the intensity of his interest in what he had heard, and began taking his leave. To his relief, Wovoka, though still friendly, did not press him to stay and Charley seemed to take it for granted that now that he had his dollar his responsibilities as guide were ended.

Striding off down the rocky slope toward the valley bottom, Kirk ticked off the meager results of his first day's survey. He was forced to admit that Warner's estimate of Wovoka's unimportance could not be far off the mark. So-called prophets were always popping up among Indians everywhere. Few attracted much attention and all were soon forgotten. But surely a prophet more inconsequential than this Wovoka could scarcely be imagined. Yet if the rumors of delegates flocking from other nations had any foundation, and his own glimpse of the blanketed Indians in the pine grove lent some substance to the possibility, something must be attracting them. It could only be that there was something special about the dance. If he was to make any sort of a report to the general he would have to hang around until at the least he had seen that. Jumping one of the mountain creeks he again saw the shadows of trout. What a good thing that he had had the sense to bring his tackle. He might have to wait a while to get a look at the dance and meanwhile he could get in some fishing.

It was growing dark but there were as yet no lights in the Wilson ranch house. His approach, however, had been noted. Two cowhands came around the corner of the house from the direction of the corrals. One carried a lantern. He used its light to peer not at Kirk's face but at his feet.

"Seen you crost the valley tailin' along after Charley Sheep," he remarked. "You must of done fifteen, twenty mile *on foot.*"

So bizarre a mode of travel seemed to him totally incomprehensible.

"My feet certainly feel like it," said Kirk amiably. "My name's Stuart Kirk. I'm here from the *San Francisco Chronicle* to write a piece about Jack Wilson."

"Mine's Joe Fisher," said the man with the lantern, "and this here's" — he jabbed a thumb toward his younger companion — "Sam Hobby."

"All you could find worth writing about Jack," volunteered Sam, "you could set down on the back of an envelope."

Joe scowled at Sam for speaking up and turned back to Kirk. "Mr. and Mrs. Wilson," he said, "they won't be back till real late. But they always take in strangers. So you come with us."

He led the way to the bunkhouse. On the flat top of a sheet-iron stove bubbled a kettle of stew.

"Mrs. Wilson left that for us when they took off for Coyote Wells this morning," Joe explained. "They's a plenty."

While Sam cut thick slabs of bread Joe ladled out tin platefuls of stew. The three settled on stools around the pine table. The stew tasted as good as it had smelled. Braving Joe's displeasure, Sam returned to the subject of Jack Wilson.

"Mr. Wilson always says that of all the dumb Indians he ever hired that Jack was the dumbest."

"The agent, Warner," said Kirk, nursing the incipient argument between the two, "seemed to have the same idea. I got the impression from him that the Indians had lost interest in this dance."

Joe belched his disgust. "Sam here ain't been in the valley more'n four month and he ain't got an idea about this that ain't come from somethin' he's been told by somebody. And that Warner he don't know no more about his Indians than what he can see from his front porch." He placed his hands flat on the table on either side of his plate of stew in preparation for the delivery of his own more considered verdict. "The Paiutes they still set plenty store by Jack. Don't let nobody fool you about that. What got them so hung on him was his having that dream of his the day of the eclipse, last New Year's. Mr. Wilson and me we was over to the agency that day deliverin' some contract beef when the dark begun to come on. The Paiutes they begun hollerin' that the sun was dying and they set up a Christawful din of howlin', shootin', and bangin' on drums and pans. A good many got the notion some sacrificin' would help. They begun cuttin' theyselves with knives and killin' their dogs and chuckin' what little they owned into their cookin' fires and one squaw throwed her month-old baby in the river. When the sun begun to come back they was mighty relieved. Then before the scare wore off they heard about Jack comin' down from the mountain claimin' he'd been the one that managed it, by telling God to put the sun back where he found it. That struck the Paiutes as the only sensible way to account for what had been happening. Indians will grab at most any reason for anything so long's it ain't a good reason."

"Back in San Francisco," said Kirk, "I heard some story about delegates from other tribes coming here to see him."

"Don't you believe it," said Joe. "To get to Jack's camp they'd have to come up the valley like you did. Sam and me and Mr. and Mrs. Wilson, we ride range all the time and we ain't seen no Indians but once in a while a stray Paiute."

Intent as he was on Joe's comments, Kirk had been so worn out by the day's extraordinary exertions that it was with difficulty he was keeping his eyes open. His attention was momentarily recaptured when, upon ushering him to his bunk, Joe remarked:

"Was on that mattress they thought Jack had died just before he got up and walked off up the mountain."

But Kirk had no sooner let himself down upon the bed that had been so near a bier than he fell into a deep sleep from which he was only awakened by the usual early morning commotion in the ranch yard. He was washing and shaving at the horse trough when Sam paused beside him with a muttered warning.

"Here comes Mr. Wilson. Watch the kind of words you use 'cause he's a rock-bottom Christer."

Kirk turned, toweling himself, as Wilson came up with hand outstretched in welcome. His mild and friendly manner conformed to Sam's forecast but his eyes sharpened as might any more worldly horse dealer's when they caught the attention Kirk was paying the bay gelding. Joe was preparing to move the horses from the corral back to pasture. At a signal from Wilson he brought the bay over for Kirk's inspection. Presently, however, Wilson proved himself, after all, that rarest of human beings, a practicing Christian. Realizing Kirk's interest was genuine, he offered him the horse at the absurdly low price of twenty-five dollars. In response to Kirk's astonished glance, he came out with an apologetic explanation:

"He's young, strong and sound but he bucks hard for up to half an hour every time you lay a saddle on him, he'll bite you or kick you every time he gets a chance, even after you've been on him for hours he's still as spooky as all get out, whenever you pull him down to a walk he goes to dancing, and he's a terrible head-tosser."

Kirk still wanted him, and proved after five lively minutes that he could cope with the bucking. He insisted on paying a good price for saddle, bridle and spurs.

At breakfast in the ranch-house kitchen, served by Mrs. Wilson, he turned the conversation to Wovoka. Wilson at once looked immeasurably pained and grieved.

"That was the most miserable thing that ever happened to me," he said. "I myself shared the sin. Jack worked here for years. His Indian name was, as you make it, Wovoka, which means cutter, but everyone in the valley knew him as Jack and added the surname Wilson because he worked here so long. We liked him. He wasn't too smart but he was strong and willing. A good worker."

Mrs. Wilson was watching her husband with deepening concern. His emotion seemed a problem with which she had been long familiar.

"We kept him cutting and hauling wood," she put in, "because he wasn't much use around the corral or mending fence or doing anything that made him have to think."

Wilson had ceased to eat and was staring at the opposite wall. "That made him so much the more my responsibility." He drew a long breath. "Anyway," he resumed, "in my house we have Bible reading and prayers every evening. Jack used to like to sit and listen. He never learned much English but it didn't seem to me his being there while the Good Book was being read and prayers were being said could do him anything but good. It looked to me like some glimmer of what was right and true and holy might rub off on him. That was my great mistake."

"Stop saying that," demanded Mrs. Wilson. "You might's well claim it would have been a mistake if you'd taken him with you to church."

"Mrs. Wilson is good at making excuses for me," said Wilson. "She ought to be after all the years she's had to make 'em. But it was a mistake. A terrible mistake. Because last winter just before Christmas he got fearful sick of some sort of fever."

"For a week we every minute thought he was dying," said Mrs. Wilson.

Wilson rose to his feet, clutching at the edge of the table. He was beginning to sweat.

"Instead, one night — it was New Year's Eve — he got up out of his bed and went off up that mountain. When he came down — God forgive me, like Moses from Sinai — he claimed he'd had a vision — that he had talked to God. That was the day of the total eclipse and he said that it had been his communion with God that had blotted out the sun and then made it shine again. I tried to make him understand that all that had happened to him was the delirium of a fever. But he wouldn't listen. Instead *he* began preaching to *me* — he, this clod who didn't

23

know his big toe from his elbow, began instructing *me* in matters of religion. I tried to stay patient but when he began saying that he was the Messiah — that he, this heathen, black Paiute, was Christ returned — that was too much. I had to send him packing."

Wilson sank heavily into his chair. As if relieved by the violence of his outburst, he suddenly became calm again.

"If you're thinking of staying a spell in the valley, Mr. Kirk," he said, "we'd be pleased to have you as our guest."

"Nothing would suit me better. That is, if it's as paying guest."

"Talk to Mrs. Wilson about that."

"Would five dollars a week seem too much?" she asked.

"Hardly," said Kirk, rising. "Thank you both, for taking me in and for all you've told me. I have to pick up the rest of my stuff at the agency but I should be back by late afternoon."

He set off down the valley but once out of sight of the ranch house circled through the foothills to pick up the mysterious trail. The bay, which Wilson had said had been named Badger to go with his mean temper, took to the steepest slope with a smooth, powerful stride. As Kirk had suspected, the trail wound up and over a shoulder of Black Mountain and then dropped down toward the head of Walker Lake. In its dust and sand were the fresh prints, made during the preceding night, of at least a dozen pairs of moccasined feet. It was obvious that this was the route used by reservation Indians whenever they wished to attend Wovoka's ceremonies.

Senator Stanford had told Dr. Wood that Indians in various parts of the West had been jumping railroad trains to come to the Paiute country but the local agent, Warner, had said nothing of such arrivals. If there had been such visitors, Kirk concluded, they could have dropped from the train before it reached the agency, surreptitiously contacted their Paiute hosts, and been guided by them over the mountains to Wovoka's camp. At any rate, the trail which the prophet's congregation had used to conceal all comings and goings ended in a patch of river-bottom tule and sage a scant two hundred yards from the agency.

Warner, despite his pose of lofty disinterest, could not altogether disguise his curiosity about Kirk's activities, which Kirk did nothing to satisfy until he was on the point of leaving.

24

"When your Indians stage their next dance," he assured the agent as he turned to mount, "I'll be back to take you to it."

He heard nothing of Warner's response on account of the immediate violence of Badger's objection to accepting the additional burden of the carpetbag and the rod case. The ensuing conflict lasted for minutes that toward the last seemed to Kirk like hours. Paiutes came running from all quarters to witness the spectacle. Many roused from their usual apathy to howl with glee or to yell encouragement to the horse. Badger's frenzied leaps and plunges demolished one wikiup and at another moment carried him up on the porch of the agency. However, in the end the horse was the one to submit. He stood, sweating and trembling, while Kirk dismounted and tied the carpetbag and rod case to the back of the saddle, and started off at an easy lope when Kirk had remounted.

Kirk kept to the line of the railroad until well out of sight before circling to pick up the mountain trail. Within a matter of hours the Indians would know of his use of it but if they relished making a more complete ass out of that fool of an agent he felt no impulse to interfere with the process.

Swinging up the slope from the river to the Wilson ranch yard, Badger strode as effortlessly as when he had set out that morning, even after a thirty-five mile day that had included two long steep climbs. Kirk dismounted at the corral gate, untied his luggage, stripped off saddle and bridle, and began cooling him. Joe and Sam climbed to perches on the corral fence and stared at horse and rider.

"He give you much trouble?" Sam asked.

"None to speak of."

Joe spat and eyed the blood-crusted spur gouges on Badger's flanks. His unwinking gaze came back to Kirk. He was baffled by the difficulty of relating Kirk's behavior to what might reasonably be expected of a man who worked for a big city newspaper.

"When I was a boy," explained Kirk, very casually, "I used to spend summers at my uncle's ranch in Wyoming."

"So?" said Joe, still dissatisfied.

Kirk was a firm believer in the military principle that any territory in which there was any possibility of action deserved a thorough reconnaissance. Early the next morning, he set off on a wide circuit of the region encompassing Wovoka's camp. He took along his rod case so that if his presence in the vicinity were discovered he could pretend that his only interest was fishing. For hours he worked his way over a remarkably rough terrain, in and out of canyons, over ridges, through patches of juniper and pine. The area was crisscrossed by old trails and cart paths, none of which had been used for years. He sighted a number of small mine workings, but all had long since been abandoned. Occasionally he found an outlook from which he could see down into Wovoka's camp. All of the blanketed Indians were stretched out on the ground. Whatever their activities, they must be reserved for nighttime, forcing the prophet's devotees to sleep away their days.

He had all but completed the circuit and was turning back toward the lower valley when he came upon a particularly promising stream. It was still early afternoon and he decided to stop long enough to try a few casts. He hobbled Badger in a clump of cottonwoods where he could occupy himself gnawing bark, unlimbered his rod, and started up the canyon toward the sound of a waterfall. The canyon narrowed and heightened. Near the fall there was a succession of three pools and in each of them he got a strike and a trout.

"Great jumping Jesus Christ," came a voice out of the air overhead, "if that ain't about the slickest way of catching fish ever I seen."

Kirk stiffened and looked up to see squatting on a ledge above a little gnome of a man clad only in a wide floppy straw hat and a burlap breechclout. A battered old Winchester lay across his knees. His skin was so sun-blackened that he would have passed for a Paiute had it not been for his extraordinarily bright blue eyes.

"Is that a real bug?" he demanded, pointing at the fly dancing in the wind at the end of Kirk's leader. "How do you make it do just what you want it to?"

"It's only a twist of horsehair," said Kirk, grinning. "It's the tip of the rod that makes it act like it does."

"Come up to my place," invited the little man. "It's just above the falls there. I got a pond with fish in it ten times the size you been catching. I want to see what happens when you tie into one of them."

His tone was so eager, if slightly combative, and his manner altogether so engaging, that Kirk had no thought of hesitating. Holding his rod thrust carefully away from him into the air, he scrambled up, and followed along the ledge around the falls until they came out upon a flat where, shaded by several big pines, there stood a weather-beaten clapboard shanty with a rusted tin chimney from which came a curl of smoke.

Behind the shanty against the mountainside was the opening of a mine shaft that had been long unworked. Vines hung over the tunnel entrance and a few odds and ends of rusted machinery lay about. Nearly half the flat was devoted to a kitchen garden in which there was evidence that during the past summer a variety of crops had been cultivated, including corn, squash, beans, potatoes and onions. On a drying rack alongside the garden, festoons of meat which might be either venison or mountain sheep were drying in the sun. On the other side of the stream was a narrow meadow in which grazed an old gray mule. All of his host's attention, meanwhile, was concentrated on his one objective. He tramped on through the drying vines of the garden to the edge of a forty-foot-wide expanse of water, where an upthrust strata of rock had dammed the stream into a deep dark pool. Here he turned to gesture challengingly.

Advancing to his side, Kirk accepted the challenge by whipping his line back and forth twice in the air and then casting it expertly so that the fly dropped just short of the overhanging bank across the pool. It had hardly settled lightly on the surface when there was a great swirl out of the depths, the tip of his line jerked and his reel began to scream. It took many minutes of the most vigilant persistence, repeatedly checking and turning at the last second the trout's frenzied charges about the pool, before Kirk had the eight-pound beauty gasping on the bank.

"Never would have believed it without seeing it with my own eyes," marveled the gnome. "Them goddam trout — they been thumbing their noses at me the past four years. I've time and again got me a stout willow pole and used waxed pack thread strong enough to hold that mule and hooks big enough to hang a side of beef to and them goddam fish they just bust my gear all to hell. And here you come along and bring in one the size of that with a sliver and a length of cobweb." He eyed the slender, varnished rod enviously. "Tell me, could I get me something like that — maybe in Carson?"

"I don't see why not," said Kirk. "This one happens to be an English rod. But there are American makes just about as good."

The little man suddenly swept off his hat, whacked it remorsefully against his thigh, and clapped it back on again. In the brief interval his head was uncovered Kirk saw that he was quite bald, the scalp a startling white in contrast to the copper tone of the rest of his skin.

"Goddam," he exclaimed. "I got me so worked up about your tricks I clean forgot my manners. My name's Clem Cheever."

"Mine's Stuart Kirk."

They shook hands formally. Clem raised his voice in several guttural bursts of Paiute. The door of the shanty opened and three Indian women came out. They were moving slowly at first but at another bark from Clem they stepped out more briskly. One was middle-aged with a wrinkled, pockmarked face. The second was large and muscular with a shy grin that showed several missing teeth. The third was slender and graceful and looked to be still in her teens. All were clad in nothing more than short grass skirts and the girl clearly had a more than passable figure.

"The old one's Minnie," said Clem, presenting them. "She's for cooking. The big one's Lettie. She's for the heavy work. The young one's Susie. She's for fun." He glanced down at the trout. "You want to take that with you or do we eat it here and now?"

"We eat it here and now."

At a peremptory gesture from Clem, Minnie scurried forward to pick up the fish and the women retired with it to a fire pit near the shanty. Clem looked longingly at the rod.

"Could I just hold it in my hand for a minute?" he asked.

"Of course. Try a few casts."

"Nope. Not me. I'd only make a hash of it. What I want to remember is the way you handled it. It ain't every day you can see something being done just right." He handed back the rod. "So, let's just set down and have us a smoke. I ain't got no liquor. No way to keep it away from the women."

When they were puffing comfortably Clem looked at Kirk with another of his childlike smiles. "You're too polite to come right out with what you're thinking. But it stands to reason," his gesture indicated the shanty, the garden, and the women, "you're curiouser than Christ on the Cross about how I came by this setup. Well, I'll tell you. I like to paw over what it took for me to come by good sense after going without even a smidgeon of any for fifty-three years. For thirty of them years I was a Nevada miner. God making the world never worked no harder than I did. Three times I ran my stake up toward a million and three times I lost it all. This," he inclined his head toward the shaft entrance back of the shanty, "was my last mine. Also the poorest. When it petered out I was just putting the barrel of my shotgun in my mouth when I remembered I still had two thousand dollars in a Carson bank. So I decided first to just lay around in the sun here while it lasted. That's what I'm still doing. I'd never loafed before in my life and it's a pleasure that keeps growing on me. You should try it sometime."

"You have the Garden of Eden without the snake," acknowledged Kirk. "But I do have one question. There's still a lot of work around here. How do you keep your women at it?"

"Well, they don't exactly mislike me." A note of masculine complacence came into Clem's tone. "For sure, the young one don't. But I do scheme a little. Every six or eight weeks I put on some clothes, get on my mule, and jog along up to Carson. I draw maybe twenty dollars at the bank and when I come back I bring, besides a little salt, coffee and sugar, a ten-pound sack of rock candy and a gallon of brandy. The women they nibble on the candy for weeks but it's the thundering big drunk we have on the brandy when I first get back that really fetches 'em. You couldn't blast 'em away from me with a charge of dynamite."

The women brought the fish on a wooden platter, along with a bark tray heaped with corn cakes. The trout had been stuffed with some kind of desert herbs and baked whole in the ashes. It was delicious. The women waited passively for some sign of Clem's further wishes. After sampling the fish and cakes he waved them away indulgently. They returned to the shanty.

"They ain't worth a goddam long's this dancing's going on," Clem grumbled. "All they want to do is sleep all day."

"Dancing?" Kirk inquired idly, taking another mouthful of trout.

29

"Down at Wovoka's camp. Have another cake. They're pretty good. That Minnie. She can cook even in her sleep." Clem, again disgruntled, looked toward the shanty. "Flat on their beds again. But come sundown, they'll be up and off, bright-eyed as weasels."

"Then there's a dance tonight?" Kirk hoped he was succeeding in sufficiently concealing his interest.

"They's one about every two weeks. Take some more fish. Funny thing what a difference there is between fresh fish and when it's even an hour old. Every dance lasts four nights. The fourth night's the big one. Tonight's is one of them."

"Have you seen any of them?" Kirk asked, still elaborately casual.

"Three or four times. It gives you the prickles when you first start to watch. Then they keep on with the same rigmarole over and over and over and it begins to get goddam tiresome. But my fool women, they wouldn't miss a minute of it."

"Sounds sort of odd, at that," said Kirk. "I'll be around for a while. Any chance you ever taking me to see one?"

"Sure. Why not?"

Kirk abandoned all caution. "I'll give you that rod if you'll take me down there tonight."

"You don't have to give me no rod. I'll get me one good enough for me up at Carson. Course I'll take you down there tonight. I don't average a visitor a year and never one the pleasure you've been. Now we better have us a little snooze because it's going to work up to a long night. The moon'll be up about three hours after dark so's we can see better then getting down there. We won't be missing nothing. It's never till long about midnight the dance ever begins to liven up. At the start everything goes so slow it's hard to stay awake enough to watch."

Clem stretched out in the sun and fell asleep at once. But Kirk found that he had too much to think about. He must certainly consider it a great stroke of luck to have met Clem. He could hit upon no reason to mistrust the old miner or even to question the soundness of his judgment. As a professional soldier he had been accustomed to taking it for granted that all Indians were either actual or potential enemies. The thought of casually strolling in on a dance-excited pack of them in the middle of the night took a little getting used to. He decided to go see how Badger was behaving but had scarcely started to get up when Clem's eyes opened.

"If you're going down to see about your horse," he said, "leave your pistol there. We won't be wanting it with us."

Kirk had thought the flat armpit holster under his shirt was something less than obvious. He grinned and nodded. He found Badger had not strayed ten feet. He was somnolently gnawing from a young cottonwood all the bark he could reach. For a horse who had some bad habits he also had some very good ones. Kirk disassembled his rod, restored it to its case, and stowed his pistol in the saddlebag. With a hundred or more Indians capering about, having a gun would be no help. Clem had been right about that.

Back at the flat he dozed fitfully until the three women, now giggling and chattering excitedly, set out. In the sunset light all the more distant mountains were an unearthly pink. Then he at last fell asleep. When Clem aroused him he got up stiffly. The desert night had turned chill. Clem had put on a pair of ragged corduroy pants, an equally tattered woolen shirt and, in place of the wide-brimmed straw hat, a knit stocking cap. He looked more than ever like a gnome. There was a folded blanket over his arm and he handed another to Kirk.

"Toward morning," he forecast, "it'll get cold enough down there to frost your mustn't touch it."

The rising three-quarter moon gave just enough light to help them down some of the steeper drops of the rugged descent.

"If I hadn't taken such a fool shine to you," grumbled Clem, "I could have been warm in bed dreaming about Susie instead of stumbling around out here in the dark trying to break my goddam neck."

They worked their way down into the canyon formed by another stream and then with even more difficulty for a mile or more down its boulder-strewn bed. But when they climbed out of the canyon the going suddenly became easier. They had come upon one of the old dirt roads that once had served some forgotten mine. For a time there was only the sound of the rushing stream behind them but then as they kept on another sound ahead began to become faintly audible. As they went on it grew slowly stronger — a wailing, eerie kind of singsong, as unearthly as the pink mountains at sunset. Clem paused to listen.

"Beginning to pick up," he pronounced with satisfaction.

He turned off the road and after another two hundred yards they came out on the crest of the cliff Kirk remembered behind Wovoka's hut. Through the tops of the pines intervening between their position and the dancing ground he could see the glow of many fires and even catch occasional glimpses of moving figures. With their arrival at the top of the cliff the sound of the singing had become less muffled. There was something senseless about the tone that made him think of the stridency of night bird calls.

"No use hanging back here," said Clem. "We might's well get close up where we can see good."

"They don't object to strangers?"

"The state they got theyselves into by now — was the whole 7th Cavalry to ride up with the band playing they wouldn't take no notice."

Clem led the way down a cleft in the face of the cliff and on into the pine grove. All around them were the shadowy hulks of the wikiups Kirk had noticed on his visit to Wovoka. The air was acrid with the stench of an Indian encampment. They kept on toward the firelight until they came out of the grove at the edge of the dancing ground.

"Don't want to get too close." Clem had to raise his voice to be heard above the singing. "When they get to really jumping around we don't want no happenstance kick in the mouth."

He found a place at the base of a pine, spread his blanket, drew Kirk down beside him, and busied himself with drawing Kirk's blanket around them. All of Kirk's attention was on the dance.

Some hundred and fifty men and women were taking part. They were in a great circle formed by clasping the hands of their partners on either side. The circle rotated first one way and then the other as in a child's game of ring-around-the-rosy. The music was all vocal. There were no drums or other instruments. The beat of the dancers' feet and the contortions of their bodies accompanied their own choral singing. Wovoka had his place in the ring. When there was an occasional break in the singing it was his voice that initiated the next chant.

What most distinguished the dance was the entranced expressions of the dancers, their glazed eyes, and spasmodic movements. They seemed in the grip of a force other than their own will. They had escaped into a different world. The endless reiterations of the same chants and the swaying, shuffling, stamping steps seemed to have produced in them a kind of self-hypnosis. While just watching and listening, Kirk found the need to resist the tug of that hypnotic effect. To shake it off he began checking over the facts he needed for his report.

"What's his Messiah claim got to do with this?" he asked Clem.

"Nothing. White folks in the valley never have got the hang of his story. Wovoka don't claim to be no Messiah. What he claims is that he's the prophet able to tell them the Messiah's coming. Maybe any day. Maybe next summer. But that for sure he's on his way."

"Does he mean Jesus Christ?"

"Nope. He means the Indian Messiah. They've got one, too. From what my women tell me it ain't too clear to them just who he is. Maybe not to Wovoka either. I remember in school reading Longfellow's 'Hiawatha.' Maybe it's something like that."

"Then like our Seventh Day Adventists the Indians believe the Second Coming is near and this dance is their way of getting ready for it?"

"Nope. There's a sight more to his deal than that. When he came down from the mountain after talking to God the day they say the sun died he brought the biggest news Indians can hear or ever dream of hearing. What he told them was that if they danced long enough and hard enough to prove they believed, then the Messiah would show up leading all the Indians who have ever died to join up with the few still left alive. Not only that but everything else — birds, fish, game, especially buffalo, trees, grass, mountains, plains — everything would be put back just like it was before the white men came to mess it all up."

"With this help from their ancestors do they count on being able to drive the white men away?"

"Nope. The biggest part of this religion of Wovoka's and the part that he keeps pounding into them is that if they want to bring this off they got to prove to the Messiah they're in earnest. To do that they've got to be good Indians. They got to love each other — to love everybody. They got to stop drinking and quarreling and cheating and stealing and whoring. But most of all they got to stop fighting. They must never again hit anybody — even a dog or a horse."

"But how then do they plan to get rid of the white men?"

"They won't have to. When the Messiah puts everything back like it was, the white men will naturally still be the other side of the ocean where they came from and where they can't be no bother no more."

Wovoka's preposterous doctrine was made to seem to Kirk even more preposterous by the matter-of-fact tone of Clem's exposition of it. Surely even the most primitive and ignorant of savages could not embrace a faith that was at once so infantile and so totally irrational. Yet, studying the rapt faces of the dancers as they stamped and chanted he could see that they did believe. When they lifted their unseeing eyes to the night sky there could be no doubt that they fully expected at any moment to witness the opening of the heavens and through the gates of the past the spirits of their countless ancestors streaming downward in ghostly procession to a reunion with them.

Staring at the writhing figures, listening to the wailing chant, Kirk was enfolded in a kind of fascination which gradually began to make the scene seem even to him less unreal, less impossible. The cadence of the dance was becoming faster, more frenzied. Each dancer was by his own postures and contortions, his own cries and groans, endeavoring to find individual expression for the ecstasy of his personal emotion. The mood of mass hypnotism was tugging ever more strongly at Kirk's sensibilities. It was becoming difficult for him to resist the feeling that he, too, was drifting into a species of trance. Later he recalled that he must have dozed. In any event, he had lost track of time for he was suddenly surprised to realize that the light of dawn was paling the glow of the fires.

The dance had reached its climax. The dancers were leaping and yelling and waving and shaking their blankets or shirts or petticoats over their heads. Then with one final crescendo of yelling, all cast aside their blankets and all articles of clothing and rushed together to the stream on the farther edge of the dancing ground and plunged into the icy waters.

"Washing their sins away," said Clem, getting up. "We might as well be on our way before they start coming back sober."

They climbed the cleft in the cliff and picked up the dirt road. Back in the cottonwood grove Kirk turned from the saddling of Badger to say good-bye to Clem.

"I certainly thank you," he said, gripping Clem's hand. "You don't know what a service you've been."

"I got some idea," said Clem, "You're from the army, ain't you?"

"Yes. I don't mind your guessing but I hope you won't spread the word around. That brings me to what I want most to know. How many of those dancers were from other tribes?"

"About half. Along in the summer outsiders began sneaking in. At first only a few, then, as word began getting around, a good many more. All were from this side the Divide, Utes, Snakes, Bannocks, Pits and even two Mohave. But for the dance before this one a batch of Plains Indians showed up. My women were all excited about that. Five Arapaho, three Cheyenne, and four Crow. Then just before this dance there turned up," Clem paused for a second to savor the significance of his next words, "seven of Custer's friends, the Sioux. That's what my women and everybody else here set the most store by of anything yet. I remember three of the names, Good Thunder, Short Bull, and Kicking Bear."

"You've certainly made me the world's champion investigator," said Kirk. "I'm leaving the rod case and tackle box there under that cottonwood whether you want them or not."

The Wilson ranch house was empty. He picked up his knapsack and carpetbag and left a five-dollar bill on the mantel. Badger made the forty-five miles to Carson City with the ease Kirk had learned to expect.

The stir of excitement that remained with him had not sprung from any of the impressions left by those hours at the dance. Nothing he had seen there had altered his feelings about Indians. Chasing Apaches, he had cornered and killed them with no more remorse than were he exterminating predatory animals. Though much less dangerous, the dancers had in his estimation betrayed the same subhuman nature by the absurdity of their antics.

What did continue to excite him was his appraisal of the possible advantage he might gain from this first independent assignment of his military career. The period of Indian wars having apparently ended with the capture of Geronimo, from now on any junior officer was certain to find the scramble for promotion even more difficult. Much could therefore depend on his report on the Wovoka religion and the dancing.

35

More important than anything else, of course, was the need to make sure that the sharp-eyed general did not suspect what he had in mind.

Writing and rewriting his report through the night in his Carson City hotel room, he took pains to keep his account terse, factual, objective. If he dwelt on the frenzy aroused among Wovoka's followers by the excesses of the dance he took equal care to state that there was no evidence that the movement represented any military threat, the essence of the new religion appearing on the contrary to be a species of pacifism. He saved for the last his mention of the startling fact that already the Plains Indians were sending delegates to Wovoka. Then, as a final spur to the general's unease, he cited the names of the three Sioux furnished by Clem, names which Kirk suspected were of prominent and possibly militant Sioux the general could have known during his famous pursuit of Sitting Bull.

He sat back, satisfied with the professional accuracy of his report and with the manner in which he had disguised his purpose. But this had left him something less than an even chance that he would succeed in nudging the general toward ordering a continuation of his intelligence mission, whether here in Nevada or, much more to be desired, among the Plains Indians. Something more was needed to win him the freedom of movement and opportunity to attract the attention of his superiors that would be denied him were he to be returned to the routine of desert service.

Finally, inspiration came to him. He drew another sheaf of paper before him and set to work upon a letter to his New York hometown neighbor, Frederic Remington, the famous western artist and war correspondent. The theme of his letter was a more detailed, more colorful and far more lurid account of what he had witnessed than he had given the general. A secondary inspiration led him to the invention of the right kind of name for it: the Ghost Dance.

Kirk's excitement mounted as he wrote. He had known Remington since as a ten-year-old he had followed Remington's football career at Yale. He was certain of Remington's response. His interest would be captured at the outset by the necessity of keeping the identity of his informant a secret. As he read on he would be fascinated. No one in the country was so absorbed in everything western. Nothing could more

36

surely fire his imagination than this weird rite, so unprecedented, so grotesque, and yet so typically Indian. With his characteristic energy and volatility, he was bound to rush off to Washington to make inquiries at the War Department, the Indian Bureau, and possibly the White House. He would learn little or nothing there, where it was unlikely anyone had as yet so much as heard of Wovoka. But this would only serve to add fuel to his curiosity. He would contact his many western friends, undoubtedly go west himself. Meanwhile, puzzled officials would have begun to investigate. Western newspapers, pretending they had known all along, would be discussing the phenomenon. Western politicians, ever on the alert to recognize Indian trouble, would be magnifying the threat. Even if the cult were dying out and the dancing had ceased, the sensation would persist. The widening ripples of public excitement would reach and affect the general.

The morning sun was pouring in the window when Kirk laid down his pen. He leaned back, well pleased with his device.

III

JOHN WINTHROP, managing his skis with a native strength and agility that partially compensated for his want of skill, worked his way back to the crest of the ridge. He paused, breathing deeply, soothed by the special satisfaction that came over him whenever able to contemplate a scene the foreground of which, at least, remained uncluttered by humanity or its works. With the approach of spring the snow on these magnificent New Hampshire hills had begun turning dingy and splotched but the late-March fall last night had restored all of winter's pristine elegance. The nearest visible habitations, miniaturized by distance, were the houses of Hanover village and the halls of Dartmouth College. He could just catch the glitter of the sun on the tiny dormer window of his attic room in Wentworth. He felt the need to remind himself constantly that though Dartmouth had been founded as an Indian school he was in this generation the only Indian among its students. Among his predecessors had been Indians as distinguished as Joseph Brant and Samson Occom but he was now the sole representative of his race.

He essayed another descent. He was beginning to gain some control over the slender twin toboggans which could behave alternately with such infuriating malevolence or such graceful precision. The downhill speed, while it lasted, was exhilarating. He was not troubled by the inevitable spills. Any fall with a horse on hard ground was more painful and no less ignominious than these rolls in the snow. When he had borrowed the skis from Ben Majors this morning he had imagined his experience with snowshoes might stand him in some stead. This had not been the case. Ben's had been the first skis to appear at Dartmouth. He had said they were a Norwegian device. Undoubtedly the Norwegians learned about them while still very young, as he had about horses.

In any event, he had not come out this morning for the sake of the skis, entertaining as his struggle with them had proved. They were merely incidental to his plan. He had often noted that he never thought so clearly as when absorbed in violent activity. Instead of brooding with emotional cloudiness his mind seemed to click on and off with flashes of true perception. It was so now. His plan was as intricately detailed as any ever involved in the theft of Crow horses, but each recurring flash reassured him that it was sound. Its success promised even more gratification than could ever have been gained from taking advantage of the Crow.

Suddenly the cutter had come into view around the bend of the Etna road. He surveyed the slopes below, selected his route, and launched his descent toward the road, directing his every faculty to avoiding a fall that would throw off his timing. He contrived so well that he hurtled from the roadside snowbank immediately in front of the fast-stepping trotter. The horse reared. The girl screamed. John disengaged from his skis and ran to seize the bridle. The horse quieted, immediately responding to the touch and tone of the expert horseman.

"I hope you can forgive me, Miss Barret," said John, touching his wool cap. He gestured toward the skis. "I'm so unused to those things that I wasn't paying attention and didn't realize how near I was to the road."

"I didn't see you either, Mr. Winthrop," said Dorcas Barret, giggling. "Not until you burst out of that snowbank like — like a cannonball." The girlish giggle became a bolder laugh as she regarded him. "You must have fallen a lot. There's snow even in your eyelashes."

She had not dropped the reins, he noted with grudging approval. She appeared to have been more diverted than frightened. For all her blond curls and pink and white prettiness she seemed endowed with unsuspected spunk. This was disconcerting, for he had counted on her being enough disturbed to permit him to offer to drive her the rest of the way in. He picked up his skis and advanced to the side of the cutter.

"These godforsaken contraptions made me lose track of time along with everything else. If I don't get back fast I'll miss this afternoon's lacrosse game. Maybe you'll prove you've forgiven me by allowing me to hitch a ride behind."

"Of course," she assented. Then, when for a second he continued to stand his ground beside the cutter with his hand on the gilt-edged dash, she yielded entirely. "But you don't have to hang on back there." She threw back the buffalo robe over her knees and made room for him beside her. "Get in."

He leaned the skis against his shoulder and settled contentedly into the seat. With her still driving and his sitting alongside as an invited passenger, he was doing even better than he had foreseen. The trotter resumed his swift pace.

"Fine horse," observed John.

"Isn't he?" agreed Dorcas enthusiastically. "His name's Sultan."

John looked from the horse around at the ornately decorated body of the cutter as though only now becoming aware.

"This looks almost like Jeffrey Bradford's outfit."

"It is his," said Dorcas, flushing happily. "He insisted on lending it to me this morning because he knew I wanted to visit my aunt in Etna."

She was still flushing. Some elation was understandable in a Hanover shopkeeper's daughter who had elicited so marked a sign of favor from the wealthiest and most celebrated of Dartmouth's current students.

"You drive very well," said John.

"We've always had horses. Though never one as good as Sultan."

It would be particularly helpful if when they made their campus entrance they were seen to be engaged in animated conversation.

"My first horse," he volunteered, "I stole from a Pawnee."

She took the bait promptly. "I'm just dying of curiosity, Mr. Winthrop. They tell so many stories about you. Jeff says most of them can't be true."

"For example," he encouraged her.

"That you were at Custer's Massacre, for instance. But that can't be. You're not that old."

"Well, I was a little late getting to Dartmouth. For one thing, I didn't start to learn English until I was nineteen. So I am old enough to have seen the battle. At the age of eleven from a hilltop, where I was holding Sitting Bull's horse while he was doing his conjuring."

"It's no wonder you and Jeff stand out so from the other boys," mused Dorcas. "You've both done so many interesting things. And you're both older."

"Did he have trouble with his English, too?"

"Of course not. You know he just came back to Dartmouth this semester. What kept him out two years was traveling in Europe with his mother. All his people — all the men, I mean — have gone to Dartmouth. His great-grandfather was here with Daniel Webster."

They were in the streets of Hanover and about to make the turn into the campus. This was the moment he must contrive to hold her continuous attention.

"I came to Dartmouth because a circus tent blew down." He was watching to make certain he had caught her interest. He had. "I was with Buffalo Bill's Wild West Show. The storm struck while we were playing Concord. A falling tent pole broke both my legs." They were on the campus now. Knots of students, coming from lunch, were drifting toward the playing field. As the equipage passed they began to gape and point. He leaned nearer, looked into her face, and made his voice deepen with earnestness. "One of the best men who ever lived, Dr. Ezra Winthrop, took me into his home. He was a born teacher. He became so fascinated ·by my ignorance that he adopted me. His tutoring was so inspired that in a year he was able to get me into St. Paul's and last year into Dartmouth. He died last Christmas but I can never forget what I owe him."

The calculated pathos in his last words had even kept her turned toward him as they passed the field, where players and onlookers were already assembling. The sensation occasioned by the spectacle of the Indian riding past in Jeffrey Bradford's cutter driven by Jeffrey Bradford's girl was unmistakable. Then, glancing past Dorcas's intent face, he realized complete success. Jeffrey Bradford, himself, the center of attention as usual, turned, laughing, lacrosse stick on shoulder, glanced over the heads of encircling admirers, stared incredulously, and whitened with rage.

John asked to be set down at the gymnasium.

"Thank you, Miss Barret," he said, "You can't know what a help you've been."

Hastily changing at his locker, he trotted out on the playing field, which had been cleared of the overnight snow by freshmen. Lacrosse had been imported from Canada too recently to permit intercollegiate competition as yet. Games at Dartmouth were practice contests between selected intramural teams.

John slowed to a walk. The players and onlookers, as though by common consent, were opening a lane between him and Bradford, meanwhile elbowing and shoving to gain an advantageous position to view what might develop. All realized the dramatic possibilities in the confrontation. When Bradford had left school two years before, his social and athletic prowess had established him as unrivaled campus idol. He had returned this semester to discover himself still the social lion but that on the playing fields a challenger had risen in the person of this upstart Indian. As the constant advocate of sportsmanlike conduct he had struggled to suppress his mounting irritation. But his unease had not escaped the sharp eyes of even his most devoted admirers. The Indian's flagrant effrontery in the affair of the cutter had now raised the expectations of everyone present. But eager as was their anticipation the moment of decision was not yet. The supreme arbiter of undergraduate behavior had regained his composure.

"Get a move on, Uncas," he called out cheerfully. "Let's get the game started."

Among all the variations in his offensiveness, nothing grated on John more than this custom of addressing him by facetious Indian names. He surveyed his adversary impassively. Bradford was a good two inches taller than John's six feet, outweighed him by thirty pounds, and carried his strongly muscled body with the easy assurance of the natural athlete.

"Sorry to have kept you waiting," said John, his veiled allusion to the occasion for his tardiness getting a louder laugh than had Bradford's sally.

The field was cleared of spectators and the players took their positions. John and Bradford faced each other as opposing centers, which meant that in the course of the game they would be in continual personal competition. Bradford was holding his stick loosely, looking about, grinning, bearing himself as though nothing more was at stake than a Saturday afternoon's fun. His attention came last to John as casually as though he had forgotten his presence.

"Okay, Tecumseh," he said, amiably. "Let's see who loses the most teeth."

For a moment John wondered if he had not underestimated his opponent. He had been certain that the trick with the cutter and the girl would have so infuriated him that only a little further goading during the game would maneuver him toward the disaster planned for him. If on the other hand Bradford proved too seasoned a competitor to permit emotion to affect his performance then all might become more difficult.

But the moment the referee had put the ball in play he was reassured. He, for his part, expertly retrieved the ball, sidestepped, and swung his stick in a horizontal arc to deliver a flat hard pass that shot the ball half the length of the field to one of his forwards who, expecting it and already in motion, caught it on the run, pivoted at the edge of the crease, and shot the goal before the goalkeeper had fully realized the game was under way. John had not seen the score, for Bradford, meanwhile, ignoring the ball, had thrown his weight into a driving body check which had sent him sprawling.

With elaborate concern, Bradford helped John to his feet.

"Sorry, Big Thunder," he said, grinning. "I seem to have taken my eyes off the ball."

"So you did," said John, patting his shoulder forgivingly. "But don't look now — it's in the net."

The ball again was put in play. John again hooked it out of Bradford's reach but this time he swerved away from the body check. Holding the ball cradled in the web of his crosse by the adroit rocking motion which only the adept could achieve while running full speed, he zigzagged about the field, his teammates meanwhile jockeying for position to receive his pass or to clear the way for his shot at goal. It was Bradford's responsibility as his immediate opponent to break up this insolent tactic and this he undertook with furious energy. But his bull-like rushes and lunges found no target more solid than empty air. Dancing, shifting his balance from side to side and his stick from hand to hand, John kept the contest as unequal as that of cat and mouse. The spectators had begun to roar with laughter and then to cheer. John's teammates were yelling their delight and Bradford's their pained exhortations to their champion.

John had not before at Dartmouth permitted himself any such display of his skill. The Canadian game of lacrosse was a derivation of the most popular and most earnestly played of all Indian sports, in which he had engaged not just these few spring days at Dartmouth but all his earlier life. He was not, however, bent on making a show of his proficiency but of Bradford's ineptitude. And he was succeeding even better than he had schemed.

Bradford had dropped the mask of sportsmanship. Accustomed to triumph, excruciated by the cheers and jeers, he was losing all sense that this was just a game. There was a glitter of hate in his eyes. John realized the moment had come to spring his trap. For the first time administering a body check, he delivered it so shrewdly that Bradford was sent staggering to his knees. As Bradford charged back, John deliberately offered an opening to the blow he saw was coming. Bradford, beside himself with rage, swung his stick at his tormentor's head. John parried the blow with the butt of his stick so that it only grazed his shoulder but he took care to fall to the ground and to get up slowly.

The other players and the onlookers swarmed about, yelling remonstrances. Bradford lifted his clenched fists and assumed the posture of a pugilist.

"Come on, Spotted Tail," he taunted, "let's settle this now."

This was the moment John had rehearsed in his mind so often.

"Don't you think," he said, "a better place might be the barn — and a better time — say, at eight tonight?"

The crowd breathed a sigh of pure bliss. The barn was the huge, empty, hay shed on an abandoned farm a mile from the campus which had long been the traditional arena for the review of those student differences which could only be resolved by personal combat.

On their way to the barn that night, Ben Majors was filled with forebodings.

"John, you don't realize what you're up against," he grieved. "Jeff's more than just a good boxer. He's a near great one. That last year he was here he was intercollegiate champion of New England. You won't be able to lay a hand on him and he'll cut you to pieces."

"Maybe not," said John.

The barn was crowded. Few of Dartmouth's three hundred students were missing. Many willing hands had set the scene. Ropes had been

44

strung to form a makeshift ring. A canvas from the gymnasium had been stretched to cover the rough floor. A number of lamps and lanterns swinging from the rafters gave a checkered light which was made more uneven by the haze of tobacco smoke.

Bradford, wrapped in a heavy woolen bathrobe, sat on a stool between his seconds. When he rose the robe swung open, revealing his boxing trunks and shoes.

"So Pocahontas did show up," he said. "We'd begun to wonder if you'd changed your mind."

John advanced to the edge of the ring and surveyed the ropes, the canvas and the lighting. Bradford slipped out of his robe and extended his taped hands for the drawing on of his gloves by his seconds.

"If you haven't got any," he said, "you can have the other pair of mine."

John shook his head. "No gloves," he proposed.

"Good for you," said Bradford, ridding himself of his. "Should save some time."

"And no rounds," added John.

"Better yet," said Bradford. "Make any rules you want. You can bite if you like."

John removed coat, shirt and pants, disclosing he was clad in breech-clout and moccasins, and crawled through the ropes. Bradford and the referee, a bearded, bespectacled graduate student, moved to the center of the ring. As John came into the stronger light his brown skin had a polished sheen.

"What's that grease you've got on?" demanded Bradford.

"Not grease," said John. "See." He calmly wiped his forearm against Bradford's shoulder. "Doesn't rub off." He grinned innocently and offered a fuller explanation. "Snake oil. Loosens the muscles. Makes you quicker."

Bradford was annoyed by the laughter John's byplay had drawn from the crowd. "The quickest you'll be," he said, "is in hitting the floor."

As they stood together, the dark, smooth, lithe figure of the Indian appeared startlingly overmatched by the towering, heavily muscled, pale bulk of his opponent. John caught a glimpse of the expression of utter dejection on Ben's face as he crouched at the corner of the ring. It was, after all, possible that Ben could be right. If so, John reflected, he had surely brought it on himself. He had taken a great deal of care to work himself into this spot where, were his calculations to turn out to be mistaken, this big white man could beat him to a pulp.

At the referee's gesture, the two contestants touched hands in a token handshake. Even while stepping back Bradford launched his first blow, a hard right straight for John's jaw. His delivery was much quicker than John had anticipated. It was due more to luck than his evasive shift that the blow, though hard enough to make his ears buzz, glanced off the side of his head. For the immediately following left he was better set. He deflected it enough with his parrying right hand and forearm to turn it harmlessly onto his shoulder. More respectful now of Bradford's speed, he concentrated on the telltale angles of the wrists behind Bradford's cocked fists, which offered some clue to the imminence of the quick, short jabs. These he feared far more than the longer-range hay-makers, which he could always see coming. He kept dancing away with Bradford in relentless pursuit, hammering at him savagely. Many of these blows seemed to be landing and the spectators were already roaring for the kill.

However, since the surprise of that first right, John's assurance had been steadily returning. As he had expected, by watching Bradford's eyes and shoulders he could invariably detect the onset of any really threatening blow. His shifting evasions were so swift and slight that even Bradford, steaming with angry impatience, was not realizing that none of his blows was connecting solidly.

Neither at St. Paul's nor at Dartmouth had John taken more than a desultory interest in boxing. It had seemed to him that a method of attack that depended on the cumbersome thrust of a clenched fist at the end of a straightening arm that must have the whole weight of the body behind it to strike any sort of a decisive blow was so ineffective as to be absurd. This conclusion had been an early result of the brawling fist-fights prevalent on the circus lot. In his estimation any man with his wits about him who would stand still until struck by the lumbering advance of a fist propelled by such telltale advance movements of arm and shoulder was a fool or a paralytic. The defensive dexterity involved was as nothing compared to the desperate quickness required to evade

46

the thrust of a knife blade or the spin of a thrown tomahawk. Even in Indian wrestling, in which hands could be used as weapons, the combatants did not indulge in aimless pounding but sought bodily areas with nerve centers cripplingly sensitive to the prodding of so much as a stiffened forefinger.

Still dancing away, keeping just at the extreme length of Bradford's long arms, John had so far demonstrated only the defensive half of his theory. He had been taking some punishment. The bruises did not show on his dark skin. But his lips and both cheekbones were bleeding and one ear was puffing. He had so far made no single aggressive move. Bradford, panting, exasperated by John's continuing flight, dropped his arms in disgust.

"Get off your bicycle, Minnehaha," he mocked. "Or didn't you come here to fight?"

John was in on him like a flash, his own extended arms delaying for a second Bradford's raising his. Before he could be shaken off he had brought up not his fist but his protruding knuckles in a hard jab into the corner of Bradford's eye. With a bellow of rage Bradford resumed his charging attack but began swinging so furiously that John was able to dart close again and jab the other eye. Both eyes were swelling and streaming and Bradford was attempting to clear his vision by wiping his forearms across them. John risked accepting a solid blow to the head to get inside his reach again. This time he drove his knuckles into the Adam's apple. Choking, clawing at his throat, Bradford saw John coming at him once more. Unconsciously raising his guard high to protect his face and throat, he was wide open. John was able to get the thrust of his legs and all his weight behind a straight-arm into the solar plexus. Bradford doubled up. John straightened and brought down the edge of his hand in a flailing chop at the nape of Bradford's neck. Under the impact of the rabbit punch Bradford slowly collapsed facedown on the canvas.

John stepped back and watched, still outwardly impassive. But the flood of exultation pouring over him was like the surge of a cataract. Here in the very center of the camp of his enemies he had overthrown their most redoubtable champion. He was nearly overcome by the atavistic impulse to throw himself into the leaps and bounds of the victory dance or to give voice to the fierce ecstasy of the scalp song. Since earliest childhood his strongest conscious emotion had been his hatred of whites. During all of the past five years he had been obliged to keep this throat-clutching animus suppressed and concealed. He had had to keep reminding himself that he was in effect a captive who had elected to remain among his enemies in order eventually to strengthen his hand against them. Only now had come this one shining moment of blessed relief. The foolish, schoolboy rivalry with Bradford had opened to him this unique, safe opportunity to be, for this brief interval, himself.

The next moment the intoxicating taste of triumph was turning bitter in his mouth. He was becoming aware that the yells shaking the barn were cheers for him. Not only Ben but scores of others were invading the ring to shake his hand, pound him on the back, deluge him with congratulations. He might be the representative of his race but it was a race held by them in such poor esteem that they could cheerily applaud any success so nearly without precedent.

At breakfast the next morning Ben was perusing the morning paper which had just arrived from Portsmouth. He was specializing in European history and took a studied interest in all the foreign dispatches.

"Can you imagine that?" he announced. "Bismarck has resigned."

No one paid any attention. Everyone else at the table was discussing last night's fight. A scattering of Bradford's friends pronounced the rabbit punch to have been an unfair advantage. This proposition received no support in any other quarter. In the opinion of the vast majority the back of the neck was certainly not below the belt. Ben had dropped the paper on the table. A minor headline near the foot of the front page caught John's eye. He bent to read:

GHOST DANCE

A number of notices appearing recently in various far western newspapers have come to our attention. According to these accounts several Indian tribes of the interior have become strangely excited by a new religion which practices a heathen rite known as the Ghost Dance. The devotees of this extraordinary superstition apparently believe that by prolonged dancing they may recall the spirits of their ancestors to assist them in their until now unsuccessful struggle against the advance of white settlement.

"Where you going?" demanded Ben, as John suddenly rose to his feet.

"I have to see Professor Temple. I want to catch him before he gets off to chapel."

He mentioned Temple only because it was the first random excuse to occur to him. He had been suddenly overwhelmed by a compulsion to get off by himself, to find time to think. But, striding across the campus in the face of a warm southwest wind that was melting the snow and bringing with it the rich, earthy odors of reviving spring, he realized that there was no need to think. He had already come to a decision. And it was one so conclusive that his disquiet could only be eased by its announcement.

Hector King Temple, professor of philosophy, a subject which he considered merely a vestibule to logic, came into his study bearing a tray with a coffeepot and two cups. He prided himself on his ability as a teacher but even more on his ability to court the personal confidence of his students. His portliness, his snow-white hair and beard, his twinkling eyes, his hearty voice, gave him somewhat the air of an academic Santa Claus. He gave John one quick, sharp look as he crossed to his desk and thereafter pretended to sense nothing unusual in his call.

"Morning, Winthrop."

"Good morning, sir."

Temple chuckled. "Rumor has it that there was some slight alteration in the campus pecking order last night."

"I should feel ashamed. I do, a little."

"Sugar? Cream?"

"Three lumps, please. No cream."

"You don't look much the worse for it."

"It was too easy. He didn't have a chance."

"So you didn't find as much pleasure in it as you had expected."

"I did while it was happening."

"There seems a general feeling that he had something of the sort coming to him so you should feel no lasting remorse." Temple took his time fussing with the coffee. When an interview promised to pose a serious problem it was his custom to linger over preliminaries. He flattered himself that he could always place the most perturbed student at ease. He sank back in his chair and regarded John co-conspiratorially over his coffee cup.

"But you didn't come to tell me about your triumphs in the arena, I take it."

John hesitated, though not because he was at loss for words. He had first to subdue his unreasoning disinclination to give any accounting to this pompous, pleasant, well-meaning man. He resented the need as he had resented it also in the case of his original benefactor, Dr. Winthrop. Both of these self-appointed mentors had felt duty bound continually to advise, admonish, and correct him. As an Indian, he wanted nothing so much as to be let alone, most of all when the impulse of the moment was utterly capricious. He had had to pay a very high price for the opportunity to learn the use of this weapon, education, with which he had resolved to arm himself.

"I'm sorry, sir, to be troubling you on a Sunday morning. But on account of our plans I decided the sooner I told you the better. It's about this coming summer vacation. I can't go to England with you."

Temple never permitted himself concern when confronted by error. He was convinced that, were personalities eschewed, error must invariably yield to logical analysis.

"I presume you have something in mind to do instead."

"Yes, sir. I propose to spend the summer in Dakota."

"No bad news from the family, I hope."

"No, sir. I have no family. My father, mother and two sisters were lost in a blizzard the winter after the Custer campaign."

"A tragedy in truth. But one long past and evidently not a factor impinging on our present problem. Have you then heard something disturbing from friends?"

"No, sir. I haven't heard anything from any Sioux for some years. I did have friends, of course, but some can't write and others have disowned me."

"They count you no longer a Sioux because of the time and effort you are devoting to getting a white education. Is that it?"

"They think I've lost my horses."

"While in your estimation you are not only quite sane but have been doing this in order ultimately to prove of greater service to your people."

"That is what I have kept telling myself."

"Then certainly there are certain aspects of your problem you have not sufficiently considered. For one, among Dr. Winthrop's most explicit wishes, as expressed in his will, was that this year you make this English visit."

John was finding the cross-examination progressively easier to endure. It was in any event clearly necessary to match wits with this man whose goodwill would again become essential when he returned to college next fall.

"I know that, sir. It was his view that as an educated man I should learn to recognize that I had certain cultural roots in the common experience of humanity in addition to those in my Sioux background."

"Very well put."

"It should be. That's the way he put it."

"You have been an apt pupil, Winthrop. That I must admit. But we must get back to our muttons. So — despite your appreciation of your foster father's wish you still propose to squander this summer in Dakota?"

"I have to, sir."

Temple swung around in his chair to stare out the window and then swung back.

"You oblige me to bring up a subject which I should have preferred not to mention. As you know, the fund dedicated to the completion of your education that was left by Dr. Winthrop was left in my keeping as trustee. You can hardly expect me to underwrite this excursion of which I am so certain he would have disapproved."

"I realize that, sir. I still have to go."

For the first time Temple betrayed something like impatience.

"Surely something put this idea into your head. Something recent. What was it?"

"You'll understand even less when I tell you."

John leaned forward, unfolded the newspaper on the desk, turned it toward Temple, and indicated the Ghost Dance item. Temple glanced through it.

"Seeing that all of a sudden reminded me of something I'd been forgetting," John was saying. "I had been forgetting what an incredible difference there is between the way we think here and the way they think out there. I need to get the feel of their way again. Call it a kind of homesickness, if you like."

Temple appeared not to be listening. His customary appearance of urbanity was replaced by an appropriately severe frown.

"You are bound to realize what my position in this matter must be. I am solely and totally governed by Dr. Winthrop's detailed plans for you. Your progress has so far been more commendable than even he had hoped. I am therefore less than ever able to countenance this nonsensical interruption of it. I am compelled categorically to forbid so arrant a frivolity." He leaned forward, palms on the desk. "Surely, my dear boy, reflection upon this immutable circumstance must lead you to change your mind?"

"Yes, sir, it has already," said John. "I'm leaving for Dakota tomorrow."

IV

THE STONY TRAIL wound back and forth among huge boulders without seeming to make much forward progress. Badger was already sweating, for Kirk had been letting him go as fast as he liked no matter how rough the ground. There could be some need for haste. At the Donelson ranch, ten miles back, where he had spent the night, they had said that eighty-year-old Zenas Williams, whom he was on his way to see, had been ill all winter. There had been some neighborly, obscene hilarity about the odd lot of heirs from points as separate as Placerville, Julesburg and Taos that had gathered about the prospective Williams's deathbed to lay claim to his celebrated property. The extreme dissimilarities among the heirs, particularly as to age and race, had stirred more amusement than astonishment. The old mountain man, in his sixty years of excessively active wandering about the West, had always been reputed to have left progeny scattered from the Canadian to the Mexican border.

The trail at last moved forward to swing around a shoulder of the hill and reveal once more the tremendous vista ahead. The rising sun behind Kirk glittered on the snow-covered rampart of the Wind River Range, rearing into the intensely blue sky out of dark pine forests broken by escarpments of red rock. Patches of snow still clung to the northern folds of the nearer foothills but everywhere on these lower slopes the first bright green of new grass was showing in swathes as vivid as though applied by a paint brush. Nearer, the earliest and hardiest of the wild flowers were flashing their spots of color, while overhead soared flocks of far-traveling sea birds en route to their summer haunts in the mountain lakes. There was a special tang of excitement about the coming of spring in these Wyoming Rockies.

Kirk pulled up Badger and got out his glasses. There was as yet no sign of the Williams ranch anywhere ahead but he picked out two herds of antelope, one of elk and three of deer. He took a deep breath of the sharp, clear air. He still felt the tingle of relief and elation that had come when he had at last recaptured the assignment for which he had so adroitly fished.

For weeks that had lengthened into months it had been touch and go. Each morning as he had reported to the general's San Francisco headquarters he had expected to be handed orders transferring him to some dismal Arizona outpost. For days at a time the general had taken no more notice of him than to return his salute when they chanced to pass. He had had his own problems. He had learned of the imminence of his promotion to major general along with his transfer to the Department of the Missouri. But months had passed while the War Department delayed activating either order. His indignation had exceeded any former seizure. Still Kirk's original report on Wovoka must have held enough of his attention for him to keep his most junior aide within call.

To Kirk the most painful feature of the long suspense had been the time it had taken for his letter to reach Remington. The artist had been traveling in Mexico and it had not finally overtaken him until he had returned to New York. It was only then that all had begun to march as Kirk had hoped. There had been bureaucratic stirrings in Washington, forebodings in western newspapers, cries of alarm from western governors and legislators. By mid-March, while the army and the Indians were still in hibernation, the Ghost Dance, about which nothing yet was tangibly known, had become a topic for anxious speculation everywhere along the frontier. This had had its effect. The general had made up his mind.

Kirk put away the glasses and let the impatient Badger start on. The next moment he was required to hold him back with all his strength. A dozen antelope had plunged without warning from a gully alongside to run on ahead, rocketing back and forth across the trail, their white tails flaunting a challenge to a race. By the time he had Badger's indignation under control the trail was dropping away to the right and finally led into the narrow canyon of a lively, sparkling stream. He made sure that this was Hell Creek by leaning from the saddle to stick his finger in the water. It was warm even this far downstream from the mountain hot springs which were its famous source. He cupped some in his palm. Though warm it was as fresh as the purest glacier water.

He rode on. The canyon began to widen with indications that ahead there was a broader upland valley. According to the directions he had been given, this must mark the location of the Williams ranch, a site once known as Williams's Hole and before that as Hell Hole. Mounting one last slight rise in the widening canyon floor, Kirk was suddenly confronted with a full view of the valley. It was a nearly flat mountain meadow, perhaps a mile wide by three miles long, encircled by pine-clad foothills and backed by the great Wind River Range. In the meadow the new grass was already a lush six inches deep. He recalled Pete Donelson saying that in addition to the hot water of Hell Creek there must be some more general subterranean heat for even in midwinter the snow never remained long on the Williams bottomland.

"Old Zenas can just set there on his butt and smoke his pipe and swig his likker," Donelson had grumbled. "He's got the best piece of land in Wyoming all because he just happened to be the first white man to come along. He don't even have to run cattle. He makes all the living he wants just winterin' other folks' cattle when they start to die off come a bad year."

The cluster of ranch buildings stood beside the stream in the center of the valley, diminished to toy size by distance and the expanse of mountain and sky. There were thirty or forty horses grazing here and there in the meadow, mainly mares and foals, but no cattle in sight. Kirk dismounted, rubbed down Badger's steaming flanks and legs with hot water from the creek, and walked him the last mile. As he approached the main ranch house he began to see what had given it so peculiar an appearance from a distance. Up close it looked even more peculiar. Across the front of the earlier adobe had been stretched a more recent verandah of blue and yellow painted wood with slender colonial pillars and much gingerbread decoration.

As he tied Badger at the hitching rack the four men in rocking chairs on the verandah ceased to rock and stared at him in undisguised hostility. They varied in apparent age from twenty to fifty, two were white and two were breeds, one of the latter with obviously a Mexican streak and the other possibly a French. It was not hard to guess that these were some of the presumptive heirs or that they were regarding him so coldly because they saw him as one more rival. From somewhere in the depths of the establishment came a brief burst of ribald song delivered in a drunken male voice. Kirk climbed the steps and, with a curt nod to the rocking-chair brigade, crossed the verandah to the heavy, iron-strapped door set in the adobe wall.

It was opened while he was still a step away by a woman he knew must be Aurora Dickson, who in recent years had been Zenas Williams's housekeeper. There had been nearly as much Donelson chat about her as about Zenas himself. They had said that among a number of other noteworthy attributes she had a temper to match his and that her marksmanship with a six-shooter was second to no man's. If she was much past forty the extra years did not show. Her sedate gown of gray taffeta could not disguise the fact that under it was a body long accustomed to and still worthy of attention. She had very white skin behind a maze of freckles, green eyes, and flaming red hair. She was regarding him no less coldly than were the men in the rocking chairs.

"Well?" she inquired.

"My name is Stuart Kirk," he said. "I have an important message for Mr. Williams."

Her unfriendly scrutiny traveled over his person to his feet and back up to his face. A second thought seemed then to have occurred to her for she thawed ever so slightly.

"Come in," she said, standing aside and closing the door behind him the moment he had entered.

After the bright sunlight outside, the big room seemed as dark as a cavern. Kirk gathered a general impression of two great, stone fireplaces at either end, heavy Spanish furniture, and a profusion of Navajo rugs, buffalo robes and bearskins.

"I'm Aurora Dickson, Mr. Williams's housekeeper," she said, moving across to open an opposite door to a wide, sunlit, interior courtyard. "Caty," she called. "My daughter," she explained to Kirk.

From the direction of the corrals came a lanky, long-legged young woman dressed in tight blue denim pants, boots, spurs, white shirt and wide-brimmed felt hat. As she came closer Kirk saw that she had the same white skin, freckles, green eyes and red hair as her mother and that her cowboy attire did no more to conceal her essential femaleness than did the prim taffeta in her mother's case.

"This is Mr. Stuart Kirk," said Aurora. "Take him to Harvey."

There was an exchange of looks between mother and daughter after which the polite smile with which Caty had greeted Kirk turned to a rebellious scowl.

"Come along," said Caty curtly.

Aurora withdrew into the house and Kirk followed Caty into the courtyard. The U-shaped extensions of the ranch house, enclosing the space on three sides, displayed at a glance the long history of the site since Zenas had first camped here in 1830. Whatever the original nucleus, the edifice had with the passage of time grown haphazardly, with additions of log, adobe, and clapboard of varying heights and with roofs ranging from woven mats to shingle or tile. Along the ell on the left stretched the stout, oaken railings, which, backed by a loopholed wall, had served to keep Indian customers in order in the era when Zenas had operated a trading post. At the end of the other wing rose a relic of the days when the place had been a frontier fort, a two-story log blockhouse, the upper room of which could only be reached by a ladder. From this upper room came another roar of song:

Hangtown girls are lovely creatures
Think they'll marry pious preachers
Heads thrown back to show their features

"That's Zenas," said Caty. "When he's that drunk he won't listen to nobody. So best you can do is talk to Harvey."

In the middle of the courtyard, seated on the coping of an abandoned well, his head hanging in utter dejection and his hands clasped over his ears to shut out the singing, was a gray-haired man in a dusty black suit. He looked up, caught sight of Kirk, and leaped toward him in anguished appeal.

"Don't tell me you're another one of them."

"I'm not," said Kirk, "I'm just a visitor."

"Then when you get back outside — anywhere away from this den of

57

iniquity — will you for the love of God tell people — tell the authorities — that I'm a prisoner — that I'm being held here against my will?"

Caty appeared in no way disturbed by the charge. She firmly disengaged the supplicant's clutch on Kirk.

"He's Sam Pelton," she explained. "He's a preacher."

There came another burst of song from the upper room:

> *Oh Kentucky, the hunters of Kentucky,*
> *We are a hardy freeborn race*
> *Each man to fear a stranger*
> *Whate'er the game we join in chase.*

The beleaguered minister of the gospel, his flare of hope blighted by Kirk's impassivity, retreated to his seat and again covered his ears. Caty resumed her explanation:

"Ma had him fetched up from Riverton so she could keep him here right on tap. She figgered maybe Zenas would get weak enough toward the last so she could get him to marry her. If that didn't work and one o' them polecats on the porch got the place she figgered either her or me might rope him, with the preacher handy to make it legal." She had been moving toward the trading-post wing and paused to look at Kirk sharply. "Is it a fact what you just said — that you ain't another of Zenas's bastards?"

"Much as you make me hate to admit it," said Kirk, "I am not. My business with him has nothing to do with any inheritance, more's the pity."

"Well, I'm surely mighty glad to hear that," said Caty. "Not for Ma — or even to get this place which I want most as much as Ma does — would I touch one of them dogs out there with the end of a pole. I ain't never yet took up with no man except when I honest to God felt like it." She looked at Kirk with a suddenly sunny smile and touched her fingers to his sleeve. "Look . . . ah . . . what did Ma say your name was?"

"Stuart Kirk."

"Look, Stu, you must of come by horse 'cause there's no other way. While you're chinnin' with Harvey I'll go get him and feed and water him."

58

"Thank you so much . . . Caty. Trouble is — he's about the orneriest horse alive."

"Hah," said Caty.

Kirk watched the lean yet graceful figure striding away toward the main house. In the upper room the singer, having hit upon a phrase that struck his fancy, was endlessly reprising it:

> *Whate'er the game we join in chase*
> *Whate'er the game*
> *Whate'er the game*
> *We join in chase*
> *The game*
> *In chase*

Kirk pushed open the trading-post door. Behind the counter within, across which bales of fur had once been exchanged for fusils and fire-water, stood a sour-faced man with graying sideburns, a green visor shading his steel-rimmed glasses, and pencils over each ear. On the counter before him was propped a brass doorplate reading:

HARVEY VICTOR BERGER
ATTORNEY AT LAW

Also on the counter were arranged several law books and a number of documents, on one of which he was meticulously making an entry with a goose-quill pen.

"My name's Stuart Kirk," said Kirk. "I have to see Mr. Williams but they said I should see you first."

Berger shoved up the visor and surveyed his caller.

"He is not at the moment in a condition to transact business. However, I am Zenas Williams's legal representative in all matters — all matters — Mr. . . . ah . . ."

"Stuart Kirk."

Berger leaned over to write the name on a pad.

"Domicile?" he inquired.

"San Francisco."

The lawyer gave Kirk another and sharper look. "No appearance of any Chinese strain," he muttered. Completing the notation on the pad, he cleared his throat and began to speak as though addressing a court.

"It will save us both time if I outline the legal and factual aspects of the situation. You can then determine whether your case is such as to warrant your further persistence." He indicated the array of documents before him. "These are six alternate wills that I have drafted to hold in readiness for the moment when my client may come to some decision and may prove able to demonstrate a competence as well as a readiness to sign the one of his election. So far as I have been able to determine his intentions, these are the only heirs in a position to advance any sort of claim to his consideration." He began indicating the wills, while Kirk listened, enthralled. "This one bequeaths the estate to Aurora Dickson, who has been my client's common-law wife since April 7, 1880. This one favors Catherine Dickson, her daughter by an earlier legal marriage, for whom my client has expressed a special affection. These next three make allowance for persons the status of whom I, pursuant to my client's express instructions, located and authenticated, at considerable effort, I may say, and thereupon, still pursuant to his instructions, invited here so that he could inspect them, inasmuch as he had never before been certain of their existence. The first of these favors one José Valdez, with whose mother, Innocentia Valdez, my client spent the winter of 1845 in Taos. The next deals with one Gaston Langlade, whose mother, Madeleine Langlade, my client visited for a week at a no longer existing trading post on Lake Coeur d'Alene in 1848. The third favors Terence McGary, whose mother, Bridget McGary, my client befriended in 1866 while he was hunting buffalo to supply a railroad construction camp near Julesburg at which she was employed as cook. This last, favoring Joseph Cramer, presents a case I have not personally investigated, but he came here of his own volition armed with an apparently authentic document in the shape of a letter written him by his mother, Amelia Cramer, just before her death, acquainting him with her assurance that my client was his father and that though said Joseph Cramer had been born in Sacramento, California, he had been conceived in 1850 near Fort Hall, Idaho, in a covered wagon that was part of a train that was proceeding to the goldfields under the guidance of my client. Now Mr. . . . ah . . . Kirk—on what do you base your expectations?"

"I don't," said Kirk. "I have to see Mr. Williams on a quite different matter."

"Then why are you wasting my time?" said Berger, pulling down the visor and resuming his writing.

Kirk returned to the yard. The singing had for the moment ceased. The preacher had disappeared. In his place on the well coping sat a tall, young cowhand, wearing goatskin chaps, a long-barreled Colt, and an air of dejection even deeper than had weighed down the Reverend Pelton. He rose to greet Kirk with a forced grin.

"I'm Jim Macy, foreman," he said. "Caty said to tell you that's about the best-mannered horse she ever met up with."

Kirk looked off toward the barn, where Caty was watering Badger at a trough. The faithless Badger was not so much as switching his tail.

"She's quite a girl," he remarked.

"She sure is," said Jim.

He, too, was looking at Caty but the longer he looked the more of his dejection returned. Caty led Badger into the barn. Jim became aware that Kirk had perceived his misery. He reddened and attempted another grin.

"She sure is," he repeated.

Caty reappeared and started past the corral toward them. Jim's utter dejection was displaced by utter confusion.

"I clean forgot," he said. "She told me something else. Said to bring you these here bags."

He turned hastily to pick up Kirk's saddlebags, lying beside the well coping, fumbled, dropped them, snatched them up again, then stood stiffly erect, blushing furiously as Caty joined them. Caty acted as though she and Kirk were alone.

"Count one for you, Stu," she said. "Man that's got a horse like that must have some idea which way is up."

Jim flinched. Some barb in the remark had been intended for him. Aurora came to the door of the main house.

"Caty," she called, "Show him some place to stay. If he sure enough wants to see Zenas he may have to hang around a while."

Jim gulped, gathered his powers, and made a statement: "Still plenty room down in the bunkhouse."

61

Caty appeared not to have heard him.

"Come with me," she said to Kirk.

Kirk took the twin bags from Jim's suddenly nerveless hands, slung them over his shoulder by the connecting leather band, and followed her to the wing extending from the main house toward the blockhouse. She paused to look up at the upper room, cocking her head to listen.

"He's gone to sleep," she said. "No telling when he'll wake up. Could be five minutes or five hours or sometime tomorrow."

She moved on across the threshold into a narrow vestibule leading to a heavy door in what had at some earlier time been the outer wall of the fort. It was now nailed shut. The companion door, which had formerly closed the inner end of the vestibule, had been removed from its hinges and discarded. The corridor, Kirk realized, had once been the entry port by which Indians who had come to trade had been detained one or two at a time until they had deposited their arms before being permitted access to the interior of the stockade. There had been loopholes in either wall of the vestibule through which weapons might be thrust. These had been boarded over and in their place, facing each other from opposite walls, were contemporary painted doors, apparently leading to rooms on either side. Caty threw open the one on the left, disclosing a clean, bare chamber, lighted only by one window in the courtyard wall but equipped with cot, chair, and washstand. On the cot were stacked folded bed linen and blankets.

"It ain't the Palace," she said, "but the company might suit you some better than out in the bunkhouse."

Kirk tossed his saddlebags through the doorway and turned upon her his most ingratiating grin.

"A whole lot better," he affirmed.

His effort was wasted. She was looking after Jim Macy, walking off toward the corral, head down, his spurred and booted feet kicking furiously at stones in his path.

"One thing I can't stand," she declared fiercely, "is a man that when something rough comes at him just lays down and rolls over."

Still angry, she threw open the other door to reveal that the opposite room was manifestly her own. There were several pieces of quite good walnut furniture, articles of feminine apparel, including underwear, scattered about, and dresses hanging in an open wardrobe. The bed had not been made and her nightgown was still draped over the foot. She took two or three stamping steps into the room, then came about to return to Kirk with a remorseful grin. Her gust of anger seemed so soon to have passed.

"Looks like hell, don't it?" she said, with a gesture toward the disordered room. "But it's not so far off that when there's anything you want all you got to do is yell."

"Anything?" he said.

Her eyes met his without wavering. There seemed in her regard only candid speculation upon his masculine potentialities. "Maybe yes. Maybe no. Sometimes takes me a while to make up my mind."

"Be any help for me to say that I made up my mind the minute I saw you?"

"Not any."

Having apparently concluded her appraisal, she stepped around him and walked rapidly toward the main house. Looking after her, Kirk could scarcely credit his luck. She was so sure of herself. She had boasted, truthfully or not, that she had only taken men she had wanted. Though so much younger, she was basically no more virginal than her mother. He went into his room and began unpacking his saddlebags. Caty reappeared with a pitcher of hot water.

"Thought you might want to wash," she said, as calmly as though there were no issue between them more significant than a casual guest's comfort. "Supper'll be toward dark. Long's we have to feed the riffraff be some relief to have somebody new at the table."

She crossed to her room and began setting it to rights. She had not closed the door. Kirk followed and leaned on it.

"Well?" she demanded.

"Just watching. Any objection?"

"Nope." She did not look up from her bed-making. "Not so long as you're that easy to please."

"Don't want to upset whatever you two might have on the fire."

Kirk turned to find Aurora at his elbow. She patted his arm and leaned past him to address Caty.

"The preacher's got away. He's on foot but he's already most to the head of the canyon."

"Tell Jim to go fetch him. He's at least man enough to rope a preacher."

"He won't do it," explained Aurora. "He claims he wants no part of what's the same as kidnapping."

"What really ails him," said Caty, resentful, as always, of anything to do with Jim, "is that he doesn't want the preacher hanging around here ready to do any kind of a marrying job. Long's it's something he don't want I'll go bring back the old codger myself."

She strode out toward the corral. Aurora looked up at Kirk and then from Caty's room to his.

"I had an idea she'd put you in here." She looked off toward Caty stalking on into the barn without a glance up at Jim seated disconsolately on a top rail of the corral. "That girl can get meaner'n a skinned catamount."

Her look came back to Kirk. He could tell that she was wondering why a man like him was off after a girl like Caty when a woman like her was at hand. He was beginning to wonder a little himself. But all she voiced was a decent concern for his welfare.

"I wouldn't want to see you gettin' yourself shot while you're here. So you better get it through your head which brand is which. When Jim Macy come to work for us last winter Caty was off to Cheyenne visiting her grandmother. Zenas was laid up with a broken leg and drinkin' hisself sick. Jim and me we got a little careless with how we passed the time. Then when Caty come back and Jim got a look at her he fell for her like a landslide off South Mountain. But the bend in the trail he couldn't get around was that he'd already bedded her ma. He decided there was nothin' left for him but to cut his own throat and Caty she gets so mad at him she's ready to hand him a knife."

"You couldn't be recommending, could you," observed Kirk, stepping back and closing the door to Caty's room, "that if I should happen to walk in my sleep I should stay away from this door."

There was a murmur of laughter in her voice as she replied. "That's exactly what I could be."

"But otherwise I'm free to wander?"

64

"Free as air." She took his arm and led him out of the corridor into the open. "Except up there."

She inclined her head toward the main house. At the top of an exterior stairway leading to the upper story was a blue door.

"Yours?" he asked.

"Mine," she said, laughing softly again.

She went into his room and began making his bed. He looked on from the doorway but neither spoke nor did their eyes again meet. She finished and started out past him.

"Thank you," he said, making way so slowly that she brushed against him.

"You're quite welcome," she replied.

He watched the movement of her hips as she walked away across the courtyard and up the stairs to the blue door. His luck, he decided, was still holding.

Supper was served at a plank table in the enormous kitchen. From an iron stove in the recesses of a vast fireplace a fat Mexican woman brought trays of tortillas, platters of roast mountain sheep, and bowls of beans and chili. Already on the table were pitchers of cool beer from a keg in the springhouse.

It was a silent gathering. Kirk was seated between Aurora and Caty. He was conscious of the nearness of each woman and amused by the hostility with which he was being eyed by the heirs, the preacher, and Jim Macy. Only the lawyer was giving his full attention to what he was eating.

In his room later, Kirk undressed, went to bed, and slept four hours. Awakening at the time he had intended, he drew on pants and shirt and knelt by the corner of the window to look out into the courtyard. The darkness was relieved only by the faintest glimmer from the stars, which made certain shadows seem a shade darker than others. After minutes of intent study of these shadows Kirk was convinced that one was the figure of the young foreman. Jim was lying prone against the coping of the well, in a position from which he could be certain to detect the occurrence were Caty's guest to attempt to cross the corridor to Caty's room.

Satisfied that all was developing as he had expected, Kirk carefully opened his door, crept barefoot from the vestibule into the courtyard, passed so near that he could have stepped on Jim, and turned toward the stairway.

Feeling with his toes for the first step, he slowly climbed upward. The skin in the middle of his back began to twitch. There was still, he was forced to admit, an element of chance in his venture. Jim's primary determination was to defend Caty's virtue but he had once been Aurora's lover and might conceivably resent a stranger's taking his place in the enjoyment of her favor. However, from the darkness below came no rasp of movement, no hoarse challenge, or, most reassuring of all, no click of a six-shooter being cocked.

Reaching the landing, Kirk detected the slight movement of the heavy curtains shrouding the window commanding the stairway. His groping had found the knob. The blue door was not locked. He opened it and slipped within.

The room was warm and smelled of some scent that was somewhere between musk and lilac. The coals in the open grate of a Franklin stove in one corner cast a shimmering pattern of light and shade across the ceiling. The ornate brass bed against the opposite wall looked strangely chaste. All coverings had been stripped from it except the lower sheet, stretched tight as a drumhead over the mattress.

Aurora stood by the window. She had drawn a long deep breath as he entered. Her hand dropped from a fold of the heavy drape. Her movement toward him was slow, trancelike. She was naked. Her red hair hung to her waist, glistening in the glow from the grate as though sparks were entangled in it. Her skin was as smooth and her figure as firm as he had suspected when seeing her clothed. The scent preceding her, seeming to come from her breasts and thighs, announced the urgency which possessed her. Had it only proved more difficult to earn his passage here, Kirk reflected, he could not have imagined a more promising moment.

"You took your time, you bastard," she whispered. "Waiting's got me in such a state you better be as good as you think you are."

He began unbuckling his belt. Her fingers flew to his assistance in the unbuttoning of his shirt. When one leg of his pants caught at his ankle she bent hastily to jerk it free. Together they walked through the shadowed glow toward the white expanse of the bed. For Kirk this encounter was still no more than a necessary preamble to his night's principal intention. The thought helped him to keep that control of the situation for which he had schooled himself so often to strive.

"Jesus," she finally gasped. "That was the third time for me. You come along, too, honey, whenever you like."

At the conclusion of their ultimate mutual paroxysm she rolled away from him and sat up on the edge of the bed.

"Good God almighty," she marveled. "Except for one night with Jim that's the first go I've had since Zenas broke his leg. I got near as excited as I used to when I was fifteen."

She rose and bent to kiss him lightly on the forehead. The luxuriance of her hair fell across his bare chest and the nipples of her magnificent breasts touched his arm. He resisted the impulse to draw her back down to him. She straightened.

"You know something?" she said. "I had a hunch the minute I set eyes on you there at the front door. And was I right."

She went into the bathroom. When she emerged Kirk was waiting with pants and shirt over his arm to take his turn. There was a big iron bathtub and a charcoal water heater. He soaped and scrubbed vigorously, trusting none of Aurora's scent would remain on him. Climbing out, he toweled himself dry, pulled on his shirt and pants, and returned to the bedroom.

Aurora had made up the bed and was lying in it, her head on a pillow and her hair in a thick braid drawn sedately over her shoulder. He had expected her to protest his leaving so soon but she merely smiled ruefully.

"You won't believe me," she said, "but whenever I bulldog a man into bed like I had to you, once it's over I get so goddamned ashamed all I want to do is crawl somewhere out of sight. So you don't have to feel any call to hang around."

He crossed to the bed, grinned down at her, gave the braid an affectionate tug, and went out.

A late half-moon had climbed above the eastern hills to wash the courtyard with a ghostly light. When he reached the foot of the stairs he made a slow circuit, keeping to the shadow of the trading-post wing. Jim was no longer by the well nor was there any sign of him anywhere in the courtyard. Turning into the deeper shadow of the vestibule, Kirk leaned against the wall and waited. Jim could have found some more hidden post from which to watch. But if so he would immediately have bolted out to make sure that Kirk had returned to his own room. There could be no further question of how effectively Jim had been impressed by Kirk's midnight excursion. Kirk's disappearance behind the blue door had left him so little doubt about Kirk's occupation for the remainder of the night that he had felt justified in abandoning his vigil.

Kirk chuckled soundlessly. All was continuing to go according to plan in every respect and in every detail. The gears of a watch could not have meshed more precisely. He went to Caty's door. The knob turned readily but the door was barred by a bolt on the inside. There was a glimmer of light through the keyhole. He rattled the knob and pressed his ear against the door.

He could hear a rustle as of bedclothing being thrown back. Then came a faint scuffing as of feet being thrust into slippers. There followed a silence of many seconds. He began to imagine he could hear breathing. She could be as near her side of the door as he was on his.

There was the sudden grate of the sliding bolt. The door opened a crack. The light within was dim and her face was only a pale blur.

"You said to yell," he whispered. "But it didn't seem a good idea to wake up everybody."

She did not reply. He pushed gently against the door. For a second she resisted. Then she swung the door wide. He stepped past her into the room. She quickly closed the door.

The light came from a stub of a candle in a yellow glass bowl. Beside the bed was a chair across which her clothing was draped. He crossed to it and sat down.

She was still leaning against the door, listening. She had on a long, blue flannel nightgown and her hair was braided in tight pigtails. Tall as she was, she still looked like a little girl. After a moment she threw open the door and peered out into the corridor. Closing the door again, she set her back against it.

"That scum," she said. "That chicken track. That creeping excuse for a mouse."

"Was what you had more in mind," suggested Kirk, "getting him to prove his manhood by shooting me?"

"I'd not have stood for his shooting you." Caty did not appear to consider this point really important. "What I did want worked into his head was that Aurora wasn't the only piece on the place."

"Still not too late to prove that."

"Seems damned late to me. Seems like I been laying there listening for a hundred years."

"It had to be not for him but for me you were listening."

She gave this an instant's startled consideration, as though he had voiced an apprehension to which she had been attempting to deny recognition. "You mean I could be more mixed up than I think?"

"I mean you better get back into bed before you get too cold to think."

She looked from him to the bed to the door. But she did not order him out. She crossed to the bed, got in, and drew the covers up to her chin. The two braids stretched out across the pillow gave her more than ever the look of a little girl.

Kirk had not stirred from his chair.

"So," he continued, "you've been lying here awake all these hours trying to make up your mind."

"No." The denial was emphatic. "You can tell by this horse blanket I'm wearing," she indicated the flannel nightgown, "that I'd made up my mind before I came to bed. Actually, as long ago as when I was making the bed and you were standing there in the doorway — that's when I knew it was no soap."

"Yet now you're not so sure."

She regarded him thoughtfully, weighing this possibility.

"You do look somehow different now than you did then."

"Once you get a man in your room doesn't he always look different?"

She did not comment but neither did she look away.

"Well," he insisted.

"Everything else has been going wrong." She closed her eyes the better to contemplate this phenomenon. When they reopened she had decided. "Put out the light."

He walked to the door, shot the bolt, and returned to blow out the candle. While discarding his pants and shirt he could sense her movements in whipping off and tossing aside the flannel nightgown. He got into bed. She was shivering but her arms were reaching out to receive him.

"You don't have to be so damned careful," she objected presently. "This isn't the first time for me."

"No? I suppose that first was long, long ago — say, when you were fifteen."

"How'd you guess? That's just when it was. My last, too."

Kirk's exultation grew. His approach had been a masterpiece. He had at every moment taken heed to her every inflection, expression, attitude. It had been like the stalking of a fleet and alert wild creature. All this had been climaxed by the discovery that she was a total delight.

Later, when with her face snuggled against his neck he had thought she had fallen asleep, she whispered:

"Will you tell me the truth?"

"I always do."

"You never do. But this time you got to."

"About what?"

"About how I stack up — compared to Ma."

"Good God, how could I know?"

"No use trying to weasel. I saw how she was looking at you yesterday. When she gets that grabby no man's got a chance."

"I can tell you one thing. You don't ever have to worry about what Jim will think."

"You mean as between me and Ma?"

"I mean between you and anybody."

"You're such a terrible liar. Anyway, why are we always talking about Jim?" She drew a long satisfied breath. "I can't wait to watch his face when I tell him about — about this."

"Don't do that."

"Oh, I'll wait till you're gone."

"Don't tell him then. Don't tell him ever."

"You don't catch on to what I'm getting at. He's been staying away from me because he thinks he's spoiled. Now I'm spoiled, too. We're both in the same boat. It'll make everything easier for him."

"It will not. You couldn't make a greater mistake. Believe me."

"I suppose you're right. How can you always be right about so many things — even me?" Her voice trailed away drowsily. "I like it better this way. Because no matter what reasons I thought I had I'm glad it happened. Now it can stay something for only us to remember — nobody else — just us."

Kirk was awakened by Caty's hand on his shoulder. He sat up in his cot. The morning sun was streaming in the window. She was dressed in a starched gingham dress and smelled of flour, as though she had been making bread. In her poise there was no hint that last night had been other than a dream.

"Zenas is beginning to wake up," she announced.

Kirk could hear from the upper room of the blockhouse a guttural mumbling. Caty had a pitcher of hot water in her other hand. She set it on the washstand and went out. By the time he had finished his hasty toilet the mumbling above had been succeeded by a bellow:

"Orrie. Orrie."

Kirk toweled his face dry and went out in the courtyard. Aurora was coming from the main house. She had a full bottle of whiskey in her hand.

"This is what he's hollering for," she explained.

"Orrie," came another and louder bellow.

"Coming," she yelled.

She handed the bottle to Kirk.

"You take it up to him. He'll want it so bad it might give you some chance to get a word with him."

Kirk climbed the ladder, pulled the latchstring of the small half door at its head, and pushed his way into the upper room. It was square, some twenty feet to a side, dimly lighted by dusty rays of sunlight coming through loopholes, and warmed by a charcoal fire in a big iron pot. Kirk's strongest impression as he straightened up was of the amazing array of weapons hanging on the walls. There were firearms ranging from a Kentucky long rifle through Hudson Bay muskets and primitive six-shooters to comparatively modern Spencers, Remingtons and Winchesters, along with every sort of variation on Indian lances, bows and arrows, tomahawks and war clubs. In one corner dangled a by-product, a long string of dried scalps. In its every aspect the room was the lair of a man who was hanging onto the memories of a lifetime of violence.

The man himself was sitting with his back against the wall at the head of a low bunk piled with a tangle of bearskins. His unclothed torso was matted with hair and crisscrossed by white scars but his once powerful body with its wide shoulders, long arms and deep chest was now scarcely more than skin stretched over bones. His long hair was still jet-black but the stubble of quarter-inch beard on his gaunt face was white, which set off the red glitter in his deeply sunken eyes and gave him a startlingly baleful appearance. His attention was centered on the bottle in Kirk's hand.

"Put her down here where I can reach her," he directed, indicating a spot on the floor beside the bunk.

Kirk advanced to the bedside but he did not put the bottle down. This stirred Zenas to look up in angry impatience and to realize that he was being served by a stranger.

"Who be you?" he demanded.

"What difference?" said Kirk. "You'll get the bottle when you answer one question."

Kirk's insolence seemed to sooth rather than arouse the old man. "Well, spit it out."

"How do I find Jared Glass? I was told that if anybody knew you would."

Zenas let out a snort of laughter. "No sweat answerin' that one." He dropped his voice to a hoarse whisper. "Mousey."

In the dim light Kirk had failed to notice as he entered that just to the right of the half door stood a cot on which lay a second man with his face to the wall. He had evidently been able to sleep on through Zenas's loudest roars but in response to the whisper he was out of his blankets and on his feet, rifle in hand, in one instant movement. He was small, lean, wiry, sunburned, wrinkled, quite bald, with big ears, a long nose, a stubby white mustache, and extraordinarily intent gray eyes.

Though possibly nearly as old as Zenas, there seemed in his slight frame a reserve of force like a coiled spring. Even in shirttail and drawers he was an impressive figure.

"Are you Jared Glass?" asked Kirk.

"That I be."

Kirk set the bottle on the floor by the bunk. Zenas seized it, took a long pull, snuggled down among his bearskins, and at once began to snore. Jared leaned the rifle against the wall, reached for his hat, put it on, sat down on the cot, and gestured toward a stool. The antithesis of Zenas in manner as well as size, he seemed politely considerate and prepared to please.

"Down in my saddlebags," said Kirk. "I've got orders for you from General Miles."

"Orders?" His voice was as low-keyed as his manner but there was in it the faintest hint that an order was never a feasible approach to him.

"I mean a letter for you. He thinks you're the best scout he ever had. He said in the '76 campaign you always knew more about where the Sioux were than they knew themselves."

"He wasn't a bad old coot to work for."

"He wants to put you back on the rolls so you can help me investigate this Ghost Dance business."

"Ghost Dance?"

"Yes. This new dance that's spreading among all the tribes."

"Ghost Dance. That's a right purty name, ain't it?"

"You mean you haven't heard about it?"

"I ain't been out o' this room — 'cept down the ladder to the privy — in more'n two months."

"Then maybe I better make a new start. My name's Kirk. I'm a lieutenant on General Miles's staff. Nobody knows yet whether all this dancing will lead to trouble or not. The general wants us to find out. He's the new commander of the Division of the Missouri, you know."

"So? What happened to Crook?"

"He died last month."

"Too bad. But Miles will do."

"It's the general's idea that I pretend to be an easterner out here on a hunting trip. And that I have hired you as guide. That way we can pack wherever we want, nose around anywhere, and keep at it until we find out what these fool Indians are really up to."

"Ghost Dance," said Jared, still intrigued by the name. A faraway look had come into his eyes. "Nothin' would suit me better. Trouble is, I can't make it. Not now."

"Why not?"

Jared nodded toward the snoring Zenas. "Him. Stud and me, we been partners off and on fer near sixty year. We been through a lavish o' fixes together. I don't aim to let him go it alone through this last one."

"But who knows how long that may be?"

"Nobody. That's a fact. He's been workin' hard at shufflin' hisself off these two months since he sent fer me. But there's fire in him yet and it could take a good bit more trompin' 'fore he gets the last sparks stomped out."

"What's he want to die for?"

"He figgers it this way. When a man can't fire the breath out o' no woman no more, and can't crack a marrow bone in his teeth no more, and ain't got the strength to toss a cow over a fence no more, then the time's come for him to go."

Zenas's snoring became uneven and ended in a great snort. He sat up in his bunk.

"Mousey, you miserable down end of a pissant, I just remembered somethin' that shoves your ass right in a bear trap."

Jared's reply was mild in tone but equally combative. "Stud, you always was pig-headed but by now you ain't got head enough left to remember your mother's name — if she ever had one."

"I got me plenty head left to remember nobody ever could miss a mark as far as you could. But even without the wits left to plug the eye of a needle you can recollect that rendezvous on the Green when that missionary doc, Whitman, and that preacher feller, Parker, showed up, can't you?"

"That I can. But only reason you got it that close to straight is 'cause the doc he dug that arrowhead out o' you. That's somethin' hard for even a 'dobe skull like you to ferget. We poured two bottles of brandy into you but when the doc began to stick his knife in, you sobered up real fast." Jared chuckled as he recalled this moment.

"It was you done the squealin' — not me. You could see the doc was pokin' right in up agin my liver. Now — you ain't denyin' that that arrowhead was shot into me two summers afore by that toad-face Blackfoot, Iron Horn, whilst we was a-buildin' that canoe on the Clearwater?"

"No, I ain't. I seen it. And I figgered you was a goner. And it had to be two summers afore the Green 'cause we first seen the Clearwater the fall after the rendezvous in Pierre's Hole where Milt Sublette and Tom Fitzpatrick and Jim Bridger got us into that shindig in the willows with that pack o' Blackfeet and Minnataree."

"So," shouted Zenas in triumph. "Now, you half-sliver off a wipin' stick, you're in up to your chin in how wrong you been. You can't claim no more that that fourth scalp from the top o' the string ain't Iron Horn's. 'Cause soon's the doc clapped that arrowhead in my hand I named myself the last turd out of a dyin' mule if I wasted a minute afore I run that Injun down and stuck it into him."

"So you did. I heard you. All the same, it be the fifth scalp from the top that's Iron Horn's — not the fourth. You're skippin' a whole year — which ain't too bad fer a sinkin' loon that gets mixed up by all of five year most the time. The way it come off was whilst we was packin' in toward the Blackfoot country you sighted that Crow gal, Red Bird, in a gooseberry patch. By the time you'd sneaked up on her and had her by the hair you'd forgot all about Iron Horn and mule turds. That's how come that winter come to be the winter we holed up on the head of the Gallatin. I ain't likely to ferget that winter 'cause I done all the trappin' whilst you rolled amongst the blankets with the gal. Come spring her husband showed up which makes that fourth scalp his'n."

Memories had momentarily diverted Zenas from the zest of argument. "She was a right lively piece," he mused. "I ain't fergettin' her — nor that fool man o' her'n. It was her that knifed him — not me. I only put him out of his misery." He shook off sentiment and returned to the fray. "But all that come the next winter — after I'd run down Iron Horn."

"Nope. It was the next winter that you got through with Red Bird and got to him."

"Mousey, you're gettin' too old and foolish to count far's two."

Relief from the hopeless impasse was provided by Caty's pushing open the door at the head of the ladder. She had the end of a rope in her hand. Pulling on this brought into view a basket containing half a ham, a sack of pemmican, a wad of jerky, a loaf of bread and a great pot of coffee.

"You want something else — just holler," she said. She set the basket on the foot of the bunk, gave Kirk a passing and entirely calm glance, and withdrew.

The two old men had drawn their knives and were falling upon the bread and meat with gusto. Despite their relative toothlessness they did not appear to be having much difficulty wolfing down the ham and even the tough jerky.

"Well," said Kirk, getting up reluctantly. "I have to be on my way."

"Set down," ordered Zenas. "And take you a sniff o' what's in that basket'n see if'n anythin' there suits you."

"Thank you," said Kirk. "All of it does."

He was hungry and the ham and dried venison were excellent. He lifted out the pot and poured the coal-black coffee. Zenas, taking his cup, regarded Kirk critically.

"You talk like an easterner," he said. "But you look some like more man than that."

"I once worked awhile at a ranch down by Cheyenne," said Kirk. "But I guess I am an easterner. I was born in Ogdensburg, New York."

"Ogdensburg," said Jared with unexpected if mild interest. "Summer afore last I packed fer a spell fer a man said he was from Ogdensburg. Miles steered him to me. Name was Remington — just like the rifle. He drawed pictures."

"Frederic Remington," said Kirk. "I know him well. When I was a boy he lived right across the street from us."

"Must o' been the same feller," said Zenas. "Last summer he come ridin' in here. Spent most a week makin' him pictures o' me. Got real excited. Said he'd never seed anybody afore that looked like a honest-to-God mountain man's supposed to look. Reckon he'd forgot about Mousey."

Jared for once did not take the bait. Having sufficiently dealt with the subject of the itinerant painter the two resumed eating.

"One thing I have to know," said Kirk, after a while. "Why do you call each other Stud and Mousey?"

The process of eating delayed their response momentarily. Jared was the first to gulp down enough to enable him to speak.

"The name the Injuns give Stud was Stallion-Always-Ready. That's the most he's ever been good fer."

"The one they tied to Mousey," said Zenas, "was Panther-Mouse. The panther end don't mean nothin' but the other end's right on the mark. Mousey's a powerful nibbler. Always nibblin' at you." His interest in the topic was already fading, however. He was again contemplating Kirk critically. "Now why'n the goddam hell, Mousey, couldn't one o' them stinkin' cockroaches turned out as likely-lookin' as this here young-un?"

"Where I lose the trail," said Jared, an unprecedented earnestness in his voice indicating the importance of the problem that had suddenly been brought into the open, "is what in the name of God Almighty and all his saints and sinners ever set you, Stud, to hirin' that courthouse coyote from Riverton to nosin' around till he brung back what he brung here?"

"Never made a worse mistake," admitted Zenas. "Me, I've made a sight o' mistakes, Mousey, but never one so bad as that."

"Of all the mebbe a hundred brats," persisted Jared, "you likely left behind you up and down the Rockies what could o' turned you to sendin' fer them three?"

"I said it was a terrible mistake," said Zenas. "It's got me to frettin' till there ain't enough whiskey in Wyoming to do me no good no more." He put aside his coffee cup, shoved the basket away, and drew a long breath of resignation. "I ain't wanted to talk about it but the time's come I got to, Mousey. Last winter when I got to thinkin' my time was comin', what I thunk most about was this place. There ain't no spot like it anywhere I ever seed. Made no sense to tail off and let somebody like them Donelsons move in on it. Would suit me was Orrie and Caty to have it but this is still a country where even women like them need a man. That was what put me to followin' the wrong tracks. Could be, I got to figgerin', I'd somewhere one time or tother planted one myself that would do. That got me to thinkin' of all them gals back through the years. That brung me next to decidin' that amongst all o' them I could recollect it was either Cenci or Mady or Biddy that had pleasured me the most. That hit me like it was as good a chance to bet on as any. So I turned loose that tin-pot lawyer. But look what come of it. I was left trappin' a creek without so much as a muskrat up it." Zenas groaned. "Now I don't dast die."

"You surely worked yourself into a fix," agreed Jared, deeply but unhelpfully sympathetic.

Suddenly Zenas sat bolt upright and began to stare at him. Jared rose uneasily from his seat on the foot of the bunk. Zenas let out a howl of elation. Into Jared's carriage came a lithe springiness as though he had scented some fearful danger from which he must leap to escape.

"Why'n't that never come to me before?" roared Zenas. "The sure way to fix everythin' — all the time right here in front o' my eyes. A skinny little runt like you, Mousey, will live forever. All I got to do is marry you to Orrie. That'll put every last cat right smack in the bag. Nothin's made me feel so good since the winter that froze all Pete Donelson's cattle. Now just give me the time to take me the first proper sleep I've had since I busted my leg. Then I'll get me up, get you and Orrie hitched, and after that I can be on my way with nothin' more to fret about."

Zenas wriggled down into the bearskins and at once began to snore. Jared, after one long incredulous stare at the sleeping giant, sprang to his cot and began with practiced haste to dress and collect his few possessions. He made this a short process and turned, rifle in hand and saddlebags in the crook of his arm, to look once more at Zenas and then at Kirk.

"General Miles has got hisself a boy," he said.

"But, how about him?" asked Kirk, glancing at Zenas.

"A man that 'ud think him up a trick like that," said Jared firmly, "ain't no friend o' mine."

He pulled open the door and backed down the ladder. He had taken no more than three steps, his head and shoulders still at the doorsill level, when suddenly he twisted, looked off toward the lower end of the meadow and stiffened to attention. Kirk crouched in the doorway so that he, too, could see. A column of nearly a hundred Indians, riding two abreast, their horses at a sharp trot, had emerged from the canyon and was coming toward the ranch house.

"Shoshone," muttered Jared.

Kirk realized that Jared was astonished but could not gather how seriously concerned. The Shoshone reservation was twenty miles the other side of Donelson's and it was impossible that so many had been given permission to leave it. The four from the rocking chairs on the verandah came running around the trading-post side of the ranch house and ran on past the corrals toward the bunkhouse. Jared had not moved, other than the slow turn of his head as his eyes followed the Indians' progress. Kirk could see now that they were not bearing down directly on the ranch house. They were keeping to the creek bank and sweeping past. They moved on another hundred yards past the farthest corral. Suddenly their leader raised his arm. All pulled up and began dismounting around the tall, white stub of a long-dead oak that stood beside the stream.

Jared slid to the ground and ran to the corner of the trading post. Kirk followed, unbuttoning his shirt to ease getting at his armpit holster. Caty and Jim ran to meet near the corrals, then turned together to face the Indians. Each had a rifle. The minister came out of the barn with a pitchfork over his shoulder. The verandah four, still running, returned from the bunkhouse. They had not been fleeing but only going for their weapons. Valdez and Langlade had rifles, Cramer and McGary gun belts. The Zenas Williams strain had evidently not altogether petered out in them.

Jared was intently watching the Indians, who were hobbling their horses as though they intended to camp around the white stub. His complete calm made it still impossible to estimate what might be his analysis of the situation. There was clearly something peculiar about these Indians' behavior that even Jared, with his fifty years' experience, could not fathom. Suddenly he jerked his head around to look over his shoulder. Whatever the possible danger he perceived from the Indians, there was no doubt that he now saw a more certain danger. Aurora had appeared in the ranch-house doorway. Jared clutched Kirk's arm.

"Come on, son," he whispered. "Let's get us on our horses and be on our way."

Kirk was remorseless.

"Our job is to study Indians," he said. "And we got Indians here to study."

Jared closed his eyes in silent despair and reopened them with a sigh of resignation.

"You're right," he admitted. He dropped his saddlebags and blanket roll to the ground and handed Kirk his rifle. "You stay here and keep everybody else back."

He set out at a brisk walk toward the Indians. Kirk decided to be guided, at least for the moment, by Jared's informed judgment. Aurora joined Kirk at the corner of the trading post. There was a gun belt swung at her hips over the gray taffeta gown.

"He said for all of us to stay back," Kirk advised.

Caty, Jim, and the others gathered beside them. All watched as Jared walked toward the white stub until he was lost to view as the Indians closed in around him. Aurora took command.

"Caty, you and Jim get down there back of the well. And you four," indicating the heirs, "get in the trading post and knock the plugs out of the loopholes on the side toward the creek. And you, Parson, take that fork and stick it into that lawyer and tell him that if the Indians only want to burn one of us it'll be him."

All obeyed except Cramer, who momentarily had a better idea.

"How about up there?" he inquired, nodding toward the loopholed blockhouse. "Better field of fire from there."

"For Chrissake no," ruled Aurora. "Just pray to God he don't wake up. If he does he'll be slidin' down the ladder and yellin' for his horse and finishin' himself off for good."

She remained with Kirk at the corner of the trading post. They could still catch occasional glimpses of Jared among the Indians.

"All the ten years I been here we never had trouble with Indians," she said. "'Cept for stealin' a calf or a colt now and then. But Zenas always says you never can tell about Indians."

"You particularly can't," agreed Kirk, "when they get stirred up by getting off the reservation."

80

He could no longer see Jared. All of the Indians had jammed together around him. Whatever the substance of the discussion it was being conducted by the Indians with every evidence of extreme excitement. They were yelling and gesticulating wildly. Kirk decided, in the face of Jared's injunction, to join him. But before he was a third of the way to the white stub Jared pushed his way free of the Indians and came walking to meet him.

"No trouble," he reported, though he himself was betraying signs of an unaccustomed excitement. "They only come here to dance."

"Ghost Dance?"

"Yup"

"But why here?"

"Their head man — Bear Tail — he had him a dream. He passes fer a sort o' prophet amongst the Shoshone. He told 'em be big medicine was they to dance here. This always was a spot the Shoshone set special store by. Remember that the first time Stud and me ever come through here."

"Wonderful," said Kirk, grinning. "I can tell the general you found me another Ghost Dance five minutes after I got hold of you."

"Ain't the first time Injuns found me afore I seen them," said Jared. He looked behind him at the Indians, who were buzzing with the excitement of a disturbed hornets' nest. "Give them time to get theyselves good and started to hollerin' and stompin' and then we can poke in close as we want and watch all we're a mind to." His usually serene eyes were bright with the intensity of his interest. "Never seed Injuns so worked up. Can't figger it out."

But as they turned toward the ranch house all the brightness went out of his face. He had caught sight of Aurora at the corner of the trading post and of the minister, standing beside her, pitchfork in hand.

"All you've got to do is say no," Kirk reminded him.

Jared was not comforted by this counsel. "You don't 'pear to get the hang o' this. First place — take a fine figger of a woman like Orrie, how's a man that's got any claim to be a man a-goin' to stand up and say to her no he don't want her? And worse'n that, when Stud he comes down that ladder and looks me in the eye and says all he wants of me is to look after his woman when he's gone — how'm I a-goin' to say no?"

Bracing himself, Jared advanced toward his fate with a firm step. Jim and Caty and the trading-post garrison had reassembled beside Aurora. "The Indians only came here to dance," explained Kirk. "They seem to regard this as a sort of sacred site."

Aurora reasserted command.

"Jim, you and Caty round up the horses in the pasture and herd them into the corral. Jared, you and Stuart keep your eye on the Indians. The rest of you scout around the yard for anything loose and in the open an Indian might steal and lock it up in the barn. Me, I'll go rustle up some grub. We likely could use some before the night's over."

By midnight the dance had broken off three times and each time had resumed with redoubled vigor. During each intermission individual Indians had sprung to the center of the circle at the foot of the white stub to deliver impassioned harangues in the vainglorious manner assumed by warriors in a scalp dance when they boast of feats of valor and enemies overthrown. Jared and Kirk were sitting at the shadowed edge of the firelit dancing ground. Aurora and the others had watched for some hours but, tiring of the endless repetitions of the dancers' postures and speeches, had returned to the ranch house for a midnight supper. Nothing could have drawn Jared away. Kirk could see that his interest was intensified by the experience and understanding which permitted him more precisely to appreciate certain astonishing features of the Indians' behavior. Only once, much earlier in the night, had he broken his silence.

"That Bear Tail," he had whispered to Kirk, indicating the gray-haired, wrinkled, sixty-year-old Shoshone chief, "he don't know it but he's Stud's oldest boy. Leastwise the first from a woman Stud got at out here in this mountain country. He was born under that white stub there when it was still a live green tree. That summer o' 1830 Stud and me was on our way to the Wind River rendezvous. Whilst we was waitin' for Bill Sublette to come up from St. Louis with his wagons Stud he tuk up with the Shoshone gal that pupped Bear Tail the next spring. Water Bug was her name." The light of pleasant reminiscence had come into his eyes and figures of that earlier scene had seemed to rise between him and the dancers. "That was my first season in the mountains. Me, I was a snot-nose of no more'n fifteen. Stud he'd tuk me under his wing. By the time the wagons showed up he'd found him another gal and he give Water Bug to me. I ain't fergettin' much o' that 'cause she was my first squaw."

As the hours had rolled on Kirk's interest had been revived by the many differences between the dance being performed here and the one he had witnessed in Nevada.

"I'm beginnin' to pick up some of the trail," said Jared at last. "I've seed scalp dances and war dances and sun dances and buffalo dances and dog dances and all manner o' dances but I have never yet seed one where they got down to as bedrock serious as this here dance."

"That white stub with all those medicine bags tied to it is a new trick," said Kirk. "What's the point of that?"

"They call that the Prayer Tree," said Jared. "Got somethin' to do with Bear Tail's dream. They keep listenin' to whatever he says 'cause he's been out to Nevada but here tonight he's been tellin' 'em things either he forgot to tell 'em before or which he's just now begun to dream up."

"The way the dance seems centered on that stub," observed Kirk, "reminds me of the way the New Mexican Indians set up a big cross and then do a heathen dance around it."

"This could be somethin' like that," said Jared. "What most the hoppin' and yellin' is about is that the Messiah is on his way and that he be bringin' with him all their dead. Only I ain't been able to figger out if when he shows up they count on sightin' him somewhere up in the sky or mebbe perched all of a sudden there on that there stub."

"When the dancing stops every now and then and they start making speeches," asked Kirk, contemplating his report to the general, "what are they saying? Is it like a war dance — are they talking about what they'll do to enemies — say white enemies?"

"The tother way 'round. What they be braggin' about is what terrible sinners they be and howlin' that from now on they aim to do nothin' but good. 'Cause nothin' else will fetch the Messiah."

"The cross," marveled Kirk. "The Messiah. The confession of sins. The conversion to innocence. Why, they're getting this a lot more mixed up with the Christian religion than even Wovoka did."

"Injuns always been leanin' that way," said Jared. "I mind back the year when Tom Fitzpatrick brung the first settlers' train over South Pass a Catholic priest from St. Louis come out to the rendezvous at Pierre's Hole and more'n a thousand Flathead come down to palaver with him. The way Injuns figger is that white religion has got more powerful medicine than what theirs has got, else why do the whites keep gettin' stronger whilst they get weaker."

The movements of the dance had been getting more and more violent until they had attained a pitch of universal convulsion. Many dancers were overcome by seizures that resembled epileptic fits. Others were making prodigious leaps while screaming continuously. Some rolled on the ground in the grip of fearful contortions which were accompanied by frothing at the mouth. Others were gashing themselves with knives. Others were leaping in and out of fires. All appeared insanely possessed by the religious ecstasy which they had so persistently sought during their hours of dancing and testifying. In the midst of all the pandemonium Jared suddenly heard something that caused him to leap to his feet and peer backward into the darkness.

The flickering light from the fires picked out the figure of Zenas. He had pulled on his pants, moccasins and an old fringed hunting shirt, had a rifle in the crook of his arm, and his carriage was as easy and relaxed as though he had never been ill. Jared and Kirk sprang to meet him.

"Whereat's the trouble," roared Zenas, lifting his voice above the din of the dance. "My big toe that the Cheyenne shot off tuk to itchin' and it's never done that 'cept when there's trouble a-comin'."

"Ain't none here," said Jared. "You can see that fer yerself."

Zenas took a look at the frenzied dancing. "Fer once you be right, Mousey," he agreed. He took another look. "They fer sure be on the prong, ain't they? Nobody can ever get religion so bad as Injuns. The way they be carryin' on minds me of oncet when I was a boy back in Pennsylvany and we throwed a skunk in a Shaker meetin'." He and Jared turned instantly toward the sound of running feet coming from the direction of the ranch house. "Told you trouble was a-comin'," added Zenas. "That toe ain't never missed."

The three advanced several steps into the darkness to meet Jim, who was breathing hard.

"A hand from Donelson's just rode in to talk to me," Jim reported. "He says Donelson's outfit along with maybe twenty, thirty more from the Bar-X and Winslow ranches are on their way here to have a go at the Indians. He said they butchered three Donelson steers on their way across his range and that anyway long's they're off the reservation it's open season on them. Donelson wanted us to know so we could stay out of the way and not get hurt. That's all the man said. He was real nervous and in a big hurry to get away from here."

Zenas grunted and strode off toward the ranch yard with the other three in his train. In the main hall of the house he faced his assembled family, guests, and retainers. The light from the oil lamps revealed how much younger he had begun to look.

"Nobody's comin' on my place to bother nobody that's come to visit me," he said with great calm. "And fer sure nobody's goin' to get at them Shoshone whilst they's no more able to look after theyselves than they be tonight. Now, ain't one chance in a hunnert Pete Donelson is comin' by any other way than by the canyon trail. He ain't got the stummick to cross them hills in the dark. All the same, Jim, you, and Caty, and Orrie, ride out along the edge of the hills. Don't tangle with nobody but if you run acrost somebody comin' in that way fire off some shots. You four," addressing the Cramer group, "stay down there by the stub and if you hear any shots do the best you can to bust up the dance and get the Injuns on their horses and off into the mountains. You and me, Mousey" — his glance took in Kirk — "and you, son, we'll ride down to the end of the canyon to meet Pete and his boys to tell them they might's well go back home."

Zenas pulled in his horse at the edge of the meadow, where the slope began to drop down into the canyon. A late half-moon touched with its pale light the rock walls framing the mouth of the canyon and deepened the darkness enshrouding the trail in the creek bottom below. Zenas dismounted and sat down in the grass. Jared and Kirk followed his example. An hour passed. And then another. No shots came from the direction of Jim's hill patrol. The fires at the Indian dancing ground had died down. The patience of Zenas and Jared seemed limitless. At times

85

they appeared to doze. The eastern sky was beginning to turn gray. Zenas lifted his head to listen. The waiting had lasted longer than he had expected.

"Figgered Pete he would want to jump the Shoshone right at daylight before they was up," he said. "He's a-goin' to be late."

"The night I spent at the Donelson ranch," said Kirk, "there was a good deal of talk about the Ghost Dance. Some of them had been on the reservation to see the Arapaho do one. They noticed the dancers were so worn out by morning that they slept all day."

Zenas grunted his acceptance of this theory. "Be like Pete to aim to walk in amongst 'em knockin' 'em in the head whilst they was flat on their backs."

The stars were disappearing. The light in the east was spreading across the sky. There came a sudden clatter of hoofs far down the canyon. Kirk started to get up. Zenas and Jared did not move. The clatter grew louder. A herd of antelope came bolting out of the shadows up the slope, recoiled at sight of the men and horses, and scattered with long, arching bounds among the rocks on either side. The succeeding silence was broken by a horse's neigh echoing from the depths of the canyon.

Zenas and Jared got up, stretching. All three tightened their saddle girths and mounted, Winchesters across their knees. It was full daylight now. Zenas and Jared moved their horses forward two or three steps to the point where the trail coming up out of the canyon reached the top of the slope and here pulled them in again. Kirk had expected them to take some sort of defensible cover among the rocks on either side. His military sense envisaged the total heedlessness of waiting there motionless in the open, outlined against the sky, in the face of thirty or forty armed adversaries. But this was clearly the posture Zenas had elected to maintain. The confused clumping of iron-shod hoofs was now sounding from just beyond the nearest bend in the canyon.

"Son," Zenas directed Kirk, "you move over there back o' the corner o' that big rock. Don't figger there's apt to be no shootin' but was some to start I want you to make sure you get back to help Jim and the women and the rest get them Injuns off into the hills."

He spoke with such absolute authority that Kirk found himself unhesitatingly obeying.

Donelson, at the head of his single-file column of horsemen, came into view around the bend. He saw the two silhouetted against the sky above but came on halfway up the slope before pulling in. The horsemen behind him, finding room as the canyon widened, began to veer off the trail to draw up on either side of him until there were a dozen abreast in the front rank.

"Howdy, Zenas," said Donelson, with a show of good cheer. "Was some worried the Indians might have got you by now. Glad to see you've come to join up with us."

"That ain't why I come," said Zenas. "I come to tell you you ain't welcome. Not at this time o' day. I don't like folks sneakin' up on my place in the night."

The stir of astonishment among the ranchers built into a general growl of rage.

"Don't try to tell me them Indians ain't on your place," said Donelson, "because we know they are. Are you telling us that Indians are welcome but your white neighbors ain't?"

Zenas made no reply. Donelson held up his hand to quiet the angry muttering of his followers.

"You've got so old, Zenas," he said, "that you've forgot how times have changed. I'm asking you just this once to listen to reason. Them Indians are off the reservation. That makes them hostiles. They might be old friends of yours but they ain't friends of no other white man. No telling how soon they'll go to burning and murdering. We got our chance this morning to get rid of the whole cattle-stealing pack and by God we ain't going to throw that chance away."

The pronouncement drew a loud rumble of support among his followers. Zenas still offered no reply.

"What I say is," declared a rancher in the second rank, "let's just ride right over 'em and get on with our pig-stickin'."

But as the front rank continued to eye the two grim figures above, and particularly the muzzles of the two Winchesters, there was no forward surge in response to this proposal. It was Zenas who broke the ensuing, increasingly oppressive silence by speaking in a conversational tone to Jared.

"Any shootin' happen to get started," he said, "I'll take Pete Donelson, you take whoever gets me, and afore I hit the ground I'll get whoever gets you."

The utter nonchalance of the two old mountain men, seasoned through the years by memories of any number of such hair-raising confrontations as this, was terrifying. It was the sheer cold-bloodedness of Zenas's matter-of-fact statement of intentions that had Donelson beginning to lick his dry lips. Sudden inspiration saved him from the humiliation of an outright backdown.

"Boys," he called out, "we've walked right into a trap. He's likely got his Indians back of every one of them rocks. Let's us get out of here while we can."

The alarming possibility claimed universal acceptance. The ranchers wheeled their horses, jockeyed desperately for position, and jammed their way back along the trail and out of view around the bend.

Riding toward the ranch house, Zenas attempted to deprecate the victory.

"Country's goin' to the dogs," he lamented. "Ain't hardly a man left in it ain't got a soft spot you could mire a buffalo in."

But the eyes of the two old men were gleaming. For one more moment they had known what it was to feel fully alive.

In the ranch yard Zenas dismounted and looked about him with unreserved satisfaction and a renewed readiness to come to decisions. He came to two immediately.

"Orrie," he said, "you get up that ladder where you belong. And by the time we be back down here, you, Jim, and, you, Caty, see that you be in your Sunday clothes. Before that preacher gets away we're goin' to get you married." He turned to shake hands formally with Kirk and Jared. "Whereat you headin' for first?"

"The Crow and Cheyenne, then the Blackfeet," said Kirk.

"Half wisht I was goin' with you. If you come to where you need any help — just yell."

V

UNDER THE GRAY SKY the low rocky hills were wreathed in dank mist and darkened by scrubby patches of tamarack, hemlock, and dwarf pine. Between the hills were brush-choked bogs, slimy with frog spawn and stinking of putrefying vegetation. In this wet weather it was as uninviting a region as could well be imagined. But for John it offered the appeal of a reentered Eden. For it was a wilderness through which, in spirit-cleansing relief, he might wander at will.

Professor Temple had so far relented as to advance him funds to cover his railroad fare west. But when he bought his ticket John had, to the logician's final bafflement, elected to travel not to the Missouri but to the shores of Lake Superior at Duluth, nearly four hundred miles from his Standing Rock destination. It had suddenly occurred to him that he was presented with an opportunity to incorporate in his homeward journey a retracing of the path taken in the ancestral removal of his people when, generations ago, they had migrated westward. Since infancy he had listened to legends dealing with that infinitely arduous emergence from a shadowed, rain-drenched forest into the vast, arid spaces of the high plains.

What had most baffled Temple had been the problem of detecting any relationship between the urgency of John's determination to rush off in midterm and the inconsistency of this time-wasting detour. Had John endeavored to explain he would only have increased the old scholar's bewilderment. His abrupt departure had not been precipitated by any apprehension that the Ghost Dance might represent an emergency confronting his people. He knew how frequently waves of superstition swept the Indian community, that these subsided quickly, and that, in any event, the arrogant Sioux were less susceptible than other Indians to such aberrations. The emergency with which he was confronted had been within himself. The insignificant newspaper item had unleashed memories and images that had made the rigid discipline of learning and reason, to which he had been submitting, seem suddenly stifling. For so long his life had been bound by duties and demands. Once he, too, had lived in a world in which what was real was not so real as what could be imagined. Once he, too, had been shielded from insecurity by the irresponsibility and irrationality that can be known only by a child, a savage, or a god. He had felt compelled, looking through the diamond-paned window behind Temple into the glimmer of the western sky, to experience once more, before it was too late, what it was like to be an Indian.

The gray clouds were beginning to thicken and lower, shortening the day. Rain that night was a certainty. The luck that had seemed with him since he had dismounted from that last of many trains still hovered. He discovered an overhanging ledge of rock which when supplemented by a thatch of leaning branches assured a dry camp. He had just started his fire when the porcupine emerged on the farther bank of the pond below. It was a long shot but the arrow sped true. Acquisition of the bow and arrow had been one of the satisfactions that had lighted his woodland journey. The second day out he had happened upon an old Menominee hunter who had been happy to exchange it for the cheap rifle that had been among his Duluth purchases. It was a soundly built, old-fashioned bow, of well-seasoned yew, strengthened with strips of elk-horn, and bound with deer sinew. The arrows were straight, properly balanced, and expertly feathered. He had had from childhood a way with a bow and arrow. He performed with the circus by shooting arrows into the air so high and fast that the tenth had left the bowstring before the first had returned to earth. There had been an added satisfaction in trading off the rifle. Admittedly, the knife and hatchet were, like the rifle, of white manufacture, but they were still the sort of weapons upon which Indians had always depended. Having got rid of the firearm he could feel that he was returning to this primitive background with equipment which was as traditional as the wind, the gusts of rain, the hills, and the trees. He broiled the quarters and loin of the porcupine, rolled into his blanket and fell asleep, more at peace with the world and himself than in many years.

His euphoria did not long endure. The next morning he emerged from the hills and swamps into the smoother, more nobly forested valley of the Mississippi which, here in the northernmost reaches of the great river, was a country of innumerable lakes. The sky had cleared and each successive lake he came upon seemed to mirror its blue more vividly than had the last. Each was set off by its frame of pine, oak, cedar, maple, white birch. Swans, ducks, and geese cruised its ripples, bass, bluegills and sunfish flirted in its shallows. Every thicket rustled with quail and partridge. Every hour he sighted deer, moose, bear. On every hand were spring flowers — trillium, arbutus, water lilies. Blueberries, raspberries, cranberries, blackberries and grapes were in blossom with the promise of fruit to come. But his appreciation of all this natural abundance and beauty was streaked with the sharpness of his sudden discontent. For this was the paradise that had been the original Sioux homeland, which they had been forced to abandon by their ancient enemies, the Chippewa, against whom they had always until then been able to prevail. They had been obliged to give way because the Chippewa, living on the shores of the Great Lakes, had been supplied with guns by the earliest white traders, who had ranged so far into the interior of the continent in their boats. Long before the Sioux had ever so much as seen a white man, the white man had been able to inflict upon them this grievous injury.

The next day his disgruntlement hardened into anger. He had come upon a tract that had been recently timbered. The forest had been cut down, the earth plowed, gouged, and torn by the marauders' dragging away of the logs, the leafless limbs and branches left in huge tangled heaps, and every once flourishing tree reduced to an unsightly stump. The shores of the gemlike lakes, no longer encircled by the green of the forest, were instead cluttered by windrows of dead brush. In another hour the scene had become yet more desolate. Here the slashings left by the lumbermen had been burned, whether by accident or design. For miles the earth was a blackened waste and every lake gray with ash. The forest fires of the past, set by lightning or for Indian game drives, had killed many of the existing trees yet had left the earth ready for the immediate rebirth of a new forest. But by these immense accumulations of dried brush the fire had been kindled to a heat that had consumed the very soil itself. The greater trees would not return for generations, if ever, while all growth remained stunted and mean. The Sioux had suffered the humiliation of dispossession by the Chippewa but even after so fearful a disaster the land itself had remained as fair as before. Only the white man was capable of devastating the earth and polluting its waters.

Each day from then on his indignation was fed by every new impression. His westward progress after crossing the Mississippi, here hardly more than a brook, was taking him into a region in which white settlers were beginning to locate. It was easy to avoid their scattered clearings but he was compelled to cross the ever more numerous wagon roads and twice to cross lines of railroad. The moan of locomotive whistles, the clatter and pound of iron wheels on iron tracks, echoed intermittently across the ravaged land, loudest of all in the silence of the night. Worse, there hung always on the horizon one or more of the billowing columns of brown smoke that proclaimed the burning sawdust heap of another sawmill.

There came a trace of comfort when he had pressed on westward to the region of the Ottertail Lakes, in which he harbored a special interest. Here lumbering operations had proceeded so much earlier that there had been an interval in which a respectable second growth had sprung up to conceal some of the scars. As a child he had listened to stories of the time, more than a hundred years ago, his great-grandfather had led a party of Sioux families back to these Ottertail Lakes to hold there for a season a defiant lodgment. They had stood their ground until, decimated by the onslaughts of their better-armed enemies, they had withdrawn again to the plains, vengefully satisfied with the number of Chippewa they had been able to kill.

He circled among the chains of lakes until he found the round one with the three small islands in its center. Beside the estuary of the stream feeding the lakes he came upon what he was seeking. The area was overgrown with willow but there remained the unmistakable vestiges of the earthen embankment his great-grandfather had ordered raised to shield his perilous encampment. John camped in the center of the low earthwork, his imagination busy with speculation on that long-past summer when his ancestors had defended this spot with arrows, tomahawks, knives and bare hands against the guns of the Chippewa. There came a sudden snuffling, grunting and rustling from the side of the embankment toward the stream. He looked up from his fire-lighting and listened, puzzled, unable to identify the animal. From a thicket on the top of the three-foot bank thrust the snout of a pig which, judging by the tusks and shoulder bristles, belonged to a strain that had run wild from some settler's keeping. John's bow and quiver were hanging beyond his reach. More in annoyance at the nature of the animal than in any pressing need for its meat, he threw his knife. The cast was true to the throat. With a gurgling squeal the pig collapsed, thrashing, down the other slope. John sprang to the low bank. The pig had rolled into the stream which, aided by the contortions of its death agonies, was carrying it into the lake. John ran in pursuit, splashing out into the estuary to shoulder depth, clutched his sinking prey, and dragged the carcass ashore. It was then that he made the depressing discovery. The knife was no longer embedded in the wound. At some point in the dying pig's tumbling career it had been dislodged.

John pressed his angry search until full darkness. The knife was not in the shrubbery between the bank and the stream's edge nor was it anywhere in the sandy bed of the stream. Searching the bottom of the estuary was a more onerous process. Several feet of mud had accumulated on the bottom as a consequence of the erosion of the watershed resulting from the timber-cutting. Beneath the mud was a matted layer of rotting branches and treetops that had been deposited by the stream's occasional flood waters. In the jagged, mud-shrouded depths of this mass were innumerable interstices into any one of which the knife might have slithered beyond recall. He dove and groped for hours before finally admitting that his quest was hopeless.

He washed and dried his clothes and the next morning faced the inevitable. He had to have a knife. To a man living in and off the wilderness a knife was an absolute necessity. On the southern horizon was one of the columns of smoke that marked a sawmill. Associated with it was undoubtedly a community in which there might be a store where he could purchase one. So far on his journey an essential satisfaction had been the success with which he had avoided any contact with people, but his present predicament left him no latitude for this self-indulgence.

He hid his pack, blanket, hatchet, bow, quiver and mackinaw. Of his remaining five dollars he put three in his pocket and left the other two in his pack. Sioux had been detested in Minnesota ever since the great massacre of settlers in 1862 but, dressed as he was in blue cotton shirt, denim pants, and lumberjack boots, he trusted he would be taken for any nondescript Chippewa, many of whom wandered about begging or seeking odd jobs.

Plodding into the hamlet of Laketon, he covertly studied the location of its principal structures and the activities of its visible inhabitants. On the right side of the dusty street was the mill, shaking with the noise of its screeching machinery, flanked at one end by the long pile of as yet unsawn logs and at the other by the yard containing the piles of finished lumber. Across the street from the mill were ranged the village's few commercial establishments. On the false front of one was the painted legend: OLAF GENERAL MERCHANDISE. Just beyond the store a dozen or more unemployed lumberjacks lounged around the door of a saloon. The building on the nearer side of the store was a small dwelling, the rear part of which was fitted with a barred window. Over the door was a wooden slat lettered: SHERIFF. On the stoop, dozing in a chair tilted back against the wall, was a gaunt, long-legged man whose white hat, calfskin vest and badge identified him as the sheriff. No one appeared to be taking any notice of John as he turned from the street into the store.

Irritated by his misadventure with the knife, by the necessity of coming here at all, by the screeching of the sawmill, and by the sight of the dozing sheriff and the idling lumberjacks, he decided on impulse to pretend ignorance of English in order to be spared the indignity of any conversation. The place was empty except for the storekeeper, evidently Olaf himself by his proprietory air, seated on a stool back of the counter reading a newspaper. Though the day was mild, in the center of the floor toward the back stood a tall, sheet-iron stove with a steaming pot of coffee on top. The storekeeper looked up with an automatic smile, which faded when he saw that his customer was an Indian. Glancing along the side of the store largely devoted to hardware, John had already spotted a tray of hunting knives in a glass showcase. He pointed to indicate his interest. Olaf removed the tray from the case and disdainfully placed it on the counter for John's inspection. John made his selection.

"That will be five dollars," said Olaf, holding up his hand with thumb and fingers spread.

John grunted a remonstrance and pointed to the price tag on the knife, which read: $2.50.

Olaf surveyed him sourly.

"So," he said. "A smart one, eh?"

John continued, dumbly, to keep his finger on the price tag. A flicker of interest crossed Olaf's glum face. He turned deliberately toward the cubicle at the end of the counter that housed the village post office, lifted a flap in the counter's top, crossed to the door, opened it, and called:

"Jake. Got me an Indian here that's making me trouble."

Olaf returned to his post back of the counter. The sheriff appeared at the door and entered slowly. He was tall, lean, grizzled, with a seamed face, a straggly mustache, thin lips that kept parting in a half-smile to disclose tobacco-stained teeth, narrow shoulders, long arms, and, hanging over his belt, the small pot belly so often an attribute of country peace officers. The lumberjacks from the saloon began crowding in after him. They were grinning expectantly. It was obvious that the sheriff was known to have an entertaining way with stray Indians. He was surveying John with apparent benevolence while waiting for his audience to gather. At length he took a step forward, hooked his thumbs in his belt, and spoke.

"What's your name, big boy?"

John shook his head uncomprehendingly. He had decided complete stupidity was as sensible a course as any. The sheriff took another step forward. He still appeared benevolent.

"Whereat you from?" he inquired, almost politely.

John shook his head again. The sheriff took another slow step nearer.

"Maybe you'd like to show me your permit to leave the reservation," he suggested.

Once more John shook his head uncomprehendingly. Without warning the sheriff jerked his right hand from his belt and slapped John hard across the face, first from the right and next from the left. There was a

95

knobby ring on one of his fingers that split John's lip. John made no slightest move, either in defense or in evidence of any emotion. The sheriff turned to regard his gallery.

"You reckon he ain't got no sense at all?" he asked.

There was a scattered, nervous laugh which immediately died out. Some of the bystanders were swallowing. Others were licking their lips. The sheriff looked back at John.

"So you won't answer a civil question," he remarked regretfully.

John merely stared, his attention fixed on the tiny veins in the sheriff's eyes. So far the atmosphere in the room had been less of menace than of diversion, as when small boys assemble to attach a split stick to the tail of a dog. But now the moment the onlookers had gathered to witness was approaching. The sheriff reached into his hip pocket and drew out a small leather pouch loaded with shot. Wrapping his fingers around the braided thong handle he tapped the sap gently against the palm of his other hand. Again he appealed to his audience.

"You reckon a couple of larrups across the mouth with this might loosen him up some?" he inquired.

John made his move. Leaping backward behind the stove, he lifted one foot and kicked it over. Boiling coffee from the pot spewed over the sheriff's feet. The stove door had sprung open as the stove toppled and coals were pouring out on the dry wooden floor. The tin stovepipe, suspended from the ceiling by loops of haywire, collapsed. Clouds of steam, smoke and soot erupted.

John whirled to the back door but found it locked and too strong to be quickly broken open. He sprang over the counter, delivered a body check which sent Olaf sprawling to the floor of the post office, and turned to the tray of knives. The sheriff, reeling back from the clouds of smoke and soot, was tugging his pistol from its holster. John snatched one of the knives from the tray and threw it, piercing the sheriff's wrist. The gun dropped into the coals and soot on the floor. The first lumberjack to recover his wits reached into an open barrel of cant-hook handles for a weapon. The second knife from the tray pinned his hand to the handle. John was taking care not to kill. He was not yet sufficiently sure of escape. But when he lifted the third knife and held it poised, ready for a target, the remaining onlookers had seen enough.

They all but broke the front door from its hinges in their concerted rush to get out of range.

John sprang over the counter and followed them out. Glancing back from the doorway, he saw the sheriff groping for his gun with his left hand and Olaf pulling down a rifle from a display rack on the wall. John ran into the street. The lumberjacks' yells had attracted the whole town's attention. Men were converging on the store from every direction. Those nearest hesitated to come too near the knife in his hand but the press was already too general for him to make a break either up or down the street.

He ran instead across the street and began climbing the log pile. As he clambered from one log end to the next above he heard the first shots. From the top he looked back. The sheriff had recovered his pistol and was shooting with his left hand, using his wounded forearm as a gun rest. The gun was kicking up and the shots going high. But Olaf was passing out rifles and ammunition to whoever was nearest and other men were emerging from other doorways with guns in their hands. Within another few seconds the manhunt would be on in deadly earnest. The area in front of him had been cleared of logs and it was four hundred yards to the nearest cover. Before he could get across that open space too many riflemen would have reached the top of the log pile with too many opportunities to bring him down.

John dropped to the ground on the farther side of the pile and ran along it toward the mill. There the way was barred by the soup hole, the great, square vat of boiling water that cleansed logs of sand and grit before they were subjected to the saws. He crossed the steaming water by toe-dancing from one bobbing log to the next and ran up the incline by which the logs were drawn into the mill. There he burst upon the mill hands, who were astounded by the sudden apparition. Knife in hand, John leaped and dodged through the labyrinth of glittering saws and spinning rollers. One bound carried him to a momentary perch on a log mounted on the steam-driven carriage that drove logs against the great, screaming disk of the main saw. His next was over the multiple saws of the edger. The chief sawyer was so startled by John's vault directly over his head that he neglected to release his grip on his control lever, sending the carriage crashing through the far wall of the mill.

John's last leap carried him over the trimmer to the discharging platform, where finished lumber poured out of the mill.

One of the tram cars that ran on wooden rails by gravity to deliver lumber from the mill to the storage yard was standing there nearly loaded. John shoved aside the attendant mill hand, kicked out the wedge blocking its wheels, gave the car a push, and squatted on the front bumper, where the load would shield him from the rear. The car gathered speed slowly, for the incline was not steep. Someone from the corner of the mill behind fired both barrels of a shotgun. The charges of buckshot thudded into the compact cargo of boards at his back. The car was still not traveling as fast as a man might run and the clump of feet on the boardwalk behind was gaining. But already the car had rolled past the front rank of lumber piles. He sprang from the car and began running through the checkerboard array of great square towers of seasoning lumber, zigzagging back and forth among the screens they provided, giving no pursuer a glimpse that was long enough to take aim.

At the further edge of the lumberyard was a stretch of brush. He dove into this haven. Beyond the brush was a field of breast-high corn. He bent double and ran through this. Beyond was woodland. It was miserable second growth, a jumble of poplar, willow, alder and miscellaneous brush, but it offered better cover than virgin forest. The yells of the pursuers, mixed with an occasional shot from an overexcited marksman, were still not far behind. But now that he was back in the woods he had no doubt that he was in control of the situation. He was making no attempt to cover his tracks. He wanted them to realize that he was fleeing northward, not westward, hoping that there might be among them a woodsman capable of following so plain a trail.

He was running easily and yet maintaining the distance between him and the pursuers. Afraid that they might give up too soon to suit his purposes, he occasionally showed himself to them from the farther shore of a lake or a clearing. The faint clamor of their angry yells gave reassuring evidence of the fury of their determination. It was a pleasure to consider the occasion for their ire. His Laketon excursion had developed into something more like a raid than a visit. The mill was probably out of action for some days. And a second column of smoke rising on the horizon beside the one from the sawdust pit was surely from Olaf's store.

Reaching his camp, he reassembled his kit, tied a slab of the pig to his pack, and was about to set off again when he stiffened to listen. Something had been added to the chase. The disciplined baying indicated a pack of hunting hounds on leash. He gave vent to a long ululating whoop of savage elation. Now his exploit could unquestionably be made perfect. From the ancient Sioux fort one more blow, a century later, was about to be delivered.

He ran hard through the afternoon, with new assurance that thanks to the dogs his trail would not be lost. He kept on directly northward, veering from his course occasionally to drag his pursuers through swamps and bogs. At dusk he reached his goal, the border of the White Earth Chippewa reservation.

While avoiding the first fringe of Chippewa villages and hunting camps, he kept to the driest ground from here on to make certain that the dogs would have the least possible difficulty in following 'him. Toward midnight, he neared a larger Chippewa community and brought his trail to an abrupt end by crossing an intervening stream and running to the edge of the sleeping town, retracing his steps, and walking in the water for some miles up the stream. Having thus used the dogs' noses to convince the pursuers that the end of their chase was the Chippewa town, he ran northward again until daylight. When he was well clear of the reservation, he hid on a thicketed island in a pond and slept through the day, waking from time to time to speculate pleasantly upon the castigation being visited upon the Chippewa by the sheriff and his men as they demanded delivery of the culprit who was so manifestly a Chippewa.

Traveling at night, he continued northward until reaching the Thief River country before at last permitting himself to turn westward. Soon thereafter he emerged from the great belt of eastern woodland. After swimming the Red River he became aware of how greatly the climate was changing with each mile he traveled westward. This was the area of the long-grass plains. In favored valleys the grass often grew shoulder-high. But this spring there was no new grass, no hint of green except about dying water holes or along the trickles of water that had once been broad streams. The remnant of old grass was brown and crumbling, indicating there had likewise been no rain the year before. He could recall no Sioux tradition of there ever before having been so dry a period.

Settlers had multiplied in this part of the Dakotas in these recent years since the intrusion of railroads. This year their fields were as barren as the hillsides. He saw a number of farms that had been altogether abandoned and several times each day another eastbound wagon with a dejected family that had given up the struggle. His growing concern for the situation of the Sioux resulting from so prolonged and severe a drought was mingled with the satisfaction that it was also giving these interloping settlers such a bad time. He had by now swung his course southwestward, expecting to strike the Missouri somewhere near the mouth of the Cannonball River, the northern border of the Standing Rock reservation.

Since reaching the plains he had become impatient to get home. With a nearly full moon rising over the undulating brown plain he continued to run on into the night. Toward midnight a glint of water in a shallow valley inspired him to drop down to investigate. The site offered as ideal a spot to camp as could be found in this parched country.

Its central feature was the remnant of an ancient beaver dam which, fortified by the interlaced roots of a copse of willow and alder, had resisted years of erosion. The ordinary course of the stream divided here to flow around it on either side, making an island of the dam segment. But this year that flow had altogether ceased. There remained above the dam only a small pond of reed-encircled clear water into which extended, like a pier, the trunk of a fallen cottonwood. He stripped off his clothes, bathed in the pond, crawled into the willow thicket, wrapped himself in his blanket, and fell asleep. After trotting for thirty uninterrupted hours, half of them in the heat of the sun, even his stamina had been depleted. He slept on well into the next day.

He was awakened by the screech of ungreased axles. Peering from his thicket he saw another settler who had given up and was on his way East. On the seat of the canvas-covered wagon sat a man driving a scrawny, unmatched team near the point of breaking down. Behind the wagon walked a barefoot woman in a tattered blue dress who was trailed in turn by a small black and white dog. Her mop of tousled hair, which had shaken down around her shoulders, was white but she moved with the only vigor being manifested in the procession by man or beast.

John was about to return to his blanket when he saw that the settler was making a mistake that would reward his watching a little longer. Misled by the dried brown of the surface vegetation extending beyond the upper edge of the residual water in the pond, the man was driving straight across it. The mat held until it was too late to turn back. The horses began to break through and then the wheels. What the settler had not realized was that the water of the pond at its upper and shallower end extended well beyond its visible margin as a seepage under the dried vegetation. Whipping his floundering team, he succeeded in churning up the muck beneath the mat until he had gotten horses and wagon hopelessly mired. John wriggled back to his blanket and fell comfortably asleep once more.

Some hours later he was again awakened, this time by the frenzied barking of the little dog, which in its ranging around the pond had picked up his scent. When he did not move, the dog, gaining courage, pressed deeper into the thicket until its insensate clamor was almost in John's ear. He snatched up a stick and caught the dog across the snout with the throw. The dog, yipping with pain and panic, fled around the shore of the pond to the wagon. His presence having been discovered, John yawned, stretched, crawled from his nest and stood up.

The settler and the woman were wallowing about in the mire up to their waists, ineffectually tugging at the wagon and their collapsed horses. The yipping dog attracted their attention, they caught sight of John and, after a brief consultation, the man began urgently to beckon. John turned his back, squatted, cleared a space on the ground with his knife, and laid a small fire. He then stripped off his clothes, walked down the prostrate cottonwood, and let himself into the water. Lurking about the bottom of the pool were a number of ten- to twenty-pound catfish, one of which he proposed to catch, boy-fashion with his bare hands, for his supper. There was an added relish to be thus pleasantly minding his own business while his white neighbors were so distractedly immersed in their difficulties.

Stretched out on the submerged end of the cottonwood, his nose and eyes just clear of the surface of the water and his right arm hanging with his relaxed hand just above the bottom, he waited with the patience of one who had early become accustomed to hunt or fish in order to eat. After some minutes one of the catfish began nosing nearer and nearer the waiting fingers. Suddenly it veered away as a shadow fell across the water. John looked up to see the settler standing on the bank. His mud-smeared figure was sturdily built, his weather-beaten face that of a man still young and strong.

"My name's Lionel Potter," he said. "We need help — real bad."

John did not reply. He was considering the disagreeable possibility that these witless whites might offer some payment for his help which it would be nonsensical to refuse. In any event, he could meanwhile indulge his resentment by letting them grovel and beg for a while. Assuming that John had not comprehended, Potter began making signs indicating the nature of his need.

"Can't you see I'm fishing?" said John.

"I know — I know," said Potter hastily. "But Hattie — that's my wife — she said for me to come and fetch you."

"Go back and tell Hattie," said John, "that I'm having my supper — once I've caught it."

Potter bowed to the ultimatum and obediently set off. John resumed his fishing posture. After several more minutes a catfish again drifted near, this time so near that John's suddenly darting fingers closed in a clutch behind its gills. He rose with the great flapping fish in his grasp and had turned to start up the cottonwood before he saw that the woman was waiting on the bank.

She was as plastered with mud as her husband, almost as sturdily built and certainly no older. The tangle of muddied, disordered hair was not white but a bleached flax. Out of her broad, sunburned face, with its wide mouth, snub nose, high cheekbones, and rugged brow, gleamed small pale blue eyes. But he was much less aware of her appearance than of his own nakedness, only partially obscured by the struggling fish clasped in his arms. He stepped past her, knelt with his back to her, and began methodically cleaning the fish, scorning to make a break for his clothes hanging beyond the fire or otherwise to betray any confusion. If this brazen white woman elected to embrace the ignominy of pressing her appeal upon a mother-naked Indian that was her privilege. There was none of her husband's whine in her voice when she spoke. Her terse words merely formulated a succession of pungent statements of fact.

"Them horses gonna die 'less we get 'em out right now. The little we got left in the world is there in that mud and we can't afford to lose it. Me, I don't intend to."

"The two of you've been working at it for hours," said John. "What makes you think I might make any difference?"

"Anybody could make a difference. That man of mine — he's always getting stumped by something anybody else could handle with one hand tied. That's why we're tailing off East after working hard's we did for two whole years on that place across the Missouri. He's always ready to quit. But me — I ain't."

John kept at his fish-cleaning, contemplating the happy probability that a great many settlers were finding this drought as great a calamity. He could tell that his silence and inattention were shifting her wrath from her husband to him. He could almost feel the waves of fury and frustration emanating from her. Had she an axe or a club in her hand he would have expected her to swing it at his head.

He rose with the boned and skinned half of the fish in his hands and started with it toward the fire. To his annoyance she ran around to face him, barring his way, and then, to his much greater annoyance, he saw that her anger was displaced while her sharp little eyes were boldly exploring his nakedness.

"That's something I've always wondered about," she announced. Her indomitable candor had suddenly become chilling. "Why, an Indian ain't made no different than a white man."

"Which race did you imagine was something other than human?"

He realized that he had instinctively clasped the fish against him to interfere with her view and, remembering with irritation that this was a reaction learned among whites, he let it dangle by one hand to permit her to stare as shamelessly as she chose.

"All I meant," she said, staring, "was that there must be some reason Indians set so much more store by it than white folks do."

"If you mean by what you call 'it' what you seem to — what makes you think Indians do?"

"All my life I've heard they were that way. I've even got an old aunt that's all the time telling about the time back in '62 when she was taken captive by the Sioux. She says the Sioux men, young and old, and even some of the little boys, kept at her so much she all but died of it."

"If you'll kindly step aside," said John, taking refuge in acid politeness, "I can cook my fish."

She appeared more concerned with her aunt's onetime experience than with what he was saying, but she drew back out of his way. He cut and peeled a willow wand and skewered the side of fish in preparation for its broiling. Not until he had unhurriedly completed this task did he step past the fire, lift the breechclout from the bush on which he had left it, and wrap it about his loins. He squatted to arrange the spit over the fire. When her silence continued he casually glanced up at her. She was staring not at him but off toward the wagon. Then she turned back to look at him again and he could see that she had come to a conclusion. But he was in no way prepared for its enormity.

"I ain't got no way to pay you for helping. Except this. You come with me now and get me out of this mess and tonight I'll come back here and make out like I'm your captive. Just for this one night, that is. What do you say?"

The challenge crackled in the air between them like an electric charge.

"I say I can cook my fish later," he replied.

He laid aside the spit and rose to his feet to accompany her. She continued to astound him.

"That other half," she said, again matter-of-fact, as she indicated the portion of the catfish still on the bank. "If you was going to throw it away — we been hungry the last two days."

He picked it up, handed it to her, and followed her bedraggled figure around the pond to the wagon. The dog retreated to a distance and resumed his tireless barking. Letting himself down into the muck beside the front wheels, John discovered the situation to be as he had surmised. When the settler had driven into the bog he had bumped down through the surface mat of dried vegetation into the ancient silt-choked stream bed which had existed before the beaver dam had backed up the water to form the marginal swamp. Upon reaching the other side his front wheels had lodged against the overhang of the opposite bank. A dozen teams could not by any direct pull have drawn the wagon past that obstruction.

John unhitched the horses and by applying the tip of his knife blade to certain particularly tender spots inspired them to such convulsive efforts that he soon had them, wheezing and shaking, out on dry footing. Returning to the wagon, which had at the outset of their dilemma been lightened of its load by the struggling Potters, he instructed them in the next process, the essentials of which he had learned during summer storms while helping with the extrication of mired circus wagons. Laying hold of the spokes of the wheels, with the three of them throwing their weights in unison, they forced the wagon backward from the submerged bank until there was enough clearance to turn the tongue and front wheels to a right angle. Working on the relatively firm sand of the old creek bottom beneath the mire, they were able then to force the wagon up the bed until it could be worked out to dry ground beside the horses. The whole operation had not required a quarter hour. Ignoring Potter's fervent protestations of gratitude and without a glance at the woman, who was already gathering wood for a cooking fire, John set off for his camp.

He bathed in the pond, washed his clout, and set it on a stick to dry by the fire. He broiled and ate the fish. He cleared a wider area behind the fire and spread the blanket. Then he settled by the coals and contemplated the pleasures that the night might bring. The twilight was already darkening and the silver rim of the moon was beginning to edge above the eastern hills. The range of possibilities offered by the hours immediately ahead was endlessly diverting. There was, of course, the possibility that she would not come but as he considered her annoying singleness of purpose he was inclined to think that she would keep her word. While he, for his part, was still in the process of deciding, he kept telling himself, just what he would do. One fact that kept recurring to him was that he had never had intercourse with a white woman. His Indian companions with the circus had occasionally visited brothels but he had not been tempted. Yet during the years he had lived among white people he had seldom been able to look at an agreeably-shaped white woman without speculating on how it might be under a blanket with her.

In his present situation, however, there was a factor of more significance than any personal notion he might entertain. Of all the bitterness of Indians toward whites there was nothing to match their resentment of settlers. They hated settlers, more than soldiers, more than traders, more than agents. For hundreds of years it had been settlers who had been their principal adversaries and their most relentless despoilers. His present problem was, therefore, to determine how most successfully to offend these two settlers. He might, for example, decline at the last moment to accept the woman's favors. Nothing could ever offend a woman much more than that. The flaw in this procedure was that it would let the husband off free. Only by possessing the wife could he adequately offend both. There was comfort in finding his mounting inclination supported by this sensible view of the matter.

These agreeable fancies were scattered by the sudden realization that she was on her way around the pond. There was still a dim glow in the western sky. She had not even waited for full night. He remained seated on the ground beyond the embers of the fire as she approachd.

"You're early," he remarked. "What about your husband? I noticed he had a rifle."

"No call to fret about him," she said. "He's asleep. That's what he's best at. Once he turns in he wouldn't stir was a cow to have a calf on him."

She walked down the cottonwood and let herself into the water. There she began vigorously to wash herself, first her hair and face, then, after stripping off her garments, her body, and, finally, the clothing. At length satisfied that she was rid of the last vestige of mud, she walked back up the cottonwood, carrying the bundle of dripping clothing. At the edge of his little clearing she paused to wring out the garments and drape them over bushes to dry. Her movements and postures were unselfconscious, as though she was unaware of his presence ten feet away. He sat, silent, motionless, watching, striving to restrain his excitement as he sought to match her composure.

Stepping back and forth arranging the clothing, she moved in and out of the rays of moonlight slanting through the willows which bathed her moist, milk-white skin in a silvery sheen. Her flaxen mane, clinging wetly to brow and neck, was like a silver helmet. Even the triangle of pubic hair was silvery. She continued to seem so unconscious that she was exposing her nudity to his view that he momentarily wondered if her immodesty might spring from a feeling that she was presenting it to the gaze not of a man but some alien creature more on the order of an animal. But he was much more actively thinking that so long as he was contemplating the novelty of possessing a white woman it was not likely that there could be anywhere one whiter than this one.

Having arranged the clothing to her satisfaction, she began stroking her skin with her palms to press the excess moisture from it. She was a big woman, strongly built, yet all her members were unexpectedly smooth and shapely and gracious. Her thighs were firm, her belly flat, and her large breasts solid and round. Appearing at last to become aware of his regard, she peered down at her body complacently.

"This part of me ain't so bad," she said. "Was I as passable from the chin up as the chin down I could maybe of looked around a while longer for more of a man than the one I settled for." For the first time she looked at him. "Well?" she asked.

He indicated the blanket. She crossed to it and stretched out upon it deliberately.

His initial essay was a catastrophe. Years of abstinence had left him with the absurd precipitancy of a boy.

"Most as quick as my husband," she murmured.

He stalked out to the cottonwood, transfixed with fury. Looking back he could see the pale blur of her body, lying there, supine, waiting. The heat of his anger rekindled the heat of his desire. He strode back and threw himself upon her. There was a certain reciprocal response in the sheer strength and resilience of her splendid body but in every volitional respect she remained inert, impassive.

"That was a mite more like what I expected," she said, when at last he had finished.

But the appraisal was no accolade. She had seemed as little stirred as were he a child she was idly permitting to take liberties with her person.

He retired to the cottonwood to gulp the cool night air and stare unseeingly at the stars while he regathered his powers. Again and again he renewed the assault. With all the violence of which his young vigor was capable he sought release upon the body of this white woman for the animosities of a lifetime. By no whimper of pain or reaction to his manhood did she recognize the tensions of his attack. Her constant defense remained the unshaken placidity of her permissiveness. Finally, exhausted, he rolled to the edge of the blanket and fell into a feverish sleep.

When he awoke it was daylight. She was removing her undergarments from the bushes, shaking them out, and pulling them on. When she saw that he was awake she lowered the ragged blue dress she was about to slip over her head and indicated her willingness to return one more time to the blanket. He was listening to the sound of the axe and looking to see that his bow was within reach. He could not shake off the conception bred in him with his mother's milk that any white man with a gun invariably represented a danger that needed to be considered.

"Better bend down," he advised. "Your husband can see you if he looks this way."

"Let him look," she said. "I want him to see. That's why I came." She drew on the dress and turned to survey the other camp. "If he don't look, I'll tell him soon's I get back. And I'll keep on telling him long's he lives — how he's a man that's so poor a stick he can't keep his wife from bedding with Indians."

She strode off around the pond toward the wagon. John sat up, his skin crawling with disgust. He had thought by degrading this woman to degrade her race. But so easily had she turned the tables. It had been he and his race that had been degraded.

VI

HAVING SLEPT UNDISTURBED by any of the disordered dreams that so often infested his nights, Sitting Bull awoke rested and momentarily free of the swirling tides of resentments that invariably engulfed his days. But before he had opened his eyes his good humor was ebbing away. His groping hand had reminded him that this had been the night of the week that his old wife was privileged to take his young wife's place in his bed.

Opening his eyes exposed him to a wider discontent. It had been bad enough when his wives had maneuvered him into moving from his tattered skin tepee into this gloomy house built of logs. But now that they had introduced that iron cookstove and that pine table and bench his home could hardly be told from the miserable abode of a white settler.

He swung his feet to the floor, stepped into his breechclout, tightened the belt, and walked out the door to the porch. His first glance was at the sky. It was cloudless. Even before sunrise the still air was dry and hot. There was in this at least some occasion for satisfaction. The length of the drought was already unprecedented and, so long as the Sioux failed to heed his warnings, his reputation as a prophet depended on its continuation. His next glance was directed at his second house, where his off-duty wife and his four younger children slept. No one was yet stirring there. Likewise, there was as yet no activity in any of the half-dozen huts and tepees behind the corral where families of his nearer relatives and immediate followers resided.

He looked around quickly to make sure the white census takers had not selected this morning to make a descent. It was one of their favorite tactics to swoop down on an Indian community at daybreak in order to make their count before the inhabitants could scatter or hide. Sioux frustration of the census was important, inasmuch as the government would surely take advantage of its conclusion to justify another reduction in the ration issue. Then he saw Bull Ghost coming along the river road.

He walked down to the stream bank to meet him. Grand River had nearly ceased to flow but the bathing hole was still full. He took his usual morning dip in the pool while listening to the report of Bull Ghost, who had just now returned from a tour of the other Sioux reservations. The envoy squatted on the bank, his single eye blinking disconsolately.

"As you told me to do, I visited the Lower Brule, the Rosebud, and Pine Ridge. When the delegates first came back from Wovoka the moon before last, people in all of them began to dance. The dance was something new and the message of Wovoka, while not easy to believe, was something that they wanted to believe. But that part of the dance that told them to love not only each other but the white man, too, began to make them feel foolish and they were getting ready to stop when the agents ordered them not to dance and that started them dancing again. Then when the agents did nothing to make them stop, they stopped. Nobody is dancing now."

Bull Ghost was sad. He was a dreamer and the accounts of the dance that had spread so dramatically across deserts and mountains and plains had meant to him an assurance that a new world of promise could open for all Indians.

"That is good," pronounced Sitting Bull, wasting no sympathy on Bull Ghost's sentimentality. "That dance — it is not for the Sioux."

He was reflecting upon how sensible his judgment had been the previous autumn when the Sioux delegates from the other reservations had been selected at the Council summoned by Red Cloud. As a result of his skepticism no delegates had gone from Standing Rock. In this instance he had agreed with the point of view of his perpetual adversary, the agent McLaughlin.

"But if the Sioux do not dance," said Bull Ghost, "what hope is left for us?"

"The hope to stay Sioux," said Sitting Bull. He stepped out on the bank to dry in the sun that was already hot. "Kicking Bear — what is he doing?"

He was interested in Kicking Bear. Unlike most of the other delegates, Kicking Bear had been an important warrior, aggressive, resourceful, stubborn, the intimate companion in arms of the immortal Crazy Horse, and all his life an inveterate hater of everything white.

"He was angry when the dancing stopped and he has gone to the Arapaho to see what they are doing."

"When he comes back he will have thought of something," said Sitting Bull. "He never gives up — that Kicking Bear. Come in with me and eat."

"Thank you," said Bull Ghost. "But I have already met Red Hawk and told him that I will rest in his lodge."

Sitting Bull grunted his understanding. He was unhappily reminded that, as was well known to all, today was not a day he could entertain his friends in his house. There was another much less welcome demand upon him. He returned to his house to find that his old wife, instead of waiting to serve him, had so far forgot herself that she had left his breakfast on the table and hurried off to the other house. Before he had morosely finished eating, both wives and the younger children trooped in. All were wearing shoes and new clothes, the gifts of that incomprehensible society in Boston whose members pretended to be friends of all Indians.

This was a special day, the last day of school. There would be speeches and songs and the presentation of cards and stars. His attendance was expected at the ceremony. He would have preferred to continue seeming merely tolerant of the existence of the Grand River school rather than exalting this white activity by his presence, but his constant impulse to humor his children had persuaded him to agree. He had not, after mature deliberation, objected last fall to their attending the school. Beneath all the fires of his hostility there had been the cold if rankling thought that when he was gone and they were grown the estate of the Sioux might have fallen so low that some white education might prove their only shield.

But he balked at riding in the new wagon with his wives and the children. His brother-in-law, Gray Eagle, brought out Roland, the gray circus horse that had been Buffalo Bill's parting gift as a souvenir of that year with the Wild West Show. Roland was old and fat and not much good as a horse but he was capable of certain astonishing tricks that captivated all Indian observers and endeared him to the heart of Sitting Bull, who as a veteran conjuror was a connoisseur of tricks.

He dressed in his second-best blue serge suit and put on the big white hat that had been another of Buffalo Bill's gifts. The gray horse and the white hat recalled those tumultuous and exultant days with the circus. For that long summer he had everywhere been the center of attention. While touring Canada he had been received by the crowds with rounds of applause and shouts of approbation and had been invited to the homes of their principal men. But what he liked even better to remember was the way it had been in the United States. There he had been introduced as The Man Who Killed Custer. There his appearance had drawn showers of epithets and insults. The waves of hatred descending upon him from those thousands of whites had been supremely gratifying.

But their detestation of him was as a grain of dust compared to the mountain of his hatred of them. Riding along this river bottom among the several miles of scattered dwellings of his native town there was thrust upon him from every side new fuel for his fury. The Sioux, so recently the wild, free rovers of the far plains, had been reduced to a starved and helpless existence more repugnant than slavery. Here the Hunkpapa, his own tribe, lived in flimsy brush huts or flimsier canvas tepees. Here were the patches of sunbaked earth which, compelled by hunger, they had scratched in their pitiful attempts to raise unfamiliar crops that had for two years running been burned up by the drought.

Today was their hungriest day. This afternoon they would set out on the forty-mile trudge to draw their bimonthly rations tomorrow at the Standing Rock agency. This meager and cheerless dole would not prove half enough to sustain them through the next two weeks. To so abject a fate had been condemned a people who no longer than seven years ago had been able to range hundreds of miles to take buffalo by the thousands to supply their every want.

It was a relief to be distracted, as he approached Pierre Chadron's little store, by the sight of the trader's daughter, Mary, coming out. She, too, was wearing shoes and a freshly starched dress, as well she might since this year she had been teaching assistant to John Carignan, the Grand River schoolmaster. Sitting Bull was additionally pleased with her because he felt that she had proved something by qualifying so quickly to teach.

Mary was not actually a member of his family but he had always considered her as though she were, inasmuch as her grandmother, Arrow Woman, had been the sister of his father's third wife. He drew up to regard her while she waited for him to speak. He noted happily how tall and supple and strong she had grown. It was too bad that aside from her very black hair and eyes she was so pale that she had something of the look of a white woman. It was not her fault, of course, that her mother, Blue Lark, had married this Frenchman who, though white, was, after all an honest enough man.

"Mary," he said, "You are a pleasure even to eyes as old as mine."

"Thank you." She smiled up at him. "And your eyes are not now looking at all old."

"Yours see too much. And mine are old because they have been dimmed by some of the things they have seen."

She caught his glance at the dress. "You are right. The agent's wife gave me this dress. She thinks that being a teacher I should look well today."

"The agent's wife. That is the only good thing about the agent."

Mary smiled again. "She has done something for me much more important to me than this dress. You know that next fall I will not be teaching here?"

He stirred angrily. "No. I did not know. I am the last to be told anything. Why not? That Carignan — I did not think him so big a fool."

"It is not his fault. At the last election the Republicans won and so there will be many new government people on the reservations — new agents, new teachers. That is what he said. Anyway, there is no longer money enough for an assistant teacher here. That is where the agent's wife came in. I do need a job. My father is poor because his customers are now so poor. She has arranged for me to help in the orphanage of Father Murphy's mission at the agency."

He nodded his approval. "It is well that you can be a comfort to your father. And that black robe — though a white man and the friend of the agent he is not all bad."

He rode on, to pull up again before the lodge of Catch-the-Bear. His was unique among all the tepees on Grand River. Only his remained entirely fashioned of buffalo hides. At the famous last buffalo hunt he had had the forethought to put away extra skins and since then his wives had taken such care, patching and sewing, that he alone among the Hunkpapa was spared the shame of depending for shelter on canvas issued by the agent. Catch-the-Bear came out, his scowl dark. He had bad news.

"Gall and Grass and Crow King," he announced. "They are here."

Sitting Bull at once understood all the implications of this. The three chiefs from the more populous camps nearer the Missouri were his principal rivals on the Standing Rock reservation and the particular favorites of the agent. All had become progressives who had come to the conclusion that the only course left open to the Sioux was an accommodation to any white demand. They had elected to pay their visit here on this day that the Hunkpapa were about to set out for the agency because they knew Sitting Bull never submitted to the indignity of appearing in person to collect a ration issue. These deputies of the agent could therefore be sure that by accompanying the Hunkpapa en route to the agency while he remained behind they could devote the journey, free of his interference, to a further attempt to undermine his influence with his own tribe.

"Come," he said grimly, "let us go bid them welcome."

Catch-the-Bear shook his head regretfully. "They are in Bull Head's house."

Catch-the-Bear had nursed a hatred of Bull Head since an altercation between them over the purchase of some Crow horses two years ago. Obviously he could not run the risk of being obliged to speak to Bull Head.

Sitting Bull rode on to the big log house that served as Bull Head's residence and the local police barracks. Lieutenant Bull Head of the agent's Indian Police lived in substantially more comfort than his neighbors as a result of having been so long on a government payroll. Sitting Bull's rage was given another twist when he saw that it was his own nephew, One Bull, wearing the hated police uniform, who was darting out to take his horse.

"Don't touch him," he said. "He'll stand."

He shouldered past One Bull and stood in the open doorway. Bull Head and his three eminent guests were seated in chairs at a table drinking coffee. Bull Head jumped up to offer his seat but Sitting Bull remained standing in the doorway, staring at them contemptuously. Gall had been a great warrior and the valiant companion of his Canadian exile before he had become the agent's pet. But Grass he had always considered a self-serving sneak and Crow King a mischievous troublemaker.

"I see," said Sitting Bull, "that when Gall and Grass and Crow King visit the Hunkpapa they like best the company of their own kind."

This reference to the police was a bitter thrust. The quick-witted Grass was the first to return the insult.

"We thought that you had become too great a prophet to have time for your friends."

"What you thought was that in my house you would not be able to talk to my people behind my back."

Gall shifted uneasily in his chair. "Once we were friends," he said. "I want still to be your friend. I will not be saying to your people anything I have not said before more times than can be counted or that I will not keep on saying as many more times. What I am saying is only the truth and the only truth."

"The truth is that all you are telling them is to kneel beside you while you stick your noses in the dirt at the agent's feet."

"And what are you telling them," demanded Grass, "that will put food in their bellies?"

"There is a power to save them," said Sitting Bull, "that is outside their bellies and beyond your understanding. Look at that sky. Have any of you ever known the rain to hold off so long?"

The arrogant reference to his now famous prophecy silenced them for a moment. But Crow King had once made a name for himself by unmasking a pack of itinerant conjurors who had been extorting contributions from his credulous neighbors. He was proud of that exploit.

"Do you then think your powers proved by one lucky guess?"

Sitting Bull fixed him with a fierce stare.

"Ask Shell King when you see him," he advised.

Shell King had been the last man who had ventured in public to doubt Sitting Bull's magic. That very night, six years ago, he and his eldest son had been killed by lightning. Letting this prediction hang in the air as a parting shot, Sitting Bull wheeled from the doorway and mounted his horse. He had debated these three in so many councils through so many hours and days and weeks that any restatement of their endless arguments would have been pointless but he could feel that in the exchange of threats and insults he had not come off too badly. Nevertheless he sought out Circling Bear and Black Bird and Circling Hawk, whose reliability he most trusted, to exhort them to take every care on the journey to the agency to counteract any attempt of the agent's three henchmen to sow new doubts among the Hunkpapa.

By the time he turned homeward he concluded that the ceremony at the school had run its course, so he was spared that trial. The Hunkpapa were beginning to stream eastward on their long trip to the agency. Most were on foot. They would return with their ration issue in sacks on their backs. A few more substantial family groups had pooled their resources and were taking wagons. The much advertised government issue of wagons to occasional favored families had so far had as a principal consequence the ruination of many horses. Indians unfamiliar with the process had had an indifferent success in breaking their riding horses to pulling loads in harness.

Suddenly he saw the stranger appearing over the hilltop on the northern rim of the valley. The distant figure was trotting with the easy stride of one who has been traveling far and he was striking directly for the river as though the Hunkpapa town were his destination. Presently, Sitting Bull saw that he was not a stranger. He was Eagle Strikes's son. Sitting Bull pulled in his horse to await his approach.

John had even sooner spotted the gray horse and white hat. He came to a stop beside Roland. Sitting Bull leaned down to clasp his hand.

"You are the first Sioux I have spoken to," said John. "That is a good omen."

Sitting Bull was regarding the prodigal with a pleasure so deep he felt obliged to conceal it.

"You have been traveling hard."

"Yes. I have come far."

"That bow is Chippewa."

"I traded with a Menominee for it."

Sitting Bull took the bow, flexed it, and handed it back.

"It is a good bow."

"I came by way of the country of lakes and woods. I wanted to see where the Sioux once lived."

Sitting Bull was not impressed.

"When the Sioux lived there in the east they crept among the swamps and fed on berries and dug for woodchucks. When they came west into the sun they rode horses and killed buffalo and struck terror among people as far off as the Shoshone and the Kiowa."

Sitting Bull started his horse on homeward, taking a side path up the lower slopes to avoid the people in the road. John walked alongside.

"Where is everybody going?" he asked.

"To the agency to draw their rations. The Sioux are now beggars."

Sitting Bull could see, as John kept glancing uneasily down the slope at the ragged people, their brush and canvas hovels and blighted garden patches, with what dismayed astonishment he was surveying these evidences of Hunkpapa destitution.

"What did you learn in your white school?" he asked, to distract John's attention from this cloud over his homecoming.

"I learned that I belong here."

"I have heard that they gave you a new name."

"The man who adopted me named me John."

"Was he a wise man?"

"Yes. He died last winter."

"Here your name is still Rides-an-Eagle."

"That is so."

"You have no family. You will live in my house."

"Yes, my father."

They went on for a few moments in silence. Sitting Bull cleared his throat hesitantly, a gesture that in anyone else might have been taken for uneasiness.

"That night of the storm when the tent pole fell on you. The circus people did not tell us about that until the train was a hundred miles off. Then they first said that you had run away. They were afraid we would leave the circus to go back to you."

"There was no need," said John. He added carefully, "There are many sorts of white people. The ones that looked after me were as decent as Indians."

Sitting Bull nodded, reluctantly, puzzled as always by the enigma presented by such occasional departures from the norm of white malevolence.

"There are white people in Boston and Philadelphia," he admitted, "who, though strangers we have never seen, have banded together to send us food and clothing and sometimes even money."

Still shaking his head, he pulled up before his house. Around the porch were gathered those of his family and followers who had not attended the school exercises, waiting for the return of those who had so that they might travel together to the agency to draw their rations. The sight of John drew from them a buzz of surprise. Sitting Bull dismounted, took John by the arm, and led him up on the porch. Here he turned to address those present.

"You all remember Rides-an-Eagle," he said. "He has come home. For years he has been living among the whites, learning all their secrets. On account of what he has learned he will be able to counsel us on how best to deal with the agent, and the soldiers, and the settlers. I will listen to his advice and consider it carefully. I expect you, too, to listen to whatever he says."

He could see that this pronouncement was being received with mixed feelings by his hearers. His seventeen-year-old son, Crow Foot, and his son-in-law and personal interpreter, Andrew Fox, were hostile. Each foresaw in the preferment shown this interloper a displacement of his own importance. Retaining his clasp on John's arm, Sitting Bull escorted him into the house, tossed the white hat on the bed, stripped off the blue serge suit, got out two backrests, handed one to John, and settled down comfortably on the floor facing him.

"Now," he said, "how much have you heard about what has been happening here?"

"Almost nothing, I am ashamed to say. For five years I have been shut up in schoolrooms without ever looking as far as a window. I did hear something about the Ghost Dance."

"That is not for the Sioux."

"So I imagined. Anyway, what I remember was being able to ride less than a hundred miles from here and killing five thousand buffalo in a single hunt. Until I got back I had no idea how bad things could have got in so short a time."

"You do not begin to know yet how bad. But I will tell you. The big trouble has been about our land. It is true that we had no use for much of it because the game was gone but so long as we held it they had to consider us. The railroads and the settlers and the state of South Dakota wanted the land but what the government most wanted was to tie every Sioux down to one little patch of ground so that from then on they could do with us whatever they liked. So it was that the year before last the head of the Carlisle Indian School, who they thought we would count our friend, was sent with a commission to talk us into selling our land. I was able to keep our people from signing any treaty and after I had gone to see the President that was the end of that. But the next year there came another commission with the governor of Ohio and the head of the American old soldiers society and General Crook. They spent months telling us we were living on charity and had no choice but to do whatever they said. There would even then have been no treaty if the agent, McLaughlin, had not arranged the signing without notice for a time I was not there because he had not notified me. So they claimed our land. Eleven million acres of land. That was bad but there was worse. We have not only lost our land but they have paid us nothing for it. In the treaty they promised us little and they have not even done the little they promised. Congress has not voted the money for our land and has instead reduced our ration. And the President has not waited. He has declared the land open for settlement though the land is still ours because we have not been paid for it. Had it not been for this drought thousands of settlers would be swarming in on us. But even that is not the worst. The worst is that we have been driven into a corner — like rats — and if we do not look out we will no longer be Sioux."

Sitting Bull became so excited he sprang to his feet and began pacing and gesticulating.

"The Great Spirit knows that I have gone more than halfway to meet these dogs. I have not been blind or crazy. I know that with the buffalo gone we who were born to ride and hunt must learn to plow and plant. I, myself, though I am a chief and a prophet, am raising cattle and chickens and planting beans and corn. I tell any Sioux who will listen that he must likewise lower himself. He must submit to this shame if he is not to submit to the deeper shame of standing with his hand out at the back door of the agency. But the whites are not satisfied to see us stooping over a hoe. Now that we seem weak and helpless they cheat and lie as much as they used to do when we were great and they were afraid of us. When they stole the Black Hills from us we killed Custer, who was the thief. But that was the last time we have been able to strike back. So now they are stealing everything we have left. What they are trying hardest to steal is our feeling that we are Sioux. I tell you that the time can come when it will be better to die free men than to live like rabbits."

The full effect of his peroration was dispersed by the sudden rumble of bounding wheels and galloping hoofs. The wagon which had taken his children to the school was returning in frantic haste. His two wives burst into the room.

"The agent — he is coming."

Through the open door Sitting Bull could see McLaughlin's buggy turning toward the ford from the road on the other side of the river. With him, instead of his regular interpreter, Louis Primeau, was his Indian wife. For Mrs. McLaughlin Sitting Bull felt a grudging tolerance. During that summer with the circus she had accompanied the Sioux party as official interpreter and unofficial manager. Except when overwhelmed by the immediate presence of her husband, her attitude toward her fellow Sioux could not be considered too objectionable.

"Bring my horse around to the corral," he directed his wives.

Taking John by the arm, he went out the back door. They remained behind the barn until the third set of messengers had come with increasingly urgent word that the agent was waiting. Sitting Bull finally hoisted himself into his saddle and rode at a slow pace around the house to confront his adversary. He did not dismount, leaving McLaughlin no other recourse than to remain in his buggy. He had always managed these unavoidable encounters in a fashion that saved his ever being obliged to ask the agent into his house.

Their eyes met. The agent was making no more effort than he to conceal his animosity. His thin face was as watchful and as mean as that of an old dog fox. His stiff white hair, which so often bristled like a prairie cock's topknot, was covered by his broad-brimmed hat but there could be no question that being made to wait had heated his short-fused temper to a glow. He was too shrewd, however, to make an issue of that.

"Tell him," he was saying to his wife without greeting or preamble, "that we drove forty miles to attend the exercises at the school but that we did not see him there."

With all whites Sitting Bull had for years maintained the pretense that he did not understand English. This had proved a posture of immense usefulness. He had been spared all aimless chitchat. And when the necessity arose to respond to statements of importance he could give due consideration to his reply during the delay required for interpretation or resort to the opportunity provided for evasions and misunderstandings.

"Tell him," he replied, "that I was on my way to school this morning when I met Gall and Grass and Crow King. I decided they needed watching more than did the children."

The insolence of this reference to his protégés tightened McLaughlin's lips to an even thinner line but his retort trailed off into a grunt of surprise. He had detected John's presence in the packed circle of intensely interested Indian onlookers.

"Rides-an-Eagle," he said, nudging his wife. "Ask him when he got back."

"This morning, Mr. McLaughlin," said John, not waiting for interpretation.

"I would have expected you to report first to the agency."

"Should that have occurred to me?"

McLaughlin suppressed his exasperation. "You appear to have gained something of an education. I am glad of that. Let's hope you put it to sensible use."

He turned his attention back to Sitting Bull. "Ask him if he can deny that that son of his, Crow Foot, came to the landing yesterday to pick up a load of chicken feed donated by one of those damned societies of Indian lovers in the East that keep on addressing their shipments directly to him."

"Why should I deny that?" replied Sitting Bull. "That is what happened. Our hens had stopped laying because they can no longer scratch anything to eat from the bare ground. My friends sent me grain to feed them. I myself let my son take the old wagon to fetch it."

The agent smiled with satisfaction. "Now ask him if it was by his direction that the boy traded the feed to the Fort Yates sutler for a rifle."

This was a thrust for which Sitting Bull had not been prepared. He turned to look down at his son. Crow Foot shrank back from that fierce stare, dropped to his knees, and scrambled under the porch. When he emerged and again stood he held cradled in his arms a shiny, new Winchester. Sitting Bull leaned down, took it from him, examined it, and handed it back.

"See that you keep it cleaned and oiled," he directed. "Tell him," he ruled, addressing Mrs. McLaughlin, "that a boy his age needs a rifle more than he needs chickens."

McLaughlin closed his eyes for a second in the intensity of his effort to maintain his temper.

"This is an order," he said. "I want that rifle returned at once."

Sitting Bull shook his head regretfully. "It could be that my son was foolish. But that is a trouble that belongs only to me. The feed, too, belonged only to me."

"Not one kernel of that feed belonged to you," pronounced McLaughlin, speaking with slow emphasis to give his wife time to interpret phrase by phrase. "These donations from those eastern societies — even though they may be addressed to you — are not for your personal use but for the benefit of all the people on this reservation. So, pay attention to what I am saying. I am giving you a second direct order. Hereafter, you will turn over such shipments to the agency so that they may be equitably distributed at the time of each ration issue."

The suggestion that anyone, least of all a white man, was more fit than he to judge the needs of his people had evened the balance. Sitting Bull was now as enraged as McLaughlin. But before he could reply he felt John's restraining hand on his knee. John stepped forward into the open space beside the buggy to address McLaughlin.

"With your permission, Mr. McLaughlin, may I say something before this becomes more of a misunderstanding than I am sure either of you would wish. While in the East I met a number of these so-called friends of the Indians. Like many philanthropists they're a stiff-backed lot. I'd doubt that they'd welcome any official interference with the manner they choose to manage their contributions."

"Why, for God's sake?" demanded McLaughlin.

"They are people whose interest in this field is largely based on their strong disagreement with the way Indian affairs are being handled by the bureau and the army. They regard themselves as better-informed regarding everything Indian."

"I've met some of them, too," declared McLaughlin. "Nobody could know less about Indians!"

"That's probably so," said John. "But what concerns you most at the moment is the special case of their dispatching donations in the personal care of Sitting Bull. This, I can assure you, is no reflection on you but purely and simply because to them he is so well known. In their estimation he is a figure of outstanding importance. In their estimation, I repeat, he is the one chief to whom every Sioux looks. He is the Indian most respected by the white public. He is regarded by his own people as a prophet. He is a famous military commander. He has traveled all over the country. He has been acclaimed by thousands. He has been received at the White House. His name is known all over the world."

"While no one outside the Dakotas ever heard of James McLaughlin," said the agent.

"That is not what I was saying."

"It's what you were driving at."

"On the contrary, Mr. McLaughlin, what I was driving at was this: There is no reason whatever that you two should be forever working at cross-purposes when as a matter of fact you both want the same thing."

"If by that you mean the good of the Sioux people you couldn't be more wrong about him." McLaughlin gathered his reins. "You seem to have his ear. Don't let him forget I've given him direct orders. He can remember on his own hook his two years in that cell at Fort Randall. So don't let him forget, either, that the road back to that cell is a short one."

He let out his team. As the buggy spun around in front of John, Mrs. McLaughlin turned toward him, her fingers under the edge of her shawl twitching with the sign-language message that she had something to tell him.

The covert signal had not escaped Sitting Bull's attention. He watched for a moment the retreat of the irate agent, then looked down at John.

"Your magic, my son," he said, "could be second only to mine."

VII

THE HOURS OF DISCUSSING the Sioux dilemma had, by the time Sitting Bull retired, left John too restless to remain under a roof. He walked up the ridge and along its crest. Below, in the four-mile-long straggle of scattered dwellings comprising the Hunkpapa town, there was the occasional dim glimmer of a fire showing through the drab walls of a canvas tepee, indicating a household in which a sick or aged inmate had been left behind when people had set out for the agency. The last time he had looked down upon a Sioux encampment at night had been in the days when tepees were still made of decorated buffalo hides that had been scraped and treated until they were so nearly transparent that the fires within made them glow with the brilliance of great paper lanterns. Light of every kind was going out for the Sioux.

The sense of guilt in having spent these past five years of their accelerating decline in the carefree ease of white schools was as persistent as a bone stuck in his throat. Looking up at the innumerable stars in the clear night sky, he wondered if among them there actually did reside some greater power which harbored a regard for the fate of a man or a people. One consequence of education had been the breeding of every sort of doubt. He sat down, dropped his head against his knees, and surrendered to his dejection. Eventually he slept and dreamed that he was riding his eagle but that the eagle was flapping like a monstrous, sickly bat through the darkness of a cavern that had no end.

The early heat of the sun awakened him. Daylight dispelled the worst of the night's morbidity. He was rested, hungry, and once more aware that he had things to do. He trotted down to the river bottom, plunged in the pool, drew on his shirt, pants and boots, and returned to the number-one house. Sitting Bull, stripped to clout and moccasins, was lolling in the sun on his front steps, breakfasting on a tin of salmon and a package of hardtack. He gestured to John to join him.

"People can no longer afford to buy things like this at Chadron's trading post," he said. "They are lucky if they can scrape enough together to trade for a handful of salt and a pint of flour and by now the trader himself is no richer than they. That is why whatever comes to me from those people in the East I trade to Chadron for what he cannot sell, like this fish which I have learned to like, and then he sells what I furnish him to our people, charging whoever comes only what he can pay. That way everybody, even the trader, gets something of what he needs but no Sioux has to feel that he is a beggar. That is better than making everybody crawl to the agent to get it, as he wants us now to do."

"Much better," agreed John. He accepted a handful of salmon and hardtack. "Why do you not tell the trader to move his post off the edge of the reservation to the other bank of the Cannonball River? The Hunkpapa can easily get to him there and we can write the people in the East that what they choose to send you they can send to you in the trader's care instead of the agent's. It will then make no difference what the agent thinks."

Sitting Bull's eyes began immediately to glow as he considered the manifold advantages of this maneuver. "Ho," he crowed. "He will fall down in a fit when he learns of this." He got to his feet. "Come, I will show you the letters they have written me so you will know how to write to them."

But when John sat down at the pine table in the house, Sitting Bull returned to the porch. John grinned his understanding. Sitting Bull always became restless when obliged to watch anybody writing. He was disturbed by the reminder that this was one form of conjuring in which he, the master, was not even a tyro.

"I will take these letters when I go to the agency tomorrow," said John from the doorway. "But I will buy the stamps at Fort Yates so the agent will not know about them."

Sitting Bull's half-smile expressed approval more clearly than any words. "The only good thing about ration day," he said, stretching with a comfortable sigh, "is that with everybody gone it is so quiet."

126

John sat on a lower step. "When I went off to the circus," he remarked, "I left my mare with the trader's daughter. The mare was old but I will need a horse, so I will have to ask her to let me have it back until I can find something to take its place."

"Mary has taken very good care of your mare. I wondered about you when you went away. There were many plump young Hunkpapa maidens who would have been glad to go into the bushes with you — whether or not you left them the mare. Yet you left it with that skinny little runt of a Mary, who was shaped like a starved grasshopper and behaved like a wildcat."

"She needed a horse," said John, "because she wanted one so much. And I did not go into the bushes with her though I may have with the others."

Sitting Bull glanced up at the cloudless sky and abruptly changed the subject.

"At your white school did they try to teach you that I am not a prophet?"

"They tried to teach me that there are many people and that they believe in many different things."

"You are trying to hide in a prairie-dog hole. What I am saying is — do you believe I am a prophet?"

"A prophet," said John, "is a man so wise that he can be a leader of his people. Of course you are a prophet."

"You are still hiding in that hole. So I must prove to you, my son, the powers that I have." Sitting Bull paused for effect, glancing again at the cloudless sky. "By noon I will have called up a thunderstorm. Not a big one. Just enough rain to remind the Hunkpapa, when they get back, of the truth I have told them about what has happened to dry up the earth." He stood up and again abruptly changed the subject. "Mary did not go with the trader and his wife when they went to the agency yesterday to draw their rations. He is proud but is now so poor he must beg like the rest of us. So . . . she is alone at the trading post." He went into his house.

John set out in quest of his mare. He was puzzled by the old chief's subjecting his magic to the test of so foredoomed a forecast but, since this appeared merely a passing irrationality, was more immediately curious about his repeated mention of Mary. He found the door of the trading post unlocked but there was no one within. He withdrew, crawled through the bars of the empty horse corral alongside the log house, and circled into the backyard. Through the leafless branches of an Osage orange hedge that had been killed by the drought he could see the figure of a girl kneeling in what in former years had been the Chadron kitchen garden.

"Mary," he said, as he came up to the waist-high hedge.

The girl sprang up to face him across it, flashing up into his view like a jack out of the box, her eyes widening incredulously, her face flushing and paling. John was as startled by the unexpected apparition, scarcely an arm's length away, of this lovely stranger.

"I beg your pardon," he added hastily. "I was looking for Mary Chadron."

Already she seemed to have recovered her composure.

"Should I take your not knowing me as an insult or a compliment?"

Her lips were parted in what was more like the tomboyish grin he remembered than the smile of the woman he was encountering for the first time. His heart was beginning to pound with an excitement he had never known before.

"I liked the little Mary so much," he said, "that I think the grown Mary should be charitable."

"Nobody told me you had come back." She was continuing to marshal her defenses. "That's why I was so startled when I heard your voice."

"I only got in yesterday." He could restrain his words but he could not restrain his gaze, which was roving raptly from the smudge of dust on her cheek, which drew attention to the old-ivory sheen of her skin, to the mist of perspiration, which sparkled like tiny jewels outlining the curves of throat and shoulder, to the careless knot in which her long black hair was twisted little-girl fashion on the top of her head, from which glossy strands had escaped to frame the harmony of eyes and nose and lips. "I took it for granted you'd gone with your family to the agency — that is, until I heard this morning you were still here."

She had evidently grown so accustomed to stares that her poise could remain unruffled by his. "I have heard they gave you a new name. What do you want me to call you?"

"Call me John. It goes better with Mary."

She let that pass by reverting to his former remark. "I stayed here today to replant the garden. This will be the third time this year and my mother has become so convinced by Sitting Bull's prophecy that I knew it would never be done again unless I did it. It has to rain sometime, you know. I have almost finished."

"I'll help you. The way I'm beginning to feel, it could rain today."

He rounded the hedge to kneel beside her, where, under her direction, he began digging holes with a stick into which she dribbled seeds from the half gourd in her hand.

"It's too late for corn," she remarked, "but maybe not for beans and squash and pumpkins and onions."

"They tell me you've become a schoolteacher," he said in English. "When I heard you had left the circus to go to school it made me want to see whether I could learn something."

"But your English is perfect. Your teacher must have been inspired."

"Poor Mr. Carignan did work very hard with me. But I learned most from a box of books I found in the schoolhouse storeroom. Everything was in it from romances and histories to a Bible, a dictionary, and a handbook on how to raise sheep. I read them all." They had come to the end of the row. "There. That's it. Thank you very much, sir."

They stood. He was regarding her as though he still could not believe the testimony of his own eyes.

"You know, seeing you has made me forget why I came — though not why I'll be coming again."

"You mean you came about your mare. I'm sorry to have to admit it, John. But your mare died last winter."

"What difference? She was old enough to go."

"Wait," said Mary.

Her eyes were dancing. She put fingers to her mouth and blew a long piercing whistle. From far up on the ridge came an answering neigh. A horse appeared on the crest of the ridge, galloped down the slope with tremendous strides, and burst through the fringe of willows edging the river bottom.

"Oh," said Mary. "He'll plow up my planting."

She ran to the farther edge of the garden plot. The horse came to a sliding stop when he reached her and, whinnying softly, began to nuzzle her shoulder. He was a magnificent young buckskin stallion. John ran to join them. The stallion whirled, teeth bared, and reared with forehoofs poised to strike.

"Don't come too close," said Mary. "He doesn't know yet that he's your horse." At a word from her the stallion quieted. Taking a handful of mane, she began leading him around the end of the garden. "We'll move into the corral, where we can give you two a chance to get acquainted."

He followed, lost in wonder whether he was admiring most the shape of the woman or the conformation of the animal. Both appeared to him incomparable. This seemed really too much to be bursting upon a man all at once. In the shade of the horse shed, Mary turned to face him, her arm over the stallion's neck.

"Now keep on talking and edging slowly closer while he begins to get used to you."

"The bigger question," said John, "is how I'm going to get used to edging closer — slowly, that is — to either of you. But first, tell me this. That mare of mine was of fair enough Spanish stock but where in the world did you find a stud to produce a get like this?"

"I'm a trifle proud of that. At least, I'm proud of the wretched little girl that managed it. The spring you left I heard of a wild horse herd out on Thunder Butte Creek that was led by a remarkable stallion. So I took the mare out there and hung around until she came in heat. Then I left her hobbled where the wild stallion could get to her."

His glance took in the tiny loft above the manger, just big enough to hold a pad and blanket.

"So long as you're confessing how much that wretched little girl has done for me, maybe you'll tell me who sleeps there."

"I do," she admitted. She stroked the satiny buckskin neck. "I like to let him run in the hills by day because that's so good for him and he's so fast no one could catch him. But I keep him here at night. And I sleep there because I'd sooner die than let someone steal him."

He had edged closer, carefully keeping Mary's averted body between him and the horse, until the front of his shirt was brushing the back of her shift, his face as he bent was almost in her hair, and he could smell the sweetness rising from her sun-warmed skin. Moving ever more slowly, he reached over her shoulder to lay his hand over her hand, which was stroking the horse's shoulder, allowing the tips of his overlapping fingers to touch the smooth buckskin. She understood his purpose and approved the experiment. The stallion trembled but quieted at a murmur from Mary. Though he was not quite touching any part of her except her hand, John guessed that she, too, was trembling. He knew that something inside him was. He continued the stroking with Mary's hand, allowing more of his fingers to come in contact with the horse's nervously twitching hide. There was the same strange ambivalence in his pleasure as when he had walked behind the two toward the corral, the mingled delights, each adding to the other, of being able to touch at the same time each of these two treasures, the very existence of which he had been unaware a short half hour ago.

"We should keep on talking," Mary reminded him.

"What do you call him?"

"He has no name. That was for you to give him."

"I think I shall name him Puma. For his color and because he is so quick — and because there is something in him fierce and proud and — and alone."

"Puma is a good name. In my mind while he was growing up I always thought of him as Wild Honey."

"I will not need to call him Honey in order to think of you every time I look at him."

He edged nearer Puma's head, drawing away from Mary lest he give way to the nearly overpowering impulse to close his arms around her. Keeping hold of her hand he extended the two clasped hands near Puma's nostrils, turning the hands gradually until his hand was uppermost. The stallion sniffed, snorted, rolled his eyes, and laid back his ears. This time it was John's murmur that quieted him.

"You do have a way with horses," said Mary. "He's never before let anybody but me come near him — not even my father and mother, who have been around him since he was born."

"No credit to me. Think of the introduction I have had to him. He is accepting me because he is thinking of me as part of you."

Her eyes fell. For the first time her so carefully maintained composure was threatened. He was reminded that the gentling of either a woman or a horse was a process that should never be hurried.

"Now," he added. "Let's see you ride him."

"But I never have."

"Why not? As I remember the little Mary, she was ready to ride anything."

"He was your horse and I thought that first time was something that should be saved for you."

"Since he is my horse we will do with him as I want. I want to see you on him so that I can always think of that whenever I look at him. Is he halterbroken?"

Mary nodded. There was a gleam of incredulous delight in her eyes. It was apparent by what a conquest of her self-will she had, through the years that she had been rearing the colt, resisted the temptation to ride him. She brought the halter from the manger and slipped it over Puma's head. John took the lead rope.

"Now lean your weight across him. I do not think he will buck. Anyway, I can keep his head down."

Mary stood on tiptoe, extended her arms, and rested her weight across the stallion's back. John slackened slightly his grip on the lead rope. Puma craned his neck, twisting his head around to regard with mild astonishment this unfamiliar development. He whinnied softly.

"See," said John. "You can do anything with my horse. Now get on him."

Mary drew back and sprang lightly astride the stallion's back. The moment was punctuated by a roll of thunder. Puma was disturbed neither by the crash of the sound nor by the advent of his rider. Again he craned his neck to regard Mary and to whinny his indulgence. The sunlight was suddenly fading. John glanced up to see a fringe of gray cloud scudding across the hot blue of the sky. He led Puma out of the shed into the open corral. They could now see, as they had not been able to see in the shed, the mass of dark cloud bearing down out of the west. There came another and nearer roll of thunder. A gust of wind ruffled Mary's hair. Occasional big drops of rain were hissing in the dust. The stallion was remaining as composed as though nothing unusual were happening.

"Miracle piled on miracle," said John. He turned to make a bow in the direction of Sitting Bull's house and looked up at Mary with a grin. "Would you believe that four hours ago he assured me there'd be a storm before noon?"

"Today I can believe anything," said Mary.

John opened the corral gate and led Puma out across the river bottom. The stallion was breathing hard and snorting occasionally but was accepting John's guidance with the same shivering equanimity with which he was submitting to Mary's presence on his back.

They kept on through the willows and up the slope. It was raining hard now and the claps of thunder and flashes of lightning were nearer and nearer. The air, so recently dry and hot and stifling, had turned ineffably cool and wet and refreshing. There was a sense, as in the beginning of spring, of life reviving. Mary lifted her face up into the rain.

"Just think," she said, "what a little while ago we were poking those seeds into the dry ground."

"And of all that has grown from them already," said John.

They paused on the crest of the ridge to look around. In every direction the horizon was bright. It was, as Sitting Bull had pronounced, a very small thunderstorm. Upon only the Hunkpapa was the rain's blessing being bestowed.

"Take a good grip on his mane," said John.

Starting back down the slope, he jogged, then ran, then ran as hard as he could. Soon, instead of leading, he was regulating the pace of the descent by holding back on the rope from a position alongside Puma's hindquarters. Mary's posture astride had pulled her shift to mid-thigh and the wetly gleaming graciousness of her leg was immediately before his eyes. Her hair had shaken loose and was whipping wildly in the wind. Had there been dryads who rode horses she could have personified one. In her exhilaration she was screaming with laughter and yelling encouragement to Puma. He realized that he, too, was whooping. The crashes of thunder and crackling of the lightning were now directly overhead, delivering gigantic salutes to their exultation.

By the time they had reached the corral the rain had ceased and the sun was out again. Mary slipped to the ground and faced him, her eyes glowing.

"This was the most wonderful thing that ever happened to me," she said.

The rain had plastered the thin cotton shift to every contour of her breasts and belly and thighs. It still seemed incredible that the meagerness of Mary at fifteen could have metamorphosed into this splendor of Mary at twenty.

"I think he's had enough excitement for one day," he forced himself to say. "And, I might add, maybe so have I. He and I both need time to think about what is happening. So, I'll come back tomorrow and we'll take him for another run."

The light went out of Mary's face.

"I can't," she said. "I have to go to Fort Yates. Mrs. McLaughlin has found me a place in the orphanage at the mission and I said I'd be there tomorrow at the latest."

"What could be better? I have to go to the agency in a day or two and it might as well be tomorrow. If we leave from here by the first daylight we can easily make it by sundown. You'll ride him and I'll lead. By the time the day's over just think of all he'll have learned without realizing it. That's the surest way to learn — for anybody."

"Is that how you learned at Dartmouth?"

"Well, not quite. I had to work at it. There was so much to learn."

He was backing toward the gate.

"Did you like learning?"

He realized with a new delight that she was talking in order to delay his leaving. He did not want ever to go away from her. Yet at the moment he had suddenly begun to feel that there was something he wanted even more. He wanted to get off by himself so that he could contemplate, examine, and gloat over the immeasurable fortune that the last hour had revealed to him.

"Yes. But there was always so much that I had not yet learned that it was — well, stupefying."

He opened the gate. She took a step after him.

"These schools like Dartmouth. Do only men go to them?"

"Yes. Of course, there were many girls in the town." He grinned at her instant blush. "But all the time I was away, wherever I went and whatever I saw, there was nothing anywhere to equal Puma — or you. Now lead him outside here. So that every time I look back I can see the both of you."

She obeyed.

"Get on him," he commanded.

She mounted. He walked rapidly away. Each time he looked back he was more tempted to return. At the edge of the river-bottom willows he turned to wave. She waved in reply. The gesture seemed to him as immensely reassuring as a pledge.

Before reaching Sitting Bull's house he turned from the trail and struck off up the ridge. On the crest he sat down. The great bowl of the sky arching over him seemed almost within his reach. He laughed and beat his fists upon the ground and raised his voice in long howls of pure elation.

There was a light in the window of the trading post when he returned the next morning. Mary's mother and father had got back from the agency only a few hours before but they were up waiting for him. The warmth of their greeting was like the jerking aside of a curtain to reveal something that he had known was there but at which he had not wanted to look. With such a daughter they must long since have become accustomed to regarding young men as potential suitors. The parental favor with which they received him forced him to face something he was not yet prepared to face. The excitement of his encounter with Mary yesterday had left no room for any speculation on the future, if he might be said to have a future. Through the night and while trotting here this morning he had been contemplating nothing beyond the delights of the single day that lay ahead. It was not even appropriate for him at this moment to be taking satisfaction in noticing that Blue Lark, Mary's mother, instead of growing dumpy and gnarled at forty, like most Sioux women, was still as erect and supple as a girl or to take further satisfaction in this reminder that Mary came from a long line of women noted for their beauty.

Then she came in and the sight of her drove from his mind everything but the promise of the day. In his thinking of her since they had parted there had been a dreamlike quality, as of a perfection that could not possibly be altogether real. But here at three in the morning she was as real as she had seemed at noon.

She set down the basket in which she had packed the personal effects that she was taking with her.

"Whatever can we do about this?" she asked. "We can't have it bouncing behind me on his back."

"That we can't," said John. "So I have spoken to Bull Head, who is going in today to make a report to the agent. He will take the basket to the mission."

Pierre Chadron laughed. "The high and mighty lieutenant of police who looks down his nose at everybody — so already you have him running errands for you."

"With John," Mary informed her parents, "people have to get used to letting him have his way."

They set out toward the red glow of dawn in the east. He crossed to the lesser-used trail on the other side of the river, on which there would be less likelihood of encountering people still straggling back from the ration issue. Puma soon learned to adapt his pace to John's so that, with slackened lead rope, John could run alongside instead of ahead. From this position he was able as often as he chose to survey the vision of such a woman on such a horse. Whatever was to come, for this whole day he was endowed with the privilege of looking at her, of knowing that so long as the day lasted she would be near.

An hour passed and then another without either speaking. Mary was revealing a new quality, unique among women. She appeared able to maintain silence and nevertheless to seem at peace. Suddenly, in mid-stride, as it were, he became aware of the resolution that with this peace he must not tamper.

Toward noon they stopped in a grove of young cottonwoods with virgin bark for Puma's entertainment.

"I was so excited when we were starting," said Mary, red-faced, "that I left in the manger the sack of sweetened cornmeal mother gave me to bring with us."

John laughed and drew a roll from his pack.

"As you must have heard, Sitting Bull's old wife has a way with pemmican."

With his knife he cut thin, curling slices of the mixed deer and bear fat, thickened with acorn meal, studded with huckleberries, and flavored with wild celery and wild ginger. It was not so easy to remain silent while sitting there facing and watching her and yet it was even less easy to hit upon something to say that would not be saying too much. The use of the knife got him on the safe subject of how he had acquired it. It was a pleasure to observe the gusto with which she appreciated his fully detailed story of the discomfiture of the sheriff and the Chippewa. There might be some white in her but there was still plenty of Sioux.

"Now," he said, putting the remnant of pemmican back in his pack, "it's time for the next step." He was doubling the lead rope and attaching it at either side of the lower loop of the halter so that it might serve as reins. "It could be that I'll never have to put a bit in his mouth. I hope so."

"So you're going to try riding him without his being led," she said, shivering with excitement.

"No. You are."

"Oh, but I couldn't. Surely this is something you must do."

"Not yet. I want him much more used to me before I run the risk of trying him. You see, when I do get on him, if he makes trouble I'll have to start in breaking his will and I'd much sooner never have to do that."

She yielded to this argument and ceased attempting to conceal her eagerness to be the one to make the trial. While he gripped the halter, she vaulted astride and took the reins. The stallion shook spasmodically but when John permitted him to look around at Mary he appeared to accept the situation. With tugs at the halter John started him walking and then drew him up to a halt, repeating the process again and again, while Mary was at the same time loosening and tightening the reins. After a while John released his hold on the halter and it became apparent that Mary was able to start and stop him with the reins alone. Puma appeared to regard all this as exceptionally foolish business and to be disposed to endure it only because it was Mary who was asking it of him.

"This is really terrible," said John.

"What's terrible? I think he's doing marvelously."

"It's what's happening to him that's terrible. His pride in being a male should be stirring him to fight every sort of submission. Instead, he's weakly surrendering because he's been taken in by affection for a female."

"Why shouldn't he want to please me? I've been pleasing him ever since he was born."

"I don't mean that what you're doing to him is terrible. I mean that what I'm doing to him is. Instead of fighting it out with him man to man I'm hiding behind your skirts. Using you is an unfair advantage. Without you as a decoy it could have taken a month's pounding on each other before I'd got him to where you have in these few minutes."

She giggled. "You should have called him Samson. That would make me Delilah, who is betraying him to you — the Philistine."

Presently she was able by gentle yet firm manipulations of the reins not only to make him start and stop but to require him to turn. In an hour she had him loping easily at a pace as fast as John, alongside, could run.

"Now," said John, "try letting him out once."

Drawing a long breath of excited anticipation, Mary loosened the reins and touched her heels to Puma's flanks. He exploded into a gallop. John, running after them, watched, his heart beginning to pound in his throat. But, after a hundred yards, Mary was able to pull him in, turn him around, and bring him galloping back. Again and again she repeated the maneuver. John, running hard, always paused to contemplate each of these returns to him. Each time she approached, she smiled down at him as she wheeled to dash off again. Her hair was flying, her face glowing, her laughter ringing.

The dusk was beginning to darken when they reached the mission. Father Murphy himself came out to greet them.

"Mary," his voice booming as though he were addressing a congregation, "you are welcome. Thrice welcome. Mr. McLaughlin and I have many times disagreed about many things but I must admit that his humoring his wife in this instance was an excellent idea."

Mary slipped down from the horse. "Thank you, Father. May I present John Winthrop."

Father Murphy gripped John's hand. "So you're back from the wars — I mean the schools. I know more about you, young man, than you may guess. I've had a letter from one of your professors — a Dr. Temple. He and I are not acquainted but he ventured to write me that you were coming. From what he says of you I'd suppose the Sioux might find use for you."

"I hope so. But first off I must ask a favor. Have you a place where I may put up my horse for the night?"

Father Murphy peered at Puma. "Indeed I have. My stable will be honored to shelter such a steed. There's an unused box stall that should suit."

Later John drew Mary aside.

"Whatever your duties here, they should not begin at daylight. If I come back then can we give him another run?"

"Yes," whispered Mary. "Yes."

Mrs. McLaughlin was said to miss very little that went on around the agency. Though it was almost full dark she noticed John's approach and was holding open the kitchen door of the agency's living quarters. Unlike most Indian agents, McLaughlin was not reputed to have sought private gain from his office but his wife was forever on the alert for practical opportunities to add to their resources and John had taken it for granted this accounted for her summons.

"Mr. McLaughlin's at Fort Yates," she said, "and long's he's not bothered to send word when to expect him no reason we shouldn't eat without him."

She moved back and forth from the stove, placing on the table before him a platter of ham and beans and beside it, she being by birth a Santee, the easternmost of the Sioux, the tray of wild rice cakes always offered a guest. The cakes were crisp and brown and particularly delicious when served, as these were, with maple syrup.

"Now that you're back," she said, coming at once to her business, "what do you figure on doing?"

It was the question he had known she would ask and he was prepared with his answer.

"I hadn't given it much thought. They expect me back in school in September."

"What I had in mind for you wouldn't take above a month. Would you like to make some money or do those folks back East give you all you need?"

"No. I could use some money."

"Who couldn't — no matter how much they got. Do you remember Bert Banks, the horse trader?"

John shook his head.

"He's been hanging around the last couple of weeks trying to pick up Sioux horses. The Sioux are so hard up that they have to keep selling anything they got left. Most of their horses ain't worth the price of their hides. But there's some good ones here and there. Those are the ones Bert's after but he ain't having much luck. If you were to scout around for him he'd give you ten dollars a head — for the real good ones twenty-five or maybe fifty."

"I hardly think I'd be able to drive the bargains he'd want."

"Why not? Everybody's cheating the Sioux. Why let it all go to strangers?"

"I still don't think I would suit him."

"Maybe not. Like I said, somebody's going to get their finger in that pie and I thought it might as well be you. But if you don't like the idea, I can't really say I blame you. And whatever you do this summer, I've got one piece of advice for you. Don't get yourself tied too close to Sitting Bull."

"Why not?"

"You could get into trouble."

"How?"

"Because Mr. McLaughlin is after him and you could get stepped on in the scuffle. Things have changed since you were here last. The agent's got real authority now. He can dole out the rations and he can call on all those soldiers at Fort Yates."

"Why is he so set on breaking Sitting Bull? Is he jealous of him?"

"Ridiculous. That's the last thing he could ever be. What you have to understand about Mr. McLaughlin is that the strongest feeling in him is that being a white man sets him a world above any Indian. He has been good to me but he feels that way even about me, his wife. When we were married we were young and hanging hard to each other. But from the first he was calling me Santy. He made out like it was just a pet name, after my being a Santee Sioux. But what he was after was being able every time he spoke to me to remind me that he was a white man and I was an Indian. No. He is bent on pulling down Sitting Bull for one reason only. He cannot stand any slightest question about his authority over the Sioux on this reservation. Sitting Bull does question that and therefore Sitting Bull has got to go." She cocked her head at the sound of hoofbeats. "There he comes now."

McLaughlin, coming in, showed neither surprise at seeing John nor any harbored resentment over John's remarks when last they had met. He crossed to him at once to shake hands.

"Father Murphy tells me that your name is now John Winthrop."

"I suppose that is my legal name."

"Does that adoption by an American back in New Hampshire make you a citizen?"

"I hadn't thought of that. Maybe it does."

"I hope so. What I mean is — you could be a great help to us here. A full-blood Sioux who is also a citizen and fluent in both languages — you could be like my right arm."

Santy was leaning over McLaughlin, serving him his dinner. John caught her warning glance.

"You're very kind, Mr. McLaughlin," he said. "The trouble is I haven't finished school. I'm due back there in September."

"Ah. That's too bad." McLaughlin chewed reflectively. An angry gleam came into his eyes. "I suppose you'll be visiting Grand River again while you're here."

"Yes, I will."

"When you do, make a point of telling Sitting Bull I have written the Indian Bureau recommending that he, along with his cronies, Circling Bear, Black Bird, and Circling Hawk, be removed from the reservation and kept so far away they can make no more trouble here. Don't say I told you to tell him. Just say you happened to find out about it."

"Will the bureau agree?"

"Who knows? Probably not right off. Since the Sioux quit dancing — and they never started here in my area — Washington thinks everything is rosy. I can't make them realize the mischief that old bastard is capable of. What I want him to realize is that I'm after him — and that I'll keep after him until I get him."

Santy pulled down a blanket from a shelf and handed it to John.

"He's worn out," she told her husband. "Half asleep there in his chair." She gave John another warning look. "You'll find an empty bed in the police barracks."

"Run along," said McLaughlin. "I'll see you in the morning."

When John reached the mission stable at dawn, Mary had Puma out of the stall and out on the road with the rope bridle already in place.

"Good," approved John. "Because we have less time than I had counted on and this morning we'll have to take all the next steps in one jump. That means taking an even more unfair advantage of him. This is what we will do: You get on him and I will run alongside. Then when he is not expecting anything I will jump up behind you. If he still accepts me as part of you so much the better. But if he starts to object, then be sure you slip off very quickly so that he and I are free to have it out."

Mary nodded and mounted. John ran alongside. They turned from the Fort Yates–agency road into the river bottom and on along a dirt track left by woodcutters. Then, so unexpectedly that even Mary was taken by surprise, John sprang astride behind her and, reaching his arms around her, took the reins. Puma came to a stiff-legged stop and stood, snorting and shivering. He was deaf to Mary's murmured appeals. John tightened his grip on the reins and touched his heels to the stallion's flanks. Evidently confused by the stronger note of authority in the dual nature of his rider, Puma started walking on.

"How sad," said Mary. "Neither of you need me anymore."

"Yes we do. He's still wondering how to get around you to get at me. Now let's get down and remind him again that there are really two of us."

They dismounted and stood at Puma's head, each with a hand on the rope bridle. Their eyes met. The interlude of their mutual training of the horse was coming to an end. The moment of truth was upon them.

"I am not going back to school," he announced abruptly.

She stared at him, incredulous, troubled. "But you haven't finished."

"I have work to do here."

Her consternation was immediately displaced by a surge of happy excitement.

"John! That is wonderful. What could be more wonderful? You can help us. You might save us."

"I can make things worse, too. For one instance, the time can come when I may have to ask the Hunkpapa to listen to me instead of to Sitting Bull."

"I can see that. But what I can see so much plainer is that what happens to the Sioux is more important than what happens to him — or to you — or to me."

Looking down into her rapt face he could not accept the possibility that anything could be more important than what happened to her.

"I have many dreams for you, Mary. One of them is not sharing a corn-husk pad in a canvas tepee while we live from hand to mouth on government rations."

He had blurted out words which a moment before he had had no intention of voicing. Her face paled and her excitement ebbed as swiftly as it had risen but her eyes were steady. He could not begin to guess what she might be thinking.

"Neither is it one of mine."

"Good for you." He struggled toward safer ground. "But what I have to think about first is what I have to do first. Now. Today. I have to get to Grand River as fast as I can to see Sitting Bull and then back here as fast to see the agent. Look for me at the mission stable by sundown tomorrow. Somehow I have to keep those two from feeding each other's ill will until they've started a fire that can burn us all. I'll have to risk taking Puma whether he's ready for me or not. So when you get back on him, sit well back. When I jump on this time I'll sit front of you. Be ready to slip off when we pass the mission — if we get that far."

Mary nodded. Puma proved less ready to accept this development. He kept tossing his head, prancing sideways, half rearing. Some premonition of the magnitude of the threat now looming appeared to have assailed him. Still he did not totally rebel. At the mission Mary slipped off and stood watching. John yelled, shook the reins, and struck inward with his heels. Screaming his response to the challenge, the stallion shot off at a tremendous gallop, as though by the very fury of his speed he thought to regain his freedom. Such a pace must in a few hours exhaust even his strength. Unfair advantage was still being taken of him. By the end of the day the last moment he might have disputed the mastery of his rider would, without his realizing, have escaped him.

At dusk the next day John was dismounting beside Mary at the mission corral. To cool the steaming Puma, they led him down the woodcutters' road into the river bottom.

"I can see that he did very well," said Mary.

"He did. He is as without parallel among horses as you are among women."

"I can also see that you are excited about much more than your horse and me."

"I am. Things are moving much faster than I had imagined. Sitting Bull wants me to visit the other western Indians — the Arapaho, the Cheyenne, the Crow, the Blackfeet and the rest. He says what he wants to know is what effect the Ghost Dance is having on them. Are they taking it seriously? How seriously? But what he really wants to know is whether or not he can count on their help if the agent drives him to the point when he must call upon the Sioux to fight."

"And you agreed to go?"

"Yes. If I had not he would have sent somebody else who might tell him what he wants to hear instead of the truth that is recognized by every Indian alive except a few like Sitting Bull who cannot give up dreaming about the past. That fact is that the whites are so many hundred times stronger than we are that no matter how we are put upon any attempt at armed resistance would be suicidal. Anyway, Sitting Bull has promised me to try to get along with the agent if I will do this for him and after I have talked with McLaughlin tonight I hope he will not push Sitting Bull too hard."

"How long will you be gone?"

"Not above two months. To save time, I will go by train wherever I can. Sitting Bull gave me money from the store he has accumulated by his transactions with his eastern benefactors. Naturally, the agent will not know what I am doing. I will ask his permission to visit the Pine Ridge reservation. Once there I will seem to start back here and will instead drop down to the railroad and be on my way. But here is where I need your help. While I am away there may be need to get messages to Sitting Bull and I will certainly want to keep him informed about when I am returning. However, the telegraph office here is in the agency and the agent reads everything that comes. So I will address my telegrams to Father Murphy and sign them Xavier, as though I were some associate of his who is keeping him informed of his travels. You will tell him that these are messages meant for you that we want to keep secret to prevent people from gossiping about us. Do you think he will agree to that?"

"I'm certain he will."

At dawn the next day they met again at the corral.

"The agent has agreed to try once more to be patient with Sitting Bull," John reported. "This was made easier for him by the Indian Bureau having disapproved his request that the chief be exiled."

"And Father Murphy is delighted to serve — as he irreligiously terms it — as Cupid's messenger in our behalf."

John gathered the reins in his hand preparatory to mounting.

"Now, before I start," he directed, "walk away from me and into the mission. I want my last sight of you to be a reminder of your being safely sheltered here while I am away."

She smiled. Again he realized that he could not possibly guess what she might be thinking. Then, obediently, she walked, without looking back, through the gate, across the garden, and into the mission.

VIII

SANTY WAS ACCUSTOMED to rising early but this morning it was not yet light when she slipped from her bed.

"What's the trouble?" mumbled McLaughlin.

"Could be that pork pie we had last night."

"Didn't bother me none."

She dressed hastily. In the kitchen she fished the glass jar from its hiding place back of the flour bin, extracted fifteen ten-dollar bills, and thrust them into her blouse. Letting herself out into the yard, she passed the outhouse, circled the police barracks, and kept on in the growing light to the farther side of the stables. It was a relief to find Cut Bear waiting there, for she had only half believed that he could have brought himself to so painful a decision.

Taking the reins from his hands she walked the horse in a tight circle and ran her hands down his limbs. The big bay gelding was one of the rare types once known among the Sioux as a three-buffalo horse. A brother-in-law of Gall, Cut Bear was in a position to own so valuable a mount and she speculated briefly on what personal difficulty might have moved him to part with it. Satisfied that the horse had developed no last-minute disabilities, she removed the money from her blouse and handed it to Cut Bear. Without counting it, he thrust the wad of bills into his shirt.

"Take him down to the willows by the ferry landing and wait for me to send for him," she said.

Cut Bear mounted and walked the horse off into the shadows. Turning, she saw McLaughlin in his nightshirt watching from the corner of the barracks. As she approached him she could see that he was rigid with rage.

"Get back in the house," he said.

In their bedroom she waited in silence while he deliberately washed, shaved, and dressed. It was his way when displeased with her to postpone his censure until he had controlled the first flush of his anger. This was one of the marks, she realized comfortably, of his esteem for her. At a curt gesture from him, she preceded him into the kitchen. He sat at the table, gripping its edge. She began kindling a fire in the cookstove.

"I should have guessed sooner," he said, "what with that Bert Banks hanging around so much. How long you been buying horses for him?"

She was prepared with her defenses.

"Nobody's been getting anything but the best of it. I know what's the top price Bert will pay. So whenever somebody's got a horse he wants to let go he gets twice what he would if I wasn't the go-between. Bert gets what he wants, the Indian that's selling gets more than he had any right to count on, and I get something. Everybody's better off. What's wrong with that?"

"I'll tell you what. You're the wife of the agent. And I'm one agent that don't hold with taking Indian money — or anybody's money — under the table. I'm running this reservation the best I know how and I don't intend to give nobody room to point any fingers at me. So you'll stop this horse trading — or any other kind of trading — right now."

"Yes, Mr. McLaughlin."

In any direct clash of wills between them she had from the day of their marriage realized the necessity of submission. It was a great pity that this horse dealing had been cut off but she had done very well with it while it had lasted and had actually feared that he would catch on sooner than he did. The one problem remaining was what to do about Cut Bear's horse now that she had promised to cease dealing with Bert.

McLaughlin gulped the last of his coffee and went into his office. Santy opened the door to the storeroom off the kitchen, which adjoined McLaughlin's office. In the common wall was a small window covered with oiled paper. From the darkness of the storeroom she could see what occurred in the office and hear whatever was said. While continuing with her household tasks she was able to keep track as well of business being transacted by the agent. McLaughlin knew of her eavesdropping and approved of it. So many of the problems arising with his Indian protégés were of a nature that made his wife's advice useful. His one great weakness as an Indian administrator was his refusal to learn the language, in which he had persisted through the years, as though any effort to speak Sioux would in his estimation have lowered him to the Indian level.

His first interview this morning was with Yellow Horn, who had brought with him his wife, Stands Looking. Yellow Horn's basic complaint, as announced by the interpreter, Louis Primeau, was that his forty-year-old wife had eloped with a fourteen-year-old boy, Frog Spawn.

"I was only on my way to visit my sister who lives in the Cheyenne River reservation," said Stands Looking. "Frog Spawn had a horse which I needed to ride there because he," she glared at her husband, "had lost his last horse gambling with Moon Dog."

"It is at most two days to the Cheyenne," argued Yellow Horn. "But after a week I found her and the boy still holed up in a dry cattail patch in the river bottom not an hour's ride from here."

McLaughlin frowned. "What did you do to Frog Spawn?" he demanded.

"Why should I do anything to him? He is only a boy. He was no more than a corncob this slut might have been pleasuring herself with."

Santy could tell by the way McLaughlin cleared his throat how relieved he was that Yellow Horn's response to his problem had not precipitated a feud with the boy's family.

"So you cannot manage your wife," said McLaughlin. "Why come to me about that?"

"I come to you so that you will tell me the truth." Yellow Horn glowered at his wife. "I was starting to cut off her nose, which is the proper thing to do with a wife when she turns whore, but Crow King stopped me. Crow King said that if I cut off her nose the census taker who counts noses would no longer be able to count hers and I could no longer draw rations for her. Is that the truth?"

"Yes," ruled McLaughlin. "That is the least that would happen to you."

Yellow Horn grunted his immense disgust and began prodding his wife ahead of him toward the door.

His place before the desk was taken by young One Bull, holding himself at stiff attention in his police uniform.

"I have talked to everybody on Grand River," he reported. "All they know is that John — he who once was Rides-an-Eagle — left for Pine Ridge two months ago."

"But I have it from the agent at Pine Ridge," objected McLaughlin, "that he was not there more than one day. What I want to know is where he is now. You have been fooled. A good policeman should know when people are lying to him."

"Nobody knows where he is if he is not at Pine Ridge," insisted One Bull, beginning to sweat. "He has not come back. Nobody has heard from him. Some say that he must have gone back to his school."

"What does your uncle, Sitting Bull, say?"

"I do not know. He will not speak to me because I am a policeman."

With a disgusted gesture McLaughlin dismissed the downcast One Bull. Second Sergeant Red Tomahawk came in, dragging with him the stumbling hulk of old Dog Ear, Standing Rock's most noted drunkard. Dog Ear's latest escapade, as reported with a kind of awed respect by the sergeant, had been to disrupt the drill of a platoon of recruits by charging on a mule stolen from Iron Fish across the Fort Yates parade ground into their formation. McLaughlin was not so much irritated by this last of Dog Ear's innumerable transgressions as he was by the sergeant's embarrassed admission that weeks of watching and searching had failed to discover the hiding place of the mysterious store of liquor on which the penniless old reprobate was able to draw whenever he elected to embark upon another spree.

Santy could see that the people still waiting on the porch for their audience with the agent suggested affairs of even less moment and turned her attention to her household duties. Then she saw Bert Banks riding toward the corral and hurried out to him. Bert, too, she was glad to notice, seemed in a hurry.

"What about that horse of Cut Bear's?" he demanded.

"He still can't make up his mind."

"Too bad. I wanted that horse. But like I've said before, the one I really want is that buckskin stallion the Chadron girl raised. I've had my eye on that one since he was two."

"He belongs to John Winthrop. He'd never sell him."

"Not if I was to go as high as — say — four hundred?"

"I doubt it. Anyway, John's not here. He's gone to Pine Ridge."

"He has, has he? Then I'll look around for him there 'cause that's where I'm headed. I hear they're dancing again at Pine Ridge. When Indians start getting worked up, then's the time to make deals. So I got to get me out to the railroad. You tell Cut Bear I can't wait longer'n the rest of today."

"I'll tell him," said Santy.

Relieved to have so easily disposed of Bert, Santy felt her satisfaction fading when she saw that White Duck, her younger servant girl, was waiting, round-eyed, at the kitchen door to speak to her.

"Crow Foot is in the hay barn," the girl whispered. "He wants to see you."

Santy's uneasy premonition was amply borne out. Crow Foot had had more drinks than his inexperience could well handle, without doubt slipped him by the Fort Yates sutler, whose sly custom it was to make use of any occasion to encourage Indian thirst. The whiskey had at once stimulated the boy's bravado and his animosity.

"That polecat that calls himself John," said Crow Foot. "My father thinks he knows so much. But me, I know something, too. A lot more than they think."

"Talking when you're drunk," said Santy, "that's not knowing much."

"I'm not drunk. I know what I'm saying. But before I tell you how much I know, you tell me something. John's getting back next Monday. They thought I was asleep when I heard my father tell Catch-the-Bear. What I want you to tell me is what will the agent do to John when he gets back if he finds out what John's been doing?"

"I can tell you what he'll do to you. He can't stand troublemakers."

"I'm not the one that's been making trouble," insisted Crow Foot with drunken logic. "You haven't been listening to what I been saying. John's the one that's been making the trouble. Big, big trouble."

Santy controlled her distaste for her necessary part in this ignominy.

"What kind of trouble? If you're not drunk you must be dreaming."

"I'm not drunk. And I'm not dreaming, neither. I know. I know that John's been visiting all the other tribes with a message from my father. My father didn't send Gray Eagle, or Black Bird, or Circling Hawk or — or me. Me, I'm his son. I'm a grown man and I got a rifle. Me, his son, he didn't even tell anything about it. John was the one he talked to. John was the one he picked to go. But I found out. I know more than they think. I know more than anybody."

"What was the message?" Santy forced herself to ask.

A delayed ray of lucidity flickered across Crow Foot's drink-befogged mind. He suddenly began to realize the enormity of the betrayal upon which he was embarked. Fear shook him. His lips quivered, his face worked, and he turned, stumbling, with a blind instinct to escape, toward the door. Santy seized his arm and jerked him around.

"Now listen to me," she commanded. "You're not to tell anybody what you've told me. Not anybody. *Not anybody.* You understand?"

He nodded dazedly.

"If you do, I'll go straight to your father and tell him what you've told me."

This threat terrified him.

"Don't do that," he begged. "Don't do that. The way he will look at me will strike me dead."

"Then remember. You're to tell nobody."

She let him go. Walking slowly back to the agency she contemplated the implacable necessity that was awaiting her. The agent was her husband. He was the responsible authority on the reservation. He could not be left unacquainted with this threat to that authority. Even though the excess of his response might hopelessly aggravate the threat, he had to be told. She owed him his chance to cope with it. Her appearance at the side door of his office brought him at once to her in the kitchen.

"I've something to tell you," she said. "But don't ask how I found out."

He nodded. He realized that she had sources of information among the Sioux of which it was wiser for him to remain in ignorance.

"I know what John's been doing. He's been carrying word from Sitting Bull to the other western tribes. He's due back Monday."

McLaughlin's face remained stony while he digested this revelation. "Hold on a minute," he said.

He went back to his office and returned with copies of several telegrams.

"I've been wondering about these messages. They don't say much." He shuffled through them. "From Cheyenne, Wyoming — Billings, Montana — Minot, North Dakota. Somebody named Xavier reporting his comings and goings. They're addressed to Father Murphy but I can't believe he knows what's going on. He's only being used. The last one says John's due back Monday all right. Not here but at Gunsight, way the other side of Pine Ridge. That's where he's getting off the train. Probably where he took it, too."

McLaughlin tossed the telegrams to the table. Now that the facts had been sorted out in his mind he began to pace the floor, permitting his rage to take command.

"That old son of a bitch. Pretending to behave these last two months. All the time laying low and laughing at me. And that John. After I'd offered him a place here with me. The two of them with their heads together. Imagining they can make a fool of me on my own reservation. I'll break up their goddam little scheme if it's the last thing I do."

"You don't know yet what word Sitting Bull was sending to the other tribes," Santy reminded him.

"What difference? No question he's hoping to stir them up. He doesn't stand a chance. He can't even stir up his own tribe. What it does prove is that he's the creeping, backstabbing troublemaker I've said all along he is. But that John's his sidekick — that's bad. The old man's twenty years behind the times but John's smart. He could really make some trouble."

He strode into the hall, shoved open the side door of his office, and called in One Bull from his sentry post on the porch.

"Tell him," McLaughlin directed Santy, "to find Bert Banks and bring him here."

When Bert appeared he hesitated uneasily in the doorway and only ambled on into the office after being relieved by McLaughlin's gesture of welcome.

"Hello, Bert. I hear you're off for Pine Ridge."

"Yes, I am."

"When do you figure to get there?"

"I'm taking the morning train out of Pierre. With lucky connections, by Saturday. Sunday for sure."

"Would you do something there for me?"

"I sure would."

"I don't know whether the new agent's showed up at Pine Ridge or not. Anyway, I don't know him. But I do know old Half-Moon, head of the Pine Ridge police. Do you?"

"Yes, I do."

"Then will you tell him something for me? Tell him one of my Indians, Rides-an-Eagle, sometimes known as John, is due to get off the train at Gunsight Monday. Half-Moon knows him. Tell him that the minute John comes on the Pine Ridge reservation I want him arrested and held until I can send for him."

"Any special charge?" asked Bert, appearing more and more eager to be helpful.

"Anything. Off the reservation without a permit, horse stealing, fornication, anything. Just so Half-Moon makes sure to hold him for me."

Back once more pacing the kitchen, McLaughlin was still thinking furiously.

" 'Course that John's likely doing some thinking himself. Could be once he got off the train at Gunsight he'd stay out in the sagebrush till he turned up at Grand River."

He went to the kitchen door, fished a silver whistle from a vest pocket, and blew three sharp blasts. Sergeant Shave Head came running from the barracks.

"Tell him," McLaughlin directed Santy, "to take an order to Bull Head at Grand River. Beginning next Tuesday I want Bull Head to put every man he's got to watching every trail from the south. I want him to post them in pairs thirty or forty miles out. When they pick up John I want him brought here." He began rubbing his hands. "This report he's bringing — he can make it to me."

Through the late afternoon Santy pretended that she had not made up her mind. But when McLaughlin left to keep a dinner engagement with Colonel Drum at the fort she knew she had not for a moment been in doubt about what she must do. As a wife it had been her duty to warn her husband. As a Sioux it was equally her duty to warn John.

Father Murphy was enjoying his usual late-evening stroll in the mission garden. Santy circled to the back door and directed a servant to summon Mary. Without preamble she explained to the startled girl the agent's orders for John's arrest.

"He has to be warned the moment he gets off that train," said Santy, "to give him some chance to look after himself and to keep this trouble between the agent and Sitting Bull from getting a hundred times worse. But for my sake, for his sake, for everybody's sake, whoever we send has to be someone we can surely and absolutely trust — first, to get there in time, then, to keep quiet about it. Who else is there?"

"No one," said Mary. "Of course. But how do I get there?"

"I have a horse. A real good one."

"What can I tell Father Murphy?"

"You have an aunt in Pine Ridge. She's sick."

"My father's sister. But she died last year."

"He doesn't know that."

"I can't lie to him."

"Come with me," said Santy firmly.

They joined Father Murphy in the garden.

"Mary has to take a trip on very important Sioux business," said Santy. "You can suppose that she is going home for a visit. That is not where she is going but it is better for you if you do not know anything more."

Father Murphy peered at them in the light from a window. He was troubled but inclined to make the best of it.

"If I cannot trust you two who then can I trust? So be it. I will wrap myself in my complete and innocent ignorance."

In the willows by the ferry landing Cut Bear was still waiting patiently. He turned over the horse and disappeared in the night. Santy had stopped at the agency to pick up several items. She was holding the impatient Mary to deliver one or two last-minute admonitions. These all had to do with practical details. In her estimation, from the moment Mary had decided to go no great problem remained. Mary had once been as far as Pine Ridge and no Indian needed to see a piece of country more than once to remember every inch of it forever. She would know how to keep below the skylines and, whenever she had to get close enough to talk to anybody, with that long knife she kept at her belt since her father had given it to her at twelve she would be as able to take care of herself as any man, better probably.

"Here's a sack of ham and turkey pemmican that's got more good to it than the priest's bread and cheese," said Santy. "And a doeskin shift that will stand the hard going better than that calico of yours and a woolen blanket in place of that thin cotton one. It's a good two hundred miles but you've got four days and nights to make it. Don't worry about pushing the horse — he'll stand up. When you get to Pine Ridge leave him with Dr. Eastman. He's been wanting me to find him a good horse. Tell him he can have him for a hundred and fifty dollars."

"But how then will I get back?" asked Mary.

"John will get you back."

"Yes," said Mary. "So he will."

IX

THE TWO-CAR TRAIN PUFFED laboriously up the grade, then rocked and rattled down the other slope over the rough roadbed hastily constructed this year in the railroad's urgent reach toward the Black Hills. Kirk peered from his window for a first glimpse of Gunsight. This third resumption of his fact-finding mission for General Miles appeared even more promising than had the first two.

When he returned to headquarters with his report on his visit with Jared to the far western tribes, he had taken it for granted that nothing could longer delay his reassignment to ordinary duty. But when Kicking Bear's reappearance in the Sioux country led to a renewal of dancing by the Sioux it also led to the general sending Kirk to evaluate this unexpected and more alarming development.

This time his contrived identity, though fortuitous, seemed a nearly perfect cover. After parting with Kirk, Jared had been engaged by Frederic Remington to guide the western artist on a projected tour of the Sioux country. Kirk's telegram had elicited Remington's indulgent approval of his hometown friend's joining the party in the ostensible role of the news photographer. Behind a camera and in the company of the famous correspondent, surely the most inquisitive observer would be unlikely to detect the young army officer.

Gunsight came into view and as the little train screeched and shuddered to a stop he looked in vain for Jared or Remington. The sun was scarcely up but what must have been most of the inhabitants of Gunsight were at the boxcar depot, waiting for the train. In the forefront of the crowd was a knot of men with a prominently displayed rope. The moment the train stopped, these dedicated fellows swarmed aboard to search the two coaches. Their excited calls back and forth indicated that they had been awaiting the scheduled arrival of a horse thief they kept referring to as Indian John. Kirk's interest faded. He knew there had been no Indian among his few fellow passengers. The crowd's interest also subsided when the depot telegrapher leaned from his window to report word from the agent at Scott's Bluff that there was an Indian with a ticket for Gunsight on the next train, due to arrive that evening.

The crowd was drifting back into town. There was still no sign of Jared or Remington. Inquiry of the telegrapher turned up no message for Stuart MacGregor, the name Kirk had assumed for his current incognito. He set off along the dusty street toward the post office. Gunsight was another of the raw, new plains communities with which he had grown fondly familiar during his recent travels, with its essential complement of twenty saloons to one church and one school, its gamblers, dance-hall girls, cowhands, teamsters, drifters, and even a scattering of homesteaders squatted in the creek bottom beyond. It had existed for only one lusty year but already there was a nostalgic sense of its imminent decline.

Many of the inhabitants had reassembled at the post office to await the distribution of the mail that had come by the morning train. While waiting with them for the window to reopen, Kirk listened with interest to their talk. All of it was about Indians. The town was in the grip of an Indian scare. There was some geographical excuse for this, inasmuch as the Pine Ridge reservation, forty-odd miles away, was occupied by six thousand Oglala, the most primitive of the Sioux. Most of the discussion in the street before the post office was devoted to a feverish exchange of this morning's crop of rumors. Of these, the one that was attracting the most attention dwelt on the secret message General Miles was purported to have sent the president of the railroad advising the immediate evacuation of the town.

When Kirk at length got to the window he struck some trace of Jared. There was a letter from him that read:

Dear Stu:

Fred he figgers to come back next week. Ed Stump has got his rig. Get it and head due north. Count on comming cross me for you get fars the Badlands.   *Jared*

The alternately darker and lighter words suggested how often he had licked his pencil, but for all the effort it answered fewer questions than it raised. However, Kirk had learned the uselessness of speculation on the genesis of Jared's impulses. At the Stump livery stable he noted with satisfaction that Remington had invested in a good sound team and a strong new buckboard with an elongated box that made it almost a wagon. His camp equipment, supplies and painting paraphernalia were already stowed away in it under a tarpaulin. Stump had been expecting Kirk and had no hesitation about turning the outfit over to him. He was a talkative fellow, which encouraged Kirk to fish for information.

"What happened to Remington?" he asked.

"All I know is whilst he was waiting for you he got a telegram that left him fit to be tied. Far's I could tell by the way he was swearing about it to Jared, seems he had to go clean back to Chicago to meet up with somebody from New York that's got something to do with *Harper's* magazine."

That accounted for Remington. There was no use asking what Jared might be up to. Stump nor anyone else would know that. While they were hitching up the team Kirk kept glancing at a handsomely muscled buckskin stallion in a stall.

"That's the horse Indian John stole," said Ed, "before he took the train out of here month before last."

"Funny," said Kirk, "his leaving a stolen horse — and such a fine one, at that — right here for anybody to notice."

"He didn't. He left him hid with a half-breed squatter down the creek a piece. But Bert Banks, he's got eyes in the back of his head when it comes to horses. He spotted him. Seems Bert had bought the horse off the Indian up at Standing Rock and then after taking the money the Indian sneaked up on Bert's camp and took him back. Before he caught the train out yesterday Bert he talked in most the bars in town about his trouble. Folks here don't like horse-stealing and they don't like Indians and it wasn't no time before they got real steamed up."

"Then once he'd brought that off he ducked out."

"He said he had some business down to Alliance that couldn't wait."

Kirk forebore attempting to satisfy more of his curiosity. The charge smelled of chicanery. Even if the accusation were justified, the lynching of an Indian at this moment of mounting frontier tension could have no very helpful consequences. It was not, however, his problem.

He drove the buckboard back to the depot to load his luggage and photographic equipment. On his way out again through town he pulled up briefly to watch the arrival of the stagecoach from Pine Ridge. He was near enough to the Indian country by now to consider anything that happened worth noticing. The usual crowd of idlers was gathering to see who might be coming. Among the boxes and bags on the roof of the stagecoach was hunched a squaw so bundled in a blanket that little could be seen of her other than a glimpse of dirt-streaked face and a few strands of gray hair.

At sight of the squaw a mutter of animosity ran through the assemblage. Indians were not welcome in Gunsight. The mood of the crowd was more malicious than menacing but the squaw naturally hesitated to jump down into the pack of jeering, jostling men. When she continued to hesitate, several began to rock the body of the stage on its leather suspension to shake her off. This maneuver brought roars of laughter from the onlookers.

So unequal a contest irritated Kirk. As he drove past the stage he motioned to the squaw to jump his way. After one look at him and down at her tormenters, she leaped from the stage to the bed of the buckboard, managing the feat with remarkable agility for an old woman. She had not even released her clutch on a small basket she carried. Kirk whipped up his horses. The crowd's howls of laughter turned to yells of protest at this interference with the fun. The horses bolted. Not until he was well out of town did Kirk get the team under control. He looked back at his passenger.

She was kneeling, clinging to the back of the driver's seat for support while looking over her shoulder toward the town. Her twisting posture had pulled the shrouding blanket away from her face. He could see at this close range that her hair was not gray. It had merely been streaked with ashes. Her face was not old. It had merely been smeared with oil and soot. She was young. It was even possible that she was not bad-looking. Before venturing into a white town she had presumably felt that she might be safer if she seemed an old squaw rather than a young girl. She turned to look up at him.

"Thank you," she said, in fluent English. "You have been very kind. But please let me out. I have to go back."

"What! I mean — why?"

"A friend," she explained. "He is arriving by train today. I have a message for him that he *must* get at once."

"Indian John?"

Nothing seemed to disturb her grave dignity. "Yes. You have seen him?"

He pulled the team to a stop.

"No. But I've heard about him. All of Gunsight will be waiting at the station to hang him as a horse thief the minute he gets off the train."

She considered this without surprise.

"Whose horse?"

"That could be a moot question. But I've seen the horse. A buckskin stallion. A marvelous animal."

Her eyes brightened for a second before clouding thoughtfully again.

"It isn't the people of the town who are doing this," she said. "It is . . . other people." She looked at him searchingly.

"Maybe if you told me your trouble," he suggested.

"I shouldn't," she replied, "but what else can I do? We must think of something. Or, at any rate, I must. John was sent by Sitting Bull on an errand to some of the other nations. He had to go without the agent's permission. I came to warn him that agency police had been ordered to take him before he could get back to Sitting Bull. I knew nothing about this horse-thief charge until you told me. The horse is his, by the way."

Kirk was struggling to hide his elation. A more extraordinary stroke of luck could not have been imagined. His mission was to seek to determine what the Indians really had in mind, if they yet knew. The chance to befriend these two emissaries of Sitting Bull could mean a possible opportunity to work his way near the most secret councils of the Sioux.

"I've already thought of something," he said hastily. "Get up here on the seat with me."

He turned the team off through the sagebrush flats, circled the town, and picked up the dirt road left along the railroad by construction gangs when the tracks had been laid a few weeks before.

"The other side of that ridge," he explained, "there's a tank where trains stop to take on water before they take their run at the grade. I noticed it when I came through this morning. When your John's train stops you can hop on, get him off — and be on your way."

She considered this. "It seems like a possible chance," she decided. She turned and again studied him.

"Why are you doing this for us?" she asked.

"Shall we say that I have a weakness for Indians?" He grinned. "Or, more likely, a weakness for girls in need of help?"

Her response to this was to appear even more remote. He tried a more serious approach.

"I could help more successfully if I knew who's working against us. Who are these 'other people' who are trying to frame John?"

"I've said too much already."

"Maybe it would help if I told you who I am. My name's MacGregor. I'm a news photographer. I sell pictures to newspapers. This outfit belongs to Frederic Remington, the famous artist and war correspondent. You've heard of him, haven't you? We've come West to find out for ourselves what's really going on with all this Indian excitement about the Ghost Dance. What we find out will get straight off to people everywhere in the East and also the government in Washington. Wouldn't you like the Sioux side of the story told?"

She shook her head noncommittally.

"Why, for example," he persisted, "would these mysterious 'other people' you talk about want John killed? Are they trying to stop a war or start a war? It's the truth I came to get. You aren't afraid of the truth are you?"

She kept shaking her head.

"Who knows what is the truth?" she said finally. "If we find John, you can ask him. He will know what to tell you."

The horses strained up the long slope, following the tortuous course of the railroad to the crest of the ridge and then began the even more winding descent. Despite the midday heat she remained huddled in the blanket, staring straight before her, all of her attention appearing concentrated upon the horses' ears. He began to realize the disquiet which gripped her. After all, she was embarked on important Indian business, which threatened the life of her collaborator, and had placed the outcome in the hands not only of a stranger but of a stranger of the enemy race.

In the late afternoon they rounded one more shoulder of the hills to find the water tank in view before them. He could hear the sudden indrawing of her breath as she sighted it. It was obvious that she had not until this moment felt any confidence in the gamble she had taken in trusting him. Swinging off the road to a little flat half a dozen yards from the tank, he pulled the sweating horses to a stop.

"Train's due sometime before dark," he said.

He began unhitching and rubbing down the horses. As she contemplated the tank there appeared in the girl's expression the first hint of animation she had permitted herself. Yielding to some sudden impulse, she sprang down from the seat, her basket in hand, and moved alongside the wooden water tank on its stiltlike ten-foot legs. Fed by a pipe from a spring up the slope, the tank's overflow vent released a miniature waterfall which ran down the side of the tank and then fell, glittering in the sun, to splash pleasantly on the rocky ground.

She tossed aside the voluminous blanket, disclosing that she wore underneath it a tattered and very dirty cotton shift that left her arms and legs bare. About her waist was a belt from which hung a long-bladed knife. She laid the belt and knife aside, stepped into the waterfall, and began energetically washing herself.

Kirk straightened from his horse-tending to stare. The vigorous scrubbing of her face, arms and legs was revealing that when clean her skin was almost white. She turned her dripping, half-washed face toward him.

"You are wondering about me," she said with her usual gravity. "My name is Mary Chadron. My mother married a white man." She glanced dispassionately at her gleaming arms and legs. "So I am maybe not all Indian." Her eyes flashed. "But I am all Sioux."

She turned back to the waterfall and resumed her bathing. Giving no heed to the circumstance that her dress was getting drenched, she stepped in and out of the little cascade as though she could not get enough of the water's cleansing freshness. In the glint of sun and water there seemed a naturalness, a kind of naïve innocence, in her every posture and movement. The soaked cotton shift was beginning to cling so closely to her body that it seemed transparent.

This was clearly developing into something of which it was imperative he get a closer view. Yet, as her self-appointed protector, it was as necessary to have some plausible excuse. He yanked his photographic equipment from the buckboard, ran nearer, set the big camera on its tripod, and swung it toward her.

"I have to have a picture of this — this transfiguration. It will be my first in the Indian country and maybe the best I'll ever get."

"Not yet," she said. "I have to get from this dress into a clean dry one. You wouldn't want your picture to . . . ah . . . catch me between the two, would you?"

"Well . . . no," he said. "So go ahead. I'll wait."

He would not have guessed that this educated Indian girl could have retained so primitive an unconcern about nudity. It seemed too good to be true. It was. Her fingers went to the fastenings of the dress but then she paused as though for the first time considering the fact that he was watching.

"I won't be looking until you say you're ready," he reassured her.

He ducked his head under the black cloth shrouding the back of the camera. Hastily he adjusted the focus. Suddenly the image of Mary came into his view in brilliant clarity. She was stepping out of the shift and back into the waterfall, her sudden complete nakedness in delightful silhouette. But there was an equally brilliant clarity in the mocking glance she threw in his direction over one wet shoulder.

"Is looking through the camera at me what your people call a Peeping Tom?"

"Yes, by God, it is," said Kirk.

He tossed off the black cloth and turned his back, by now in the grip of genuine excitement. The composed insolence of her challenge had been unmistakable. She had deliberately permitted him that brief glimpse. Yet she remained certain that she retained control of the situation. She was no shrinking prairie flower. She was knowing and wary and bold. She was not only fair game. She was big game.

Already he was swiftly calculating his options in the hours immediately ahead. When they rescued her fellow conspirator from the train he must contrive ways to keep the two of them with him for a day or two. Fortunately, this was also his military duty in order that he might determine the significance of John's mission.

"You can turn around now, if you wish," she said.

He swung back toward her. She had donned a white deerskin shift that hung in simple, classic lines from shoulder to knee. Wringing the last water from her long hair, she began braiding it. He surveyed with new interest the graceful angles of her arms and wrists, the curves of throat and shoulder, the tilt of her head.

"The real reason you feel so safe," he said, "is that long knife."

She paused in the braiding of her hair to give this statement fair consideration.

"Who can tell?"

There was still that note of challenge. He was starting toward her, even though every memory of such moments warned him his move was premature. The train's distant whistle saved him.

He dashed to hitch up the team. She snatched up the blanket, vigorously shook the dust from it, and once more enveloped herself in its folds. But as they watched, at first expectantly and then aghast, the train, instead of slowing as it approached the water tank, gathered speed for its run at the grade and rumbled past in clouds of smoke and showers of sparks.

She turned to stare at him accusingly.

"How in hell was I to know?" he demanded.

Her eyes were narrowing with fury and her fingers slipping under the blanket toward the handle of her knife. There was no use attempting to convince her that his purpose in bringing her to the water tank had been honest. He jumped to a stand on the seat of the buckboard to look after the train. Confirming his observations during his two passages, he saw that the track, after winding far to the left in its switchback assault on the grade, swung finally back to a shoulder of the mountain a few hundred feet directly above the tank.

"Come on," he yelled.

He jumped to the ground and began scrambling up the steep slope. Mary dropped the blanket and followed. He still retained most of his desert-bred stamina but so violent and sustained was his effort that he was gasping when at last he sprawled across the tracks above. Mary was still right behind him. He saw a large flat rock in the embankment above, pulled it loose, and slid it down on one of the rails.

"Run up the track," he ordered, "so you can hop aboard the moment the train slows."

He took off his bandanna, and ran after her toward the oncoming train, waving his red flag. The train screeched to a stop. As the engineer and fireman dismounted, he could see Mary darting into the single coach. By the time the trainmen had tugged the rock from the track and had turned to thank their savior, Kirk had dropped from their sight.

When he reached the water tank the two Indians were there awaiting him. He was taken aback by his first sight of John. He had expected, if not a wrinkled, old chief, at least a personage of seasoned maturity. Indians were not accustomed to assigning important missions to any but tribal elders. But John was lithe and sinewy and certainly less than thirty. Under the wrinkled bagginess of a blue serge suit he also looked as supremely sure of himself as though he were wearing a war bonnet and in his way he was as handsome as was Mary in hers. Surveying the two standing side by side before him, Kirk realized with a renewed surge of excitement how much the stakes had again been raised.

"Mr. MacGregor," said Mary, "this is John Winthrop."

John's handclasp was quick and firm.

"Glad to know you, sir." A suspicion of a grin flickered across his aquiline face as he glanced from Kirk to Mary and back to Kirk. "I can guess what you're thinking. God damn — *another* school Indian."

"We've got more than that to guess," said Kirk, indicating the buckboard. "When that train gets in everybody in Gunsight will know you got off here. First thing in the morning there'll be a hundred men riding out to look for us. We've got to get as far as we can as fast as we can."

John shook his head with the instant decisiveness of the born commander.

"No use. Your wagon will leave a trail like a prairie schooner that even they can follow. They'll run us down before noon."

"Got a better idea?"

"I think so."

With one quick glance John surveyed the surrounding slopes stretching from the ridges above to the sagebrush flats below. The surplus from the spring became a tiny stream below the railroad which trickled away into a winding little canyon choked with scrub pine and chaparral. The canyon deepened as it descended. John dropped down into it. In five minutes he was back. He did have a better idea, as Kirk was at once compelled to agree.

They unhitched the horses, removed the wheels from the wagon, and separated the cargo into bundles. By then it was getting safely dark. Mary led the horses one at a time down into the canyon. The men made trip after trip carrying the wagon parts and impediments. John took care that no branches were broken as they forced their way through the thick brush. After their last load he took even more care to remove every trace of their passage from the road beside the tank to the thickets below. When the operation was complete they were encamped in a lower and deeper bend of the canyon, where the screen of overhanging pines concealed them from view from any higher point anywhere around. Their concealment was so secure that they could even afford a small fire.

While rummaging in Remington's supply box, Kirk could hear the low-voiced colloquy in Sioux between Mary and John. She must be giving him more complete detail on the various receptions planned for him at Standing Rock, Pine Ridge and Gunsight. His replies were monosyllabic, indicating that he was taking no time to tell her anything about his western mission. It seemed that Kirk would learn little about the trip except directly from John.

He had come upon a shelf of tinned delicacies that the artist had evidently brought along for special occasions — ham, chicken, butter, jam, English biscuits, sugar, coffee. Mary immediately joined him to take them from him, appearing to take it for granted that it was her place to serve the two men. As she bent over Kirk her face remained as expressionless as when she had sat those hours beside him on the seat of the buckboard. John wolfed what was put before him and by the time he was reaching for his coffee was ready to get down to business.

"Where did you find out about my horse?" he asked.

"When I arrived at the station I saw the necktie party waiting for you. Then at Ed Stump's stable, where I called for Remington's outfit, I saw the horse. Stump said a trader named Bert Banks claimed you sold him the horse two months ago at Standing Rock."

"But you didn't see Bert?"

"After spreading his story around town he'd gone off to Alliance."

"Bert's always hanging around the reservations trying to pick up horses for a quarter of what they're worth," said John. "Sooner or later I'll run across him."

Having disposed of this item he turned to the next most pressing.

"Where were you headed when you came across Mary?"

"Just north. Somewhere before striking the edge of the Badlands I expect to meet Remington's guide. He's an old mountain man, Jared Glass. Maybe you've heard of him?"

"Yes, I've heard Sitting Bull mention him."

John's reply had come without hesitation or any appearance of special interest. One disadvantage of traveling with Jared was that he was known to so many older Indians. Apparently, however, John had not during his western tour learned of Jared's earlier passing. Kirk decided the time had come to try his first cast.

"If my way north is anywhere near yours," he said, "maybe you might think it just as well if we stuck together for a day or two while getting clear of Gunsight?"

John's glance went from the bulge of the holster under Kirk's arm to Remington's Winchester leaning in its scabbard against a tree. "I do think so," he said. "I also think you're very kind. That's not much to say after you've saved first Mary, then me. No use my harping on it but that's been something I'll not forget."

Having finished his repast and his speech, John rose and without ceremony peeled off the blue serge suit and cotton shirt, leaving him stripped to a breechclout, folded the garments carefully, and stowed them in his carpetbag along with his shoes, hat and socks. Having thus ministered to his comfort, he stretched out lazily on the ground. In the movements of his smoothly muscled body there was the controlled and flowing grace of a dancer. Mary was moving in and out of the firelight, washing and repacking the dishes. Kirk noted that John had taken a position from which he could watch her without seeming to watch. A pair of more perfectly suited mates could not be imagined. They looked like something out of mythology. The tableau became even more striking when Mary sank to her knees near John's feet and began to unbraid her hair.

Some kind of tension had developed between them. She began rebraiding her hair with wisps of sweet grass she had found by the stream. John rose, the suddenness of his movement suggesting a retreat from the vision or the scent. He drew from his carpetbag a blanket, a belt with knife, and a pair of moccasins. He put on the belt and moccasins, spread the blanket at the far edge of the firelight, and, rolling into it, seemed to drop off at once to sleep. While finishing the braiding of her hair Mary regarded the back turned toward her. Then, becoming aware that Kirk was covertly watching her, she spread her blanket and appeared also to have fallen asleep at once.

Kirk leaned against a rock behind him and thought about the events of the day and the light they might cast on his expectations in the days ahead. He was in effect embarked upon a quite different yet simultaneous pursuit of John and Mary. If he, as General Miles's secret agent, were to take full advantage of his contact with these two Sioux secret agents, he must make sure that he didn't make the slightest misstep in the sensitive area of their attitudes toward each other. His personal purpose demanded, for the same reason, as much circumspection. What seemed most likely was that these two had been lovers who had become in some way estranged. It was not yet clear to him how this might help or hinder either of his designs. There was the chance, for example, that if John remained obdurate her resentment might make her more susceptible. But what was clear was that John was as dangerous as a man as Mary was difficult as a woman. All in all, it appeared a more promising situation than any in which he had ever before become entangled. Having come to this satisfying conclusion, he, too, fell asleep.

When he awoke, cramped, Mary was sitting by the embers of the fire. John's blanket was unoccupied.

"Standing guard?" asked Kirk, indicating John's empty place.

"He went to Gunsight."

"What! That's more than twenty miles."

"For him — maybe three hours. That's his horse. He wants it." She did not seem greatly concerned by the risk John was running. "He'll be back by daylight."

She returned to her bed. When Kirk roused again there was a streak of dawn. Mary was sitting up in her blanket.

"He is coming," she said.

Presently Kirk, too, could hear. John appeared from down canyon, leading the buckskin stallion. The horse whinnied. Mary leaped up.

"Let me cool him," she said.

John handed her the reins and she walked the horse back down the canyon, murmuring to him as she went.

"That livery stable was right in the middle of town," said Kirk. "However'd you manage?"

"No trouble," said John. "When it comes to stealing horses you white men are all amateurs."

He stretched out on his blanket and fell asleep. Mary returned with the horse, tethered him, and withdrew to a spot below the camp where the stream widened into a pool. While bathing she caught a dozen trout with a forked stick. She came back to broil the trout. Kirk climbed to the canyon rim. There was nothing to see. He returned to the fire. At the precise moment the trout were ready John woke up. They breakfasted. John glanced at the sky.

"They ought to be getting here," he said.

The three climbed to the rim. The revenge-seeking riders from Gunsight were in view. Twenty or more were galloping along the construction road. Another sixty or seventy had dropped straight down from the switchback above and were moving across the flats below in a widely spaced line, as in a rabbit drive. The nearer twenty paused at the water tank to examine the ground and then galloped on east along the construction road.

The day's further developments demonstrated the sagacity of John's stratagem, as the fugitives contentedly noted when they climbed intermittently from the camp to peer over the rim. Remote spirals of dust indicated how widely and stubbornly the hunters were circling in their vain search for the trail of their prey.

"Only one way for them to figure it out," said Kirk. "The buckboard went up in a balloon."

In late afternoon the disgruntled posse came straggling past along the road up the ridge, walking their wearied horses back to Gunsight. Kirk and John began packing the wagon parts and cargo to the mouth of the canyon. By dusk they were ready. In the failing light they took one more look at Kirk's map.

"We have to get back over the hills to the valley of the White," said Kirk, "in order to strike north toward where Jared will be looking for me. But I hate to take the way we came along the railroad. It's long and takes us too near Gunsight. You must have cut straight over both times last night. What kind of going did you find?"

"Bad," said John. He indicated a spot on the map some miles to the northeast. "About here there used to be a buffalo trail running between the Niobrara and the White. They generally found as easy a way across country as was to be had."

Kirk realized enviously that John, young as he was, must, of course, have been able as a boy to range across these high plains at a time the buffalo still numbered in the hundreds of thousands.

"Let's try for it," he decided.

Getting across the sagebrush flats proved a reasonably simple matter. John rode ahead, selecting the most feasible path for the buckboard. A first-quarter moon hanging in the western sky gave enough light in that clear air to keep him in view even when his pathfinding led him a hundred yards in advance. They came upon the buffalo trail where John had expected to find it. It was overgrown with grass and weeds but remained sufficiently perceptible to follow. After some preliminary meandering it eventually led them up a long slanting ridge to the crest of the range and by equally convenient contours down the other side to the nearly dry bed of the White. The hills, which Kirk had considered their greatest obstacle, had proved no barrier at all.

Beyond the White they crossed the stage road connecting Gunsight and the Pine Ridge agency. After another two hundred yards, Kirk, at John's suggestion, pulled up and waited while John and Mary went back to remove all traces of their passing that might attract the attention of anyone among tomorrow's users of the road. It was a process that was costing a delay of nearly an hour. The moon was setting and they were about to be deprived of its faint but helpful light. Kirk had begun to fidget by the time they returned. Before remounting, John paused beside the buckboard.

"Just ahead," he said, "in the direction you want to go, is a belt of really rough country — maybe seven or eight miles deep, as I remember it. Be a job to get a wagon over it by day and it'll soon be too dark to see past your horses' heads. I think I can get you through. Otherwise, we'll have to circle ten miles back toward Gunsight and another ten miles up the other side." He waited for Kirk's verdict.

"Let's have a try at it," said Kirk.

He soon began to regret the decision. Their course was leading them into a maze of sand hills interspersed by deeply eroded gullies — a miniature Badlands. It was a region which, as John had said, might by day have seemed impassable for any wheeled vehicle. The moon had set, leaving the night too dark to distinguish John at even a dozen yards. Yet he had to weave and circle a quarter of a mile ahead in his urgent search for a conceivable route for the buckboard that might not end in some impasse in the hills which might require them to turn back altogether. To make possible this guidance from an invisible distance he was resorting to the night cries of the little ground owl. These were interpreted in whispers by Mary to Kirk to direct his management of the team.

"A little to the right," she would whisper. "A little more. Now straight ahead. Now to the left. Now ahead again. Now wait."

Kirk wrestled with his doubts but continued to lend himself to this nerve-racking procedure. The intermittent rasp of squeaks and chirps and hisses coming eerily out of the night ahead was strangely chilling, suggesting irrationally something inhuman luring him step by step to the brink of some final disaster. At times he sensed that the wheels were crunching along the very edge of declivities which in the darkness appeared bottomless. At other times they stood still for long desolating moments, the horses shivering and snorting, waiting for the owl's unearthly summons to be renewed. For all his disquiet, he found himself anticipating each moment Mary might again lean toward him to whisper instructions. Each time he became more conscious of her physical nearness as though a palpable warmth were radiating from her body to his.

Finally, there came from John, far ahead, not another weird owl's cry but a low yell of distinctly human elation. Kirk turned his horses down a long, suddenly smooth slope which continued until John loomed in the darkness, waiting for them.

"The great trace," he announced.

Kirk could not see in the darkness but he knew what John meant.

"I've heard of that," he said. "The route taken by the herds to get back and forth between the North Platte and the Cheyenne."

"Yes," said John. "It stretches almost due north to where your guide will be looking for you."

"It also stretches due south right past Gunsight," said Kirk. "Maybe you should drop down it a ways and check if we're being hunted in this direction. By daylight you should reach high enough ground to see if our friends in the town have any clever ideas."

"Yes, sir," said John. If there was a trace of irony in his tone it was too faint to grate.

"We'll keep on north," added Kirk, "until we find either Jared or a likely spot to camp."

John swung his horse south along the trace. Kirk turned the other way. The hundred-yard-wide, once deeply trodden trace was rough and pitted and choked with low brush, but compared to what they had been enduring it seemed a smooth highway.

The east finally began to pale. As the darkness yielded, previously unseen buttes and mesas sprang into existence on either hand. The growing light blackened the jagged skyline to the east and spread blue and mauve and presently pink shadows across the country ahead as far as the dark bulk of the Black Hills.

Kirk, rid of John for at least the next couple of hours, deliberately waited for a more sufficient light before even turning to look at Mary. She was once more enveloped in the blanket. Jolting on the hard seat, swaying to the bouncing of the wagon, her eyes were closed as though she were able to sleep. What he could see of her face was thinly powdered with dust. In this cold early-morning light there was not too much to distinguish her from any of the hundreds of other young squaws of whom he had taken so little notice during his recent travels with Jared.

Yet he could not look at her without seeing under the shapeless folds of the blanket the glistening nymph of the waterfall. He would never be able to look at her without seeing that vision nor would he be able to rest until he had recaptured the opportunity of that moment. Her eyes opened and, becoming aware of his regard, she gave him a half smile.

"I didn't want to wake you up," he said.

"You didn't, Mr. MacGregor."

"That won't do. I call you Mary and him John. So — my name's Mac." She considered this doubtfully.

"Yes," he insisted. "John, Mary and Mac." He slightly emphasized the alliteration.

"If you wish . . . Mac," she assented.

"Good. Now don't think I'm prying — though I'm going to sound like it. But . . . my boss, Remington, has come out here to write about Indians. If, when he shows up in a day or two, I can't answer any of the questions he's bound to ask about you and John and Sitting Bull he'll ship me back to Ogdensburg."

"Ogdensburg?"

"Where he and I live."

"What sort of questions would he want you to ask?"

"Maybe some you wouldn't want answered. So stop and think. And if something slips out you wish you hadn't said — just tell me so and I'll forget it. By now you know you can trust me. Or do you?"

She looked at him as searchingly as when first they had met. "After what you have done for us, it would not be easy to think anything else."

"Well, then — first off — who is John?"

"He is an orphan. He lives in Sitting Bull's house."

"Do you live there, too?"

"No. I work in the orphanage at Father Murphy's mission."

"Where'd John learn all that English?"

"Dartmouth."

"Good Lord. And how about yours? Wellesley?"

"Hardly. At our village school."

"No!"

"There and from a box of books."

Kirk could see that the longer they talked the more at ease with him she was becoming.

"Now, about Sitting Bull. Everybody in the country is talking about him. What kind of man is he really?"

Mary's face softened. "Arrogant. Obstinate. Superstitious. Cunning. Childish. A wonderful man. A truly great man."

"He's certainly got second sight when it comes to picking people to work for him. But why was somebody so bent on keeping John from getting back to him?"

"You already know about that. The agent at Standing Rock ordered John arrested because he had left the reservation without permission. The trader called John a horse thief because he wanted his horse."

"Then it wasn't because this trip John's coming back from was so important?"

"That is something you will have to ask John."

"How can I? He'll be in such a hurry to get back to Sitting Bull that the minute he catches up to us he'll be rushing off again."

"It is true that he is in a great hurry but first he will want to go to Pine Ridge."

"How can he do that now that he knows the Indian police are looking for him?"

"Now that he knows, he will have no trouble keeping out of their sight. And there is someone at Pine Ridge he has to see."

"Is this another big secret?"

Mary smiled. "No. This is something very simple and pleasant, for a change. Since John came through here, Dr. Charles Eastman has been given the post of reservation doctor at Pine Ridge. He graduated from Dartmouth the year before John started there and went on to Boston University to study medicine. He's a Santee and a distant relative of Mrs. McLaughlin, wife of the agent at Standing Rock. He and John have heard so much about each other that they naturally want to meet."

"I can see that." He had at least discovered John's imminent movements, which had been what he had needed most to learn, and, equally satisfying, the longer and more innocently they had talked the more Mary's vigilance had been relaxing. "I'm also beginning to see that whatever else Remington may want to know he'll have to dig out for himself. That leaves me with what I want to know." ·

"For instance?" said Mary, still off guard.

Kirk glanced toward the sun, which had climbed well above the sand hills.

"It's turning warm. So, for one instance, why don't you come out of that blasted cocoon?"

Ready to humor him in so small a matter, Mary stood up to unwind the enshrouding blanket. Kirk had been taking note, just ahead of the team, of a rock the size of a keg. Since it had gotten light he had been automatically twitching the reins to avoid such obstructions. This time he twitched them toward this one.

The wheel above which Mary was standing struck the rock and her side of the buckboard heaved violently upward. She was already off-balance while turning to drop the blanket behind the seat and the sudden jolt pitched her toward Kirk.

During the seconds since he had noticed the rock he had been waiting for this good fortune. He caught her in his arms and held her across his lap, her upturned face only inches from his. Her eyes were staring, startled, into his and her mouth opening in an exclamation of outrage. Upon those parted lips he pressed a kiss. It was a long, almost savage, kiss. She began immediately to struggle and he as immediately released her.

She sat up in the seat, looking away from him, breathing hard. But he saw that her hands were clasped in her lap. She was not reaching for the knife even though she had just been made so much more aware of his intentions than she could have been by any number of wheedling speeches.

"I suppose," she said in a low but strangely firm voice, "you think I deserved that."

"If by deserve you mean by the way you look — you most certainly did."

"No. I mean by the way I acted yesterday at the water tank. That was what made you think . . . what you do."

"Then you're doubly right. I've thought of nothing else since."

"I can think of nothing since but how foolish I was. There is no use my saying that Indians do not see the difference between clothes and no clothes that you whites see. That's no excuse for me. I knew well enough what you would think when you looked. But what I was most thinking about was that John was coming back."

"You thought you could have the go at your teasing because when he joined us you'd be safe?"

"No. I was safe then — as I still am. What I wanted was for him to notice when he joined us how you would keep looking at me."

Kirk could hear his own grunt, which came out as from a blow to his solar plexus. Never had his self-esteem suffered a sharper shock.

"So I'm left holding the sack. The whole frolic was just to trick me into making John jealous."

"Yes. But there was where I was the most foolish. I could see that he noticed but I could also see that he did not care who looked at me."

Kirk began reassembling his scattered forces.

"Not quite so fast. Give me a minute to get used to this. And you'd be smarter if you gave him a little more time, too."

"What for? As soon as I saw him again I was reminded how stubborn he can be. You cannot know how stubborn."

"Now wait a minute. You're just jumping at conclusions. How can you tell for sure so quick? After all, he's a man, isn't he? Give this scheme of yours more of a chance. I'll help any way I can. You don't have to worry about me now that I know what's up. I've never yet taken a real jump at a woman before she was ready. Though I must say I'm not sure you were as upset by that kiss as you thought you were." Kirk pointed. "Anyway, there's John coming — not from behind but over the hills from the east. He must have circled clear around by the Pine Ridge road. That horse of his can really cover ground. See, he's going to wait for us at that clump of cottonwood, where there's probably a spring and a place to camp. So we've got until we get there to work out how we're going to handle this."

"Don't make me feel more ashamed than I do."

"Nonsense. Hasn't been a woman since Eve who hasn't tried what you did. Now, how about this for a starter? John's going to Pine Ridge and then to Standing Rock. Remington and I will be headed the same way, though not, of course, so fast. Getting you home could hold John up some. So why don't I ask John if he's got any objection to our taking you with us as camp cook?"

Mary vigorously shook her head. "That is impossible. It is so impossible it does not make even a little sense."

"Don't keep going off half-cocked. You didn't listen to what I said. I didn't ask you if you wanted the job or would take the job. I asked you to let me put it up to John. He'll have to say no and then say why he's saying no and that'll put a stop to his straddling. That's what you want, isn't it?" For the first time since the kiss she had turned to look at him. "And don't look at me as if you were still in so much doubt about how far you can trust me."

They drove into the shade of the cottonwoods. Having cooled Puma, John released him to graze up the hillside and turned to help with the team.

"Nobody stirring toward Gunsight," he reported. "Nor along the Pine Ridge road." He glanced past Kirk toward the hills to the southwest. "But that might be your man."

On the distant horizon there was a speck which soon disappeared in a fold of the land. Mary began building a fire. John watered and rubbed down the team. Kirk cut and carried wood. When the speck next appeared it was from a clump of scrub juniper not a hundred yards away.

"He knows his way around, that one," murmured John.

Jared cantered forward and leaned from his saddle to grip Kirk's hand. He then ceremoniously greeted the two Indians. His Sioux was practical but required the occasional supplement of an elaborate resort to sign language. They replied agreeably in kind. Kirk let the semaphoring discussion run along awhile before he broke the news to Jared that he was being had.

"John and Mary tell me that Sitting Bull thinks very well of you," he said.

"What he actually says of you," said John in English, "is that you're the only honest white man he's ever known."

"He's also got a scar on his neck," said Mary, "that he says came from a time when being too young to know better he tried to steal a horse from you."

Jared chuckled, as much diverted as they by his recent sign language

rigmarole. "He ain't no liar." He pulled back his shirt to show a red
seam along his collarbone. "This here's the mate to his." He regarded
the two young Indians with new interest. "Me, I uster think I knowed
some about Indians. But . . . could be times is changin'."

He dismounted and untied the haunch of freshly killed antelope
swung at his saddle horn. Mary unobtrusively took it from him and
turned toward the fire.

"If you've nothing more on your mind than wandering about," said
Kirk, "why didn't you meet me at Gunsight?"

"The older I get, the curiouser I get," said Jared. "Bein' as how we
aim to travel some in Indian country, seemed like there'd be no harm in
tryin' to guess what the Indians got on their minds. No quicker way to
catch on to that than to take a herd o' six hundred cattle within a day's
ride o' six thousand hungry Sioux. So when I heard a fool cattleman
named Dabney had took off from the end of the railroad for the Black
Hills with beef for the mining camps I took off after him to have me a
look."

"What did you find out? John, here, is just as interested as we are."

"Old Two Strike, who's got so old he can't remember much since the
last time he was chased by Custer, let hisself get talked into ridin' off
with a pack of young braves not old enough to have anything to remember. They hid in the edge of the Badlands waitin' to jump Dabney's
cattle. But Red Cloud, who's as old as Two Strike and near blind besides
but has still got all his senses, he took off after them and kept them
arguin' so long the cattle got on past and out o' reach."

"A near thing," said Kirk.

He could see that John was regarding the incident even more gravely.
Two of the most respected and influential chiefs of the Sioux had been
involved and the more moderate had barely prevailed. Had the herd
been attacked and the cowhands tried to resist, the death of the white
men would have lifted the current frontier nervousness to the pitch of
total hysteria. It was apparent that John had not been fully prepared for
the change in the disposition of the Sioux that had developed during the
few weeks he had been away.

Jared attended to his horse and helped Kirk set up the tent. John
stretched out to sleep in the sun until Mary was ready to serve portions

of broiled antelope. Kirk could see the growing approval with which Jared was regarding the two young Indians. To consolidate the impression he described in some detail the genesis of his own acquaintance with them.

"Never knowed nobody 'cept old Stud hisself could get into more different kinds of trouble than you can," said Jared. He cast a reflective glance at Mary. "Nor nobody but him could come out of it with a likelier luck." He stood up, wiping his mouth. "Thankee, ma'am. That antelope tasted a sight better than if'n I'd of cooked it." He turned to Kirk. "With the wagon and that tired team it'll take you the rest of today and most of tomorrow forenoon to get over the hills to Pine Ridge. So maybe I better ride on ahead to the agency to see if there ain't some word from Fred. Could be I'll have to go down to Gunsight to meet him. If no, then I'll meet you somewhere tomorrow morning."

They watched him ride away.

"He is a good man," said John.

He was getting up, looking toward the grazing Puma. Kirk's eyes met Mary's. Hers were troubled and doubtful but she nodded. Kirk rose beside John.

"I have a proposition to make. We need a camp cook. Would you have any objection, John, to my offering Mary the job?"

John's glance went swiftly from Kirk to Mary and back to Kirk, though his face remained expressionless.

"Why should I have any objection? I hope she takes it. Nothing would suit me better."

He was getting together his saddle and gear as though the matter were already settled. Kirk's and Mary's eyes met again. Her dismay made it easier to conceal from her how contented he was with the results of his gamble.

X

JOHN WALKED BEYOND the edge of the cottonwoods before whistling for Puma. He had had the two months that he had been away to get used to the idea that in the days and maybe years ahead he could not permit himself to depend on Mary, or, what was infinitely more important, permit her to depend on him. That early dawn in her father's trading post he had been shaken by the sudden realization that he was too poor to take a wife, certainly one who deserved what Mary did. Thereafter a more implacable barrier had loomed. In his travels through the other Sioux reservations and the western nations he had been made appallingly aware of how desperate was the Indian situation. All, including the once mighty Sioux, were destitute, hopeless, dependent from day to day on the sufferance of the ancient enemy that now so closely encircled them. There was no way to evade what was demanded of him. As one of the few Indians with personal acquaintance with the white world's complexities he must devote whatever future he could foresee to counseling and defending his doomed people. In such a future there was no place for wife and family.

He had schooled himself to the acceptance of this idea. It was a totally reasonable idea, sound, responsible, incontrovertible. Yet when he had seen her again, awaking from his doze in the railroad car to find her miraculously bending over him, he had in that instant realized that he had not become in the slightest resigned to being without her, or ever could.

He knew Mary would follow him from camp and was glad that Puma reached him before she did. But for once she paid no attention to the stallion. She was looking only at him.

"The white man," she said, as though the three words made a complete statement. "Can't you see? He does not want me by his fire. He wants me in his tent."

John was placing bridle and saddle on Puma.

"Many men have wanted you. For years. Always before you have known what to do about that."

"You have the same as given me to him. That has never happened before."

"I will never be far away. Anyway, at night."

"There will be no need for you to watch. I will not stay with him."

"Yes, you will. If you will listen I will tell you why you will."

"Nothing you can say —"

"Will you listen? When I visited the western nations there was much talk everywhere of a white man who had passed the same way as I a month before. He pretended to be on a hunting trip but in one reservation after another he was always hanging around the dancing. This same Jared, who's now supposed to be Remington's guide, was that man's guide. There could be no question that he was spying upon Indians for somebody. It could have been the railroads, or the Indian Bureau, or some Indian aid society, or . . . the army."

Mary turned to look back at Kirk shaving at a mirror hung to his tent pole.

"What makes you so sure he was that man?"

"You know that when Indians talk about how anybody looks they go into detail that even a camera would miss. There can be no question. I realized that the moment I saw him."

"And now that you've seen more of him, listened to him talk, noticed his manner, you've made up your mind that he is an army officer."

"Yes."

"And telling me makes you feel safer about leaving me with him. Knowing he's not only a white man but a white soldier will make me less likely to go into his tent. Is that it?"

"You're not a slut, so don't talk like one. I'm telling you so you'll know that you have to stay with him. So that you'll realize what you have to do. You don't have to crawl under his blanket. You only have to work for him and stay as near him as you can. You must not let him see that you suspect him but you must be alert to catch his every attitude. He's an enemy spy. And now he's spying in our country — the Sioux country. You must notice and estimate and anticipate — what he is thinking as well as what he is saying and doing. Because when the time comes we must be able to guess what kind of a report he may be making to his superiors. With a war possible you can understand how much may depend on that, can't you?"

"Yes," said Mary. "I can. I will do my best."

John vaulted on Puma and was off. He could feel in the middle of his back the impact of Mary's following gaze. It was a sensation that could have seemed no greater an ordeal were he riding away from the bent bows of a hundred enemies, from which as many arrows were taking flight.

He was nearing the border of the reservation before he was forced to realize that no matter what the risk of wasting another whole day he could not go on. He circled back and watched from a high ridge until in the far distance the tiny spot that was the wagon came into view. Thereafter he kept it in sight until in the evening Kirk stopped to camp.

For once John tethered Puma, to make sure he did not stray or possibly drift toward the scent of the campfire. Then he crept to a nearer hilltop. Kirk was taking care of his team. Mary was building a fire and preparing to broil what remained of the antelope. As it grew darker, John edged nearer, though, knowing the acuteness of Mary's senses, not so near that there was the faintest chance of her detecting his presence.

When they had finished eating, they sat for a while talking. He was too far away to hear what they were saying but their lack of animation made it seem a casual, even desultory, conversation. When they rose to retire the tent had still not been set up. Kirk brought the tarpaulin from the wagon and spread it by the fire. Mary settled upon it and drew her blanket over her. Kirk rolled in his under the wagon a good fifty feet away.

John dozed through the night. With the first streak of daylight he withdrew to his hilltop. Kirk and Mary rose, breakfasted, broke camp, hitched up, and drove on. John recovered Puma and galloped on ahead, keeping behind the screen of hills and circling to the north to avoid any chance of encountering Jared, in the event he might be returning. The uneventfulness of his night's surveillance had left him oddly dissatisfied, not only with himself but with Mary and even with Kirk. He realized that he had subconsciously hoped that something would occur to require him to rush in and reassume responsibility for Mary.

At the first herd of grazing Oglala horses he came upon, he sent the herdsboy to summon Half-Moon. Within an hour the lieutenant of the Pine Ridge Indian Police came cantering over the hill to pull up his horse where John was waiting. The policeman was fat and fifty and regarded the world about him with an air of amiable dignity. There was nothing in the benevolent complacency of his outward demeanor to suggest that stowed in the bottom of the medicine bag at the head of his bed was a clump of more white scalps than had ever been taken by any other Oglala or that since he had become a policeman his authority had been questioned in the single instance of a wandering Miniconjou whose wits had been scattered by sunstroke.

"I hear you have an order to arrest me," said John.

"And that I will," said Half-Moon, beaming, "when you pound on the agent's door, push into his office, and tell him that you want him to order me to take you."

He handed over the Chippewa bow and quiver which John had left with him on his way through Pine Ridge two months before to take the train at Gunsight. John slipped the strap of the quiver over his shoulder and began stringing the bow.

"The horse trader, Banks — is he here?"

"He came through yesterday but he did not stop. He said he was going to the Rosebud but he took the north trail so it is more likely that he was headed for the Cheyenne River reservation."

"I also hear that the Oglala are dancing again," said John.

"Every night," said Half-Moon. "In the spring they only danced to pass the time and to bother the agent. But now it is different. They are seeing visions."

"What's the agent doing?"

"He does not know what to do. He has been waiting for the new agent to come. But today he decided that he had to do something. So tonight he will go to the dance ground and tell them to stop."

"What about the police?"

"He will take us with him."

"What will happen?"

"Nothing." Half-Moon beamed again. "What can thirty police do if a thousand Oglala do not want to stop?"

John took his leave and circled again so that he might approach from the rear the house of Red Cloud on the bluff above the agency. The many promises in the treaties wrung from the government by Red Cloud's victories in the Plains wars of the sixties had been soon dishonored by the white signers but the personal benefits still being showered upon him were marks of the concern with which the aging commander's prowess was still regarded. The Oglala chief had been endowed with this commodious frame residence and as recently as the year before had been voted twenty-eight thousand five hundred dollars by Congress, ostensibly in reimbursement for horses confiscated from his band during the Custer campaign but actually as a bribe to solicit his continued good behavior. His career had been a glittering example of the truism that among Indians it was never the meek or the humble who inherited government favor.

Several families of Red Cloud's relatives had usurped as their residence the big feed barn flanking the corral, while clustered about were a dozen tepees of his immediate followers. It was past noon but most cooking fires had just been lighted and people were only now arising, a sure sign that the night had been devoted to dancing. But there was an instant excited gathering about John as he turned Puma into the corral. The acclaim was not for him but for the horse, which any Sioux could see at a glance was one in a thousand.

The pillars, roof and most of the floor of the back porch of the house had been dismantled, evidently to meet the previous winter's overriding need for firewood. Red Cloud's favorite horse was tethered by the kitchen door, a mark of the old warrior's lifelong habit of having his best mount always at hand not only for instant use but to keep him safe from theft. The oldest wife peered from the doorway and hurried off to announce the visitor's arrival.

The main room of the house, stretching across its front, looked like an ill-kept warehouse superimposed upon the disordered interior of an oversize tepee. In the center of the floor on a square of sheet iron burned a small fire, the smoke from which rose to curl in wreaths about the blackened ceiling. Ranged about the fire were a number of low lounging pads covered with moth-eaten buffalo robes and bearskins. Scattered about the room, leaning in corners, hanging on the walls, suspended from the rafters, were lances, shields, bows, war clubs, medicine bags, storage baskets, skins of grease, pots, saddles, feathered headdresses, pictographs. Incongruously obtrusive among this jumble of primary Sioux furnishings were articles of white manufacture, including two new brassbound trunks, a rocking chair, an unused sewing machine, a mahogany chest of drawers, a never-assembled brass bed, a Franklin stove still in its unopened, dust-covered shipping crate.

"The young man from Sitting Bull's camp," announced the old woman.

Red Cloud rose from his backrest in the darkest corner of the room and extended his hand in welcome. He was tall and emaciated but still erect and his wrinkled face still presented the fierce profile of a hawk though his eyes were bleared and so nearly sightless that John was obliged to reach for his groping hand. He returned to his seat and John sat on a corner of a pad before him. The old woman served them bowls of leek soup and chunks of hastily warmed corn cake.

Their conversation initially dwelt upon the ritualistic civilities decreed by custom. They exchanged polite references to the weather, to Sitting Bull's health, to the excellence of John's stallion, which had attracted wide attention during his former brief visit, to the manifest comforts of Red Cloud's house, to the new Indian doctor who was fulfilling so great a need. After the presentation of pipes, John at length ventured an approach to the business upon which he had come.

"I have heard that Two Strike was of a mind to take the miners' cattle herd."

Red Cloud responded with immediate angry vigor.

"His people are hungry. And so are my people. But in his old age he has become so foolish that he can no longer remember what moon it is. How can a man who has been to war as many times as Two Strike ever forget that when winter is upon us is no time to start one. In the winter there is no feed for our horses, no shelter for our people. The soldiers like the winter. They wait for it. When the snow is deep it is easier for them to catch and kill our women and children."

The old commander's grasp of strategy had been tempered by the bitter memories of many tragedies. The greatest Indian disasters of the last quarter-century had occurred in the depths of winter, when the better supplied and clothed army could take the field while the Indians were obliged by blizzards to cower in their flimsy encampments.

"It will be worse now," suggested John, "with all these new railroads, by which the soldiers can travel hundreds of miles in a day and the telegraph, which enables the generals to speak to each other across any distance."

Red Cloud did not appear impressed by the significance of these modern novelties. He was concerned by the inherent hazards of winter campaigning but all of his conceptions of warfare seemed still attached to the days when Indian forces could under all ordinary circumstances move so much more swiftly than white and when their supply depots, the buffalo herds, were always at hand.

"My good friend, Sitting Bull — what does he think?" he asked, pursuing his own train of thought.

"He thinks we should plow and plant," said John, "so that we no longer have to beg at the white man's door. He thinks only when we need ask the white man for nothing can we become Sioux again."

Red Cloud considered this view and wagged his head regretfully. "He may still be a prophet. But he is no longer a warrior."

This distinction between their areas of leadership so excited him that he got to his feet, so that he might more expressively gesticulate, and launched into a rhetorical account of his storied exploits as a warrior and a leader of warriors. He presently became so impassioned that he had forgotten John's presence. He was omitting no slightest detail as he relived those days of glory. There was some excuse for his exultation. Others had won battles but the only war ever won by the Indians of the plains against the army of the United States had been under his command.

John, politely attending the protracted unfolding of the epic, edged nearer the window which offered an expansive view of the agency area below, a panorama the appreciation of which had been denied the house's master by his failing eyesight. Pine Ridge was a more pretentious establishment that the one at Standing Rock. The Oglala were the most primitive and intransigent of the Sioux and more care had been taken to satisfy their needs. There was a two-story frame boarding school topped by a belfry, a very large commissary, an equally large storehouse, barracks, barns, corrals, a trading post, a tavern, a church, a mission, the agent's residence, a water tower, and, rising from the middle of the compound, a tall flagpole from which rippled the American flag. It was still not midafternoon but dancing was already under way on the wide dancing ground beside White Clay Creek, though so far there seemed more onlookers than dancers. Then he saw the wagon coming down the slope from the west and his attention centered on that.

With Jared riding at the tailgate, it pulled alongside a small detached house which had a small corral behind it, holding one horse. Mary ran from the wagon to talk to this horse, which must be the one she had ridden from Standing Rock, so evidently the house was Dr. Eastman's residence. After a few moments Mary and Kirk crossed the compound on foot to the administration building, before one door of which a line of people was waiting. This was apparently the doctor's office. After another few minutes they came out again, returned to the wagon and then, with the camera tripod over Kirk's shoulder, the two of them made their way to the dancing ground. Jared remained with the wagon, attending to the horses and setting up camp.

Red Cloud came at last to the end of his declamation, an end which he punctuated with a scalp halloo delivered with such vigor that his voice cracked. He dropped wearily back into his seat.

"Those were great days," said John. "The Sioux were many. The buffalo were many. And the white men — they were not so many."

Red Cloud appeared not to have heard. He was still dwelling on the thought that had precipitated his outburst.

"Sitting Bull makes medicine. He does not make war."

His voice trailed off and he began to nod.

"I can see that they are dancing down there by the creek," said John.

This brought the old chief's head up and a final flare of vibrancy into his speech.

"That is good. That is very good. They must dance harder and harder. All through the winter they must dance. Because that will bring the millennium in the spring, when the Messiah will come. He will lead us. He will make the white men weak as water. The summer will be before us and we will drive them forever from our land."

Exhausted, Red Cloud again nodded and this time he slept.

John tiptoed out, dropped down the steep trail to the agency grounds, and took his place at the tail of the line of patients waiting outside the doctor's door. With a fold of his blanket wrapped about his mouth, as Indians were accustomed to do when afflicted by bronchial ailments, he was safe even from having it noticed that he was a stranger. He waited patiently while the line hitched forward. When his turn had come to enter the doctor's office, he pulled aside the blanket and announced himself:

"Dr. Eastman, I'm John Winthrop."

The doctor jumped up from the kitchen table that served him as a desk to rush forward with outstretched hand. He was tall and lean and quick and had a look about him that made John think of how Red Cloud must have looked thirty years ago. On Charles Eastman a war bonnet might have seemed more natural than did his white coat.

"I'm really happy to know you, John," he exclaimed. "Would you believe it — when I heard of your business in the barn with Jeff Bradford I sold my only good pair of shoes to make the trip up from Boston to congratulate you. But you'd already left Dartmouth. What had struck you?"

"It all of a sudden came over me that I needed air."

"I can remember the same symptom. Tell me. You sweated in white schools almost as long as I did. What most helped you to stand it?"

"Constantly reminding myself that I was better than any of them. I believe that's true. I think we all are."

"You mean that they've kept licking us only because they outnumber us?"

"That. Plus the fact that they fight to win. We fight either for fun or to prove we're not scared."

"While the more scared they get the more unspeakable the advantages they take. And don't forget. We're better than they in more important ways than fighting. And by better I mean more civilized, more honorable. It can pretty well be summed up in one count. We keep our word. They never do. But once I get on this subject I can't stop. Excuse me a moment."

Eastman went to the door, spoke briefly to the three patients who had joined the line behind John, and came back in. "Nothing wrong with any of them that can't wait till morning. There's enough real sickness around to break your heart but half the patients that come to see me just come to get a close look at the fool Indian who imagines he's learned enough to set up shop as a physician."

"But what a good thing for them you stuck it out — I mean until you could set up your shop here."

"I suppose so. Though there's so much more to be done than one man can do. And the healing they most need is beyond the treatment of any human physician."

"Or any help. People who have lost all hope are already dying."

The doctor drew a long breath so slowly that pain seemed to have permeated even the air around him. "That may not be quite as true as it sounds. Weak as he is, a man is a curiously invulnerable animal. He can endure almost anything. Someday the Indians who manage to survive will begin to pick up the pieces and try putting them together again." He fumbled for his pipe. "Mary says you've been traveling. What do you make of this dance?"

"On the western reservations it's a species of peace dance. They've patched a hodgepodge of bastard Christianity on equally bastard Indian supernaturalism. Their basic tenet is that if we can learn to love everybody — even the whites — we can yet be saved."

"By taking enough opium we can at least disguise our distress. Is that it?"

"Yes. But the Sioux are not natural pacifists. What they'll make of it can be something quite different. This has been Kicking Bear's second try at planting it here. Since his first go missed fire he may have come back with more interesting bait."

"I gather he did. I met him while he was preaching here last week before rushing on to inculcate the Brulé. He's a genuine mystic. Though the ferocity of his hatred of whites drops him something short of the role of holy man. However, if the dance keeps them preoccupied until winter drives them to cover, may it not be serving some purpose?"

"Possibly. Red Cloud, for example, foresees the Oglala dancing as a kind of girding for next summer's campaign season."

Eastman poked somberly at his pipe. "They never learn, do they? Here we're in as helpless a fix as if we'd already been herded off to Indian Territory. Yet you have to admire some of these old chiefs. No matter how prostrate they've been beaten they can't forget that once they were free and to them that means free to obey the natural impulse to strike back."

"But neither must we forget that what they are dreaming can mean our final extermination and the only problem that will solve will be the white man's."

"That leaves the dance still a godsend. It can be at least postponing the evil moment."

John shook his head. "Only in the Indian case. The dance can cut both ways. You can tell by all the hullabaloo being raised about it by frontier politicians, border newspapers, western congressmen, and the railroad people, that the country is being prepared for any excuse to sic their soldiers on us."

There came a knock at the door. After a brief colloquy outside, Eastman returned, taking off his white coat.

"Speak of the devil and up he pops. The agent is taking his police to back his order that the dancing stop. He wants me to accompany him. He must think there could be need for a doctor."

"What he more likely thinks is that he'll be safer with you at his elbow. He knows what the Oglala think of you. But ten to one there'll be no trouble. Trust Half-Moon for that."

"From what I've seen of the old rascal, I'd guess you're right. If so, come around to my house tonight after the dust settles. One of my patients has given me a haunch of venison and your Mary is cooking it for me."

They went out into the slanting light from a sun dipping behind the western hills. Eastman headed for the agent's house and John for the dancing ground. Some hundreds of Oglala had already assembled and more were streaming in. With the approach of darkness there had developed a tendency for warriors to replace women and children in the central circles of active dancers.

With his first glance John began to appreciate the underlying differences between this Sioux rite and the Ghost Dances he had previously observed. In all outward trappings and attitudes it was the same. There were the same beseeching gestures toward the upper reaches of the sky, the same red circles, crescents, and crosses painted on the dancers' forehead, cheeks, and chin to represent the sun, moon, and morning star, the same eagle feather in the hair to suggest the dancers' readiness to fly upward into the heavens to meet the hosts of their returning ancestors, the same gaunt Prayer Tree to mark the site of the Messiah's reappearance, and the same white Ghost Shirts to symbolize the dancers' capacity to transport their mortal bodies into the spirit world. But here these supernatural aspirations were infused with other attitudes more demanding and more aggressive. Essential elements in Wovoka's doctrine had been the disavowal of every form of violence and the renunciation of all articles of white manufacture, particularly firearms. But the Oglala men had come armed to this dancing ground. Some handed their weapons to their onlooking wives but others continued boldly to clutch rifle or bow or tomahawk while dancing.

Upon his return from his second western pilgrimage Kicking Bear must indeed have taken care to advocate modifications of doctrine more appealing to the Sioux than the dance had originally been for them in the spring. John soon detected with what demonic cunning he had proclaimed the foremost among these revised tenets. This was the persuasion that prolonged dancing could render the wearer's Ghost Shirt bulletproof. To so innately belligerent a people as the Sioux no promise could have a greater appeal. Having successfully stirred the Oglala to this intensity of excitement, Kicking Bear was pressing on to preach the same doctrine of unreason to the Brulé and the Miniconjou. John was possessed by a chilling apprehension that he was picking up a trail that was leading inexorably to ultimate disaster. Among the Sioux the Ghost Dance could be on its way to becoming the war dance that ignorant and self-serving whites had from the outset alleged it to be.

He began edging his way through the crowd encircling the dancing ground, listening to the general talk and noting the reactions to the dancing. Every evidence was discouraging. The Oglala were more than excited. They were in a frenzy of anticipation. There was a universal disposition to envisage the Ghost Dance as a means to assure the assistance of supernatural power, allied with which they could be certain of overthrowing the white man. While listening to what people were saying and studying the expressions on their faces, he all but stumbled over Mary and Kirk before he realized that he had come upon them.

It had been more than an hour since the light had been strong enough for photography and they were sitting side by side under the tripod, ostensibly watching the dancing but much more engrossed in each other. Mary was leaning toward him, smiling, nodding, her entire attention upon whatever he was saying. There was a familiarity, even an intimacy, in their attitudes that contrasted strikingly with their deportment by the campfire last night. During the morning drive they must have become much better acquainted.

He was beginning to back away carefully when he saw over the heads of the dancers the column of police appearing around the corner of the barracks to start down the long slope toward the dancing ground. The agent and Dr. Eastman had come out of the agent's house and were angling across toward the tail of the column. John worked his way back nearer Mary. For all of Half-Moon's confidence, when two bodies of armed men came face to face there could always be some misguided dolt who fires a first shot to put an end to all restraint. Mary caught a glimpse of the moccasins below the edge of his blanket.

"John," she exclaimed, getting to her feet.

"Thought the police were after you," said Kirk, looking up.

"The agent has something else for them to do," said John, nodding toward the approaching column.

Kirk sprang to his feet and looked, scowling.

"The goddam fool," he said. He shoved Mary toward John. "Look after her."

He shouldered backward through the press and started running around outside the crowd encircling the dancing ground, apparently with some idea of remonstrating with the agent. The dancers continued their dance, though they had ceased their singing and testifying, giving their soundless contortions a dreamlike quality. The women and children among the onlookers on the side toward which the police were advancing were scurrying between the dancers to the refuge of the opposite side, where John and Mary stood. At the same time men from their side were running across to join their comrades facing the oncoming police. Soon a solid rank of several hundred warriors was interposed between the police and the dancing ground. The array bristled with weapons.

As the confrontation became step by step more imminent so complete a hush had settled that the thin wail of an infant in a tepee a half-mile away was audible. The police came stolidly on until the head of the column was within a hundred yards and then fifty. Among the waiting Oglala there was no stir, not by so much as the twitch of a finger. Half-Moon's shout of command was loud in the silence. The police swung from the marching column into a line facing the rank of warriors. At a second command they came to a halt. At a third, the policemen smartly lowered their carbines from their shoulders, planted the butts on the ground, and folded their hands over the barrels in the formalized attitude of parade rest.

"Good old Half-Moon," John murmured to Mary.

The significance of the police posture of nonviolence was unmistakable. The threat had been ludicrously brief and was already ended. A laugh started among the Oglala, rose to a roar, and died away in a medley of taunts and jeers. Half-Moon appeared not to have heard. The agent was equipped with enough common sense to realize immediately the necessity of cutting his loss. To save some face, if not to retrieve much from the fiasco, he stepped in front of the police to address the Oglala. In an expressionless monotone Dr. Eastman interpreted for him.

"I came here this evening to remind you once more that this dancing can cause you nothing but trouble. You have again refused to listen to my advice. You leave me nothing to do but to report your misconduct to the government of the United States, which will take such measures as seem appropriate. That is all."

Flanked now by Kirk, who had reached his side, as well as by Dr. Eastman, the agent turned to begin the long walk back to his house. At the bark of one more of Half-Moon's commands, the police about-faced, wheeled into column, and marched toward their barracks. The warriors broke into groups to embark upon exultant discussions of their victory.

"You don't look pleased," said Mary.

"The Oglala have made a fool of the agent," said John. "He, maybe because he wanted it that way, has made it harder for his successor. But the situation for the Sioux has been made much worse."

He put the tripod on his shoulder and started with Mary for the wagon. The twilight was rapidly darkening. When they were free of the crowd he slowed his pace.

"What do you make of him so far?" he demanded.

"You mean Mac?"

"Whatever he calls himself."

"When he first looked at the dancing he pretended only to be taking pictures but underneath he was excited. It was not at all as though he had seen the Ghost Dance many times before among the western nations."

"No wonder. This one excited me, too. Because it was so different from what either of us saw out there. The Sioux have turned a religious dance into a war dance."

"That was how it looked to me. It made me feel at first sad and then . . . well, terrified."

"What I want most to know is how it made him feel. He is in a position where with a few words he can do the Sioux very much harm. What I really mean is how does he feel about Indians? How did he look while he was watching the dance? Is he like some whites who think of us as partly human or like most who think of us as no more than dogs?"

"He is maybe somewhere in between. When he looks at the dancers he does not see any of the hopelessness, the despair, that they are trying to escape. But he speaks respectfully of Sioux like Sitting Bull or Red

Cloud. And he most certainly does not think you are a dog. He thinks you are wonderful."

"And you?"

"What he thinks about me is no longer so plain as it was at first. From the moment we were alone after you left us he became almost like we were old friends who had known each other a long time. Before, the way he had looked at me made me want to hide or reach for my knife. But last night we talked about things that had nothing to do with my being a woman and his being a man. Today we talked about many other things. We even laughed because when he laughed I was able also to laugh."

"Don't be so easily fooled," said John. "I know his kind. He has had his way with many women. He has seen that you are not to be had just by reaching for you. So he is now willing to wait until you are more used to him. You must be more than ever on your guard."

"What do you want of me," said Mary, suddenly angry. "First you tell me to stay close to him. Then you tell me to stay away from him. What kind of a dog in the manger are you?"

"I will tell you what kind," said John, as quickly angered. "If I thought this white man's intentions were honest I would say to take him because never among your own people will you ever be able to marry half as well."

The wagon loomed before them. Jared was not in evidence but the shadowy figures of Kirk and Eastman were approaching from the direction of the agent's house.

"Even a greenhorn easterner like me," Kirk was saying, "could see what a howling mistake that was." He saw the two in the shadows. "Good for you, Mary. You brought the wanderer along. Thank you, John, for lugging in the camera."

"Come in, come in," said Eastman, opening the back door of his house. "It is better to celebrate a small victory than to bewail a great one."

It was Kirk's fingers that touched Mary's arm in guidance up the single step as they followed their host. The darkness within was relieved by the flare of a match.

"Of all the momentous inventions of civilization," said Eastman, "none equals the convenience of the humble match."

The glow from a kerosene lamp illuminated the room. Entering behind Mary and Kirk, John saw how instantly in the first flare of light she looked at Kirk.

The single room of the cottage was barely furnished with a small iron cookstove in one corner, a cot against the opposite wall, a pine table, two stools and a pair of wooden boxes to serve as chairs, and a shelf on which was ranged a few dishes and kitchen utensils.

"There's the venison," said Eastman. In his excessive cheerfulness there was an undercurrent of excitement as though he were anticipating some unusual event. "With grazing what it's been this year you'll probably have to boil it for hours. Only I haven't a pot big enough. We may have to rely on Mr. MacGregor's generosity."

Kirk, too, was in high spirits, though with more immediately apparent reason. "Anything your camp affords is always at Mary's disposal. My friend Remington planned to travel like a prince and his food box is crammed with hopeful items."

Mary pulled away the paper and examined the meat.

"It's not too old," she pronounced, poking it with a finger, "and not too terribly lean. We can lard it with bacon, stick a few cloves in it, and bake it in the oven like a ham."

"So epicurean a prospect demands a libation, however modest," said Eastman. He knelt, groped under the cot, and rose with a squat black bottle which he shook speculatively. "Prescription brandy — enough for a spoonful apiece. Which we will have as soon as I can get back."

He set the bottle on the table and was turning toward the front door when from outside came the sound of running footsteps. The door flew open as Eastman was reaching for the knob. A chestnut-haired, blue-eyed, fresh-faced young woman darted in and clasped his arms.

"Charles, Charles," she exclaimed. "I was so glad to see your light. I'd been so worried about you."

Too late she realized the presence of the other people in the room, snatched her hands from his arms, and blushed furiously.

"I was on my way to get you, Elaine," said Eastman, taking the awkward moment in stride. "But what a good thing I was slow for otherwise we'd have missed your so charming entrance. May I make you acquainted with my new friends, Miss Chadron, Mr. MacGregor, and Mr. Winthrop. This is Miss Elaine Goodall, a teacher at the boarding school. Once we were fellow Bostonians but I did not have the good fortune to meet her until the government in its infinite wisdom assigned us to our posts here."

Recovering her equanimity, Elaine smiled, acknowledging the introductions with a pleasing simplicity, her glance returning to Mary repeatedly, whose contrasting garb and color and fluent English appeared immediately to intrigue her. Eastman further eased the situation by administering the brandy spoonful by spoonful to his guests. Supper preparations were resumed. John brought in wood. Kirk and Mary raided the Remington food box. Eastman and Elaine became involved, with much whispering together, in sorting and arranging the few dishes.

When all had reassembled, John sat on the cot in the background, watching the others as they hovered about Mary while she prepared the venison for the oven. Their gay talk and gay laughter was incessant. The significance of the tableau had become inescapable. To John, Kirk and Mary seemed no less than Eastman and Elaine to be lovers in the early throes of discovering each other. The intermixture of race was making the experience the more intriguing, the more dramatic.

He was more certain than before that Kirk had no other thought than a passing seduction, though clearly he had by now been so captivated that he was prepared to devote to the project whatever patience and persistence might prove required. John was as certain that Mary would, for some while longer, at the worst, continue to resist, though at the moment her behavior was bound to raise her suitor's hopes. There was the chance, of course, that some of her heedlessness sprang from the circumstance that he, John, was looking on.

Jared scratched at the door. Kirk went out and returned.

"Would you excuse us, Dr. Eastman, Miss Goodall," he said. "We'll be only a minute. Mary, John, will you come outside?"

They stood by the wagon in the faint light from a window.

"We'll have to revise our route a little," said Kirk. "The wire from Remington says he'll get to Fort Bennett next Saturday. He says he'll wait for Jared and me there but obviously we can't let him wait long. So we'll have to shorten our stay here and cut north from here for the Cheyenne River reservation, leaving a visit to the Rosebud until later."

He peered inquiringly at John, who shook his head.

"I have to get back to Standing Rock as soon as possible so I'll have to take in the Rosebud on my way. There's no use my trying to report to Sitting Bull without knowing what's happening on these southern reservations. However, if I leave right now I can make the Rosebud and still get to Fort Bennett before you."

"What about Mary? Does she stay here, go with you or go with me?"

"Ask Mary."

Both looked at her. In the dim light her face was perfectly composed.

"I'll go with Mac," she said. She met Kirk's look. "That is, if you still want me."

"Of course I want you. Then everything's settled."

John said good-bye to Eastman and Elaine, climbed the bluff to Red Cloud's corral, and rode eastward through hills that were ghostly in the starlight. At noon next day he paused to rest but, discovering he could not sleep, continued on foot, leading Puma, trusting that if he ran long enough and hard enough he might get exhausted enough to sleep. Still he found no rest.

As he approached the Rosebud the next dawn the first Brulé he encountered was a man out looking for a strayed colt who turned out to be Broken Axe, whom he had known when both were with the circus. Broken Axe walked his horse alongside for a time while with great relish he described some of the many entertaining developments of recent days on the Rosebud reservation.

"We have no agent at all now," he said. "George Wright, our old agent, was suspended when the census takers' count showed only fifty-two hundred and fifty Brulé, while the agent had been drawing rations for seventy-five hundred. It hadn't been the agent's fault but all the same the government blamed him for it. So everybody's doing just as they please. The police are paying no attention to anything. They're having as good a time as anybody."

"How about the dancing?"

"They're dancing all the time. Naturally everybody got excited when they heard Kicking Bear explain about the Messiah coming in the spring and how when that happens we can put on our Ghost Shirts and chase the whites clear back to Washington."

"Do you believe that?"

"Why not? Kicking Bear isn't the only one. Short Bull and Mash-the-Kettle know about the Messiah too. They have seen him and talked to him. They were afraid to tell us before because they were afraid we wouldn't believe them. But after Kicking Bear came they began to talk. They told how when they went to the Rocky Mountains last summer they saw this vision. That was when they saw what the Messiah was doing. He was beginning to roll up the earth and push it east towards us. Behind where he was rolling it up they saw herds of buffalo and bright streams and lots of grass and everything just like it used to be." Broken Axe pulled in his horse. "But I got to find me that colt so I can get back in time for the ration issue. The contract cattle were delivered to the agency last night and with nobody to look after the issue I don't want to miss what can happen."

Riding toward the agency, John saw evidence on every hand of the new exuberance that had taken possession of the Brulé. Men were dashing about purposelessly on horseback. Children were laughing and screaming. Women were clustered in gleefully gossiping groups. The few police were strolling about with unbuttoned uniforms and foolish grins. The whole atmosphere was that of a carnival. The Brulé were ripe for mischief to an even more dangerous degree than the Oglala.

Everybody was drifting toward the big commissary corral, where the ration cattle were penned. The contract delivery had consisted of some three hundred Texas longhorns. They were huge animals, gaunt, rangy, fierce, and largely inedible. The contractor and his cowhands had departed. The problem of equable distribution was now one for the Brulé to solve.

The senior chief of the Brulé, ancient Two Strike, sat on his horse beside the corral, listening vaguely to the suggestions being showered on him from all quarters. Ordinarily cattle were killed within the enclosure, butchered by the women, and the distribution of the meat by family allotment supervised by the agent with the assistance of his police.

The increasingly vociferous arguments about procedure were brought to a sudden explosive conclusion, which ended all debate. Someone had been inspired to throw open the gate of the corral. The restlessly milling longhorns instantly bolted through it, charged through the crowd, and stampeded toward the hills.

The Brulé greeted the breakout with howls of delight. The utter bliss of the opportunity was at once appreciated by all. Men leaped on their horses and set off in pursuit, brandishing their rifles or bows. The occasion offered all of the long-lost gratification of a buffalo hunt with the added advantage that these great beasts with their enormous spread of horns were an infinitely more dangerous prey.

Puma snorted. John found the temptation irresistible. With Puma's speed he was soon in the van. Stringing his bow at full gallop he overtook animal after animal, ranging alongside, evading the thrusting horns by a hairsbreadth, shooting them down, whooping with as much gusto as any of his companions. He had not for months been so light of heart. For this one heedless, wild moment he was an Indian again.

XI

WHEN THE TWO RIDERS pulled in at the top of the ridge their horses were beginning to sweat in the early morning sun. The autumn weather had remained remarkably mild, a circumstance as unprecedented in this clime as had been the duration of the drought. Since leaving Fort Bennett, ten miles behind, they had entered an area that had been recently watered by one of the wandering local storms that had become more frequent with the passing of summer. Viewed from the crest of the ridge, the nearer hills rolling away westward were as freshly green as though this were spring instead of fall. Surveying the tremendous vista extending over the horizon toward the forks of the Cheyenne and the Black Hills, Frederic Remington drew a long slow breath of contentment.

"I never come back to this country without wondering why I ever leave it," he said. "Mankind has certainly hit upon the most preposterous way to live — in ruts, in towns, in crowds, in stinks."

"I figgered that out whilst I was still fourteen," said Jared comfortably. "We'll find Stu camped just back of that third hill."

Remington studied the terrain ahead and wagged his head.

"Either you're just guessing or you knew where he planned to stop."

"Take a look at his wheel tracks in this new grass," suggested Jared. "They go behind the hill and they don't come out. And at that smoke against the sky."

Remington continued to stare and then grunted disgustedly.

"My eyesight's better than average. It's been trained for years to observe detail. And I've been in the West enough to allow for the clear air and the distances. What tracks? What smoke?"

But when they came over the third hill there was the camp immediately below them. Kirk and John were leaning against the tailgate, conferring earnestly. Mary was bending near a small campfire. The two Indians were aware the moment the riders appeared over the skyline. Then Kirk looked around. Surprised to see that Remington was riding Badger, he walked out to meet the newcomers. Before taking the train to Gunsight, Kirk had shipped Badger to Fort Bennett so the horse would be quickly available if needed. Remington swung to the ground to shake hands. Jared rode on into camp. Kirk laid his hand against Badger's neck.

"How'd you make out with him?" he asked, grinning.

"He's only the second horse that's ever dumped me but he tossed me three times as a kind of get-acquainted gesture. From then on we got along fine. He's a good horse." Remington's glance went to the grazing Puma. "But there's a great one."

"Belongs to John. There's quite a story connected with him."

"First let me tell you mine." Remington lowered his voice slightly to make sure it would not carry to those in camp. "I waited an extra day in Chicago for General Miles to get back from Washington. Long's I'm doing these special articles on the Sioux I thought it wouldn't hurt to get a line on the commanding general's attitude. As an old friend he couldn't very well hold out on me."

"What is his attitude — aside from disapproving of everything in Washington?"

"Same as always — that nobody else in the army knows anything about Indians. Though he does want to hear what you have to tell him. He'll be at Pine Ridge day after tomorrow. That's why I brought your horse out to you. To save you time getting there."

The message appeared to have had a singular effect upon Kirk. His eyes closed as though he were in pain. He turned and bent over. "As probably my earliest well-wisher will you kindly give me a good hard kick?"

"What's the matter? Did Miles catch you so soon you haven't got anything to tell him?"

Kirk straightened and began to appear resigned to whatever had so disturbed him.

"No. It's not that. I've pretty well caught the drift of things. I've seen the Oglala myself. John has just told me about the Brulé. And Kicking

Bear's now getting to the Miniconjou to continue the pattern. So I'll have enough to tell him. Anyway, I have to go. And I'll have to take Jared with me. The general likely takes more stock in his opinion than in mine. We'll have to ride hard to make it in two days. That'll leave you stranded with the wagon."

They turned toward camp. Remington nodded toward the waiting figures of John and Mary.

"I'll make out. From what Jared tells me about your two Indian prodigies I couldn't be left in better hands. Matter of fact, I'm delighted to be rid of you."

Kirk made the introductions.

"Mary Chadron, John Winthrop, Frederic Remington. Don't be misled, Mary, by his looking like a cross between a Norse hero and a Greek god. That roving eye pursues only something to paint and he's been happily married seven years. As for you, Fred, you'll be reassured to learn that their true names are Star-at-Dawn and Rides-an-Eagle."

"Capital," said Remington, keeping hold of Mary's hand and stepping back to survey first her and then John. "Being an artist gives me license denied this Philistine, MacGregor. I couldn't myself have named you more appropriately."

Kirk broke in with: "He doesn't usually take the trouble to fascinate his victims but when he does, look out. I wish I could stay to watch. But I can't. There's been another change in plans. Jared and I have to start for Pine Ridge at once. John, I hope you and Mary can stay with Mr. Remington, at least for the moment. It'll be five days at the earliest before Jared can get back to him."

Remington had not yet released Mary's hand and was still scanning, as though already beginning to sketch her, the fine planes of her face. He could sense her slight, convulsive start and see the shadow come into her eyes. The sudden imminence of Kirk's departure was a painful shock to her. More than likely this accounted also for Kirk's reception of the news.

Remington was disappointed. So commonplace a complication seemed to him to have taken some of the light out of the scene. From his first glance he had been delighted by the striking figures of the two young Indians. For all their outer gloss of education they seemed to him captivating examples of savage grace and beauty. Mary's pale skin made her primitive quality the more provocative. John might stand as the prototype of the wild horseman of the plains. They belonged together, to be studied together against the backdrop of that expanse of green hills and blue sky. His imagination was already busy with the range of poses and attitudes in which they might be painted. For Kirk's roving impulses there could be no place in any such composition.

"You don't have to decide on the spur of the moment," he was assuring John and Mary. "We've got time to talk it over."

Mary had withdrawn her hand and, though seeming to listen politely, was hearing nothing he was saying. John, however, was not only attentive but astonishingly friendly.

"We'd like nothing better than to accompany you, Mr. Remington. Only thing is — we have to keep going to Standing Rock, where we're already overdue."

"That would suit me fine," said Remington. "Long's I've come out to write pieces about the Sioux I might's well start at the top with Sitting Bull."

Mary was still only seeming to listen. Though she had not once glanced toward Kirk, she was remaining aware of his every movement, as he pulled back the tarpaulin, uncovered his valise, and began transferring from it to his saddlebags those essential effects he needed to take with him.

"We might's well be off, too," said Remington, hoping to distract her. "Let's pack and be on our way."

Given occupation, she seemed to regain her Indian reserve. Remington helped her with stowing the dishes and kitchen utensils. John brought in the team and began harnessing. Jared removed Remington's saddlebags from Badger and tucked them under the tarpaulin. Suddenly Mary straightened, her eyes widening. So soon, Kirk was ready. John moved nearer Mary. Kirk crossed to them. He showed no emotion beyond a repressed excitement over the precipitancy of his unexpected departure.

"What a pity I have to rush off this way," he said, with more cheer than regret. "Never in my life have I enjoyed a trip as much as this one with you two." He shook John's hand. "It's been wonderful the way you've taken a stranger under your wing." He lifted Mary's hands in both his own, bent to brush his lips lightly against each, and smiled down at her. "John's been fine. But you, my dear, are the one I'll never forget. I can only hope something one day will bring me to Standing Rock."

"We hope so, too," said John.

Mary said nothing.

Kirk gave her hands one more squeeze and turned to give Remington a mock salute.

"Be seeing you, Fred."

He mounted and rode off with Jared. The moment they were out of earshot John addressed Mary harshly. Remington, watching the fluidity of their changing expressions and attitudes, so foreign to the popular conception of Indian stolidity, guessed their colloquy to be in the nature of a lovers' quarrel. But to his great disappointment he could not understand what they were saying. They were speaking in Sioux.

"What will he report to his general?" John was demanding.

She stared at him remorsefully. "I do not know."

"Why not?"

"I did not ask him."

"You didn't? Your blanket is still in his tent."

Her eyes dilated, then closed.

"Yes. I slept there last night — during the storm."

"And still you did not ask him?"

"He did not come in." Her eyes opened. "You believe me?"

"Yes. At least you do not lie." His scowl darkened. "If he had come in what would have happened?"

She looked toward the tent as though herself seeking the answer.

"I lay there all through the night . . . wondering. I could not be sure then. I am not sure now."

"Are you in love with him?"

"Why must I listen to your questions?" Her voice shook with sudden anger. "Already you have found me another white man." She jerked her head toward Remington. "Do you now want me to sleep in his tent?"

"You are a fool but you do not have to be so big a fool. You have heard from your white man all about this one. This one is a famous artist. He writes for magazines and newspapers. He knows generals and people in Washington. The whole country will listen to him. Are you too silly to realize how much we need to make him our friend so that he will tell the truth about the Sioux?"

"You are worse than a fool. You are a toad — a puffed-up toad. What gives you the right to think that only you have feelings for the Sioux? I am as ready as you to do anything I can — to give anything I have to give. What have you to offer that is so much greater than that?" Her voice broke. "Oh, John, what evil manitou has got into us? Can we no longer even be friends?"

Their eyes met. His face softened.

"We must be," he said.

They shook hands.

Mary turned, again outwardly calm, to resume packing.

"I hope you can pardon our speaking Sioux for the moment," said John to Remington. "Something came up we had to settle."

"And apparently succeeded," said Remington, grinning.

They set out north toward the Cheyenne. Remington sat in Kirk's place on the seat of the buckboard beside Mary. John rode on ahead and was soon lost to sight. Remington had from his first glimpse of them been enthralled by the physical attractiveness of the two Indians. His primary reaction was always to the shape and color and composition of whatever came to his attention. Suspecting how absorbing was their personal involvement with each other and with Kirk was adding scope to his appreciation. He was avid to know more about them but John, who seemed willing to talk, was out of sight as well as hearing and his occasional sidewise glance could tell him nothing about Mary. She was staring straight before her, as though at a gnat or a dust mote suspended in the air between her and the heads of the horses, her profile as impassive as one on a coin. He was tempted to engage her in conversation so that, turning toward him, she might reveal to his perceptive eye some further unveiling of her personality. But he restrained the impulse. Then his forbearance was rewarded. It was she who addressed him.

"You drive very well, Mr. Remington."

"Not like a tenderfoot, you mean. I haven't always been a writer and illustrator. When I was younger and brighter I spent some time in the West. Worked as cowhand and scout. Even descended to running a sheep and mule ranch for a while."

"You speak of when you were young as though that were a long time ago. You don't look so old."

"Whether I look it or not I've aged fast — trying to do too many different things. That's what they say about a jack-of-all-trades, you know. Master of none."

"Neither do you look like a man who doesn't know what he wants to do."

Remington was breathing easier. Even an Indian girl could hardly chat so calmly if her heart had been broken. As a romanticist with a special predilection for everything western he could much more comfortably contemplate this lovely creature being possessed by the young warrior than by the young officer.

"That buckskin stallion of John's," he said, to keep her talking and turned toward him. "MacGregor says there's a story behind him."

"There is." Without apparent reluctance she embarked upon an unselfconscious account of the breeding of the mare to the wild stallion and then of the first ride on Puma down the ridge in the tumult of the storm. Remington was fascinated. These were incidents suggesting the most compelling subjects for pictures. More immediate was the temptation to get out his sketch pad so that he might try to capture the flow of expression passing across her face.

"Ah," she said suddenly, breaking off the narrative to look at something in the distance ahead.

They had been angling down the slope of a shallow valley toward the dry stream bed of a tributary of the Cheyenne. He had been too intent on her to notice that John had reappeared on a slope ahead. He was alternately walking and trotting Puma, keeping his distance behind a white man on foot who was running and stumbling a hundred yards before him. The man presently veered up the slope to the east as though desperate to break out of the valley in the direction of Fort Bennett. John circled above him and turned him back to the valley bottom, as a cowhand might shepherd a stray calf along the course he wanted him to take. There was some indication that he was deliberately driving his victim in the direction of the wagon. If so, the fugitive himself simplified the process. He had been so preoccupied with looking over his shoulder at his pursuer that he had not at first sighted the wagon but when at length he did he summoned new energies and ran despairingly toward it. Remington pulled his team in on the floor of the valley and waited. In his frantic haste the man kept stumbling, falling, scrambling to his feet, and lunging on.

"The horse trader," murmured Mary.

"The one Jared was telling me about?"

She nodded. Bert made a final effort and with his left hand grasped the wheel beside Remington's foot.

"Help me," he begged. "You got to help me."

"Why?" said Remington. "You have a gun."

Bert had evidently forgotten the derringer still clutched in his right hand. He stared at it foolishly and let it drop to the ground.

"No shells left." He twisted to look over his shoulder at John walking Puma slowly forward. A new wave of terror engulfed him. "That red devil kept off at long pistol shot and was still able to drive them goddam arrows clean through the boards of my wagon box."

The episode had apparently proved a shock from which Bert had not been able to rally. John was coming remorselessly on. Bert ducked under the wagon and collapsed on the ground in moaning panic. John rode alongside, bent, reached under the wagon, took Bert by the collar, and stood him on his feet again beside the wagon.

"Don't let him kill me," Bert implored.

"I won't even cut off your ears," said John. "That is if for once you start telling the truth."

A ray of hope penetrated the haze of Bert's terror. He ceased his babbling and demonstrated his anxiety to please by spasmodic nods of his head.

"Have you something to write on?" John asked Remington.

Remington bent among his gear back of the seat and came up with his sketch pad and a crayon.

"That'll do fine," said John. "He can write large and clear."

He thrust the pad and crayon upon Bert.

"Now, write what I say." Bert took the pad with trembling hands. John began to dictate slowly. "To whom it may concern. I at no time ever purchased the buckskin stallion from the Indian, John Winthrop. It was therefore impossible for him to have stolen the horse from me. Neither has John Winthrop at any time under any circumstances stolen any property of any description from me. I am making this statement of my own free will and before witnesses. Signed. Bert Banks."

John took the pad, examined what was written on it, and handed it to Remington.

"Would you keep it — at least for the time being. I could be arrested and it just might get mislaid. It will be safe with you."

Remington tore off the sheet, folded it, and put it in his pocket. "It certainly will be," he said.

"Can I go now?" asked Bert.

"Not quite yet," said John. "Mr. Remington is a newspaper reporter. He will be interested to hear where you were going with that wagonload of new Winchesters."

Bert blinked, gulped, drew a long unhappy breath, and realized even more unhappily how steadily John was regarding him.

"Up the Cheyenne to the camp of Big Foot."

"That's a lie," said John. "Since Big Foot left the reservation his camp has been watched by a troop of cavalry. Neither you nor Big Foot is stupid enough to try to run a wagonload of guns past them."

Bert licked his lips.

"Big Foot and some of his boys sneaked out last night. They was waitin' for me at Mud Creek when you chased me off my wagon."

"That's better. If you'd had eyes for anything but me you'd have noticed that they were watching when I rode out of the willows to pass the time of day with you. How were they going to pay you?"

"Horses. They had some good ones they wouldn't sell for money but they'd trade them for guns."

"You're getting off the track again. Big Foot's been out there all summer and the grazing's been so poor his people haven't got a horse left in a condition worth trading for a popgun."

This reflection on his trading judgment stirred in Bert a flicker of protest. "They was still good horses. They could of been fed and fattened."

"Well, we'll pass that for the moment. Now tell Mr. Remington what will interest him most. Where'd you get the guns?"

Bert had foreseen this most difficult of all questions and was ready with his answer.

"At Pierre. Pete Jenkins's hardware store. He'd got him in a big shipment on account of the settlers they're all so scared they're all buying rifles."

John shook his head reproachfully. "You're really lying now. On three counts. In the first place the newspapers are full of stories about how Congress is appropriating money to supply arms to the settlers, so it's not likely there's any rifle-buying spree. In the second, any storekeeper knows that if he furnished the Sioux rifles his fellow citizens would burn down his place within the hour. And in the third, no storekeeper could afford to supply you with new Winchesters at a price that would leave you a profit in trading with Big Foot. You'll have to come up with something better than that."

Bert cast about desperately for a more satisfactory accounting. Then he realized that John's cold stare was focused on his left ear. He clapped his hand over the ear and capitulated.

"They come in two coffins that George Morton he brung in a baggage car."

John pondered this explanation and nodded.

"That sounds more like it. Anyway, you can go."

Bert edged hesitantly along the side of the wagon, ducked around the tailgate, and bolted up the slope. Remington had been listening with interest to the intricacies of this small frontier conspiracy but had found the final revelation sensational.

"George Morton," he said. "I've heard of him. Jacob Morrison's handyman. And Morrison's the Washington lawyer who works on Congress for most of these western railroads. But it makes no sense. Everybody knows the tricks to which the railroads will stoop to sell land. Still, how in the world will arming the Indians have any other result than to stop land sales?"

"Very simple. The better the Sioux are armed, the more likely they are to resist. The moment they resist, the army will move in and they can all be packed off to Indian Territory. Then can come the real land boom in the Dakotas."

Remington gathered the reins. John rode alongside.

"I can't very well print the gun-running story," said Remington. "Not until I've got more to go on than the word of one rascal. But I can get private word of my own belief in it to General Miles — and to the President."

"You are learning bits and pieces of the truth," said John. "There will be more."

"What about this Big Foot? Why did he move his camp from the reservation out on the plains? Is he as dangerous a character as the newspapers make out?"

"He is dangerous because he does not want much but is determined to have what he wants, which is to be let alone. He wants this so much that among the principal Sioux chiefs he has been the most willing to accommodate, to knuckle down, to cater to white authority, even to sell Sioux land. All he has gained is the discovery that on the reservation he will never be let alone. So he has left and he will die before he will come back."

"If he's such a pacifist why does he want rifles?"

"Any Sioux wants a rifle. It is bred in him. Without a weapon in his hand he is no longer a Sioux. But Big Foot's people are feeling a special need. They moved to the plains to get away from being badgered by agents and teachers and missionaries and police. They are willing to go hungry if only they may starve in peace. But when the cavalry was sent to watch them they were frightened. You must remember how many times in the last forty years the army has descended on defenseless Indian camps, taking them by surprise, shooting men, women, children, dogs, horses, everything that moved, burning their lodges, bedding, food, everything they possessed, carrying off the survivors in chains. When an Indian sees soldiers coming he is transfixed by the same horror as when a settler looks from his doorway to see a pack of painted warriors riding into his yard."

"Everything you say is unfortunately all too true. It is an historic process known as the pacification of savages. But getting hold of more guns won't save them. Not any longer."

"Agreed. It only makes their case worse. But there was no help for that in this instance. Once a Sioux gets his hands on a shiny new Winchester nothing can persuade him to let go. The moment Big Foot's young men sighted the trader's wagon it became too late. All I could do was to indulge in the minor gesture of seeing to it that they didn't have to give up their horses."

"I'd like to see this Big Foot."

"You will in a minute."

The valley of the dry creek opened as they came around a bend. Before them was the Cheyenne. Where the creek met the river there was a muddy slough. From a low bluff above this estuary a group of dismounted Indians was pushing a wagon. It toppled into the muddy water and sank from sight. Several mounted Indians were meantime driving the unharnessed horses of the trader's team off to the eastward, where they might be expected to keep on until they had eventually found their way to their home stable.

"Disposing of all the evidence," said Remington approvingly. "The horses will turn up safe. The wagon will never be found. The trader won't dare complain. And the Indians can't be accused of stealing rifles nobody dares admit ever existed."

Big Foot wheeled away from his followers and cantered forward alone to meet the wagon.

"I told him you were a friend of General Miles and of the President," said John. "Also that you were a man the Sioux could trust. He believed me."

Remington pulled in his team, handed the reins to Mary, and jumped to the ground. Big Foot was tall and cadaverous, with a length of arm and leg that made the small horse he bestrode seem no more than a pony. Upon dismounting he paused to cough and spit. He was apparently afflicted with one of the respiratory ailments to which Indians had become so much more subject since they had been herded together on reservations. When the paroxysm of coughing had ended he wiped his mouth apologetically on the sleeve of his doeskin hunting shirt and came forward. His deeply sunken eyes were infinitely sad but they lighted up faintly as he stretched out his hand. John interpreted.

"I wanted to take your hand so that I could tell you I am glad you are visiting our country," said Big Foot. "And to ask you to take my greetings to your friend, the President, who is also my friend."

Remington realized that he was referring to the visit to the White House of a delegation of Sioux chiefs during the land-sale negotiations.

"Thank you," he said. "I will tell him, and I can assure you that he sends his warmest regards to you."

"When we went into the big house with the white posts in front," said Big Foot, yielding to reminiscence, "they took us into a room where there were a number of white men. All looked alike. All had black suits. All had high white collars. All had beards. All had shoes that squeaked. We could not tell which one was President until our guides pushed us into line and he started shaking our hands. I have heard that his grandfather was a great soldier who beat Tecumseh and the English but this one did not look like a commander."

"He is our head man, though," said Remington. "He was made paramount chief by the election of all the people."

"No doubt he is a great man even though he looks like somebody behind a counter in a store. He smiled at us with his lips. His tongue said he was our friend. And he offered us twenty-five cents an acre more for our land. Only we have not yet seen a penny of the money."

"The Congress is his council. He keeps telling them to vote you your payment. Did you enjoy your trip to Washington?"

"No. From the windows of the train, when we walked in the streets, everywhere we went, wherever we looked, there were more people. There are more white people the other side of the Missouri than there are prairie dogs on this side."

"Most of them wish you well."

"That is what they always said when they shook our hands. Not only in Washington but wherever the train stopped. Still, they keep sending their soldiers. And their soldiers keep killing us. And there are so many white people that soon there will be no place for Indians. We must have room — and air — else we can no longer breathe."

The thought was so disturbing to him that it set off another spasm of coughing. This time when he wiped his mouth on his sleeve there were flecks of blood.

"There will always be room for Indians," said Remington. "There has to be."

Big Foot shook his hand again.

"I am grieved that I cannot stay longer with you. Your talk is good. But the soldiers have scouts out looking for us and my young men are beginning to squirm."

He mounted and rode away, the toes at the end of his long legs almost touching the ground.

"So that gentle man," said Remington, "is the terrible menace to the frontier the newspapers are prattling about."

Big Foot's little band was already fading wraithlike from view among the folds of the hills.

"Do not be misled," said John. "He will fight if fighting is forced on him. That is true of all Sioux."

As they crossed the Cheyenne and continued northward they avoided the more inhabited areas of the Cheyenne River reservation. John kept altogether out of sight.

"The nearer we get to Standing Rock," he had explained, "the more chance of McLaughlin's police trying to collar me."

They camped that night in the seclusion of a cedar grove in the Missouri River bottoms. With darkness John had rejoined them. After supper Remington was happily intent with his pad, sketching various poses of the Indians and horses in the shadowed reflections from the campfire. John had been pacing about restlessly but eventually seemed to have come to some conclusion which involved Remington, for he settled beside him to ask for a piece of paper. On it he wrote a bill of sale for Puma and handed it to Remington.

"You will say I sold him to you because I needed the money. That I'd heard about the order for my arrest and had decided not to stay in the Sioux country."

Remington refused to take the paper.

"I know what you think of that horse. Are you crazy?"

"No. As your horse he will be safer than if I tried to keep him with me. I can maybe keep under cover but it is not easy to hide a horse like him."

"But meantime you may be needing him."

"When I do I'll take him."

"Okay," said Remington. "I'm beginning to gather you usually know what you're doing."

"Now about Mary," said John.

"He always gets around to me," said Mary, "right after his horse."

"I don't want her punished for leaving the reservation without a pass in order to bring me a warning. When you drive in tomorrow, try to deliver her to Father Murphy before you run into McLaughlin. He's an impulsive man and can make a fearful commotion before anyone's had a chance to try to explain anything. Not that there's any excuse for what we've done — that is, from his point of view."

"I'll see that she's let alone," said Remington. "But what are you going to do?"

John shook his head.

"When you drive into the agency tomorrow you'll be obliged for Mary's sake to protest your innocence as far as having had anything to do with me is concerned. The less you know about my plans the more credible your protestations will sound."

The next morning Remington nested Mary in the bed of the buckboard under a corner of the tarpaulin, tied Puma to the tailgate, and drove boldly past the agency headquarters. Sergeant Shave Head, on duty at the door marshaling the line of Indians waiting to see the agent, looked at Remington with sharp curiosity and then, as his glance fell on the horse, ran inside for instructions. Remington whipped his team on to the mission.

Father Murphy was overjoyed by his first glimpse of Mary and intrigued when he realized the identity of her protector.

"So," he charged Mary, "from what I hear, the only mischief you got into while you were away was to wander all over the Dakotas and Nebraska without a pass, while busying yourself with stealing horses, robbing trains, harboring criminals, and inciting riots. I am so pleased to have you back safe that I have already forgiven you your incredible misdeeds. But all the same the sooner we brave McLaughlin's wrath the straighter face with which we can deny our guilt."

The three climbed to the seat of the wagon. As it drew up in front of the agency, McLaughlin came rushing out, bursting through the group of Indians around the door, his countenance convulsed with rage. With his bristling shock of white hair, he reminded Remington of some of the historic portraits of Andrew Jackson. There was in his spare, acidulous features the same furious refusal to tolerate any hint of insubordination. He gestured to Shave Head to take charge of Mary and glared up at Remington.

"So you're the other horse thief that helped Mary hold up that train?"

Remington's temper was as easily triggered. He shoved the reins into the priest's hands and jumped down to confront McLaughlin.

"Are you admitting, then, that you're the official jackal who schemed to get John murdered?"

On the other side of the buckboard, Shave Head was reaching up, waiting for Mary to jump down into his custody. But, reacting to the altercation which was so obviously nearing the verge of a physical attack by Remington on McLaughlin, she turned, pushed past Father Murphy, and jumped down between the two antagonists.

"Wait," she begged. "Mr. McLaughlin, you're making a great mistake. Mr. Remington had nothing to do with the train. And he owns the horse. He's got papers to prove it."

"I don't give a goddam who owns the horse. What I want to know is what makes you and John — and Father Murphy — and even this outsider — think you can —" His yelling broke off in midsentence as the significance of the name Mary had mentioned belatedly struck him. "Remington? Frederic Remington?" He gaped at Remington, still unwilling to believe the extent of his ill luck, then muttered dejectedly, "I'd been warned he was on his way West." He forced his stiffened facial muscles into a smile of greeting and offered his hand. "Welcome to Standing Rock, Mr. Remington. If there's anything we can do for you I trust you will let us know."

Remington ignored the hand. The change in the agent's demeanor, as sudden and complete as an exchange of masks, had been so abrupt as to appear ludicrous. Then Remington began to make allowances for a veteran officeholder's years of experience with the exigencies of dealing with superiors, politicians, generals, newspapers. Only by the payment of constant tribute to public relations could he survive. Any visitor as capable as a noted correspondent of gaining so wide a hearing in the East was clearly one it was imperative to cultivate. The generally known fact that he was a personal friend of General Miles and Theodore Roosevelt and had access to the White House must have made the agent's situation appear to him more desperate.

"No question there are explanations for these shenanigans that have been bothering me," McLaughlin was saying. "Could be some on my side, too, I don't doubt. But all that can wait." He gestured to Shave Head to take charge of Remington's horses and to his wife, who had appeared in the door of the agency. "Santy, Mr. Remington will be having dinner with us." He saw Remington was still scowling. "And set places for Father Murphy and Mary. It will give us a chance to talk things over without any more rumpus. But first, Mr. Remington, let me show you your quarters." Remington still looked grim. "Father, Mary, come with us and help me talk Mr. Remington into staying with us a while."

He led the way around a corner of the agency. The others followed, Remington and Father Murphy exchanging broad winks. Adjoining the police barracks was a small, unused frame house with a corral behind it. The interior was neat and clean and sufficiently furnished. Remington raised a back window and threw open the storm shutters to disclose a good north light. This comfortable location at the nerve center of the reservation, with ready access to mission, telegraph office, and Fort Yates was so ideally suited to his needs that he finally permitted himself to thaw appreciably.

"You're very kind, Mr. McLaughlin. I'll be glad to take advantage of your hospitality."

The new atmosphere of amicability was immediately dissipated as by a thunderclap. Through the open back window John vaulted into the room. Remington's surprise was so natural, as John had foreseen, that the agent could not possibly suspect he could have had foreknowledge of this development.

"I'm here to submit to arrest," said John. He indicated Remington and Father Murphy. "Before witnesses."

The implication that this might prove a factor shaping the treatment to which he might otherwise have been subjected did not temper McLaughlin's outrage. He snatched out a whistle and blew a blast. Shave Head and One Bull came pounding across from the agency.

"Not so fast," said John. "First listen."

"There's nothing you can say I want to hear," shouted McLaughlin. Then he recalled Remington's presence and struggled to control his rage. "Well?"

"You know that I've come back to report to Sitting Bull." John was ticking off the points on his fingers. "I have not yet seen him, as your police watching his house can certainly assure you. You are bound to have the greatest official interest in what I tell him. This, therefore, is what I propose. Let us go now together to Sitting Bull so that you may hear whatever I say. There can be no tricks because I will speak only in English. Father Murphy will interpret for Sitting Bull and confirm to you in English his responses. Mr. Remington, who in a sense represents the outside world, will hear everything that is said and can draw his own conclusions. Well, what do you say?"

"I say it's a pack of nonsense. You're a prisoner and it's my duty to see that neither you nor that old scoundrel makes any more trouble."

He gestured for Shave Head and One Bull to take John away. John shook off their grasp. He was still staring at McLaughlin.

"You know well enough," he said, "that you cannot be sure which of your Indian police or servants you can fully trust. You know that no matter how you lock me up it will only be a matter of hours before I get whatever word I choose to Sitting Bull. But you will never know what it is. Have you then some objection to knowing?"

Even in his exasperation McLaughlin could not miss how thoughtfully Remington was regarding him.

"Very well," he assented. "Though I still say it's a great waste of time."

The still enraged McLaughlin insisted that they start at once. Remington was unwilling to ride John's horse in John's view. McLaughlin vetoed John's riding him on the theory that so exceptionally mounted he could escape at will. Remington therefore left Puma with Mary and borrowed an agency mount. The little cavalcade, Remington, John, McLaughlin, Father Murphy and the two policemen rode so hard that they were dismounting before Sitting Bull's house by midafternoon.

Sitting Bull must have been warned of their approach by one of his videttes, for almost at once the door opened and he came out on his porch. Remington was disappointed. At first glance the great Sitting Bull, in whom the public had become so interested that he could be made the principal attraction of a circus, seemed just another expressionless old Indian. But his second did not miss the flicker of arrogance in the chief's eyes as he looked at and through McLaughlin. Sitting Bull had been followed out by his scowling young son, Crow Foot, and by his younger wife, carrying a stool. Upon this he sat calmly, while his visitors necessarily remained standing on the ground below. The gesture intensely annoyed McLaughlin, for it was like a bald announcement that the chief considered he was giving audience to a visitor of lesser rank.

Thirty or forty of Sitting Bull's followers were gathering. Three members of Lieutenant Bull Head's Grand River contingent came running from their watching stations in nearby woods to take positions from which they could keep the resentful Hunkpapa onlookers in order. There was some shoving and muttering. It was apparent that special ill will existed between the uniformed police and their fellow Sioux.

"Well, get on with it," said McLaughlin to John.

John spoke slowly so that Father Murphy might interpret, sentence by sentence. "I visited the Cheyenne, the Crow, the Arapaho, the Blackfeet, and the Shoshone. All are dancing. All are praying. All are hoping. All are waiting. But they pray and hope and wait only for a miracle. All the chiefs and all the warriors remain by their lodges. All are of one mind. Whatever comes — good or bad — it can come only in peace. Not even the oldest and most bitter or the youngest and most foolish talk of war."

Sitting Bull's face had remained impassive until the last word, then he nodded his decisive and vigorous approval.

"That is good," Father Murphy began interpreting his reply. "They are wise. Let them pray. Let them hope. But let them also wait. There are too many white soldiers. There are too many white people. We, too, must wait, for we Sioux are of the same mind."

The apparent sincerity of this formal announcement of peaceful intentions impressed Remington and Father Murphy. But the proffered conciliation only darkened McLaughlin's scowl.

"A prearranged performance," he pronounced, addressing Remington. "You can't imagine the lies that old devil has tried to tell me through the years."

John interposed, challenging McLaughlin.

"No matter what he has tried to tell you, you have never listened. He has just chosen peace. Does that offend you?"

"What offends me is his eternal hypocrisy. I'll prove to you what he is choosing. Everybody knows the Ghost Dance can lead to war. The Sioux are dancing on every other reservation. So far this one has been free of the plague. So this is what I say. If he really wants peace let him help me keep it out." McLaughlin turned to Father Murphy. "Tell him that I know his people are talking about dancing and that some of them want him to invite Kicking Bear here to teach them how. Tell him to have nothing to do with Kicking Bear and to see to it that his people do not dance. Tell him that is an order."

Father Murphy's expressions and gestures during his interpretation suggested his abhorrence of heathen rites and yet his underlying sympathy with Sitting Bull's dilemma. Sitting Bull rose. For a moment all the arrogance and ferocity of his past flamed in him.

"He says the dancing is their religion," said Father Murphy. "He says Indians have as much right to their religion as white people have to theirs. He says if his people choose to dance he will never stop them."

McLaughlin shot a triumphant glance at Remington and a scornful one at John.

"Well, there's your answer." He turned again to Father Murphy. "Be so good as to remind him that I have given him an order."

Sitting Bull turned his back contemptuously and reentered his house.

"From what I've been told," remarked Remington, "he's always been opposed to the dancing on the grounds it was beneath the dignity of a warrior people."

"Dance or no dance he's still a troublemaker at heart," said McLaughlin, for the moment curt even with his pampered guest. "And it'll do him no harm for once to do as he's told."

The agency party remounted and set out on the long ride back. McLaughlin rode out of earshot ahead with John, engaged in an earnest conversation. After a time he dropped back to Remington.

"What you witnessed back there was staged largely for your benefit," he said. "Now there is something *I* want to show you."

Allowing the others to proceed without them, McLaughlin led the way up a long slope which brought them out eventually on the crest of a high bald hill. Here he pulled up.

"You came out to this country to size up the Sioux situation. From what I gather you're some more bent on getting hold of the way things really are than most of these jackass reporters who keep looking only for something to scare their readers."

"That's right," said Remington.

"Then I can hand you the whole kit and caboodle in a nutshell. First look that way."

To the west the vast expanse of the high plains stretched away toward the wreath of thin clouds on the horizon that marked the Black Hills.

"Until ten years ago those plains swarmed with buffalo. Up to eight years ago we could still kill 'em by the thousand a day's ride from here. Now there is not one left. Then, the Indians could range wherever they pleased because always and everywhere there was meat for their bellies and skins for their lodges. Now they must huddle around agencies because without the issue of government beef they will starve. Now look the other way."

To the east, dwarfed by the distance, could be glimpsed the walls of Fort Yates.

"At that fort and a dozen more like it," continued McLaughlin, waving his hand to indicate every horizon, "ringing the remnant of the Indian country, are soldiers — too many and too well-armed for the Indians to have the faintest hope of resisting. Now look south. The land the Sioux sold last year runs in a strip seventy miles wide from the Missouri to the Black Hills. The strip altogether divides the northern Sioux on the Standing Rock and Cheyenne River reservations from the southern Sioux on the other reservations. Due to the drought there's been no rush of settlers yet but in two or three years the white inhabitants of that strip will outnumber all the Sioux by more than ten to one. Finally, look down there."

At the foot of the hill was an Indian hamlet of three brush huts and half a dozen tattered canvas tepees surrounded by as many acres of crudely scratched ground.

"There," said McLaughlin, as though pleased by the meager prospect, "that represents their one hope of surviving. They must learn to plant and reap and work — as other people have to do. The Sioux cry about the loss of so much of their land — another eleven million acres at one swoop just last year. But I tell you there's more hope for them in one planted acre," his gesture swept from the cultivated patch to the vista of the plains, "than in all that. However, they'll never face the facts of their future so long as they are excited by this idiotic dance or by the crazy schemes of Sitting Bull. That's why I'm determined to deal with both of these poisonous influences. I am determined because if I fail it could mean the final extermination of the Sioux. Now do you begin to understand?"

When Remington did not at once reply McLaughlin looked around at him sharply. Remington was staring down at the dismal little Indian farms at the foot of the ridge.

"What I am wondering," he said, "is what I would do if I were a Sioux."

It was long after dark before they approached the agency. McLaughlin turned off on the road to Fort Yates.

"I have to talk to Colonel Drum," he said. "Mrs. McLaughlin will have something for you to eat."

At Remington's house One Bull was waiting to take his horse. Santy came out her kitchen door with a lantern.

"Where's John?" asked Remington.

She inclined her head toward the police barracks, handed him the lantern, and went back into her kitchen. A room at one end of the barracks had a door with a barred window. When Remington held up the lantern John got up from his cot and came to the window. Remington was indignant to find John still a prisoner.

"I'll wire General Miles," he vowed. "I'll wire Washington. I'll make the bastard turn you loose."

"Don't," said John. "McLaughlin has a reason for keeping me here and it's one with which I agree."

"You trust him that far? After he tried to get you lynched?"

"He had nothing directly to do with that horse thief charge. I don't trust his methods or his temper but I do trust his intentions. He wants to head off a war almost as much as I do. A war would destroy his life's work, prove him a failure."

"What's all that got to do with keeping you shut up?"

"I will try to explain," said John, patiently. "If he turned me loose I'd have to go back to Sitting Bull's house. I could serve no purpose there because the moment Sitting Bull found me giving people advice different from his he would roar with outrage. Meanwhile the Hunkpapa would not listen to me because they think me fooled by living so long among whites. But as a prisoner here who is being put upon by the agent maybe they will listen — I must make them listen."

"What is this advice contrary to Sitting Bull's you want to give them?"

"One plea only. Nothing else counts. Keep the peace. No matter how they're cheated and mistreated and insulted. No matter what degradations they suffer. Keep the peace. It's their one hope to stay alive."

"So you don't think Sitting Bull realizes that?"

"With his mind, yes. He wants to give the government no excuse to set the army on us. He even knows McLaughlin wants that no more than does he. But he cannot forget that he is a Sioux chief. He cannot endure being ordered to do anything — least of all by the agent. You may be sure that before we were out of his sight he had sent for Kicking Bear. Before the week is out the Hunkpapa will be dancing."

Remington devoted the next three days to working up his firelit sketches of John and Mary while his impressions were still fresh, to paying a courtesy call on Lieutenant Colonel Drum at Fort Yates, to gossiping with Santy, to a long and talkative dinner with Father Murphy during which he drew on the priest's years of experience with his Indian parish, and to the writing of his first dispatch for *Harper's*. Due to his fortuitous early contacts with Jared, Kirk, John, Big Foot, Father

Murphy, McLaughlin, Sitting Bull, and Santy, he felt that even this initial estimate of the Sioux situation was a sound one. He also insisted upon Mary taking out Puma for a daily ride.

"He needs the exercise," he urged. "But I'm not the one to give it to him. A horse like him should have but one master — and one mistress."

The fourth day John's forecast was confirmed. While Remington was at breakfast with McLaughlin, a policeman on a lathered horse brought word from Lieutenant Bull Head at Grand River that Kicking Bear had arrived and that dancing had immediately commenced.

McLaughlin received the tidings with unprecedented calm.

"You expected this?" asked Remington.

"I always expect that old son of a bitch to do what he thinks I least want him to do."

"That's what you were thinking when you pounded on him with that order?"

"Yes. The way it's working out is giving me a chance to nail him. With him out of the way I can handle the dancing." McLaughlin rose, closing the subject. "I'll have to go take me a look. Want to come along?"

"I certainly do."

McLaughlin took his official interpreter, Louis Primeau, and the young policeman, One Bull, as his only attendants. On the long ride the agent broke his thoughtful silence only as they crossed Oak Creek.

"Sitting Bull's camp is so far from the agency that I ought to have a halfway police shelter about here," he remarked. "Have to tell Bull Head to get to work on it."

Sitting Bull's houses, along with the adjoining outbuildings, corrals, and tepees, appeared totally deserted as they rode past. As they kept along the river road, other habitations, as well as the school and the trading post, were likewise empty.

"That's where Mary's parents live?" asked Remington.

"He's moved his store across the Cannonball," said McLaughlin shortly.

The road forded the stream and entered a grove of willows. While still in the woods they could begin to hear the low-keyed chanting of the dancers. Coming out of the willows they found the dancing ground on a cleared stretch of river bottoms immediately before them. They rode slowly toward the nearer fringe of onlookers and dismounted, leaving their horses with One Bull. Remington and Primeau followed McLaughlin as he walked deliberately forward.

The nearer onlookers edged nervously away from the agent's immediate proximity. But no other perceptible notice was taken of his arrival. All others in the circle of onlookers continued to keep their eyes carefully fixed on the dancers, and the dancers were involved in one of the intermittent periods of suspended animation that marked the Ghost Dance, during which the participants merely shuffled and hummed and stared at the sky. Only some of the younger children among the bystanders peered wide-eyed around their elders' legs at McLaughlin.

The effect was inescapable. The two parties to this confrontation were like poker players, each confident of his holding, each reserving for the moment the right to declare the stakes at issue. The Hunkpapa appeared determined to get it established that they had been in no way disturbed by the arrival of the agent. And he appeared not yet ready to show his hand. He was still maintaining an icy calm, though his eyes glittered as he watched and a thin contemptuous smile came occasionally to his lips.

Then Bull Ghost, Sitting Bull's one-eyed spiritual adviser, leaped into the ring and at once the momentum of the dance was accelerated. The dancers began to leap and to toss their arms upward as though about to leave the earth, to groan and moan and cry out in ecstasy.

Everything Remington saw conformed to the many descriptions of the Ghost Dance he had read and heard. There was the Prayer Tree with its unhallowed suggestion of the Cross. There were the cabalistic designs in red paint on the dancers' contorted faces. There were the agonies of those who had not yet achieved the mystic deliverance they were so frantically seeking. There were the shrieked professions of others that they were attaining those levels of supernatural experience. There was the brandishing of weapons as incongruous accompaniments to the desperate invocations of the Messiah. There were the white Ghost Shirts that had been seized upon by the American public's imagination as the most sensational feature of the whole extraordinary phenomenon. But most of all there were the authentic trances into which scores of dancers were falling. They had been overwhelmed by the conviction that they were in the process of being transported to another world.

"What about your police?" asked Remington, still the realist even at so unreal a moment.

"Bull Head's keeping them shut up in his house," said McLaughlin.

"You're not going to order them to stop this?"

"No. It's my guess they'd back off and if they didn't there'd be shooting. I'm not ready to risk either chance — that is not yet."

The Grand River schoolteacher, John Carignan, came around the dance ground to join them. McLaughlin eyed him.

"No school today?"

"No children. Sixty last week. Three yesterday. None today. With all this going on you can't expect school to keep."

The tumult of the dance again subsided and the shuffling and humming was resumed. Sitting Bull and Kicking Bear came out of the Prayer Lodge. Kicking Bear walked deliberately into the center of the ring and raised his arms in supplication toward the sky. There was in the gesture a proclamation of his assurance that he had been invested with the power to intercede with the supreme authority enthroned on high. A hush of rapt attention settled upon the assemblage, dancers and onlookers alike. Embarking upon the performance for which in the past two months he had become famous, Kicking Bear began to speak in a loud singsong.

"He is saying that when in the Rocky Mountains he saw the Messiah," whispered Louis Primeau. "That in a high valley no man had ever entered before the Messiah took him by the hand and commanded him to tell the Sioux that he was on his way to save them. That —"

"Shut up," growled McLaughlin. "We've heard all about that over and over again. It's the same cock-and-bull story he's been spouting every day for months — to the Oglala, to the Brulé, to the Miniconjou — and now here. We don't have to listen to it again."

"Yes, sir," said Primeau, crestfallen.

It was dusk before Kicking Bear had concluded and had stalked impressively back to the Prayer Lodge. The dance resumed with new fervor. Sitting Bull had been staring across at McLaughlin. He now suddenly walked forward into the center of the ring. Again the momentum of the dance diminished. His action had been unexpected and had made him even more the center of attention than had been Kicking Bear.

"I'd say he was showing off for my benefit," said McLaughlin, "if it wasn't that he never can stand it unless he's right in the middle of whatever's going on."

Sitting Bull presented himself ritualistically to the four directions, in each of which the Great Spirit was known equally to rule, and then looked around and down at a young Hunkpapa woman who, overwrought by her dancing, had fallen to the ground, where for the past hour she had lain, twitching and moaning. He bent and touched her shoulder. She instantly rose to her feet and stood before him, her eyes fixed on his, her attitude totally submissive. He passed his hands over her face. She became rigid and began to speak in a shrill voice.

"She is saying that she is doing what he has told her to do," said Primeau. "That she is flying across the sky far above the clouds. That she is seeing in the distance a great light. That she is now coming nearer and that she can see the light comes from a man with a face too bright for her to look at. That he is dressed in shining white cloth shaped like a Ghost Shirt."

"He's hypnotized her," whispered Remington.

"The old fraud's got more tricks up his sleeve than any ten other conjurors," said McLaughlin. "Me, I've seen enough. I'm going to Bull Head's house and turn in." He saw Remington was not ready to leave. "You want to look a while longer, Carignan here will show you the way when you're ready."

Sitting Bull did not prolong his extemporaneous drama. Once he had produced his major effect of demonstrating his ability to select at random a personal messenger to be dispatched into the very presence of the Messiah he released his subject from her trance and permitted her to walk off dazedly into the arms of her awed family.

Electrified by the mysteries revealed successively by Kicking Bear and Sitting Bull, the dancers were carried away by an excitement that mounted to utter frenzy. Full darkness had descended and the evolutions of the dance were more fantastic in the crosslights from the fires in the four corners of the dancing ground. Remington watched, fascinated, storing away in his memory every impression and every detail, until toward midnight most of the dancers had collapsed in total exhaustion. He spent the rest of the night in his bunk, sketching on the backs of sheets torn from a pad of Bull Head's ration returns.

The next morning they drew up again before Sitting Bull's house. When he came out he appeared very much at ease. He nodded almost benignly to Remington, Louis Primeau and Shave Head. He did not scowl even when he looked at McLaughlin.

"Whether or not your aim is to start a war," said McLaughlin, "you've got one going with me."

Sitting Bull's benevolence remained unruffled. His reply was so unexpected that it set Primeau to stuttering as he struggled with the interpretation.

"Who wants a war? Not I. Not the Sioux. I cannot think that even you do. The Messiah commands us to love one another. I see that you do not believe in him. So I tell you what we must do. You and I, together, we must go to the Rocky Mountains and find the Messiah. That way you can see for yourself and no longer be troubled by doubt."

"The trip we're going to take together," said McLaughlin, "is when I take you back to Fort Randall."

Sitting Bull wagged his head sorrowfully. "Your heart has been hardened by the Evil One. But when the Messiah comes I will tell him that you have tried to be a friend of the Sioux."

Exasperated by his failure to provoke his opponent, McLaughlin fired a more telling shot.

"This morning Kicking Bear was put under arrest and packed off to his own reservation."

The chief's eyes gleamed for a second.

"You managed to take him by surprise? With how many policemen?"

"Only one. Your nephew. When One Bull walked up to him, Kicking Bear got on his horse and rode off with him as quiet as a day-old fawn."

Sitting Bull had already regained his calm.

"Kicking Bear has much else to do. The Hunkpapa dancers no longer need his guidance. They have Sitting Bull's."

He turned and reentered his house.

"It's near impossible to get the best of that old coyote," muttered McLaughlin as they rode away. "But I'm going to."

When they dismounted at the agency, Remington hurried to his quarters, tacked his sketches on the wall, set up his easel, stretched his canvas, and at once began to paint, applying himself furiously while his impressions of the dance were still fresh and vivid. An hour later, McLaughlin came in, rubbing his hands.

"Got off a wire to the bureau informing them that Sitting Bull has started dancing. I've been telling them since June that there'd be no end to his mischief until he was shut up again and they've kept right on shilly-shallying. But now even in Washington they've got to open their eyes. By this time tomorrow we'll have him on his way down the river."

"Really," said Remington without looking around.

Miffed that the importance of his news had been so little appreciated, McLaughlin went out. In another hour Santy came to announce supper.

"Thank you, Mrs. McLaughlin," said Remington, continuing to squeeze vermilion from a tube.

Santy watched while he transferred one splash of color from palette to canvas.

"Busy as a conjuror making really big medicine," she murmured.

He worked without pause until the daylight faded. When it became too dark to paint he worked on through the night with charcoal sketches, experimenting with effects and details. With the return of daylight he resumed painting.

In his conception of the Ghost Dance, which he was successfully capturing on canvas, the human dancers were tiny, almost indistinct figures at the bottom of the picture. Nine tenths of the painting was devoted to the huge inverted bowl of the sky, out of which was charging in ghostly phalanx a countless legion of gigantic horsemen — the fabulous mounted warriors of the heroic Sioux past, with their zebra-striped shields, their streaming eagle-feather headdresses, their brandished lances, their hideously painted faces, their grizzly-claw necklaces, red blankets, medicine bags and beaded quivers. The effect he was achieving dramatized an onrushing storm of elation, pride and ferocity that was at once irresistible and overwhelming.

Toward noon McLaughlin came in angrily waving a telegram.

"The jugheads. They're still squatting under their desks. Nothing can jar them loose. They still say let everything ride and maybe it'll all blow over. So that old fart can go on laughing at me."

"So?" said Remington, intent on the detail of a horse's nostril.

McLaughlin peered over his shoulder and clucked in sudden amazement.

"Well, I'll be goddamned. For months I've been trying to make people catch on to the kind of dangerous ideas this Ghost Dance is giving the Sioux. But I ain't been able to get anybody to listen. Now with a few daubs of a brush you make the whole thing so plain not even them dimwits in Washington could miss it."

Remington leaned back to contemplate, scowling, what he had done. Never had he more successfully gained an effect for which he had striven. McLaughlin clapped him on the shoulder and went out. Remington, still staring at his picture, sensed his enthusiasm ebbing. He could still feel McLaughlin's congratulatory pat. Slowly he took the canvas from the easel and set it on the floor, face to the wall. It was to become the only one of his major works never to be finished.

XII

FROM THE MOMENT he had ridden away from the camp that was no longer his, Kirk dwelt on the realization that he was a fool. This was not an easy admission for a man whose career had previously been distinguished by so many agreeable experiences. There could be no escape, nevertheless, from the inexorable truth. Only a fool could have been capable of so monumental a misjudgment.

Even now that two weeks had passed he could not force himself to give up the constant retracing, step by step, of the events that had led to the disaster. Each step was always accompanied by an image of Mary, sitting beside him in the wagon, talking to him under the camera tripod, laughing with him at Eastman's, but most of all as she had looked in the wind and rain that last night in camp.

That night Jared had some hours before gone on ahead to meet Remington at Fort Bennett. John had not overtaken them and could not possibly do so before the next day at the earliest. When at evening they had unhitched and begun setting up camp, Mary had accepted with composure the circumstance that they were about to spend a second night alone together. That first night after John had left them in the sand hills they had been strangers. It had not counted. But this had been different.

As they were finishing supper there had come out of the west the first rumbles and flares of another of those little autumn thunderstorms. This one had veered toward them. There had been the hissing of the first drops in the fire. With no perceptible hesitation Mary had run to help him set up the tent that had never before been taken out of the wagon. All these days and nights later he could still see, in the lightning flashes, her hair blowing in the wind as she worked beside him. Once it had whipped across his face. They had got the flapping canvas staked and their gear under cover. To his amazement she had then, again without hesitation, picked up her blanket and walked into the tent. He had not needed to think to realize what a tactical error it would have been to follow too soon and had instead made his bed under the tarpaulin spread just outside the tent doorway.

There he had lain awake, during and after the brief storm, debating the time element in the possibilities before him. Since that morning drive together to Pine Ridge she had appeared progressively more prepared to accept at face value his professions of ordinary friendliness. Since that evening at Eastman's she had seemed altogether at ease in his company. The readiness of her resort to the shelter of the tent had been the clincher. Lying there in the dripping darkness, so near her that he could imagine he could hear her breathing, he had come to his conclusion. According to all the signs and symptoms with which he had in former such crises become familiar, he had only to hit upon an appropriate moment to find her responsive. From this self-assurance had sprung the fatal decision. In so important a matter there was always need to be absolutely sure. There could be no second-guessing. He had therefore decided to wait a little longer. The way things had been going, he had concluded, in another couple of days she would become so much more ready that his enjoyment could be that much greater.

But the next morning Remington and Jared had appeared with the thunderbolt of the general's summons. Riding away from her, he had at once begun haplessly to appreciate the full dimensions of his defeat. What had only a few hours before seemed literally at his fingertips had been suddenly snatched away to a remote distance. He had of his own volition denied himself satisfaction of the most insistent desire he had ever harbored. There was, moreover, no likelihood that the opportunity he had squandered might ever again return.

His discontent had been intensified by the revelation at Pine Ridge that there had been no necessity for the haste of his departure. General Miles's arrival there had been delayed, first for a week and then for another, evidently by certain obscure developments in the perpetual struggle between the Interior Department and the War Department for control over the management of Indian affairs. Occasional contacts with

Dr. Eastman and Elaine Goodall, which in so small an official community he could not altogether evade, had been no help. The euphoria in which they were exploring their personal situation merely emphasized the aridity of his. He had become so irritable that even Jared had begun to shun his company, electing instead to drift off on visits to various old friends among the Sioux.

An easier exasperation to contend with during the days of marking time had been the blunders of the new Pine Ridge agent. David P. Royer had been at times a druggist, a doctor, a newspaperman, and a state legislator but neither by these experiences nor by his character had he been prepared to be an Indian agent. He had no sooner been confronted by the spectacle of the Oglala dancing than he conceived of it as an affront to his official dignity, a desecration of the flag, a sin against heaven, and a certain threat that universal massacre was in the wind. He had begun shrilly demanding that it forthwith be stopped and as his demands were ignored his hysteria mounted. He persisted in the constant screaming of orders which nobody heeded. His police ceased wearing their uniforms, some even joined the dancers, and Half-Moon sardonically went off on an ostensible hunting trip. Kirk remained deaf to Royer's appeals for support. He pointed out that though he was now in uniform again, he was here only as a temporary observer and, as an army officer, was without authority on the reservation. Royer began seeing the Oglala exuberance as a threat not only to his office but to his life. They gleefully dubbed him "Young Man Afraid of Indians." The most dangerous consequence of the agent's witlessness was to plant deeper in the Indian mind the thought that by their dancing they were successfully defying the federal government. He was leading the Sioux to regard the Ghost Dance as an act of rebellion.

The agent's mistakes, preposterous as they were, suddenly assumed importance in the overall situation when the general at length arrived. Miles was the more incensed by Royer's conduct because it was in such extreme conflict with his own opinions. He had been assuring Washington of his confidence that any threat of war could be averted were his judgment, based on his long experience with Indians, given the consideration that was its due. His irate disapproval of Royer enabled Kirk to catch the drift of the general's thinking before being obliged to make his own report. It was easy for him to tell the general what the general wanted to hear because it was what he himself believed.

"Both Jared and I have seen what's been going on here," he said. "He's had a look at the Cheyenne reservation. A very intelligent young Indian, John Winthrop — he studied at Dartmouth, by the way — has told me about the Rosebud. It's the same at all three. The Sioux dancing is a horse of a different color from what Jared and I saw among the western nations. There it was only a kind of religious whoop-de-do. Here it's a war dance. There's not the slightest question the Sioux are getting dangerously excited. They're even beginning to believe that white shirt will turn bullets. They've certainly come to believe their Messiah is on his way. But people can't stay at that pitch of excitement indefinitely. So the greatest danger is that while they're still so worked up something will happen to blow the lid off. Using the army to stop the dancing would do just that. The least that would come of it would be that the Sioux would bolt every reservation, while if they're let alone there's still a good chance that they'll begin to cool off and the dancing will gradually peter out. Especially with winter coming on. Jared agrees with me."

Jared nodded.

The general struck the tabletop with the flat of his hand. "Exactly what I've been telling Washington. Exactly."

As an old soldier he was even more impressed by Kirk's account of Red Cloud's view that the already starving Sioux were too war-wise to consider a winter campaign.

"Of course, I can only recommend," he said, his tone indicating how unfortunate for the service and the country was this circumstance. "It is for the Secretary of War and the President to decide."

He caught the next train back to Chicago, leaving Kirk at Pine Ridge to watch the "rat hole," as Miles termed the friction between Royer and the Oglala, out of which could emerge some threat requiring immediate response. Royer, whose panic had been raised to a higher pitch by the general's scorn, locked himself in his quarters to compose frantic tele-grams to Washington declaring the Sioux in total insurrection and demanding the immediate dispatch of troops to save the agency and neighboring settlements. Kirk was not too disturbed by these outpourings for he knew that the last thing in the world wanted by the agent's superiors in the Department of the Interior was to turn the Sioux reservations over to the army.

His confidence in the validity of his recommendations to the general was not seriously undermined when, during the ensuing week, some hundreds of Oglala and Brulé, summoned by Short Bull, the Brulé chief who had gained sudden prominence by the aggressiveness of his anti-white declamations, left their respective agencies to encamp at Pass Creek, or even when Jared reported that many of the warriors at the encampment were trading their wagons and stock for rifles. The Sioux knew as well as did anybody who paused to think that with the season already so far advanced any day could bring the winter's first blizzard, with below-zero cold making existence on the open plains unendurable.

But another aspect of the situation was brought into focus late one evening when Tod Ward knocked on the door of Kirk's wretched little room in Jim Finley's bush hotel at the edge of the agency grounds. When the general had been transferred to Chicago he had contrived to take with him the two veteran captains, Ward and Hoyt.

"I'm on my way to the Black Hills," Ward explained, "to pick out a site for the general's field headquarters. Thought I might's well stop off to see what you thought about how things were going here."

His manner was dry and practical, neutral rather than hostile. Kirk decided that if he did nurse any suspicion concerning the affair in the Sierras with the wife of his friend, Wade, he was too old a soldier to betray any open dislike for a fellow officer so obviously in the general's favor.

"Why a headquarters in the Black Hills?" asked Kirk.

"Because when the time comes that's where he'll want to hold a line. If the Sioux jump their reservations he'll want to make sure they don't break past the Black Hills out across the West."

"When I last saw him he wasn't thinking about the Sioux jumping anywhere."

"I know. And we both know how little patience he's got with anybody that thinks different than he does. All the same, there are some reasonably smart people in and out of the army who don't agree with him. They think there might be a surer way to head off a war than to let the Indians go on running wild."

"Have you stopped off to ask me to begin seeing things out here that might need troops to handle?"

"I haven't stopped off to ask you for anything — except to do some thinking. I don't want a war any more than he does. If one starts it'll be a miserable, stinking business with no credit in it for anybody, the country, the army, him, you, or me. But I've been campaigning with the general since before you were knee-high. He's the one I'm thinking about. He's decided, going partly on what you've told him about what you've seen hanging around these goddam Ghost Dances, that there's no need to send troops. But if he sticks to this he's going to get overruled by Washington. That's the sort of insult I'd like to see him spared."

"So would I. But he's no fool. He knows Washington. He should — after all the fights he's had with them."

"With him it's never a question of knowing. It's never wanting to change his mind. And with you — you've been poking around out here on the plains so long you've no idea what's going on. The whole country's in a god-awful uproar. Everybody this side of Chicago figures war's due to break out any minute. The newspapers are full of it. Settlers by the thousands are running like they were already being chased. Citizens are staging mass meetings, getting up petitions, howling for the army to come save them. Every western legislator, every western governor, every western politician of either party is bellowing. You can imagine the heat on Washington. And how much worse it will get just two weeks and two days from today when Congress comes back for their next session. You know as well as I do what the President is going to do before that. So, if we're going to get troops no matter what, why not let the general get the credit for it?"

"What good getting him credit for a mistake?"

Ward looked at him thoughtfully.

"You couldn't have been hanging around Indians so long you're beginning to take a shine to them, could you?"

Kirk was himself startled by his surge of rage at this insinuation.

"I have to leave the listening at keyholes and peeking through transoms business to you planners at headquarters," he said. "I don't know any other way to soldier than to take orders. He's ordered me to tell him what I think the Indians are up to. That's what I'm doing. If what he wanted was an excuse on the record to chase the Sioux from here to Alaska I'd wire him tonight that they're talking about burning every agent and after that Minneapolis and Omaha. But so long as what he wants is the truth that's what he'll get from me."

"There isn't any very good answer to that," admitted Ward.

He went out, closing the door softly.

Kirk was too sound a soldier to run any unnecessary risks. The next day he rode out with Jared to have another look at the Pass Creek encampment. From a nearby hilltop they surveyed the circle of tepees surrounding a central dancing ground pulsating with dancers. Among these rolling hills, far from the ugly clutter of agency shacks, barns, corrals and frame buildings, the camp had the free, wild appearance of a Sioux plains bivouac of an earlier generation. The dancers were leaping with enthusiastic abandon. Groups of warriors were galloping about, armed, painted, adorned, all wearing Ghost Shirts. Several rode up the hill to greet Kirk and Jared with broad, challenging grins. The whole scene was invested not so much with menace as with an air of arcadian festivity. It had not escaped Kirk's attention that for all the intransigence of Short Bull's orations he had taken care to locate his camp on the dividing line between the two reservations so that neither the Oglala nor the Brulé who attended it could be considered hostiles who had broken bounds.

At Pine Ridge that night Kirk wired the general that the situation had not materially changed, that in his opinion there still was no immediate danger of a Sioux outbreak. But instead of a direct reply there came instead an order to report to General Miles, not at Chicago, but at St. Louis.

He waited in the hotel corridor until the general, rumpled, red-faced, sweating, came out of his hours-long conference with Secretary of War Redfield Proctor. Grasping Kirk by the arm, Miles pushed through the throng of reporters into his own room across the hall and slammed the door.

"The President's been listening to the plate-lickers instead of to me," he announced. "He's ordered troops sent to Pine Ridge and Rosebud. You don't agree with that. Neither do I. But we've got to make the best of it. We've got to remember we're soldiers." In spite of his protestations there was a glint of excitement in the general's eyes. The old campaigner was discovering anew how much greater the zest in commanding troops in the field than in the barracks. "I'm giving command of the expedition to General Brooke. No question soon's they sight troops the Sioux will take to the hills. But I'm giving Brooke the strictest instructions that his primary mission is to occupy and protect government property and that on no account is he to start in chasing Indians unless they actually attack him. Now listen to this. I'm assigning you to his staff. I want you to report to him on how your Indians are taking this. I also want you to wire me every morning and every night, every hour if necessary, about how things are going. I've told Brooke I'm doing this so you don't have to worry about stepping on anybody's toes. In my opinion there's still some room to get out of this without any shooting and I want to make sure my judgment's given a chance. Understand?"

"Yes, sir." said Kirk.

In the Omaha yards, where the troops were entraining, he found that the private car of the manager of the Fremont, Elkhorn and Missouri Valley Railroad, so recently extended past the southern border of the Sioux country, had been placed at the disposal of General Brooke, his staff, and senior officers. Stewards came aboard laden with cases of champagne and hampers of turkey, ham, and pâté de foie gras. There were repeated shouts of greeting between old acquaintances assembled here from widely separated posts.

At first, after the train pulled out, the talk centered on a professional rehearsal of the tactical dispositions involved in the expedition. The three troop trains were transporting elements of the 9th Cavalry, the 2nd Infantry and the 8th Infantry, supported by a Gatling gun and two Hotchkiss cannons. Large reinforcements were known to be on the way.

The entire 7th Cavalry, Custer's famous command, was coming from Fort Riley, Kansas, and other regiments were being drawn from points as distant as San Francisco. General Miles had determined that so long as the army was showing its hand in the Sioux country it should be shown with such overwhelming force that the Sioux dare entertain no idea of resistance. There was hearty approval of this judgment on the part of the older officers, though some of the younger were depressed by the possibility that there might be no fighting.

But under the influence of the railroad's hospitality, interest presently shifted from strategy and tactics to the champagne and pâté. As the three troop trains rumbled on through the night the atmosphere in the headquarters car became progressively more convivial. There was ever livelier badinage, the exchange of increasingly bawdy anecdotes, louder and louder snatches of song, and, among the more sedate, the institution of a poker game. The gathering seemed less one of commanders on the eve of leading their men against an enemy than of carefree participants in a holiday excursion.

Kirk went out on the back platform. Swirls of dust from the dry roadbed and clouds of smoke from the laboring locomotive eddied in his face but the air seemed to him cleaner than it had in the car. Light from the windows flickered across clumps of greasewood, tufts of buffalo grass, the shadowed depths of gullies, evidence that there stretched away in the darkness the expanses of the Nebraska plains across which they were hurtling. Once a bewildered antelope raced alongside for a moment among the fitful gleams of light. But even so fleet a creature was soon outdistanced. The general had taken care to have the Sioux warned that troops were on the way, lest they be too disturbed by a first sight of the threat, but they could hardly imagine the breakneck speed at which the soldiers were coming. The building of the railroads had changed all the processes of plains warfare as much as had the Indians' original procurement of the horse. Tracks like these were now encircling the Sioux country on every side. Before a shot was fired the Sioux were entrapped. Through the bars of their cage they might be prodded at will by their captors.

Pete Hoyt came out to join him.

"Brooke's made me supply officer at the railhead," he volunteered. "I didn't kick too hard. This ain't going to work up into any sort of a war."

"The general doesn't think it's going to work up into any war at all."

"I hope he's right. I ain't enjoyed shooting Sioux since they did the army a service by taking Custer out of our hair. All the same, I wish the old man had taken command out here himself."

"Why?"

"Whether the Sioux quit without a shot or have to be rounded up, it would have been him that everybody was looking to and hearing about." Hoyt put a hand on Kirk's arm and, though there was no one else on the platform, lowered his voice. "There was a senator I met at my wife's uncle's house back in Chicago. He got to talking about what a handsome man the general is. Called him the most distinguished-looking figure in American public life. Spoke of how often before the country had gone for a candidate who'd made a name as a soldier. He figured either party might grab him. Wouldn't be so bad for any of us, would it, if the old man happened to turn up in the White House?"

"The country could do much worse," agreed Kirk.

Hoyt rejoined the celebration in the car. Kirk speculated òn who or what might have prompted two of the general's most trusted staff officers to come to him with messages of which the general himself had surely had no knowledge. So short a time ago, he had assumed that the behavior of the Indians resulting from their reaction to the Ghost Dance represented the core of the problem. But in these last three days there had been these glimpses of the enormous complexity of the forces at work. There was so little anybody could do to resist or even to delay them. Not only he, John, Mary, Sitting Bull, the Sioux, but the Indian Bureau, the army, the general, the President, were alike in the grip of events which were no more meaningful than a succession of accidents. The white public's hysteria was as beyond any appeal to reason as was the Indian belief that the spirits of their ancestors were on the march to their rescue. This was the way wars started. They were not so much willed or declared as fallen into.

As for himself, he needed to be guided only by the general's orders.

That was one of the comforts of being a soldier. There was no compulsion to be constantly making up your mind.

The troops detrained at Rushville, the little border town most convenient to Pine Ridge for northbound traffic. Brooke was embraced by the overjoyed Royer, as hysterical now in his deliverance as he had before been in his fright. The inhabitants of the town, more than doubled by refugees from outlying homesteads and ranches, greeted the soldiers with as much acclaim as though the place had been for months besieged. Jared, too, was waiting with Badger.

Kirk mounted and the two rode off to reach Pine Ridge well in advance of the troops. From a hilltop they looked back at the already marching column. It was headed by troopers of the 9th Cavalry, the famous Negro regiment. They were clad in their winter uniforms, the muskrat caps and buffalo-skin overcoats which had led the Indians to term them "Buffalo Soldiers." From a distance the hairy riders had the look of Mongols or Tartars.

From a later hilltop they looked down on Pine Ridge. The place appeared deserted except for one curl of smoke from the schoolhouse. The hundreds of tepees that had formerly dotted the valley of White Clay Creek had vanished.

Jared grunted his satisfaction. "Leastwise," he said, "they wasn't fool enough to burn the buildings before they took off."

A lone Indian sentinel sat on his horse on a higher slope. He rode down to intercept them. Kirk saw that the horse was the one delivered by Mary to Dr. Eastman before he realized that the bareheaded, breech-clouted figure with a rifle across his knees was Eastman himself. He pulled up and looked somberly at Kirk, who understood his unspoken question.

"The army will occupy the agency property," said Kirk. "But General Miles has ordered no armed pursuit or search until every means has been exhausted to persuade the Indians to return peaceably."

Eastman drew a long breath. "Knowing you, I have to believe you. As you can see, I had decided that my place was out there with them. I let Elaine stay at the school, agreeing that she'd be as safe there as at Rushville. Soon as I have told her what you've said I'll go with you to help you spread the word."

In the agent's empty office, Kirk tacked his first message to General Miles beside the silent telegraph key:

ALL SIOUX FLED AGENCY BEFORE FIRST TROOPS ARRIVED. AM FOLLOWING WITH JARED AND DR. EASTMAN TO TELL THEM YOUR ORDERS.

KIRK

Within a few miles they began overtaking the last Oglala to leave the agency. Men, women, and children alike were so gripped by fear that it was difficult to make them listen even to Eastman's attempts to reassure them.

"For them," said Eastman, "frightened to death is more than just a phrase. They know that pursuit by soldiers has always meant the shooting or sabering of whoever of any age or sex could be overtaken. They know because they've seen it, lost relatives, or survived being themselves struck down."

The rest of that day, all through the night and most of the next day, the three rode up and down the valley of the White, along the borders of the reservation, carrying their message to the thousands of Sioux milling wildly among the hills. A few were yelling their defiant determination to fight to the end, others had resumed dancing as though seeking in this a refuge, but most were half-crazed by fear. These, were they to be approached or threatened by soldiers, would prove the deadliest and most desperate of antagonists. Gradually, however, with the word of their own scouts confirming the words of Kirk, Eastman and Jared, they began to realize that there was no immediate threat. This relative quiet, however, served merely to reveal more starkly the deep divisions among the Sioux. Those inclined to trust the army's offer of safety became more pacific and those at the other extreme of opinion more belligerent. Short Bull arrived with his Pass Creek band to add weight to the intransigent faction. In the main Sioux encampment at the mouth of White Clay Creek three groupings were becoming apparent. Those who favored submission were beginning to edge away in the direction of the agency; those who could see no other recourse than to fight were moving across the river in readiness for a dash to the Badlands, and the greater number, who could not make up their minds, continued to hold endless tribal councils. Upon his return to the agency Kirk summarized his conclusions in his message to Miles:

> With Jared and Dr. Eastman have talked with most bands who have left reservations. A few of the most friendly are already coming in. It is my opinion, supported by Jared and Dr. Eastman, that if let alone more than half will come in within the week. However, a band of the most hostile, numbering possibly a thousand warriors, led by Two Strike, Short Bull, Mash-the-Kettle, and Red Cloud, has taken up an entrenched position on a mesa at the edge of the Badlands. The steep approaches so favor defense that their elevated camp has already earned the name of The Stronghold. They are dancing more furiously than ever and challenging the army to come to get them. Kicking Bear, who has joined them, is now preaching that the Messiah will come not next spring but any day. Nevertheless, it is our opinion that if not attacked they will weaken as winter sets in. It is my further impression that Red Cloud went with them for the purpose of presently persuading them of the military hopelessness of their situation.
>
> *Kirk*

He handed the message to the army telegrapher and left the agent's quarters. The first crisp touch of frost was in the evening air. The whole agency area had become an armed camp, with precise rows of army tents in the place of the random clusters of Indian tepees. Smells from field kitchens, horse lines, and latrines swirled in the faint puffs of wind. The command had already settled into quiet for the night. The only animation came from the roistering group of a dozen or more reporters gathered in Jim Asag's trading post. After their headlong dash from distant cities to the front these aspiring war correspondents had been disappointed to discover there was as yet no war, and to cover the lack of one were writing lurid accounts of the great battles they forecast as imminent. General Brooke had had the good sense to deny them the use of the military telegraph, so they were obliged to get off their dispatches by courier to Rushville.

Kirk staggered across to Eastman's house where, exhausted by so many days and nights with only snatches of sleep, he collapsed on the floor. Awakened by a pounding on the door, he realized that it was morning and that at some earlier time Eastman must have lifted him from the floor to the cot. The summons was from General Brooke, who had established his headquarters in Royer's house. Kirk hastily shaved and gulped the cup of coffee and slice of bread smeared with pemmican which Eastman had come in to force on him.

Closeted with Brooke was Colonel George A. Forsyth, commander of the 7th Cavalry, who had come on ahead of his regiment. The regular army was so small that the personalities of older officers were familiar to even such juniors as Kirk. Forsyth was reputed to be a capable commander but his friends were prone to whisper that his fits of depression and bursts of temper were undoubtedly due to the head wound he had suffered from the Cheyenne more than twenty years ago at the Battle of Beecher Island.

"Sit down, Lieutenant," said Brooke. The room was small, overheated by a sheet-iron stove, and the portly general was sweating. "I've just been telling Colonel Forsyth what it looks like we're up against here and I wanted you to hear how our situation strikes him."

Kirk was prepared to listen respectfully to a veteran of Forsyth's campaign experience but was at the same time speculating on what could be behind this readiness of a brigadier general and a colonel to air their opinions for the benefit of a second lieutenant.

"First off let me say that I'm just as anxious as you and General Miles to get out of this without any fighting if there's any way we can do that," said Forsyth. He was addressing Brooke as though Kirk were not in the room. "I agree that it looks like the Sioux in that main White Clay camp are waiting to see what we're up to and that if we don't do anything to get their wind up a good many might start straggling in before the week's out. But those hard-noses out on the mesa are another story. If they decide to cut and run from there and start rampaging around the Dakotas, those that have come in could get so excited they could break out to join the hostiles and there'd be hell to pay before we could get them all rounded up again. The way some of your younger officers talk, they figure the army has such an advantage that this campaign is a kind of picnic. They'd do better to remember that fooling around with Sioux has never been a picnic. They can count four thousand warriors and that's more soldiers than we can lay hands on. All of them that's got Winchesters are better armed than we are. And this guff about they can't fight for long because they haven't got enough to eat is balderdash. There're enough cattle on the ranches between here and the Canadian border to keep them better fed than when they had buffalo to chase. You asked for my views and now you got 'em."

Brooke looked at Kirk. "I wanted you to hear this because you'll shortly be seeing General Miles. He has ordered you to report to him in Chicago at once. If he asks you any questions you can tell him privately that I and most of my officers entirely agree with what you've just heard from the colonel. Naturally, I'll go on sitting back here until he tells me different. It's his funeral. Thank you, Lieutenant."

Kirk realized that he was being made the cat's-paw to get Brooke's professional opinion to Miles's attention without Brooke having to run the career risk of formally disagreeing in writing with his superior. He found Jared rolled in his blanket alongside Eastman's corral, in which their three horses were penned. Jared appeared always able, whenever there was need, to go indefinitely without sleep but then he was equally able to sleep indefinitely when circumstances permitted.

"The general wants to see me in Chicago," said Kirk. "I've no idea what for. Now, Brooke has dozens of scouts — Crow, Pawnee, Cheyenne, traders, squaw men — to keep him informed on what's going on here. While I'm away, why don't you cut across to the Cheyenne? The bands of Big Foot and Hump are out there somewhere. Probably by now there'll be some smaller bands wandering around. Take a look and come out at Fort Bennett, where I'll send word for you on whatever General Miles wants next."

Jared grinned and stretched. This was the sort of lone prowling far from the constraints of anybody's headquarters he liked best.

When Kirk stepped down to the station platform in Chicago the next midnight he was astonished to find himself in the clutch of a waiting Leonard Wood, clad in a resplendent dress uniform and smelling strongly of wine.

"Hurry," Wood cried. "I'll tell you about it after we get in the cab."

Wood rushed him through the station to the waiting hansom.

"An extra two dollars if you get us to the Northwestern depot by 12:30," he called up to the driver, who whipped up his horse as his fares settled into the seat.

"Where's the general going?" asked Kirk.

"To bed, I hope," said Wood. "What kind of an Indian sign have you got on him that whatever fix he gets into makes him think of you? Anyway, you're the one that's going."

"Going where?"

"Standing Rock."

The night was dark and chill and drizzly but the unexpected revelation that he might so soon see Mary again came to Kirk with the effect of a grenade at his feet.

"In the few minutes we have I'll try to explain, though there are cases where the working of the general's mind couldn't be explained in as many weeks. He decided after all that Brooke could be trusted to do as he's told, so he called you in because he had something more immediate for you to do."

"I have private word from Brooke for the general," Kirk interjected.

"He knows all about that. He needs you to help him with Indians, not to run the army. It seems the Indian Bureau has come up with the idea that the best way to ease the situation is to make a list of the chiefs who are the main troublemakers and then hand the list to the army so that the army could put them all under arrest. Miles wanted your advice on how to go about this."

"How, indeed? Big Foot and Hump are out on the plains with their bands and the worst of the rest are all up on that mesa, where it would take a two-regiment assault to get at them."

"He knows all that, too. But the worst of them all is squatting at home where he's easy to get at. Sitting Bull."

"Still, why me? He's got Colonel Drum and his Fort Yates garrison almost on Sitting Bull's doorstep."

"My boy, after what you've been through these past few months you should realize nothing in this situation can ever be as simple as that. Actually, the general didn't think of you for this particular chore until

246

about an hour ago, when he remembered you'd be getting off that train and he could get his hands on you. He was at a Shriners' banquet at the Congress Hotel when a telegram was delivered him from McLaughlin, the agent up there. McLaughlin said Sitting Bull had to be arrested at once because any day he was apt to take off with his followers to join Big Foot or Hump or the wild men on the mesa. The general hates to take advice from agents, least of all this pushy McLaughlin. Still, he doesn't want to come out looking like a fool. That's where you come in. Here's his orders to Drum, which you're to hand Drum after you've talked to him and are convinced he agrees the arrest is really necessary and you both decide it won't start more trouble than it will stop."

The cab pulled up before the station. Wood ran on ahead to try to hold the train while Kirk picked up his knapsack and bedding roll. The train was beginning to move when he jumped aboard. Wood ran along-side for a few steps.

"Don't look so sour," he called, waving and laughing. "You handle Sitting Bull right and you could wind up with a job with Buffalo Bill's circus."

The succession of local trains bearing Kirk north and west made many stops and poor connections. But he was scarcely aware of the discomforts of hard seats, smoke, cinders, and long waits on station platforms. He was entirely engrossed in his contemplation of the prospect that he was presently to see Mary again. The significance of his official errand did not recapture his attention until he was seated across the breakfast table from Colonel Drum at Fort Yates.

"What's the general hung on?" said Drum. "For the last month he's been swearing because the Indian Bureau objected to his ordering Sitting Bull arrested. But now the bureau wants it."

"Do you really think Sitting Bull's about to bolt off for the plains?"

"Well . . . you always have to expect the enemy to do what you'd least like, don't you? Anyway, McLaughlin in his telegram rode that chance hard because he was so anxious to get authority to make the arrest at a time of our own choice."

"You have a time in mind?"

"Yes, we do. Next ration day — that's a week from Saturday — all the

Hunkpapa will come in and Sitting Bull will be alone at his house out there. That's when we'll pick him up and have him off the reservation before his people know what's happened. That way he won't get hurt, we won't get hurt, nobody'll get hurt."

Kirk gathered his wandering wits to consider this. Like the introduction of troops to Pine Ridge, the arrest of Sitting Bull was sooner or later inevitable. The McLaughlin-Drum scheme seemed as sensible a solution to the problem as might be devised. He handed over the order.

On his way to the mission he saw Remington waving from his doorway. Remington, too, had his problems.

"I've been hanging on here," he said, "because I can't get it out of my head that the central business in this whole Sioux situation is what goes on with Sitting Bull. But so far all he's done is dance all the time and wear out McLaughlin's temper. He's doing nothing to show his hand. Meanwhile you've moved the army into Pine Ridge and Rosebud and the great danger spot seems to be that place they call The Stronghold. Yet here I still sit, two hundred miles from where the news is breaking."

"Your hunch could have been right from the first," said Kirk. "Everybody on both sides seems to be waiting for Sitting Bull to make his move. Tell me, why are they keeping John shut up?"

"That's a put-up job. He wants it that way. The Hunkpapa listen to him just because he is the agent's prisoner. On ration days when they all come in he practically holds court. They squat by the hundreds around his cell door. It could be that it's his influence with Sitting Bull's own people that keeps Sitting Bull hanging fire. Before you do anything else, by the way, be sure you see him."

Kirk crossed to the barracks. John came to the window in his door. He did not reach through the bars to shake hands.

"So you couldn't hold off your army."

"It could have been worse. So far the army has only appeared. There has been no threat. If the Sioux can realize that, there is still hope."

"I've done no better with Sitting Bull. He started dancing. But still he can't make up his mind. He's smart enough to comprehend the terrible risk. But he hates the whites too much to dismiss the opportunity. As you say, there may still be hope."

"Something I've been wanting to ask you," said Kirk. "When did you catch on that I was an army officer?"

"I guessed when first I saw you at the water tank. I was sure when you started giving me orders the next morning on the great trace."

"Did you tell Mary?"

"At our second camp."

"So she knew from then on."

This had given Kirk something to think about. John was watching him closely.

"It didn't seem to me at the time to bother her as much as I expected," he volunteered. "Have you seen her yet?"

"I thought I better see you first."

"She knows you are here." John's eyes held Kirk's. "When you see her stop to think about what you say. I don't imagine that you, any more than I, would want to have her hurt."

"How could I do that?"

"When you rode away that morning she was very sad to see you go. That is what she has been thinking ever since."

"So I should take care not to arouse any false hopes. Could that be what you're getting at?"

"Exactly."

There was a sudden glow in John's eyes. The single word had been as sharp as the crack of a whip.

"Thank you. I will remember."

At the mission an Indian servant girl let him in. They passed an open doorway through which he caught a glimpse of Indian children on pine benches. He was ushered into a small, whitewashed room, furnished with two straight-backed chairs and a wall table on which stood a china statue of the Virgin. After a while the murmur from the classroom ceased. Somewhere on the farther side of the mission the children burst into the open with glad cries. Then Mary stood in the doorway.

She wore a white linen dress. Her hair was drawn into a sedate knot at the nape of her neck. Her eyes were thoughtful, her lips unsmiling. She was infinitely more beautiful than he had remembered. At the first sight of her the desire which he had for weeks struggled to suppress came sweeping through him like a tide. He took a step toward her but she slipped quickly into the nearer chair. He remained standing before her.

"For weeks I have thought of nothing but this moment," he said.

Her eyes widened with surprise but did not meet his.

"When I left you that morning," he continued, "I thought that after a while I would get over it."

"That was what I thought, too."

Her voice was scarcely above a whisper, as on that night in the sand hills.

"Why should either of us try?" he demanded. "Can you tell me that? Don't you see when you look at me? Can't you guess why I'm here? I'm here for one reason only. I'm here to ask you to marry me."

She closed her eyes and shrank against the back of her chair as though cringing from a blow.

"I know I shouldn't have blurted it out like that. You don't have to answer. I only want you to think about it — the way I have."

She opened her eyes and looked steadily up at him.

"There's no use saving my answer. I, too, have been thinking — since that day you went away. It always comes out the same. I could imagine being happy with you easier than I could imagine being happy without you. But I cannot imagine living with a man who is not only white but a white soldier."

"That's nonsense. For example, I bring you the best wishes of Dr. Eastman and Elaine. They are very happy."

"I was sure they could be."

"You mean if I were a doctor or a teacher you might feel differently?"

"Please don't look at me that way. How can I know?"

"Why can't you know? You've had weeks to think. Seemed like years to me. It didn't seem I could possibly wait to get back to you. So what do I find? In that white dress you look as unapproachable as a nun. And this — this white room is like a cell. Can't we get out somewhere — where there are trees and sunlight and air?"

"I am still trying to think. And it is quieter here. I do not feel like a nun. I wish I did. This morning when I heard you were here, I was afraid. Then, when for a while you did not come, I was more afraid."

He bent over her, driven by a compulsion to snatch her up into his embrace. The outright panic in her expression as she shrank back deterred him. She slipped from the chair to the doorway.

"Maybe we should go outside," she whispered.

They walked in silence along the road and turned off at the first path that offered. It led to the low bluff overlooking the Missouri on which stood, on its pedestal, the misshapen block of native granite known as the Standing Rock, for which the reservation had been named. Mary grasped at this safer topic.

"It's supposed to look like a woman and child and to have certain magic qualities which have been largely forgotten. It used to stick out of a hill some miles away but Mr. McLaughlin had it moved here. Sitting Bull officiated at the ceremony. It was probably the last time they ever did anything together."

Kirk looked about him. "I've also been told that around the fort this is known as Proposal Hill."

"What you mean is . . . where soldiers bring their Indian girls."

"Along with being the loveliest you're the most perverse creature God ever made. Have you so soon forgotten? I'm here just for that. To make a proposal. I want you to marry me. I can't help being white but if this damned uniform makes any difference I'll take it off. I'll resign from the army. I want you so much more than I want anything else that nothing else counts."

He reached for her but she shivered so uncontrollably when his arms closed around her that he drew back.

"Well?" he demanded. "Can you for once give me a straight answer?"

"I can. It's no."

"Why?"

"Your career. You'd never forgive me for ending it. If you did, I wouldn't forgive myself. And just now what you are doing is important. So much more important than either of us. Oh, there are many reasons."

"Then can you tell me this? Can you tell me that you don't love me?"

"No, I can't. It must be that I do. Only I'm so foolish that I can't be completely sure about anything. There were all those years I idolized

John. Then you came along and after you left me I could no longer help myself. Of course, I love you. I can't look at you without knowing that must be so."

Again Kirk put his arms around her. This time her resistance amounted to no more than a slight stiffening. There was the loud clearing of a throat. Kirk spun around to discover at his elbow an orderly from Fort Yates saluting and clicking his heels.

"Excuse me, Lieutenant." He spoke mechanically, as one who had carefully memorized a message. "Colonel Drum's compliments, sir. There's a wire ordering you to report to General Miles at Rapid City. He's setting up field headquarters in the Black Hills."

The orderly saluted, about-faced, and marched off. Kirk turned back to Mary. Something had happened to her. She was different. It was as though the simple military routine of the orderly's delivery of the message had roused her, as from a dream. She was staring at Kirk's uniform as though it were something that had unaccountably slipped her mind and had only now been recalled. Her eyes met his. Her gaze was calm and steady. Almost imperceptibly she was shaking her head. The refusal was not so much of him as of herself. There was no mistaking what had occurred. His moment had passed.

They walked, again in silence, back to the mission. At the gateway she faced him, studied his face gravely, and placed her hands on his shoulders.

"Please kiss me once."

He did. Her lips were cool. She seemed more remote from him than she had ever seemed before.

"I don't say that will be our only kiss," she said. "Though it could be." Her eyes misted with tears. She turned and ran into the mission.

Striding toward the agency he examined his behavior as coldly as though it had been that of a stranger. There on the hill, had she, as a consequence of his declarations, relaxed in his arms and accepted his caresses, he would have taken her right then. It was for that he had made his unmeant offers of marriage and resignation. But had, at the moment of their parting, the priest come out with an offer to marry them, he would have stood with her at the altar with as little hesitation. He was no longer his own master.

XIII

HEARING FROM KIRK that General Miles was setting up field headquarters at Rapid City had stretched Remington's impatience to the breaking point. The nose for news that had kept him at Standing Rock to await the development of Sitting Bull's intentions appeared this time to have failed him. Nothing was happening here, while along that long arc of troops extending from the Rosebud clear around the Badlands into the Black Hills, established by Miles to bar any possible Sioux attempt to break out to the westward, it was becoming more and more likely that anything might happen any minute. He spent half the night stowing his equipment and camping outfit in the buckboard, determined to start south the first thing in the morning.

But at dawn he was awakened by Jared bending over him.

"Where've you been?" demanded Remington.

"Just smellin' around. On my way now to have a chin with Sitting Bull. Thought you might want to go along."

"Would I?" Remington jumped up and began hastily dressing. "But what's McLaughlin going to say? He's been insisting that I, along with every other outsider, stay away from Grand River."

"Ask him," said Jared.

Remington turned to see McLaughlin standing in the doorway.

"Drum and me, we've worked up a little different idea," said the agent. "From all we hear, what with all this dancing and conjuring, Sitting Bull's getting himself more worked up every day. Be a help to get his mind on something else for a while. Anyway, what strikes us is that if you was to go out there bent on painting his picture, he's so full of flapdoodle he'd likely puff up like a turkey cock. What we want is just what you will want. We want him sitting still and looking pleasant. Feel like trying it?"

"Naturally, I do. If you hadn't kept your police following me around I'd have been out there long ago. Come on, Jared — let's hitch up and be on our way."

"I'll lend you a horse," said McLaughlin, "With that wagon it'll be late afternoon before you can get there. They'll be dancing by then and you won't be able to get to him till noon tomorrow. If this is going to work, the sooner you get at him the better. Most any day he could be jumping in the pail with both feet."

The note of urgency heightened Remington's interest. "I can get along the first day with only my sketch pad but by tomorrow I'll need the rest of my stuff."

"I'll get your wagon out to you by then," said McLaughlin.

A mile from Sitting Bull's house, Jared pulled his horse down to a walk.

"Give them time to spot us," he said, "figger out who we are, tell Sitting Bull, and give him time to think. Never good to surprise an Indian."

They pulled up before Sitting Bull's house. Waiting for them on the porch were Crow Foot, Sitting Bull's son, in moccasins, leggings, breechclout, and blanket, with the Wovoka-sanctioned eagle feather in his hair, and a slightly older Sioux, dressed in worn striped trousers, shabby Prince Albert coat, and a Panama hat with a hole in it. These white man's garments he had evidently donned in some haste, for he was still buttoning his fly. Jared began politely addressing the two in Sioux and sign language. The Indian in the straw hat stopped him with a reproving gesture.

"Me," he explained in English, "Andrew Fox. Official interpreter to Sitting Bull. You tell me. I tell Sitting Bull."

Jared grinned and agreeably resumed in English.

"Then tell him Jared Glass is here to visit him. Tell him this is Frederic Remington. He is a painter who has come from New York to make a picture of Sitting Bull."

Fox went into the house. Crow Foot stood beside the door, eyeing the visitors coldly. Remington was reminded that on each of his three former appearances before Sitting Bull he had been in the unpopular company of McLaughlin. Fox came out to announce the verdict.

"He very glad to see old friend Jared Glass. Please to come in his house." He made a gesture of repugnance toward Remington. "No want see this friend to the agent. He stay here to hold the horses."

Jared proved equal to the emergency.

"Go back," he said, raising his voice slightly as though to carry into the house. "Tell Sitting Bull this man is my friend. He is a friend of General Miles. He is a friend of the President. He is the best picture-maker in the world. Tell him when the President heard he was at Standing Rock he sent him a telegram sayin' the President wants a picture of Sitting Bull to hang in the White House."

Fox was starting to shake his head when a guttural word from within caused him to bolt back into the house. Crow Foot followed. There was a longer and louder murmur of voices within. When the door reopened it was Sitting Bull himself who first came through it. He was followed by Fox and Crow Foot, both of whom appeared to be expostulating, though more and more weakly. When they persisted there was a display of the noted Sitting Bull temper. It took but one abrupt growl from him to send the interpreter scurrying from the porch and out of sight around the house. He then turned to welcome his guests.

Crow Foot ran to take their horses. They dismounted and climbed the steps. Remington was received with a handshake almost as cordial as the one given Jared. They were ushered into the house. Sitting Bull's two wives hovered in the background. Jared and Sitting Bull became engaged in an amiable and animated conversation in Sioux and sign language. Remington slipped his sketching pad from its leather case. These were the sort of natural and off-guard moments of which he wished to catch impressions. The old chief was much thinner than when he had seen him last. Evidently the stories of his dancing night after night were true.

"He remembers all those pictures on the White House walls from the times he was there," said Jared. "He likes the idea of one of his hangin' there."

What developed next, however, materially diminished Remington's satisfaction. The wives had come forward and were beginning to dress Sitting Bull in a broadcloth suit. He was handed a huge white hat, which he clapped on his head. From the corner of his eye Remington saw through a window that Crow Foot was leading a fat, gray horse around to the front of the house.

"He's a-puttin' on his best bib and tucker," explained Jared, indicating the broadcloth suit and the white hat. "What he wants is his picture a-settin' on that old circus horse of his'n."

No effect could have been farther from the one Remington wanted. "Explain to him," he implored, "that first I want to work on his face — here where the light's better than out there where he'll be squinting in the sun."

But having succeeded in arranging the start of the sitting, Jared was disposed to be more amused than helpful.

"Keep at him," he advised, "Crow Foot here, he knows a little English. He'll help. Me, I'm moseyin' down the crik a ways to pass the time with old Catch-the-Bear. Oncet back in '68 me and a platoon o' Pawnee scouts chased him up and down the Powder for most a week. Then one night he stampeded our horse herd and bothered us all the next week it took us to get back afoot to Fort Laramie."

He had told the story in Sioux at the same time as in English. Sitting Bull was amused. Jared chuckled and went out. Patiently, Remington maneuvered Sitting Bull to a stool where there was a good light on his face. He soon discovered that Sitting Bull was quick to grasp the significance of his pantomime and gestures and that he could be more easily persuaded by these than by Crow Foot's stumbling interpretation. He got rid of the big hat on the plea that it shadowed the subject's face. He was learning that any appeal to Sitting Bull's vanity worked.

It was his noticing longingly the dust-covered array of weapons, ornaments, and barbaric regalia hanging on the walls that gave him his central inspiration. While seeming to be sketching Sitting Bull's face he swiftly depicted a young warrior costumed and armed as would have been a Sioux hero a generation earlier. When shown the sketch, Sitting Bull eyed it with a grunt of immediate interest.

At a gesture from him, his wives began removing the broadcloth suit. Remington, making judicious selections of the more flamboyant and extravagant among the array of ornaments and weapons on the walls, handed these to the women, who placed them on Sitting Bull or in his hands. Presently the old chief was accoutered in the full martial panoply he might have displayed at the Battle of the Little Bighorn. Remington was delighted with the success of his device. For a moment Sitting Bill, too, was pleased with his new role. Then his face clouded.

Suddenly he spoke in English.

"Once — as you can see — I was proud. I was brave."

"Good lord," said Remington. "You speak English."

"When it pleases me." The chief seemed to be more soliloquizing than addressing Remington. "I never thought I would die in bed. Would you come far to paint me dying in bed?"

"No, I suppose not," murmured Remington. He was trying to catch the play of changing expression over his subject's face.

"Once I was a man." Sitting Bull had suddenly straightened. His gaze appeared to fix on something in the distance. "A man knows only one way to die. Facing his enemies."

With an abrupt gesture he demanded that his wives bring him his primping box. While one held a small mirror in which he intently studied his visage and the other held his box of paints from which he selected colors, he began to stripe his face in the grotesque fashion which by Indian tradition represented the warrior's declaration of his martial prowess and his challenge to any antagonist. At last satisfied, he waved aside the box and mirror and faced Remington, ready to have his portrait painted.

The transition in his outward appearance had been producing an accompanying transition in his mood. His every movement had become jerky, restless. He was becoming strangely excited. Into his eyes had come an unearthly gleam. He appeared to have forgotten Remington. He began talking to himself. Then he was on his feet. He dropped his weapons on his bed and from a hanging medicine bag drew a Ghost Shirt. This he slipped over his head, striking his wives away when they offered to help him. Then, catching up his weapons, he began brandishing them, striding about the room, raising his voice in a singsong chant. The residents of his immediate camp came running, to cluster at the door or to peek in the windows, their eyes widening with awe. Whatever the significance of the chanting it was causing a sensation among the Hunkpapa. Remington, exultant, had throughout been sketching furiously.

Jared appeared in the doorway after shoving his way through the press gathered on the porch. At the sight of the chief's Ghost-Shirted figure the old plainsman stiffened like a hunting dog.

"What's he doing?" asked Remington.

"Countin' coups," said Jared. "He thinks he's a young buck."

"Great," said Remington.

Some note in Jared's voice caused him on second thought to glance around at him again. He was astonished to see how intense seemed Jared's concern. Through a window behind Jared he caught a glimpse of groups of warriors running up the road from more distant areas of the Hunkpapa town. Jared was attending intently to Sitting Bull's wild chant.

"What's he saying?" asked Remington, tearing off another sheet from his pad and tucking it into the case. "Whatever ails him, it's wonderful."

Suddenly Jared leaned nearer, picked up the case, snatched the pad from his grasp, and darted out the door. Remington, astounded, jumped up and set off in pursuit. He had much more difficulty than had Jared in forcing his way through the crowd packed around the door. The Indian failure to step aside seemed not to spring from animus. They seemed unaware of his passage. All their attention was on Sitting Bull's performance.

He had been delayed long enough so that by the time he had got to the horses, Jared had the girths tightened and the bridles replaced. He had tied the sketching case to the back of Remington's saddle.

"Have you lost your mind?" raged Remington.

"After what you got started in there," said Jared, "this ain't no place for a white man to be hangin' around."

"What I got started in there," insisted Remington, "is something I'm not going to leave until I've finished."

He began jerking at the rawhide holding the case, then turned, astounded. Jared was coming around the head of his horse toward him. His look showed a side of his nature which Remington had never before seen. The core of fire and steel in the old man was a trait only his adversaries had ever experienced.

"Me," said Jared, "I'm gettin' back to Fort Yates. And you're a-comin' along — if'n I have to knock you in the head and tie you in the saddle."

"You scare me more than the Sioux do," said Remington, trying to laugh it off.

But he mounted. They walked their horses to the road, Jared with his Winchester across his lap, unobtrusively eyeing the Sioux around Sitting Bull's house. Remington was forgetting his discomfiture in this new interest. His old friend, whom before he had only thought that he had known, was actually in his way as exciting as Sitting Bull.

The moment that they were out of sight Jared whipped his horse into a gallop. He kept up the breakneck pace even after darkness had fallen. The demands being made on their horses were plainly excessive. The second hour after dark Remington's agency mount pulled up lame. Jared dismounted to examine him, then led him a hundred yards from the road into a thicket of juniper, where he cut his throat.

"Don't want him doin' any neighin'," he said. "I ain't real sure they're a-chasin' us but they could be. If they do, better they run on past." He handed Remington his Winchester. "You stay squatted here. Don't try no shootin' 'less they come right at you. Me, I'm gettin' on to Fort Yates. I'll get fresh horses and come back for you."

He was ·gone before Remington could lodge either protests or questions. He found a rock at the edge of the juniper and settled behind it. The time passed slowly. No signs of pursuit developed. He could not see the face of his watch and forebore to light a match. In what he judged was possibly two hours there came the sound of hoofbeats from the direction of Fort Yates. For a moment he thought it could be Jared returning. Then he realized it was only one horse. A lone rider swept past at a furious gallop and on toward Grand River. In another half hour there came the clatter of two horses. This time it was Jared. They set out once more for Fort Yates, at a more reasonable pace.

"Now, for God's sake," said Remington, "maybe you'll tell me what all this is about."

"It's about what Sitting Bull was singin'," said Jared. "Back there after you got him dressed up. He was makin' up his mind that his place was down there on that mesa with the rest of the hostiles. And he was figgerin' on takin' with him as many of his Hunkpapa as would go."

"So that was the news you were in such a gut-busting hurry to get to Fort Yates."

259

"Seemed like a good idee."

"What are Drum and McLaughlin going to do about it?"

"Didn't wait to find out. Wanted to get back to look after you. Took me a mite longer than I liked. Stable sergeant had orders to let no horses off the post tonight. So I had to steal a couple."

"Thank you," said Remington sarcastically, still disgruntled by having been treated so much like a tenderfoot.

Jared pulled up to listen to something in the road ahead. "We'll be seein' in a minute what Drum and McLaughlin are up to."

Remington soon could also hear the distant faint thumping of many hoofbeats in the sandy road. The sound swelled. They swung their horses out of the road. Jared called out their names. There was an answering cheerful hail. A column of cavalry came trotting past. Remington prided himself on his acquaintance with the army. Even in the darkness he could distinguish enough to make identifications.

"Troops F and G of the 8th Cavalry," he pronounced when the column had passed. "A Hotchkiss gun, a Gatling gun, two wagons, and an ambulance. A hundred men with artillery. They're really not fooling. Come on, let's go with them."

Jared's hand shot out to close over Remington's reins. "No," he said. "Got to get these horses back 'fore daylight. That sergeant's a good boy. Don't want him losin' his stripes 'count of me."

Whether or not this represented his primary reason, when this new Jared assumed command mutiny was useless.

"Never made a worse mistake," grumbled Remington, "than ever getting mixed up with you."

At Fort Yates they found Drum and McLaughlin, weary but complacent, drinking coffee in Drum's quarters.

"Have some," said Drum. "Sorry to have got you into that mess, Mr. Remington. We can see now it was a mistake."

Remington was further irritated by the dry tone of Drum's last allusion.

"You must have had some purpose in mind," he said.

"We did. It was, as I believe McLaughlin told you, to gain time. We owe you an explanation and now we can give it to you. When Kirk was here he brought orders to arrest Sitting Bull. McLaughlin and I determined this could best be managed next ration day — that would have been the day after tomorrow. McLaughlin got his police concentrated in the neighborhood with the excuse of sending the detachment stationed here to work on that halfway post at the forks. We thought we were all set to do a quick, neat job. Then we began getting reports that Kicking Bear and Short Bull were pressing him to join the hostiles on The Stronghold. There was also this new talk about the Messiah putting in an appearance down there any day. That's when we got the thought that your painting his portrait might keep him . . . er . . . entertained — for the two extra days we needed."

"So you made me your monkey on a stick," said Remington, now thoroughly angry.

"Well, hardly that. Our plans were necessarily very secret. In your case, as we can see now, our not explaining was obviously a mistake."

Again, there was the tacit reference to the heedless resurrection of Sitting Bull's martial past, to which Remington had no sufficient defense. He was saved by the appearance of an orderly in the doorway.

"Excuse me, Colonel Drum. There's an Indian girl at the gate says she has to talk with Mr. Remington."

Remington jumped up. "Be a relief to talk to a friend," he growled, giving Jared a look as he went out.

He found a distraught Mary waiting beside the sentry at the gate.

"I didn't know what else to do," she said, clutching his arm, "except to come to you. When I heard about those soldiers riding out in the middle of the night I was sure they were going to take Sitting Bull. Are they?"

"Yes," said Remington grimly.

"Then why don't they let John out?"

Instantly grasping what she meant, he towed her after him into Drum's office.

"Why don't you turn John loose?" he demanded of McLaughlin. "On that horse of his he could still get there ahead of your soldiers. With him there to talk to the Hunkpapa there might be less chance of trouble."

"We had planned it that way for ration day," said McLaughlin. "But it's too late for that tonight. He can't possibly get out there in time. Sitting Bull will actually be arrested by my police at the first streak of daylight. The troops were only sent as a backup in case they were needed."

"But, Mr. McLaughlin," protested Mary, prepared to speak out even in this company. "You know how the Sioux feel about the police. To the soldiers they might give up Sitting Bull, but to the police — never."

"We sent along the troops," put in Drum, "just in case they got any such foolish ideas. One way or another they'll be obliged to give him up."

Remington's cumulative anger over the way he had been so cavalierly treated in the last few hours by the agent, the colonel, and even his old friend, Jared, boiled over. With his knuckles whitening on the table, he leaned across it to confront McLaughlin.

"You planned it this way because this was the way you wanted it," he charged. "You don't want Sitting Bull arrested. You want him destroyed. That's why you're shoving your police at him. You've hated him for years. You've failed to beat him down. Now you're out to finish him off."

McLaughlin maintained the calm of a man who feels himself fully justified.

"You couldn't be more wrong, Mr. Remington. If the army takes him what good would that do? The army's been kicking the Sioux around for forty years without accomplishing anything more than killing half of them. What the Sioux have got to learn is that they have to submit to the law. My police are law officers. I am a law officer. What Sitting Bull has got to be made to realize is not that the police are bigger than he is, or that I am bigger than he is, but that the law is bigger than he is. I pray to God that there won't be bad trouble out there this morning. If there is, all I've been trying to do winds up a failure. But to let him get away would make me a worse failure. If he gets off down there to the mesa there's sure to be a war. That's what's got to be stopped. That's what I'm doing my damnedest to stop."

"You make a case that's not so easy to answer," admitted Remington.

He straightened to realize that Mary was no longer in the room. From the doorway, she was not in sight on the parade ground. He obeyed the impulse at least to try to comfort her. He ran to the gate.

"Did the Indian girl come back out?" he asked.

"If you mean Mary Chadron," said the sentry, "she took off running down the road toward the agency."

Running as hard as ever in his footballs days, he overtook her at the edge of the agency compound.

"John," she gasped. "Maybe he can think of something."

What John, a prisoner, could do was not clear, though he could realize her need and nodded understandingly. But their pilgrimage was stillborn. Puma was no longer in the shed back of his house. The door of John's cell was ajar. He was not in it. Santy came out with a lantern.

"For once I didn't catch on to what Mr. McLaughlin was up to," she said. "Not until it was too late. But when finally I did I turned John loose." She nodded toward the west. "Whatever's going on out there, he's got a right to his part in it."

She went back into her kitchen.

"I have to look for him," said Mary. "Let me have your team."

"I have to look for him, too," said Remington. "Too much of this is my doing."

"No," she insisted. "A white man won't be safe."

"A fool like me is safe anywhere. Besides it's my job to keep up with the news. Come help me hitch up."

Not long after they had turned into the Grand River road there came the sound of hoofbeats behind. Jared drew alongside.

"Figgered maybe you could use some company," he said.

XIV

GALLOPING THROUGH THE NIGHT along this road with which since childhood he had been so familiar, One Bull was suffused by wave after wave of pride. His reasons to be proud seemed to him so many that it was necessary to count them on his fingers. He was proud to be wearing this police uniform, to which he was at last proving himself entitled. He was proud to be astride a finer horse than he had ever before been granted the fortune to ride. He was proud because it was the agent's own personal horse and it had been the agent himself who had placed so prized a mount at his disposal. But most of all he was proud to have been entrusted with a mission of more importance than any other of which he could conceive.

At the forks he pulled up for a moment at the camp of the police detail presumed to be constructing the halfway house. Sergeant Shave Head leaped from his blanket to stand beside the sweating horse. One Bull leaned down from the saddle, very conscious that the sergeant who had so often reproved him was now breathlessly listening to him.

"Agent's orders," he whispered. "Meet Lieutenant Bull Head at Gray Eagle's house — soon as you can get there."

The depth of Shave Head's grunt indicated how instantly he realized the full gravity of the summons. One Bull rode on. The stars were beginning to fade behind a gathering mist but he could tell by his last glimpse of them that he was making this ride faster than it had ever been made before except by John on Puma. A long mile before reaching Sitting Bull's house he left the road to cross the river to the other side. The mist was settling closer to the ground, making it darker than ever. He circled the firelit dancing ground, where the dancers were reaching the late-night peak of their excitement. At Carignan's house he rode alongside the room in which he knew the schoolmaster slept and tapped

264

on the window. Carignan threw it open. One Bull handed him the agent's letter and rode on to Bull Head's house. Red Bear was on guard duty. He came out of the corral shadows as One Bull dismounted. One Bull handed him the reins of his horse and went up the steps. The moment offered him not the least of the night's many satisfactions. The privilege of taking it for granted that someone else would take care of his horse was one that had never before been his.

He felt his way through the darkness within the house to Bull Head's bed and placed his hand on the lieutenant's shoulder. Starting up in his bed, Bull Head's left hand closed on One Bull's wrist and his right snatched his revolver from under his pillow.

"One Bull reporting, sir," said One Bull, remembering his military manners and speaking slowly and carefully in order fully to savor the significance of his part in this occasion. "I bring orders from the agent. He commands you to arrest Sitting Bull at daylight and to escort him to Fort Yates."

Bull Head found a match, lighted his lantern, and held it up to study One Bull's face. His own was strained, as though he had a pain in his belly. He seemed to be hoping that he would discover that One Bull could be mistaken, or could be drunk, or could be out of his mind.

"The soldiers are coming from Fort Yates," continued One Bull. "They will wait behind the ridge beyond Sitting Bull's house in case you have to send for them."

There was a finality about this that gave cold and utter reality to all the necessities involved. Bull Head began to dress. Carignan came in with the agent's written order, which he read to Bull Head. It merely served to confirm One Bull's version. The schoolmaster, pleased with the prospect, went to the stove and began brewing a pot of coffee.

"What's the matter?" he demanded, eyeing Bull Head. "You've known for a week this was something you'd have to do the day after tomorrow."

"When I go to sleep it was two days away," said Bull Head. "When I wake up it is two hours away." He returned Carignan's look. "You will be able to sit here drinking coffee. You will not be creeping up in the night to drag your bishop from his bed."

He went into the bunk room next door and began rousing his men.

Red Bear was sent to take another look at the dance. Others were sent to summon those members of the force who slept in their homes with their families. When the horses had been saddled, all gathered in the bunk room, sipping the hot coffee and furtively watching their leaders, Bull Head and Red Tomahawk. Red Bear came back to report.

"Sitting Bull danced until he had a vision that the Messiah is coming to Pine Ridge this moon. People say that then he fell down and got as stiff as a dead man. After that he went home to rest. People also say that he will start for Pine Ridge after he has rested."

The demand of duty had been repulsive. With these words it became implacable. Bull Head put down his cup. The time had come to start. The pleasurable excitement stirred in One Bull by his new self-importance was beginning to fail him.

The police rode off one by one, each circling separately through the darkness, to reassemble at the house of Gray Eagle, across the river from Sitting Bull's house. Here they rendezvoused with Shave Head's detachment from the halfway camp. They now numbered forty-three. But they gained little reassurance from the increase in their strength. It seemed rather to aggravate the sum total of their individual misgivings.

One Bull could see none of the faces of his companions clustered about him. But he could hear how hoarsely their breath was coming out of tightened throats. They had enlisted in the police because they liked the pay, the rations, the uniforms and the authority over their fellow Sioux. Now they were stricken by the enormity of a deed to which they could not have foreseen themselves ever being committed. But One Bull could not detect in them any inclination to draw back. Becoming police had not made them any the less Sioux of the warrior class. To yield at this last moment to fear in the immediate face of danger remained for them a greater fear.

Gray Eagle, who was a Christian convert, came out on his doorstep to propose that they pray. He was Sitting Bull's brother-in-law, who had broken with his kinsman as a result of disagreement over the Ghost Dance, which Gray Eagle condemned as a heathen abomination. The only Christian prayer he knew was the Sioux version of the one that the missionary called the Lord's Prayer. All dismounted and knelt. Few of the policemen were converts but all felt equally in need of divine sustenance.

They mounted and walked their horses toward the river. The mist had grown thicker and colder until it had become a freezing drizzle. There came to their ears an unnatural hooting of owls in the river-bottom willows and in the distance a peculiarly sustained howling of coyotes. The slow pace of the column was like a death march accompanied by the eerie wails of lost souls. One Bull could hear the muttered whispering of Red Bear riding beside him. Red Bear had resumed praying, invoking the aid not of the white man's God but of the Great Spirit whose concern was for the Sioux. So deeply was he disturbed, however, that in his supplication he was resorting to the traditional words of the plea voiced by the hunter stalking a grizzly, in which he begs in advance the monster's forgiveness for presuming to attack him. The dire hoots and howls continued to echo through the dripping darkness of the mist. One Bull was himself endeavoring desperately to recall in detail the words-of his grandfather, a noted conjuror, when instructing him how to recognize the meaning of warnings from the dead, which in moments of immense peril could be announced by the cries of birds and animals of the night. The last of his earlier excitement had drained away. He found himself childishly wishing that he might awake in his barracks bunk to discover this night had been only a dream.

The lead horses were splashing into the ford. Bull Head, with a sudden grunt of resolution, lifted his to a gallop. The riders behind him seemed jerked into following as though the column of horses were attached end to end by lead ropes. For all his mounting dread of what might lie ahead, One Bull felt no impulse to wheel back. He had a greater dread of being alone. There was some comfort, at the worst, in the company of his fellows.

There broke out a frantic tumult of barking from the dogs in Sitting Bull's camp. The first pallid light was beginning to penetrate the mist as the police encircled his house. Now that the time for action had come men began to breath with less difficulty. The operation had been planned with care and each knew exactly what was expected of him. Red Bear and White Bird ran to the corral to bring Sitting Bull's horse. Bull Head, flanked by Sergeant Shave Head and Second Sergeant Red

Tomahawk, all three with drawn revolvers in their hands, ran up the steps, pounded on the door, shoved it open, and went in. One Bull followed as far as the open doorway.

"We have come to take you to Fort Yates," Bull Head announced, feeling his way across the room, into which the morning's first dim light was creeping from the graying windows.

Sitting Bull was in bed with his two wives, Seen-by-Her-Nation and Four Times. As they started up it became apparent that they had been sleeping nude. The women backed fearfully away from the policemen. Sitting Bull got slowly to his feet. He was neither surprised nor angry but seemed rather to be recognizing a moment he had long expected. He kept shaking his head as though not fully awake or as though he might be still under the effect of the herb decoction sometimes drunk by the Ghost Dancers to hasten visions. After peering from a window at the cordon of police surrounding his house, he spoke mildly.

"Give me time to dress."

Relieved by his submissive attitude, Bull Head made a gesture of assent. The process of dressing, however, was delayed by Sitting Bull's changing his mind about the selection of clothing and his insisting on sending Four Times to the other house to bring his broadcloth suit and white hat.

Meanwhile, the delay had allowed time for the situation outside to become critical. Word of the police descent had reached the dancing ground. Groups of warriors were swarming to Sitting Bull's camp. The police around the house faced about with weapons ready to confront this imminent threat. Within the house Sitting Bull's dressing seemed to proceed ever more slowly. Bull Head, aware of the growing danger outside, became peremptory in his demands that Sitting Bull come with him without further delay.

At last, Bull Head and Shave Head seized him by the arms and started him toward the door. Crow Foot, crouched in a corner, called upon his father to resist. But Sitting Bull, still seeming half dazed, merely looked reproachfully at the policemen. When Crow Foot leaped up, Bull Head gestured with the revolver in his free hand toward the open door. The boy stared at the muzzle of the gun as though at a snake, then choked

268

and ran out. Red Tomahawk followed. One Bull stepped to one side. In the room behind, Sitting Bull's wives began to howl the death song.

When Sitting Bull appeared on the porch in the grasp of the two policemen there came from the assembled Sioux, now numbering more than a hundred, a continuing low growl like that of a wolf pack worrying a carcass. The rank of police between the prisoner and his followers thickened as it was joined by those formerly watching the rear of the house. It was now full daylight, though still a cold, damp, gray morning. Sitting Bull was conducted down the steps to the ground but there then developed another delay. To Bull Head's furious disgust the horse had not yet been brought. Sitting Bull raised his face to the sky as though looking for some omen. Catch-the-Bear began in a loud voice to call upon the Hunkpapa to rescue their chief. The police began lifting their carbines.

Roland came into view around the corner of the house, led by Red Bear and White Bird. Bull Head and Shave Head began pulling their prisoner toward the horse. For the first time Sitting Bull held back. When they continued to jerk him along, he cried out in protest. Catch-the-Bear was overcome by the spectacle of his best friend, Sitting Bull, being manhandled by his worst enemy, Bull Head. He lifted his Winchester and shot Bull Head.

Falling, Bull Head jammed his revolver into Sitting Bull's side and pulled the trigger. As the chief collapsed, Shave Head, on the other side, shot him in the back of the head. The nearest policeman, Lone Man, sprang at Catch-the-Bear. The old warrior's rifle misfired. Lone Man clubbed him to the ground and shot him.

By now every weapon in the hands of either Sioux or police was blazing. At such close range the fire was deadly. The police were outnumbered but their discipline was enabling them for the moment to hold their own. One Bull was shot through the chest, fell from the porch, and crawled under the edge of the steps.

The first fury of the battle was interrupted by the phenomenon of Roland's behavior. The old circus horse, accustomed to regard gunfire as his cue, went into his act. He sat back on his haunches beside Sitting Bull's corpse and raised his right forehoof in a military salute. The firing ceased as Indians on both sides paused to ponder fearfully the possibility that the spirit of the dead Sitting Bull had already taken possession of the horse.

The dying Bull Head, by now seven times wounded, took advantage of the momentary respite to order his police into the house, which they were able to make an impromptu fortress. With the police now firing from behind walls the Sioux were obliged to draw back to the shelter of the adjacent strip of woods. From this cover they resumed their fire. The battle had become a siege of the beleaguered police. In the confusion of the Sioux withdrawal, however, a policeman, Hawk Man, mounted Roland and got away alive to summon the soldiers.

One Bull, from his position under the steps, fell deliriously to counting the dead and dying who lay within his view. He could see eight Sioux and six police on the blood-soaked ground. Of these, one was the greatest of all Sioux, another was his son, and two, Catch-the-Bear and Bull Head, were among the most important of the Hunkpapa. This, he realized in an agony more painful than the torment in his chest, was what had resulted from his ride through the night.

He drifted away into unconsciousness to be shocked back to reality by a fearful explosion. A flying fragment of shell casing tore away most of his left leg. He rolled over to see soldiers on the ridge opposite the strip of woods. They were firing a cannon. They had evidently not realized that the police had taken refuge in the house, for their first shot had been at the porch, which was beginning to burn. A policeman ran out of the house to wave a white rag. The soldiers seemed to recognize the signal, for after a moment the shells began exploding at the edge of the woods. Dismounted troopers commenced volley firing from the ridge. The Sioux in the woods returned the fire.

Then One Bull witnessed the sight that lowered him into the ultimate depths of despair. Bull Ghost, wearing his Ghost Shirt, made famous by the exceptional decorations lavished upon it, rode from the woods out into the open to gallop in a wide circle halfway to Sitting Bull's house. All the fire of the soldiers on the ridge and the police in the house was centered upon him. But he continued to brandish his lance and to yell his contempt. The Ghost Shirt, he howled, kept him forever safe from any bullet fired in the service of white men. He regained the woods unharmed. Twice more he emerged to repeat the scornful excursion. On these second two rides he was subjected to the rapid fire of the Gatling gun on the ridge in addition to the hail of bullets from individual riflemen. But at no time during the three rides was he hit.

Thereafter the soldiers charged down from the ridge and on past the house to drive the Sioux from the woods. But to this One Bull paid no attention. The magic of Bull Ghost had convinced him. He knew he was dying. He was glad. For now he knew how unforgivable had been his sin when in electing to put on the police uniform he had renounced those mystic powers heaven had reserved to the Sioux.

XV

THE FIRST STREAKS OF DAWN were breaking while Remington, Mary, and Jared were still some miles from Grand River.

"Bull Head will be movin' in by now," said Jared.

A few minutes later they heard the faint mutter of distant gunfire.

"A proper set-to," pronounced Jared, cocking his head, "As many Sioux Winchesters as police carbines."

In another half hour there came the louder thumps of the Hotchkiss shells.

"So they did have to call in the army," observed Remington.

Mary sat in the seat beside him with closed eyes. She did not open them until when, a mile from Sitting Bull's house, they encountered the macabre funeral cortege. The troopers did not look like soldiers returning from a victory. They rode past, silent, morose, staring straight ahead. In one of the wagons had been placed the blanket-wrapped police dead. Also in the wagon was the corpse of Sitting Bull, propped up so that any who looked could see his wounds and the horrible manner in which his head and face had been pounded after his death.

Remington had driven off the road to make way for the passing column. As she watched, Mary's first grief and horror was somewhat relieved by her anger.

"Nothing you white people have ever done to us," she said, "can equal what we so often do to one another."

She began to weep and drooped into the encircling comfort of Remington's free arm. Jared rode for a time with the police and troopers to inquire about John. Mary had regained control by the time he returned.

"John didn't get there till after the shootin' had stopped," Jared reported. "He tried to get them to give him Sitting Bull's body so's he could bury it. After they wouldn't stand for that, the last anybody seen of him he was ridin' west up the river."

"We have to keep after him," said Remington. "Did anybody tell you what was the idea of mashing in Sitting Bull's face that way?"

"Wasn't police or soldiers that done that. It was old Holy Medicine. He went to poundin' on him with a neck yoke before anybody could stop him. One of the police that got killed was his only boy."

They drove past the smoking ruins of Sitting Bull's house and on through the Hunkpapa settlement beyond. All the tepees had disappeared. There was no sign of life around the houses, the brush huts, or the edges of the fields.

"Somebody down there in them willows," said Jared. "Mebbe you better be the one to go take a look, Mary."

Mary slipped out of the white linen dress, disclosing that beneath it she was wearing the doeskin shift, and set out on her investigation. After some time, she emerged to report.

"Just a few old women and some children. They are so scared they can hardly talk. All the other Hunkpapa are gone. Some just to hide. Some are on their way to Pine Ridge or The Stronghold. Most are joining Big Foot."

"Gettin' him a pack o' Sitting Bull's people ain't goin' to make him any easier to manage," said Jared.

"Can you blame him — or them?"

"Nope, I can't."

"Now about John," resumed Mary. "They say this morning he came through here walking his horse. He was singing a song." She hesitated. "This is hard to explain. But it was the song a very young man sings before he goes out into the hills to keep his first vigil. That's the time of fasting and praying a boy must undertake in order to become a man."

"He's man enough for me as he is," said Remington.

"I know him," continued Mary. "I know what he's feeling. He's feeling that everything he's tried to do with his life has turned out a total failure. He's gone out to try — somehow — to find a new beginning."

"You don't mean an end?"

"I can't believe that — at least, not yet."

"Anyway, let's get started looking for him."

"I'd like to. This is not a time for him to be alone. But he was born somewhere far up the Cheyenne. I'm sure that's where he will go. And that's a country I don't know."

"Jared does."

"Let's go take us a look," said Jared. "That's one Indian we don't want to lose."

They struck off southwest toward the Cheyenne, Jared ranging widely ahead. He had not smiled since hearing the distant murmur of gunfire at Sitting Bull's house. Sighting the river their third day out, he waited on a hilltop for the buckboard to come up with him. His depression was still more evident.

"First time I seen the Cheyenne," he said, speaking as much to himself as to his companions, "more'n fifty year ago — that river bottom was a-crawlin' with grizzlies. They'd come at you in packs o' six or eight. And that stretch o' country off there to the northwest — toward that smudge of engine smoke against the sky — all that was alive with herds of elk and deer and antelope — when it wasn't black with buffalo. They'd been hunted so seldom you could walk right in amongst 'em. In them days a Sioux could ride off a thousand mile with nothin' ever to make him stop — 'less mebbe it was steppin' in a gopher hole. There was room in this country then. Oncet I packed clean to the head of the Yellowstone and all the way back to Independence without once seein' no Indian or no trail o' one less'n a week old. This country ain't no more like it was then than it's like the hindside o' the moon. What ruint it was babies. The Indians never had enough and the white folks had too many. They's more white people now in the newest county in South Dakota than there ever was Sioux from here to the Rocky Mountains. When people all of a sudden start spillin' into empty country by trains of wagons and then trains of cars there ain't nothin' can save room in it for bears or buffalo or Indians or old fools like me."

He became aware with a sudden start of his rapt audience, was briefly confused, and hastily gathered up his reins. "But all the gab in the world won't bring nothin' back. Thing for us to keep in mind is findin' John."

Mary came to his rescue with a practical remark.

"I've heard him say that his home camp when he was a boy was within sight of the Cheyenne on a branch he called Grouse Creek. On the cliff above was a rock with a hole in it."

"Only about a hundred window rocks up and down the Cheyenne," said Jared.

"But below this one there was an old beaver dam — so old that trees had grown on it — and a pond with many fish."

"Ah," said Jared.

Around the next bend of the creek above the second window rock Jared had turned off to investigate was a beaver pond. Above the pond he sighted Puma in a brush-encompassed meadow. After some circling he spotted, from the creek bottom below, the tiny silhouette on the skyline above. As they approached the hilltop on foot Remington and Jared held back.

Mary went to the crest. The lonely figure was sitting, bowed, entirely enveloped, head, face, and limbs, in a blanket. John, as Mary had forecast, had returned in his despair to the scenes of his childhood to attempt again the vigil of fasting and prayer prescribed for the young Sioux striving to become a man.

Mary knelt beside him. There was a low-voiced colloquy, the words indistinguishable to the waiting Remington and Jared. Their only impression was of the poignancy of Mary's anguish and the intensity of John's bitterness. At length John threw off the blanket with a sudden impatient gesture. The two below joined the two above, where Mary was rising to her feet, as pale as though she had come upon John dead.

He was wasted from his long fast and the longer conflict of his emotions. He looked up at his two white friends with no more sign of recognition than if he had never seen them before. When he spoke it was so wildly that the words seemed torn from him against his will.

"When I came to this hilltop as a boy I had many dreams. All three nights. This time I had none. I was then able to pray. I can no longer. For Indians there is nothing left. Not even dreams. Not even prayers. There is no help in taking thought to our mistakes. It is our very existence that has become a mistake. For us there can be no new beginnings. Only an end. I thought I came here to seek light on what I must do. Actually I came here to escape what I know I must do, which is something more shameful than I can endure." He looked at Mary. "You

275

thought I came here to die. I wish I had. But even that is denied me. I am neither decently savage nor successfully civilized. I am only half a man." He got to his feet and suddenly spoke coldly and rationally. "We have to find Big Foot. The old fool is going to get the rest of our people killed."

It was not difficult to overtake Big Foot. Riding ahead, John and Jared, with their developed instinct for appraising any terrain, were able by surveying the country to the westward to keep foreseeing the course taken by the fleeing band without needing to follow every twist and turn of the tortuous trail. By getting into the fringe of the Badlands Big Foot had succeeded in eluding the cavalry searching for him. But he was moving ever more slowly. Many of his women and children were on foot and they all had had so little to eat that the band was unable to travel as fast as in their first dash.

Upon rising at dawn of the second morning since they had come to the edge of the Badlands, John and Jared were moved by one of those sudden determinations the origin of which Remington could never fathom. They struck off at a right angle to the course they had been pursuing the day before. Rounding the corner of a mesa they came upon a fresh trail. From the top of the next low rise they sighted the fugitive band strung out across an alkali flat, crawling onward. Remington had lost track of the passage of time. Fishing a calendar card from his wallet he realized with a start that this was the third day after Christmas.

John rode to the front of the straggling Sioux procession and presently signaled the buckboard to join him. The Indian women and children sank down to rest. They were so weary and starved that they regarded the passing of the two white men with scarcely more than a dull curiosity. The warriors, however, particularly those Hunkpapa who had joined Big Foot after the death of Sitting Bull, were suspicious and potentially hostile. They were far from disposed to take it for granted that John and Mary, any more than the two white men, could be implicitly trusted. By the time the buckboard, with Jared riding closely alongside, had come to a stop at the head of the column it had been closely surrounded by the coldly staring horsemen.

Big Foot, too ill to ride, had been bumping along on a travois. John dismounted and stood over him. The substance of his harsh and acrid speech was interpreted in a whisper for Remington by Mary.

"You are sick. And what you are doing is sick. You must be sick also in your head if you would pick so wrong a time to think of fighting. Just behind those hills are more soldiers than your warriors have fingers and toes. The trains are bringing more every day. They can take you whenever they wish no matter how you try to hide. But it is still not too late for you. These two white men are friends of General Miles. He has sent them to tell you that you can come back and that if you do no harm will come to you."

Big Foot struggled to his feet and after a fit of coughing made his reply.

"Why do the soldiers follow us?" he complained. "Why do they not let us alone?"

The bouncing of his sick body on the travois had depleted his spirits. But if his response had been weak, other voices of more determination were at once raised. Yellow Bird, the band's most respected medicine man, presently gained general attention by the stridency of his protestations.

"We have not been running away. We have not been trying to hide. We have been going where we pleased. For three moons that is what we have been doing. Since the summer the soldiers have all the time known where we were. Many times they have sighted us. Sometimes they have talked to us. But they have never tried to take us. Do you want me to tell you why? I will tell you. It is not we who have had reason to be afraid. It is the soldiers who are afraid. That is why they have never come close to us. They know that when we put on our Ghost Shirts there is nothing they can do to us. They know that any day the Messiah will come in a flame of light that will blind them. If ever we come face to face with them it will be the soldiers who will run away."

There came a chorus of wild yells approving this estimate of the situation, especially from the vengeful Hunkpapa.

"Hate to think we stepped into a bear trap," murmured Jared.

"Don't," said Mary. "Look at John."

John was standing, arms folded, staring impassively at the jeering tumult about him. To imprecations shouted in his face he made no reply. When jostled he stared so scornfully at the molester that the man drew away. Big Foot, swaying with weakness, sat down again on the travois. Gradually the uproar subsided. All looked at Big Foot.

"Sit down," he proposed. "Let us talk. Let us ask each other what we think we must do."

Even those who had recently been the most excitedly belligerent yielded to this suggestion. The older warriors squatted in a circle, roughly in the order of their seniority. The younger stood behind them. The women, realizing a council was getting under way, crowded around the rim of the circle.

"Indians will stop anything to hold a council," said Mary. "They so like to talk. They know each will be given a chance to have his say and that everybody will be obliged to listen to him. Indians like to talk more than they like —" she hesitated in slight confusion — "more than they like anything."

All of the early speakers were militants. They gloried in the freedom that they had enjoyed since leaving the reservation. They expatiated upon the efficacy of the Ghost Shirts. They pronounced the murder of Sitting Bull a certain proof of the fate awaiting every Sioux who submitted. They declared the appearance of the Messiah could now be expected at any moment. But as speaker after speaker rose to voice his belligerence it was becoming more and more apparent that a full half of the older warriors were remaining silent. By the gravity of their demeanor, it was evident that they were having second thoughts. Big Foot was sensing this. Finally, he addressed John.

"You have spoken once. Have you no more to say?"

"I have." He did not unfold his arms or otherwise unbend. His voice was clear but without passion. He seemed merely to be reciting a succession of irrefutable facts. "No one can grieve for Sitting Bull more than I. He was like my father. No one can despise the whites as a people more than I. I lived long among them. But I still say you must look at what is there before your eyes. What can be the use of beating your heads against the rock? The rock is what is sure to happen to you and to your women and children. You think that by standing here you are free. But you stand here alone. Your chief is sick. Of all the greatest warriors of the Sioux not one is with you. Not Gall, not Hump, not Red Cloud. Not any other Sioux. Gall, who was once the boldest of all, now speaks only in white councils. You have expected Hump and his band to join you. He will not. He has returned to his agency. He was once a chief of scouts for the army. He will be that again. When they hunt you down he will track you for the hunters. At Pine Ridge, where there are thousands of soldiers waiting, more than seven hundred Sioux tepees have returned to the agency. Other hundreds are coming in every day. Of the angry men on The Stronghold more than half are starting to come in, with Red Cloud himself at their head. Kicking Bear and Short Bull will have too few warriors left to hold it. They will have to come in. Only you will be left. And what awaits you if you stay in these hills? If the soldiers do not find you, you will in any case freeze and starve. What will happen to you if you go into Pine Ridge? You will live. You will feed upon the beef herd of General Miles. The worst that will happen to you will be to fill your children's bellies."

There were renewed howls of disagreement from Yellow Bird and his fellow militants but these were overwhelmed by a far greater commotion. At John's last words the women burst in upon the council, screaming, gesticulating, beating upon their spouses, demanding that their children be fed. The onslaught was irresistible. On the march the women performed so many of the services essential to survival, the handling of the baggage, the erection of tepees, the care of the stock, the tending of cooking fires, that their cooperation was indispensable. Their united will was bound eventually to prove decisive. When some order had at last been restored Big Foot was helped to his feet to announce his verdict. As usual with him it was a resort to compromise.

"Those who want to go to Pine Ridge will go," he said. "Those who do not want to go to Pine Ridge will stay. I will go."

There were still many swirls and eddies of argument and dissension as the order of march was reorganized for the turn south out of the Badlands but by the time the new start was made it had become apparent that all were remaining with the band. Many were still reluctant and some openly mutinous but no one elected to remain behind. John supervised the movement of Big Foot to a bed in Remington's wagon, where it was thought he might travel with less discomfort than on the jolting travois.

"He wants me to go to The Stronghold to tell Kicking Bear and Short Bull that he's coming in," said John. "So long's he's quitting he hopes that they'll quit, too. It's the old case of misery loving company. I don't know what I can do there but it's worth a try."

"Tell me this," said Remington. "We've been out of touch with everything for nine days. How in hell did you know about Hump and Red Cloud?"

"I didn't. But I know both of them. Hump likes nothing so much as to be patted on the head by white generals. Red Cloud can never forget that he's the great commander and therefore cannot accept the insanity of a winter war. So I'm as sure of what they're doing as if I'd heard direct news. It was perfectly safe to say what I did there in council. I could count on Big Foot's people knowing them, too. That's why they didn't for a minute doubt what I was telling them."

John rode off to carry Big Foot's message to The Stronghold. Big Foot's band emerged from the Badlands by a route so unexpected that his forerunning screen of warriors was able to take by surprise a camp of four army scouts. When the crestfallen plainsmen were brought to Big Foot they explained, through Jared, that they had been sent by Major Samuel Whiteside, who was encamped with four troops of the 7th Cavalry on Wounded Knee Creek, resting after many hard-riding days of looking in vain for the fugitive band. The scouts also volunteered confirmation of John's story that Hump had surrendered, that more than two thousand Sioux from the White Clay camp had returned to Pine Ridge, and that hundreds of warriors under Red Cloud were abandoning The Stronghold.

All of this further assured Big Foot that he had made the correct decision in determining to come in. To avert any possibility of an accidental clash with the 7th, he directed that the scouts be released with instructions to inform Whiteside that the band was on its way to Pine Ridge to surrender.

In spite of this pacific word sent Whiteside by the released scouts, toward midafternoon the Indian outriders some miles ahead of the column began giving warning signals by waving their blankets. Soon thereafter cavalry became visible on the distant skyline ahead. The Sioux, already made so uneasy by divided counsels, became at once as agitated as though they were already under fire. Women wailed, mothers gathered their children together. Several families broke from the column for the shelter of a nearby gully. Groups of warriors, yelling and shaking their rifles aloft, galloped up adjacent slopes to gain a clearer view. Big Foot raised himself to stare at the distant apparition and groaned resignedly. It was too late to retreat or embark on a new flight. His only positive reaction was to raise his arm in a gesture bringing the march to a halt. The vacuum in command was filled by Yellow Bird, who gathered the warriors and led them forward to form a battle line interposed between the oncoming soldiers and the Sioux women and children.

"We could have used better luck," said Remington, "than to have the 7th Regiment turn up. Half their officers have been with it since Custer was around. They can never forget the score they have to settle with the Sioux."

"This Whiteside, though," said Jared, "he ain't too bad."

Already the crisis was passing. It was becoming apparent that the white commander had no immediate intention of attacking. His troopers separated into two columns, which rode past on either side at a distance out of rifle shot. Having gained this position on the Sioux flanks, they wheeled and halted, ready to remain abreast of the Sioux march when it was resumed. The warriors had moved back, continuing to face whatever threat might develop on either hand. Big Foot directed the raising of a white flag. Whiteside, accompanied by an aide, rode down to the wagon to parley.

"Hello, Jared," he said. "Odd company you keep." He looked sharply at Remington. "Could you be Frederic Remington?"

"None other," said Remington.

"We'd been told you were lost and to keep an eye out for you."

"Now you've found me," said Remington, adding with some satisfaction, "along with Big Foot."

Big Foot had been convulsed by a coughing fit and blood was running from his mouth and nose, making it difficult for him to speak.

"We are on our way to Pine Ridge to surrender," he protested. "So why do you come with your soldiers? Whenever we see soldiers we do not know what will happen!"

"I'm only here to make sure you don't change your mind," said Whiteside. He added in an aside to Jared. "My orders are to find him and when I find him to disarm his people."

Jared glanced back along the restive Sioux column. It was bristling with Winchesters.

"Out here you'll have a fight on your hands," said Jared. "Be a sight less trouble was you to wait till you get 'em to Pine Ridge."

Whiteside rubbed his chin thoughtfully. "I think you could be right," he concluded.

He returned to his command. Big Foot looked at Remington, who gathered his reins. The Sioux march was resumed. The warriors circled warily but the troopers continued to keep their distance.

At Wounded Knee the Indian encampment was set up in a tight cluster of tepees in front of a deep, dry ravine extending from the creek back into the hills. Whiteside established his lines on surrounding slopes to guard against the possibility of an Indian breakout during the night. Rations were issued the hungry Indian families. Big Foot was taken to a heated tent and treated by an army surgeon. The Indians who had been so disturbed upon first sighting the soldiers were seeming to settle down.

Remington drove the buckboard to a slope across the creek near the trading post of Louis Mosseau, behind which Whiteside had set up his headquarters. Mary, feeling her presence might serve to reassure the women and children, had elected to remain in the Sioux encampment. Remington pitched his tent and got to work on his dispatch for *Harper's*. He had the two biggest stories of the campaign to write, having had firsthand experience with both, the death of Sitting Bull and the surrender of Big Foot.

Later in the night the other half of the 7th arrived from Pine Ridge, led by Colonel Forsyth who, as senior officer, assumed command of the entire force. Accompanying the arriving column were three newspapermen and Jim Asag, the Pine Ridge trader, with a keg of whiskey. For some hours the officers of the regiment noisily celebrated their "capture" of Big Foot. Remington finished his dispatch, found a staff officer who agreed to send it in by the next courier, and went to sleep.

He was awakened the next morning by Jared shaking him.

"Trouble," said Jared.

Through the open flap of the tent Remington caught a glimpse of Big Foot staggering off down the slope toward his own camp in the grasp of two soldiers. He jerked on his pants, shoes and coat and ran out. Jared pulled Remington's rifle from its case and followed to thrust it in his hands. Remington scarcely noticed. He was staring about, appalled by how much the situation had changed since Forsyth had taken command.

A battery of four Hotchkiss guns had been set up on a knoll directly commanding the Sioux camp. Long lines of soldiers were advancing down the slopes from all sides to establish a tightening cordon around it. The warriors were being required to leave their families and to sit in a group on the flat, fifty yards or so in front of their camp. On all sides of the flat, lines of soldiers were closing in to within ten feet of the seated Indian men. Big Foot was roughly shoved within this ring.

Remington rushed down, looking for Forsyth, with some idea of expostulating with the commander for so obviously courting violence. Big Foot, through an interpreter, was insisting that none of his people had firearms, even though yesterday on the march Whiteside's forces had seen how many were openly brandishing Winchesters. It was a cold morning and all the warriors were wrapped in blankets. They were seated so close together that their shoulders were touching and their blankets overlapping. It was impossible for the observing officers to guess what arms might be concealed among them.

"Colonel Forsyth," demanded Remington, "can't you see what you can be stirring up?"

"My orders are to disarm the rascals," said Forsyth. "And by God, that's what I'm going to do." He eyed Remington coldly. "Please stand aside, Mr. Remington. This is not your problem." He turned back to an aide. "Their guns have to be somewhere. Before we have a go at what's under those blankets let's take a look at how many are hidden in their camp."

A detail of troopers, obviously relishing their task, rushed into the camp, ransacking tepees, tossing possessions about, ripping apart bedding, searching women. No arms of consequence were found.

The seated warriors could hear the screams from their women and children but could not see past the soldiers ringing them on every side. Yellow Bird, the only Sioux on his feet, was dancing about, singing his incantations, reminding them that the Ghost Shirts under their blankets were invulnerable to white bullets. Big Foot struggled weakly to his knees to make feeble gestures urging his warriors to restrain their growing rage. The tension was becoming unbearable, as Remington was certain Forsyth had foreseen.

XVI

FROM THE HOUR JOHN had addressed Big Foot's council, Kirk had likewise been on his way to Wounded Knee. At his Rapid City headquarters General Miles had become irritably concerned over the disappearance of Remington, whose possible fate, as day after day passed without word of him, had become a news event rivaling in national attention the army's continuing failure to round up Big Foot. He had called Kirk into his office.

"The damned fool," grumbled the general. "I remember back in Arizona we had to watch him all the time to keep him from wandering off among the Apaches. Here we've got everything working out not too badly. Hump's come in. Red Cloud's come in. Nine-tenths of the Oglala are back at Pine Ridge. The Hunkpapa, except those who joined Big Foot, have shown up at Fort Yates. And we're bound to catch up with Big Foot any day. That miserable business with Sitting Bull wasn't our doing. Except for that, we've been able to head off a war without the army literally having to fire a shot. *But* — if a public figure as well known as Remington manages to get himself killed, it will take off a good bit of the shine. His being a personal friend of mine will make it look worse. I want him found."

"Yes, sir," said Kirk.

The general pawed among the papers on his desk. "What we know for sure is that the day Sitting Bull was killed he shoved off into the back country. Jared was with him then. The only word we've had since was from a Hunkpapa who, when he ran away from Grand River, decided to hide out with his family instead of joining Big Foot on coming in to Fort Yates. He saw Jared somewhere up toward the forks of the Cheyenne. But that was nine days ago. We don't know for sure that Jared's still with Remington. Even if he is, Jared's only human. Any number of small packs of Sioux are hiding out all over that country. Remington's chances of getting into trouble are unlimited. I want him located. You get down to Pine Ridge and circulate among your Indian friends. Keep after them until you pick up some word of him. I want him brought in."

"Yes, sir," said Kirk.

When he got off the train at Gunsight he found Badger waiting for him at the station hitching rail as he had expected, having wired Pine Ridge of his coming. The disadvantage of being considered the general's pet were balanced by certain advantages. The orderly who had delivered the horse saluted.

"Friend of yours over at the livery stable, sir, says he wants to see the lieutenant."

At Ed Stump's stable Kirk let out a yelp of delight upon realizing that the friend who had left word for him was Zenas Williams. The old mountain man was profanely absorbed in the final stages of buying a horse.

"How be you, son," said Zenas. "Seen that bay horse o' your'n goin' past in the street and figgered you must be somewheres around. Me, I stove up mine gettin' me acrost Wyoming." He contemplated the big, strong, but ungainly gray he had just purchased. "Only trouble with these here Nebrasky horses is they ain't none o' them fit to plow with." He waved aside Stump's injured protestations. "I'm growed up and the money I'm throwin' away is my own. Just make sure you take good care o' that old cayuse I'm leavin' with you till I git back to pick him up."

He swung his gaunt frame into the saddle and rode beside Kirk out of town.

"Last I seen o' Mousey was he was pushin' off from my place that day with you. Got any idee whereat he could be now?"

"Somewhere up the Cheyenne with Remington. According to the newspapers, they're lost."

"That's what somebody that come past my place was tellin' me. Mousey he don't know no better'n to stick his ass into places would scare the liver out'n any man with sense. But the newspapers got the wrong hitch on it. No matter where he's at, he ain't lost."

"Not likely. All the same, General Miles sent me down here to start looking for them."

Zenas cleared his throat and spat.

"Could be you might feel like lettin' me poke along."

"Could be," said Kirk.

But upon their arrival that night at Pine Ridge they learned no search was necessary. General Brooke told Kirk of the heliograph message from Westside reporting the sighting of Big Foot, his surrender, and the presence of Remington and Jared with the band. The afternoon dispatch to the scene of the other half of the 7th left it apparent that there could be little doubt of anybody's safety at Wounded Knee. With all accommodations at Pine Ridge so overcrowded, Kirk and Zenas slept on the floor of Eastman's house. Eastman was away tending the sick among the remnant of Sioux still at the White Clay camp.

The doctor came in toward dawn to scold Kirk for not occupying the cot and to express his pleasure at the privilege of meeting the legendary Zenas Williams. Then, while starting to make coffee, he announced an item of news that set Kirk instantly running to saddle Badger. The day before, Eastman had had a letter from Santy reporting that when Remington and Jared had set out to look for John, Mary had accompanied them.

Kirk and Zenas circled the great Sioux camp below the agency and rode north through the sunrise chill. Kirk was setting the fastest pace that still permitted Zenas to keep up with him. His many rides with Jared across the outer reaches of the reservation had made him familiar with the area. After a dozen miles he left the road by a cutoff. Rounding the shoulder of a hill he dropped into the head of one of the innumerable ravines that everywhere cut jagged gashes in the heavily eroded region. Following the defile downward, they came to a final turn, which opened abruptly to bring them out on a gravelly slope just above and no more than a hundred yards from the edge of the Wounded Knee encampment. The spectacle had been brought suddenly into their view with every detail as visible as though all had been arranged on the top of a map table.

Kirk's trained eye immediately took in the significance of every disposition. He saw the closely packed stand of tepees, among which cowered the women and children, the even more closely packed assembly of seated, blanketed warriors on the ground before the tepees, the capering conjuror leaping and chanting, the threatening ring of soldiers pressing inward until their rifle barrels were thrust almost into Indian faces, the troops of cavalry held in reserve on the surrounding slopes, the platoons of troopers ransacking the tepees. But most of all he saw the Hotchkiss battery on the knoll, the guns trained, the crews standing ready.

As though he were the last actor for whose entrance the commencement of the drama had waited, he had scarcely begun to stare before there came the sharp crack of a single shot. He could not see who had fired. It could have been no more than a carelessly dropped weapon striking the hard ground.

All of the encircling troopers instantly fired in response. Many of the seated warriors were killed by this first point-blank volley from gun muzzles not ten feet away. A number of soldiers on opposite sides of the ring also fell, victims of their own comrades' cross fire. Every Indian still able to move sprang up, casting aside his blanket to reveal his Ghost Shirt. Those who had believed in the magic of these sacred garments must have been instantly and fearfully disillusioned. On many of the white shirts there were already great splotches of blood. Among the Indians springing up were those who had had Winchesters hidden under their blankets. These repeating rifles were able to fire so much more rapidly than could the troopers' single-shot Springfields that some of the soldiers were beginning to recoil.

The Hotchkiss guns on the knoll had also opened fire after that mysterious first shot. But they had been trained not on the flat where the warriors had been assembled but on the camp now occupied only by the Indian women and children. The exploding shells, crashing in at nearly fifty a minute, were tearing the encampment to shreds, setting everything combustible afire, killing or mutilating the terrified inmates.

The warriors still living were breaking through the partly disorganized ring of soldiers, running around the exploding camp, and diving into the dry ravine behind the camp, where they were being joined by as many of the women and children as had survived the bombardment. The Hotchkiss guns lifted their fire to the ravine and the soldiers were being regrouped by their officers to undertake the new task of rooting the remaining Sioux from the cover they had reached. The massacre was in the process of shifting from the former area, now littered with dead and dying, to the new cockpit in the ravine.

Kirk and Zenas leaped from their horses and started running down the slope toward the ruins of the Indian camp. Suddenly Zenas threw himself to the ground. Kirk heard the zing of a bullet that all but nicked his ear. He saw the conjuror firing from the doorway of a Sibley tent. Kirk threw himself down beside Zenas. The conjuror ducked into the tent and, gaining invisibility behind its canvas walls, continued to fire at any soldier unwary enough to pass within range on his way to the ravine.

Zenas grunted and began with great energy to crawl forward. He seemed to be proceeding with some purpose, so Kirk crawled in his wake. Then he caught sight of what had animated Zenas. Remington and Jared, prone behind the shelter of several bales of hay dumped here by the horse tenders, were pinned to the ground not twenty feet from the fire-spitting tent. Zenas lifted his head.

"Goddammit, Mousey, what the hell kind of a war is this you got yourself into?"

Jared looked around without surprise.

"It ain't a good kind. And it'll git worse 'less you keep your head down. What brung you out o' your hole?"

Zenas had come upon another hay bale and, pushing it before him, wriggled nearer.

"Told you to yell when you needed help. Good thing I didn't wait till you did 'cause it surely looks like you need some now." With his knife he began hacking a bundle of loose hay from his bale.

Kirk's momentary interest faded. His attention returned from this minor conflict to the greater of which it was so small a part. His Arizona campaigns had been little more than a series of manhunts. This was his first battle. It was the tremendous adventure toward which he had looked with so much anticipation and excitement since as a boy he had determined to be a soldier. He was now in the midst of it. Yet his major reactions seemed to be an almost hysterical wish that the head-splitting din of the Hotchkiss guns would cease and a kind of astonishment that the smell of human blood and entrails was so much like that of the slaughter pen in a stockyard. He crawled back up the slope.

When once he looked over his shoulder he saw that Zenas, under cover of a fusillade from Jared and Remington, had pushed his bale before him until he was close to the Sibley tent. He was lighting the bundle of hay and preparing to thrust it with the end of his rifle barrel around the bale and against the tent wall.

Kirk remounted Badger. All action was now centered along the rim of the ravine. He swung behind the knoll from which the battery was firing and came to the head of the ravine. A heliograph was winking. The bombardment suddenly ceased. The staccato crackle of rifle and pistol shots began to die away. In the ravine bottom he could see numbers of prostrate Sioux, most motionless, some still squirming or crawling.

Kirk forced Badger down the bank, paying no heed to the warning yells of the soldiers above that the wounded Sioux were continuing to shoot as long as they had the strength to lift a weapon. He could appreciate at once how terribly the Sioux who had sought refuge in the ravine had suffered from the plunging shrapnel fire and the point-blank volleys from soldiers ranging along the rim. The gully floor was strewn with Indian dead and wounded.

His frantic search for Mary was made more horrible by the great proportion of the stricken who were women and children. Mothers were clutching the corpses of their infants, mangled children were screaming, live babies were striving to suckle dead mothers. He kept on retracing the fearful swath of dead and dying that marked the tide of battle as it had poured from the council ground across the campsite and on into the ravine.

Then, when he had climbed from the ravine, through the drifting smoke and slowly settling clouds of dust he saw that Remington, Zenas and Jared had got past the barrier of the sniper in the tent and were in the middle of the camp, tearing at the ruins of a tepee. He jumped from Badger and ran forward among the heaps of shell-torn dead and moaning wounded. He reached them just as they were uncovering Mary.

She was drenched with blood from other bodies which, in falling over her, had possibly shielded her from later shell fragments. Her worst injury seemed to have been a blow on her head, evidently from a lodge-pole sent whirling by a shell explosion. But she was not breathing and her heart had stopped.

"She's dead," said Remington.

Zenas was staring down at her.

"Git away," he said suddenly.

He shoved the others aside, knelt beside her, and stuck a finger into her mouth to straighten her tongue. After wiping his mouth on his sleeve, he bent to place it over hers and breathed in hard. With his hands he squeezed the sides of her chest and again forced his breath into her mouth. He kept this up until at last she shivered and drew a gasping breath. She did not regain consciousness but she was breathing again. Zenas sat back on his haunches and regarded her.

"All on a sudden recollected how a Sioux gal oncet got me to breathin' again that way," he said. "Was one time when a grizzly took a swipe at me that mashed my head against a rock." He rubbed his chin thoughtfully. "The goddamnedest things can happen to a man if he lives long enough," he marveled. "Way back there when I was too green to know my ass from my elbow one Sioux gal learned me how to look after another Sioux gal here more'n sixty year later."

"You couldn't of picked a better time to recollect," said Jared, blinking as he looked down at Mary.

"We have to get her up to the hospital tent," said Remington.

"No," objected Kirk. "The army surgeons will be too busy with their own wounded. Better to try to get her in to Dr. Eastman."

Remington and Jared ran for the wagon. Mary was gently lifted and cradled in it in a nest of blankets. With the other three riding alongside, Remington turned his horses toward Pine Ridge.

They had not left the battlefield far behind before bands of warriors, called to action from their Pine Ridge camp by the sound of cannon, began appearing in the distance over the hills ahead. The success of General Miles's weeks of patient reassurance, which had persuaded most Sioux to return to the agency, had been blown to bits in moments by the guns of Wounded Knee. Other bands of Sioux were riding over the northwestern horizon from the direction of The Stronghold. From one of these a single horseman separated and galloped down the slope to the wagon. Long before the rider could be identified the horse was unmistakable.

John stared down at Mary.

"Do you think she will die?" he asked, with no more outward emotion than though he were asking the time.

"We're taking her to Dr. Eastman," said Kirk.

"The only good idea anybody has had today. Except this one."

John wheeled Puma and started off at a gallop along the road to Wounded Knee, holding his bow high over his head in his clenched fist in the traditional Sioux command gesture meaning "follow me." The band from which he had separated rode after him, yelling. Other hard-riding warriors from Pine Ridge began streaming past, paying no attention to the wagon or its attendants. Presently from the battlefield came a new crackle of gunfire. The Sioux were once more challenging their old adversary, the 7th.

At the outskirts of Pine Ridge they encountered Eastman, starting north toward the battlefield. After a glance at Mary he turned back with them. They crossed the area where that morning had stood more than a thousand Sioux tepees. Now not one was left. The troops stationed at Pine Ridge had been assembled into ready formations but were not marching out. Brooke was heeding, with whatever personal reservations, Miles's telegraphed insistence that there still be no aggressive moves to aggravate the Sioux excitement.

Mary was placed on the cot in Eastman's house and Elaine summoned to help attend her. The doctor explored her skull and neck with sensitive fingertips and with his stethoscope listened long and carefully to her tenuous breathing and the faint beating of her heart.

"No fracture, no concussion, no organic destruction," was his diagnosis. "She can have suffered a greater injury from what she witnessed than from any physical hurt. Sometimes things can seem so bad that we hide from them in any way we can. We can only wait and see."

Kirk and his companions went out. Remington leaned into his wagon, drew out one of his pads, and then stood still, staring at the blank page.

"How," he demanded, "do you go about writing a story you hate as

292

much as I hate this one? How do you go about telling the country their army's guilty of murder?"

No one answered. Kirk looked at Zenas and Jared. They nodded. The three mounted and rode off toward the northeastern hills. To the northwest, where the Sioux were harrying the withdrawal of the 7th from Wounded Knee, the distant sound of intermittent gunfire was apparently nearer. The agency area was astir with marching infantry, troops of cavalry wheeling into position on nearby slopes, shouted commands, bugle calls, tapping drums. Entrenchments were being dug and batteries placed. Brooke might be obeying his orders to initiate no attack on the Sioux but was taking care to prepare his defenses in the event they attacked him.

Kirk, Zenas and Jared circled through the hills and approached from the east the main encampment at the mouth of White Clay Creek, to which the Sioux had resorted when they had stampeded from the reservation. Dismounting and crawling to the top of a ridge they surveyed the camp. Nearly a thousand tepees had sprouted. Except for the few hundreds at The Stronghold, the greater part of the Oglala and Brulé Sioux had gathered here, frenzied by rage, fear and defiance. Scores of mounted warriors were galloping off to the west to join the harassment of the 7th. Other hundreds were ranging the hills to the south, evidently expecting an attack by the main American force at Pine Ridge.

The self-appointed scouts hid their horses in a cedar grove and, working their way from one patch of cover to the next, pressed forward on foot toward the camp. Kirk kept well back lest some distant glimpse of his uniform excite new alarm or hostility. Eventually a hiding place was found for him in a juniper thicket near the mouth of a gully. Zenas and Jared crept on toward the camp, seeming to melt almost at once into the landscape. Within an hour they had returned with a frightened squaw they had caught gathering wood. They required her to look closely at Kirk and to listen as closely to the message they had brought her to hear.

"This soldier," they said, "is the same as son to General Miles. He has come here to tell you that what happened at Wounded Knee was a terrible accident. It has filled General Miles with as much grief as it has the Sioux. He has also come to tell you that the soldiers at Pine Ridge will not attack the Sioux. If instead the Sioux will come back to Pine Ridge they will not be harmed. They will be welcomed and fed and every care taken of them. Now, when you go back to your camp be sure you tell everybody who will listen the good news you have heard here."

There was some doubt of how much of the message the squaw had assimilated. When released she ran as though pursued by wolves. A new hiding place was found for Kirk and the process was repeated with a herdsboy, a crippled old man, and then other stragglers. After darkness fell Zenas and Jared were able to move about with less stealth and began bringing in their captive listeners at ten- and fifteen-minute intervals. When the peace story had been planted on the twentieth involuntary emissary Kirk decided, before making further impromptu attempts to spread his peace gospel among the Sioux, to return to Pine Ridge to make sure that in the meantime there had been no inconsistent alterations in General Brooke's orders or intentions.

It was midnight when they reached Eastman's house. Remington was getting into his bedroll in his wagon. He sat up.

"Where the hell have you been?"

"Just a-visitin' around," said Jared.

"How's Mary?" asked Kirk.

"The same."

"What else has been going on?"

"The Sioux from here and The Stronghold," Remington reported, "got to Wounded Knee before Forsyth could get his wagons loaded for the start back. They hustled the 7th so hard that you might say they chased it off the battlefield. The Sioux kept on crowding it all the way here. Then, when Forsyth got his wagon train safely in, he turned back to take a crack at the Indians that had been after him. He got himself cooped up in a valley with Indians on all the hills around and was in real trouble until Brooke got the 9th Cavalry out to his support. You can hardly say that the 7th has too much to be proud of on a day that started with their butchering women and children and wound up with their necks being saved by a colored regiment that some people think the best in the army. Brooke has his defense lines here pretty well organized by now. The Sioux are surely too smart to risk a general attack on entrenched soldiers supported by artillery. But the hills out there are swarming with them, all of them crazy mad after seeing what was left on the ground at Wounded Knee. And by the way, Miles will have his headquarters moved here by some time tomorrow."

Remington settled down. Zenas and Jared turned the horses into the corral and themselves into their blankets under the wagon. Kirk went into the house. Elaine sat beside the cot. He looked down at Mary. The utter composure of her expression appeared the manifestation of a state nearer death than life. She must indeed, as Eastman had suggested, have been driven to seek refuge in some infinitely distant sanctuary. He was starting to turn away when her eyes opened and her lips quivered for a moment. She at once relapsed into the coma but Elaine agreed that Eastman should be summoned. Kirk crossed the agency grounds to the Episcopal mission chapel, which had been converted into a hospital for the Sioux wounded brought from the battlefield by the 7th's wagon train.

Fearful as were his memories of Wounded Knee, Kirk was appalled by the spectacle in the little church. Most of the invalids were women and children, since few wounded Indian men had survived the bitterness of the closing moments of the conflict. They had been bedded on straw on the floor. Many had been mutilated, some terribly, by the cannon fire but not all had suffered from the impersonal selectivity of flying shell fragments. For there were young girls and boys and even babies who bore powder-blackened gunshot wounds indicating that they had been fired upon at arm's length by soldiers crazed by the fury of combat. The walls above the moaning victims were draped with strings of popcorn and cranberries, wreaths of redberry, sprays of evergreen, and other homemade Christmas decorations. Behind the pulpit stretched a cheese-cloth banner on which gilt paper letters proclaimed: Peace on Earth, Goodwill toward Men.

Eastman, his arms red to the elbow, came to Kirk at the door, heard his plea, looked back at his windrows of patients tended by his scattering of volunteer nurses, and nodded. "I've patched them up as well as I can. I need a breath of air. And I should have another look at Mary."

He washed, pulled on his blanket coat, and set out with Kirk. A frigidly cold wind was beginning to blow.

"Be a blizzard by morning," said Eastman, linking his arm with Kirk's. Either his reaction to the excruciating hours of his struggle with the Indian wounded had left him excitedly garrulous or he was unable to dwell on the scene in the church, for he launched into another less painful subject. "I've been hearing what's happened to John. Just during one day he's become a principal war chief. You know among Indians, leaders in war are recognized or not according to their individual appeal. Warriors will flock to one they estimate capable of special cunning and daring. John attracted attention by that damned bow, which in his hands is more deadly than any firearm. They like that. Then there's that magnificent horse. They like that. But most of all they like his foolhardiness. He's been exposing himself as if he wanted to be killed. Maybe he does. He must feel himself responsible for leading Big Foot's people into that death trap. In any event, after what happened at Wounded Knee the Ghost Shirt cult has lost out with the Sioux. They need some new myth. And John is providing it."

His examination disclosed no change in Mary. He kissed Elaine, to whom he had become publicly engaged on Christmas Eve, ordered her to get some sleep, either in a chair or on a blanket beside the cot, and went back to his hospital.

The blizzard struck at dawn. The wind howled but the cold was so intense that there was little snow. Kirk crawled from his blanket beside Zenas and Jared but did not rouse them until he was able to return from the officers' mess with a great hunk of cold roast beef. They ate, mounted, and rode off through the storm toward the White Clay encampment.

The cold was keeping the Sioux huddled around their fires. The thin layer of fallen snow was dry and powdery and when caught up in the wind filled the air with blinding and stinging clouds. In weather so severe they were able to ride unchallenged almost into the outskirts of the Sioux camp. They slowly circled it, accosting anyone who came out to gather wood or tend stock. It was no longer necessary to capture listeners. Those they encountered stood shivering and sniveling, staring dumbly up through the swirling snow at the white horsemen, appearing to be giving unwilling heed to the message that was being urged upon them.

Toward noon Kirk ordered a retirement to the shelter of a gully where they built a fire, rubbed down their horses, ate the rest of the beef, and dozed.

"Give them time to talk it over," he said.

At nightfall they made another slow circuit of the camp's outskirts. Their listeners were no longer solitary. Groups of half a dozen men and women sometimes gathered about the riders to scowl and mutter and finger their weapons but still to listen. There was no evidence that they were yet beginning to believe anything of what they were being told. Since Wounded Knee, any white promise of safe-conduct seemed a mockery even to Kirk.

The peace messengers returned after midnight for a third slow circling of the camp. This time there developed the first faint shadow of a return on their freezing effort. Red Cloud himself came out to them. They dismounted and talked with him long and desperately. He asked questions that were impossible to answer. He revealed emotions that were more discouraging than suspicion and anger and hatred. There was in his mood the conviction that in whatever event the Sioux were doomed. He himself seemed near death from the cold. And when he left them to return to the Sioux council fire he had given them no slightest indication of what he might be thinking.

"If they haven't got the idea by now," said Kirk, "we'll only make it worse by keeping at them."

On the ride back they were so near exhaustion that they came as near to freezing as the Indians. But toward morning the gale ceased as suddenly as it had begun. As they dismounted at Eastman's door the first flush of day was coming to a world that had become quiet again. Kirk went in.

There was no change evident in Mary. She remained suspended in that state of utter peace that seemed so far from life. Elaine had apparently at last been prevailed upon to go to her room to rest. The doctor was asleep on the floor by Mary's cot.

Kirk stood by the stove. Warmth began slowly to displace the cold that had seemed to have penetrated to the marrow of his bones. There was hot coffee. He drank cup after cup. There was also hot water. Presently he shaved. Then, turning to look again at Mary, he ran to bend over her cot. She had not stirred. But there was color in her cheeks and she was breathing naturally. There could be no question. She was no longer in a coma. She was merely sleeping.

He awoke Eastman. The doctor rose, sagging with fatigue. After one glance at her, he straightened. He took her pulse, laid his hand on her forehead, applied the stethoscope.

"Perfectly normal," he said. "Temperature back. Pulse back. Breathing back. Everything back. It could be that we have been witness to a miracle — that it has indeed been nature's way of shielding her from something that otherwise she could not have endured. We'll know when she wakes."

"When will that be?"

"Maybe hours. Maybe minutes. I'll go get Elaine."

Kirk studied her face. It no longer had the impassivity of a death mask. There was life in it. It was Mary's face. Eastman's words tolled in his head. She had been exposed to a horror so fearful that the contemplation of it had swept her over the threshold of death, from which she had been retrieved only by the craft of old Zenas. Her only salvation since had been that providence had kept her at that threshold until what she had experienced could become bearable. The abomination to which she had been subjected had been visited upon her and her people by him and his people, the latest in a long history of such abominations. Whatever chance there might ever have been to bridge the gulf that gaped between them had been forever eliminated by the other chance that had branded upon her for all time the memories of Wounded Knee.

She opened her eyes. They met his. Her gaze was focused and lucid.

"Mac," she whispered.

"Yes, Mary."

She looked around her. Her return to consciousness had been as entire as the filling of a room with light when a lamp is brought in.

"Why, this is Dr. Eastman's house," she said in a stronger voice.

"Yes. He's been taking care of you."

"How did I get here?"

"We brought you here. Remington and Jared and Zenas — and I."

"Zenas?"

"Yes, he's that old man in Wyoming I told you about — the one who saved the Shoshone."

"You brought me?" Suddenly she closed her eyes and began to tremble.

He gathered her hands into his clasp. "Let's not talk about that."

She opened her eyes and ceased to shudder.

"I don't want to either — not now. But John. What about him? Where's he?"

He released her hands and forced a smile. "He's all right. He's out with the Sioux. You see, they all left the agency again."

"But what's he doing?"

"We don't know exactly. There's been a storm the last two days — a terrible blizzard that's kept everybody under cover."

She tugged at his sleeve impatiently, dissatisfied with his temporizing.

"But what was he doing when last you knew?"

"I mustn't let you talk so much. You've been very sick."

"I don't feel sick." She sat up in bed and was surprised by the effort it took. "I am a little weak," she confessed.

Eastman and Elaine came in. He crossed to the cot and a broad grin spread over his face.

"Well, my girl. What a turn you've given us. But it's worth it to see you coming out of it so perky."

"What's John doing?" she demanded.

Eastman studied her for a moment with the searching scrutiny of a physician appraising the condition of a patient. He came to a conclusion.

"I'll tell you what he's doing. He's making himself the principal war chief of the Sioux. He's led a number of attacks — all successful. Among other feats, he's chased the 7th twenty miles. He's rallying the sort of following Red Cloud was able to command when he was young."

"Oh, no," she groaned.

"What's wrong with that? I'm proud of him. I wish I were with him."

"I'm not thinking only of him. The Sioux people. The families. The children. There's been so much killing."

There came a knock on the door. An orderly stood in it.

"General Miles's compliments, sir. Will Lieutenant Kirk please report to him?"

Kirk came upon Remington sitting in a chair in the anteroom to the general's office. With a finger to his lips, he pulled Kirk down beside him.

"Listen," he whispered. "The old man's just called Forsyth in on the carpet."

Through the thin partition behind them they could hear the rumble of the general's famous temper.

"Colonel Forsyth, I have here a message from the commanding general of the army congratulating you on your glorious victory over the Indians at Wounded Knee. I have to say, as your more immediate commanding officer, that I have a totally contrary opinion. In my estimation it is not a victory when you kill more women and children than you do armed enemies. It is not a victory when your dispositions are so unmilitary that any number of your own soldiers are shot down by their own cross fire. And it is farthest of all from a victory to have started a war that we had been taking such pains to avoid. As of this moment I am relieving you of command and I shall prefer charges against you. That is all."

Colonel Forsyth came out, his face ashen but his eyes burning.

Remington's hand closed over Kirk's arm.

"Let me have that horse of yours. I have to get to the telegraph office at Rushville. I've now got a story for a change which I can't stand losing a minute getting out."

Kirk nodded. Remington rushed out. An aide called Kirk.

"Sit down," said the general. He took a second look at Kirk's face. "You're not sick, are you?"

"No, sir."

"I trust not because I've got a job for you. As far as I can gather, this seems to be the situation this morning. That blizzard was a godsend. By stopping everything for twenty-four hours it's taken some of the edge off that idiocy at Wounded Knee. It's also impressed on the Sioux how hungry and cold they can get. Anyway, I've just had word from Red Cloud that he's bringing six or seven hundred tepees back to the agency not later than tomorrow. Kicking Bear and Short Bull are still hanging back but they'll come around. Red Cloud's message, by the way, kept talking about something you'd said to him. That must have been before Wounded Knee when the Sioux were still here."

"No, sir. It was last night in their White Clay camp."

"Good God." The general stared at him. "Who told you to run any such damn fool risk as that? Brooke?"

"No, sir. You did. When you first sent me here."

"So I did. Well, to get back to what we're still stuck with. It is something new and damned annoying. In that fighting day before yesterday a young buck named Rides-an-Eagle made himself such a nuisance that the Sioux began following him around, first to watch him, then to join him. Is he that John that you and Jared got so friendly with?"

"Yes, sir. He is."

"Well, when he saw that most of the Sioux were going to come back in, he took advantage of the storm to slip off into the Badlands with upwards of five hundred followers of the stripe that are still burning to fight. Most of them are young, so the proportion of women and children is small and he could have maybe four hundred warriors. They all have Winchesters because any extra ones they needed were given them by the Sioux who were coming in and knew they would be confiscated when they got here. That well armed and with a leader as smart as this John seems to be they can make us a slather of trouble. From wherever they're holed up in the Badlands they can strike out in any direction at Dakota ranches or Black Hills mining camps. If they start that we'll have to go in after them and that could cost us losses we could do without. Any new fighting could also stampede all the Sioux who've come in and we'd be worse off than we've ever been. Are you following me?"

"Yes, sir. I am."

"This is not an order. I'm only asking your opinion. You and Jared are his friends. Do you think it safe for you two to go in there after him and see if it's possible to talk some sense into him?"

"We'd be safe with him. We might get shot at on the way in. But

Jared can probably steer us away from most of that. Anyway, I want to try."

"Good. You can tell this John for me that if he comes back he'll be treated as well as if he'd never left the reservation."

"I do have two suggestions, sir."

"What are they?"

"Jared's old sidekick, Zenas Williams, is here. There'd be no way of keeping him from going wherever Jared went."

The general's tired eyes lighted up for a second. "That old reprobate. Be like taking two Jareds."

"I'd also like to take Mary Chadron. John's known her since they were children on Grand River. She's been sick but, if her doctor permits, she could be the most help of all. She has more influence with John than anybody."

"You're the one the load's being piled on and you can carry it in whatever way you think best." He rose and came around the desk with outstretched hand. "Only take care of yourself."

At the house, Kirk called Eastman out and explained the project.

"I know it's something Mary would want to do," he finished, "but I don't know whether you'd think she's up to it."

"A blessing straight from heaven," was Eastman's instant verdict. "Nothing could restore her faster. Anything's better than lying there brooding and wondering. What she needs most is comfort and for her there could be no comfort greater than to realize there's something she herself can do for the Sioux — and for John. Be no medicine to compare." He put a hand on Kirk's arm. "But you understand what you may be doing, don't you?"

"Yes," said Kirk. "I do."

When the proposal was made to Mary, she started up, her eyes brightening with resolution.

"Of course I'm going," she said. "I'd crawl all the way if I had to."

The problem of clothing for Mary was solved by Elaine's inspiration. Gifts to the doctor from grateful patients had included items which when assembled comprised a classic Indian woman's wardrobe. He had given Elaine the ensemble as an engagement present. She was able to attire Mary in moccasins, leggings, dress and overvest, all of the whitest and softest doeskin, all intricately embroidered in colored beads and quills. Then, wrapped in several blankets, she was placed on a mattress in the wagon.

Eastman rode with them for the first hour but could detect no occasion for concern. Mary seemed not only able to stand the journey but she had gained so much peace of mind that she presently fell comfortably asleep. There was therefore no reason to circle widely around the gruesome sights on the battlefield for her sake. The dead still littered the ground, all frozen into grotesquely contorted attitudes. An army contractor with wagon and crew of laborers was engaged in collecting the rigid corpses for burial in a common pit.

They kept on, now veering west of the tragic trail by which Big Foot had emerged from the Badlands. In another hour the first red escarpments began to gleam along the horizon.

"You recollect, Stud," remarked Jared, "that hole we wintered in the year them Crow stole our horses over in the Black Hills? We had to find somewhere to hide quick and we ducked into the Badlands. Place we finally camped — only way you could git to it was by a windin' canyon no wider'n this wagon but with walls runnin' straight up most as far as you could see. Could be the sort of place John might pick."

"They was food and water and grass," said Zenas, as promptly as though this had been what he, too, had been pondering, "and the mountain sheep kept a-comin' down to keep us fed clean through the winter. I been a-wonderin', Mousey, when you'd git around to thinkin' o' that."

The day had turned milder and in the dazzling sunlight the last vestige of the blizzard's thin powdering of snow was disappearing. Ahead the cliffs loomed ever higher. Jared and Zenas began riding farther in advance. In midafternoon they waited on a hilltop for the wagon's approach. A few miles beyond, across a shallow valley, there had appeared in the red cliffs a narrow cleft out of which issued a small stream.

When the wagon stopped Mary awoke, refreshed. She sat up in her blankets and hungrily ate two slabs of the ham and bread that were being passed around. Zenas and Jared dismounted and built a fire in a hole which they then smothered with the leaves of an oily shrub, producing a thick column of smoke. Thereupon, by passing a blanket back and forth over the hole, Jared projected at irregular intervals various-sized puffs of smoke into the air. He continued patiently until after twenty or thirty minutes, from somewhere behind the red cliffs, answering puffs of smoke ascended.

"I told him we had Mary with us," said Jared. "He said come ahead."

When they started on, Mary demanded that she be allowed to sit in her accustomed place on the seat of the wagon. The wheels grated down the stony slope and on across the valley toward the red gateway. Kirk could feel her presence beside him as acutely as on that night of her whispering.

She finally spoke.

"There is so much we might be saying — and yet . . . nothing we can say."

"Nothing," he agreed grimly.

"There's one thing I can say. I love you, Mac. I always will. But there must be something terribly wrong with me because . . . I love him, too." She looked at him. "Don't ever forget me."

"Not much danger of that."

The wheels grated on. The red gateway was near.

"One other thing I can say — I must say. What you are doing — you know, don't you — in spite of your always pretending so hard to be thinking only of yourself — proves how truly good you really are."

There was no harm in her thinking that. Nothing mattered anymore. The retribution being visited upon him was tinged with the irony of justice. He had wanted this woman more than he had ever wanted one before or ever would again. In place of winning her he was delivering her forever into the keeping of another. It was a punishment that he had himself prepared.

XVII

WHEN JOHN HAD AT LENGTH been awakened to be informed of the smoke signal, he had rushed out, incredulous, to see for himself the message in the sky. His weariness fell from him. He leaped on Puma and rode down the canyon.

At the end of that terrible march through the storm which had beaten upon them so mercilessly while at the same time bestowing upon them the incalculable blessing of obliterating their trail, he had not, like the others, sunk down exhausted around the hastily kindled fires. At the first streak of daylight he had set out on foot to range through the cratered and pinnacled heights encircling their refuge. It was a land, as he had remembered, corroded by the weather of uncounted centuries into a maze of crevices and cliffs, all its surfaces as contorted as a gale-whipped sea.

Having been reassured that the narrow canyon was the one feasible approach to the camp, his riding down it now by day confirmed at every turn his memory of it. Invaders venturing to penetrate the natural battlements of this winding and precipitous defile must face hopeless disadvantages. A handful of riflemen hidden among the crags above could keep an army indefinitely at bay.

Before reaching the next sharp bend, he left Puma and climbed to the shoulder above, from which he could see down the next stretch of the canyon. The wagon came into view, splashing through the sandy shallows of the stream. The blanket wrapped around her and over her head left him no glimpse of Mary's face but even at this distance he could see how easily she was keeping her balance against the swaying and jolting of the buckboard. That she could be holding herself so erect at the end of so hard a journey discounted the unwelcome possibility that they had brought her to be displayed to him as an invalid in the hope of enlisting his sympathy.

He slid down to Puma and galloped back up the canyon. At the entrance to the little valley he pulled up to savor the prospect. The canyon here abruptly widened to embrace a grassy flat some hundreds of yards wide, across which the stream meandered. The walls of the defile did not diminish in height as they receded. They gleamed more red than ever in the rays from the setting sun. Among the groves of sycamore and pine stood the sixty-three tepees. Along the foot of the cliffs grazed the horses. The smoke of many fires curled lazily upward. This, for the moment, was the home of his people. They were truly his people because to gain the privilege of freely willing themselves to be his they had defied the whole world.

During that day they had harried the retreating 7th he had been so blinded by rage and hate that he had heeded nothing apart from the violence of his own compulsions. It was only when riding back to the main Sioux camp that evening, his sweat cooling, his breathing a trifle more easy, his thirst for vengence at least partially slaked, that he had begun to realize. More than a hundred Sioux were riding in his train. In the camp that night there had been many council fires. Hundreds had gathered about the fires of Kicking Bear and Short Bull, thousands about that of Red Cloud. Then he had looked up from the tiny fire, by whose light he was sharpening his new stock of arrows, to discover how many were squatted in the encircling shadows, their gaze fixed upon him.

The command to which he had in that moment been ordained had not been over those who were among all the Sioux the strongest, the wisest, the boldest. There had been among them boys of fifteen and men of sixty, simpletons addicted to magic and graduates of Carlisle. The one distinction that they had in common was that each of the nearly four hundred was a man who could no longer know peace unless he struck, and struck again, and kept on striking, at the enemy that every Sioux had since birth been given so much reason to hate. To have been elevated to command by the united and instinctive volition of such men had been for him a soul-shaking experience. Surveying in this reddening glow the tepees and fires of their camp, this lair from which they would range like packs of wolves and panthers, it seemed to him that only in these last few hours had he been permitted fully and completely to live. All this had been given him. And now he was to have Mary, too.

He dispatched a boy to guide the wagon to a campsite near the foot of the little valley and a crier to inform his own camp that the visitors were to be left strictly to their own devices. He entered his command tepee, which he shared with the eight other young bachelors who were his aides and subalterns, and sat down, remaining silently impassive in the face of their staring curiosity. When he saw through the smoke vent that the evening sky was growing dark, he rose and, though the air had turned chill with the dropping sun, stripped to breechclout and moccasins. As his only badge of office he hung from his neck the grizzly's tusk which Crazy Horse had always worn into battle. Through the deepening twilight he strode alone down to the camp where there awaited the white ambassadors with the gift they had brought to him.

Their tent had been set up. Their horses were hitched to the tailgate of the wagon. The four were seated about their fire. They had eaten and a pot of coffee was being kept warm at the edge of the ashes. Mary sat on the farther side, still so shrouded in her blanket that he could not even yet catch a glimpse of her face. Kirk got to his feet. John did not offer his hand. Kirk sat down again. Mary stirred and for a second John caught the shine of the firelight in her eyes.

"Did you come to spy on us?" he asked. "Or with word from General Miles?"

"I have a message from the general," said Kirk. "But first, as your friend, I have something of my own to say."

"Well?"

"First and foremost — how are you going to eat?"

"Better than you think. There are many secret ways out of this place. The army cannot watch them all. The whites in Dakota and Nebraska have many herds of cattle. We will eat."

"The minute you start that the army will come in after you."

"That is what we hope. You have seen for yourself as you came in how easy it will be for us to kill whoever comes. When we have killed as many of yours as you did of ours at Wounded Knee, then maybe we will talk."

"It will then be too late to talk."

"Not about giving General Miles my permission to carry off his dead."

Kirk got to his feet.

"For God's sake, John. Stop talking like a maniac. Listen to me. There's been a big change in the country that you don't know about. People were shocked by the murder of Sitting Bull. They didn't like the sneaking way it was done or anything else about it. He was a folk hero. They didn't want to lose him. Then they were horrified by Wounded Knee. No matter how many newspapers called it a glorious victory they could tell it was plain murder. You might almost say your people who died there did not die in vain. Because what they had suffered has turned the country around. The President is in a dither. Congress is upset. Miles has ordered Forsyth court-martialed. Politicians are switching. Even the railroads are talking about justice for the Sioux. Can't you see how crazy you'd be to throw this away? Can't you see that it's the time instead for the Sioux to take advantage of it? Try to get this through your head. The American people are now on your side."

"You're really eloquent. You could have missed your vocation. A pity you haven't a sounder case. The American people have always enjoyed a tender conscience. They cry very easily. They cried over Chief Joseph. Over Crazy Horse. Over Dull Knife. Over the Red River, Washita, and Sand Creek massacres. But in a week they forget. Maybe here we can give them something they will not so soon forget. Have you more to say or do we now come to the message from General Miles?"

Kirk seemed to be counting ten before replying evenly: "General Miles gives you his word that if you come in you will be given food and shelter, punished in no way, and in every respect accepted as friend."

"He is very generous. Please thank General Miles. Tell him if he should wish to visit me I will likewise assure him safe-conduct."

Kirk sat down. John looked across at Mary.

"Have you also something to say to me?"

"Yes," said Mary.

"Then come with me and I will listen."

He looked at Kirk as though waiting for him to object. Kirk merely continued to stare into the fire, his face so set and gaunt that he seemed to have aged twenty years since John last had seen him.

"You carry your repentance very far," said John. "You must feel the guilt of your people along with your own."

Kirk's head turned so slowly it seemed a movement against his will. He looked up at John.

"See that yours does not become greater."

"In your people's view it is already greater," replied John.

He turned toward his camp. Mary fell into step at his heels.

"Hold on," said Zenas.

He got to his feet. The two turned to face him.

"This is Zenas Williams," Mary said in a quick aside to John. "You remember Mac telling about him."

"I am happy to meet you," said John, offering his hand.

Zenas shook it briefly but kept his attention on Mary.

"Long's you're traipsin' off with this-here young buck I want you to know you got no call to take no more sass from him than you're a mind to. You got Mousey and me here to look after you."

Jared rose beside him. "What Stud is a-tryin' to say is that the way we feel about you ain't no different than was we your kinfolk."

Mary drew back the blanket from a face that for a second had lost its frozen calm. "Though I love my father I have always been ashamed of my white blood. But if it were really yours I could only be proud."

She turned and followed John.

At sight of Mary, John's tepee-mates leaped up and, with furtive envious glances at him in passing, hurried out. She remained in the entrance. John crossed, threw several sticks on the fire, and sat on a bearskin.

Mary spoke in a low voice. "Did you mind — so very much — what Zenas and Jared said?"

"No. How could I? I walked away only because after what they and you had said there wasn't anything left for anybody else to say."

Mary removed the blanket, folded it, and laid it over her arm. He stared at her costume.

"So — decked out like a bride."

"Yes," she said steadily. "I have even brought the blanket."

"You couldn't be forgetting that it is the man who offers the blanket?"

"It's you who could be forgetting. There is no longer time. Not for you. Not for me. Not for anybody who has followed you here."

"Was bringing you here Kirk's idea?"

"Yes."

"What's wrong with the man?"

"There's less wrong with him than anybody I have ever known."

"Did you never love him? Or did you stop loving him?"

"Neither. But there is no use — not any longer — trying to believe what cannot be so. I could never have belonged with him. I do belong with you. We belong together. What is it that the Christian service says? For better or for worse."

He rose. "You're shivering. These canvas tepees let in more cold than they keep out. We might at least keep warm."

She came around the fire toward him. He took the blanket from her. In response to his gesture, she laid down on the bearskin. He shook out the blanket, stretched out beside her, and drew it over them up to their shoulders. He was lying well away from her.

"You were admiring this dress," she said. "It was Elaine's. She gave it to me. It had been given to Dr. Eastman by some of his patients. He had given it to her as an engagement present. Their betrothal was announced in the church on Christmas Eve. They both took such good care of me. She sat beside me day and night. And he was so wonderful. There's so much a physician can do for you besides dosing you with medicine. It was his understanding more than anything else that brought me back. And Zenas and Jared and Fred —"

"Are you talking so much because you're scared?"

"Yes."

"Why?"

"How could I not be? My coming to you. It was not because I have been able to make myself feel so bold. Inside I am shaking. Always I have been able to think. But I have never before thought of anything like this. I have, of course, thought much about you — and about Mac, too. But I have never thought — not really thought — about lying down beside you or him or any man. I must still be so hopelessly . . . the virgin. While you — for you this is nothing new. You have —"

"Whatever gave you the idea that I was such a snorting stallion?"

"Well. I would not say snorting. But stallion — yes. After all we grew up in the same village. You seemed then so very much older than me that you might have been of another generation. But from the time I was ten I was taking the most horrid interest in whatever you did. I so well remember that no Hunkpapa maiden or young wife who happened to catch your eye was long safe from you. Then — during those years you were away — there were all those white women."

John chuckled. "Under our immediate circumstances, I should be glad to be regarded with such awe. On the other hand, illusions can be a sad risk. So I will ease your disquiet. I've never had but one white woman and when I tell you about her you will realize how mistaken you are about my — ah — about your misconceptions."

With the same attention to color and detail as when he once had told her of his adventure with the Minnesota sheriff and the Chippewa, he told her of his misadventure with the settler's wife.

"So you see," he finished, "how little you have to fear."

She was laughing. "Oh, John, for all my innocence I'm not so innocent as you. To punish her husband the miserable woman had only to come to your camp. She did not have to stay. But she stayed and stayed and stayed because she could not stand not having more — and more — and more."

He raised on his elbow to scan her face. "Don't stop laughing," he begged. "You were looking just as you did that day I first saw you over the hedge — and we took Puma up on the ridge in the storm — and the rain soaked you to the skin — and you were not afraid of anything — and I was so crazy about you that I could hardly breathe. Mary, Mary, there's never been such a — such a miracle — as you."

He drew the blanket completely over them.

In the morning John rose to pace restlessly about the tepee. Mary, he knew, was only pretending to be still asleep. A stir outside caused him to jerk aside the flap at the entrance. Gathered in a semicircle before the doorway, at a respectful distance and waiting in utter silence, were twenty or so young children. They stared at him wide-eyed.

"Was it also part of your scheme," he said over his shoulder, "to have these children herded here to gawk at me?"

"No," said Mary. "Though it seems quite a good idea — of the sort that might have occurred to their mothers."

One child, so young as to be scarcely able to hold himself erect, escaped the grasp of his ten-year-old sister and toddled forward with eager uncertainty toward John. There was in his stumbling carriage the triumphant confidence of the infant learning to walk who makes an accelerating beeline for the nearest adult. John abruptly dropped the tent flap between him and his advancing adversary.

He wheeled and stared at Mary. She was kneeling on the bearskin, braiding her hair. She looked to him in no slightest respect changed from the way she had looked to him yesterday. The shared delights of the night, of which his own memories were so fresh and so disturbing, appeared to have left no faintest mark on her.

"Then the whole of your plan was the thought that you might give me a wish to live?" he said.

She removed a braid from her teeth so that she could reply.

"Do you still want to talk about what you are doing?"

"If you have anything sensible to say."

"Who could have more than this: Sitting Bull chose to die because he was old and had so little to live for. Your death wish is, of course, much more heroic because you have a future to sacrifice. But those children out there — there will be nothing heroic about their end. We both saw that at Wounded Knee."

He resumed his restless pacing.

"What's so important about death? It comes to everybody. What's important is what happens while you're alive. For the men of my camp out there, one day on these cliffs picking off white soldiers trying to get up that canyon will prove an experience more rewarding than the sum total of all the rest of their lives."

"While their mothers and wives and children — they do not count."

"Not now. Not when we're at war. And never as much as they like to think. I must make you understand. I owe you that much. A man may sometimes need a woman or want children. But always it is being a man that comes first with him. He can be seized by no emotion so deep as for those other men who stand beside him in battle. There can for him be no attachment, no dependence, to equal this bond. Not even such a fulfillment as we knew last night."

"You are driven by more than a fellowship with warriors. It is this hate that has possessed you. How can you continue to nurse it? How can you forget all that Fred has tried to do for us? Or all that Mac has done?"

"They have seemed friends, to be sure. But they are white. They are on the other side. They are still our enemies."

Mary covered her face with her hands as though to shut out the sight of him.

"You have no more to say?" he asked, after a moment.

"As you told Big Foot's people — what good can come of beating upon a rock?"

"Then let's go down and get the general's emissaries on their way."

The children had disappeared. The camp seemed absorbed in its usual morning preoccupations. There was evident great care on the part of everyone in sight to refrain from staring at the passing of their chief and his bride. The sunlight was paler today and there was an occasional gust of wind. Scattered shreds of gray cloud were scudding across the sky.

Kirk, Zenas, and Jared rose from their fire. John and Mary came to a halt facing them. Kirk was holding himself erect, as though his spine had turned to stone. After one swift glance at Mary his attention remained fixed on John.

"Tell General Miles," said John, "that I thank him for his consideration. I remain — what is the term? — his obedient servant. Or is it humble servant? Still, if he wants to see me, it will have to be here."

"This is your last word?"

"Except for this: I hope you will not be with the force sent in after us."

"Mary is staying with you?"

"Yes," said Mary.

While John and Mary watched in silence, Zenas and Jared helped Kirk harness his horses and hitch the team to the wagon. Then, instead of saddling their horses, they shook hands with Kirk and, to his obvious astonishment, came back to sit down by the fire. Kirk stared at them.

"Stud and me," said Jared, "we be stayin', too."

"What are you trying to do to me?" demanded John, his voice thick with sudden anger.

"We be aimin' to join up with you," said Jared. "This be the kind of fight a man has got to take one side or tother. Stud and me, we got us such a bellyful o' them soldiers that we can't herd with them when they come to hunt you out o' these here rocks. So that leaves us nowhere less we throw in with you at standin' off the soldiers."

"Mousey he never gits him the whole straight o' nothin'," said Zenas. "What he's a-tryin' to say is that him and me we got to figgerin' that the way this country is a'turnin' out, there ain't much left in it worth fightin' for. About the only part left that's anything like what we remember back when this country was fit to live in is what you got here in this goddam hole in the middle o' nothin'. So we aim to shove in with you and hang on to this much long's we can."

"Are you crazy?" shouted John. "Or do you think I am? It must be that I am. Nothing like this could happen to a man who was still sane. You talk of remembering. Ever since I can remember I've hated the whole bastardly white race. That's been the mainstay of my life. For centuries white men have taken every conceivable advantage of us. There has been no limit to the range of means to which they have stooped to beat us. But never has there been an equal to this."

Jared and Zenas grinned sheepishly, as though he were showering endearments upon them. Kirk took one last look at Mary and gathered his reins.

"Wait," said John.

"What for? Don't you want your answer to get to General Miles?"

The wind moaned in the nearest pine. John looked at the sky, across which the shreds of cloud, now larger, were beginning to course more swiftly. He closed his eyes for a moment, as though communing with some higher power.

"Can't you see there's another blizzard coming?" he said. "You'd never make it. So you'll have to stay, too. Miles can wait for his answer until the storm is over. Better move your camp to the shelter of that north wall. We could get snowed in for days. That'll give you some time" — once more he glared at Jared and Zenas — "to do some thinking, if thinking isn't altogether beyond you. And them time" — he jerked his head toward his camp — "to begin to get used to" — for a second he seemed to have lost control of his voice — "to what — to what is happening to their commander." His scowl smoothed as he looked at Mary's suddenly glowing face. "And us time for what we have to get used to."

(Afterword)

Of the characters involved in the foregoing story, Wovoka, Sitting Bull, Red Cloud, Big Foot, Kicking Bear, Short Bull, Crow Foot, Gall, Grass, Crow King, Bull Head, Shave Head, Red Tomahawk, One Bull, Bull Ghost, Andrew Fox, General Miles, General Brooke, Colonel Forsyth, Major Whiteside, McLaughlin, Mrs. McLaughlin, Dr. Eastman, Elaine Goodall, Carignan, and Royer were historical figures with whose activities and personalities few liberties have been taken.

Remington, the noted painter of the West, covered the 1890 war as correspondent for *Harper's* but there is no evidence that he took as active a part in the incidents of the campaign as the story has presumed.

John, Mary, Kirk, Jared, Zenas, Wade, Hoyt, Ward, Clem, and Father Murphy are, on the other hand, wholly fictional characters.

As John had forecast, the country's sympathy and remorse soon faded. In the official aftermath of Wounded Knee, Forsyth's conduct, in spite of Miles's criticism, was commended by the War Department and eighteen soldiers of the 7th were awarded the Medal of Honor for their services in the engagement.

Miles's violent differences with his superiors persisted and his presidential aspirations were disappointed but he eventually became commanding general of the army, the rank he held during the Spanish-American War.

The Sioux were not punished for their brief belligerence and were permitted to remain on their Dakota reservations, where they still reside.